Cicadas
Sing
of
Summer
Graves

Cicadas Sing of Summer Graves

QUINN CONNOR

sourcebooks
landmark

Published by Sourcebooks Landmark, an imprint of Sourcebooks
P.O. Box 4410, Naperville, Illinois 60567-4410
(630) 961-3900
sourcebooks.com

Library of Congress Cataloging-in-Publication Data

Names: Connor, Quinn, author.
Title: Cicadas sing of summer graves / Quinn Connor.
Description: Naperville, Illinois : Sourcebooks Landmark, [2023]
Identifiers: LCCN 2022061855 (print) | LCCN 2022061856
(ebook) | (trade paperback) | (epub)
Subjects: LCGFT: Gothic fiction. | Novels.
Classification: LCC PS3603.O5483 C53 2023 (print) | LCC PS3603.O5483
(ebook) | DDC 813/.6--dc23/eng/20230104
LC record available at https://lccn.loc.gov/2022061855
LC ebook record available at https://lccn.loc.gov/2022061856

Printed and bound in the United States of America.
WOZ 10 9 8 7 6 5 4 3 2 1

To my dad: the man, the mystery,
the only one of your kind.
Thank you for a lifetime of little talks.

—A.

For Rob Barrow, my daddy, who
taught me to dream boldly.

—R.

AUTHOR'S NOTE

Dear friend,

Alex and Robyn both spent happy family summers on man-made lakes in Texas and Arkansas. But there were always ghost stories. They are in the land whether or not we know them. Treading in warm, sunscreen-scented water, Robyn would suddenly drift into a cold spot and wonder if a spectral engine wandered on a rusting train track two hundred feet below. It was her childhood shiver that led to this novel.

The town of Prosper was inspired by Buckville, Arkansas, which was flooded in the 1950s by the Blakely Mountain Dam and is now beneath Lake Ouachita. The upper Ouachita valley is a part of the homelands of the Indigenous Caddo Nation, which has been systematically displaced by settlers for hundreds of years. The dam resulted in the mass dislocation of Garland County residents, mainly struggling white farmers but also many who were Black and Native American, from their homes. We wanted to wrestle with submerged histories, memory lost and found, and the impact of "progress" on communities and land.

Through this novel, we seek to honor and sensitively engage with these complicated histories so deeply entrenched in the places we come from. During our research for this novel, we contacted both local Black history bearers in Hot Springs and the leading historian of Garland County. But Buckville under Lake Ouachita is only one story. It is essential to remember that, all over the country, "development-induced displacements" disproportionately targeted and harmed Black and Indigenous communities.

Indigenous and Black historians and activists continue to ensure their stories are remembered. Oscarville, Georgia, was the home of a thriving Black community until a white mob drove them out and eventually flooded their land to create Lake Lanier. Almost 80 percent of the Fort Berthold Reservation residents—more than three hundred Hidatsa, Mandan, and Arikara families—were forcibly displaced when a dam was built to form Lake Sakakawea in North Dakota. In 1948, when the dikes holding Smith Lake back from Vanport, Oregon—a 40 percent Black town— threatened to fail, officials evacuated six hundred horses from a nearby racetrack but assured forty thousand people that they were safe. When the dike broke the next day, Vanport was washed away, displacing more than 18,500 residents, 6,300 of whom were Black. The death toll is unknown.

Too often, the dispossessed were not duly compensated for what they were forced to leave behind. With deepest respect, we acknowledge these wrongs. This book is set in a fraught land and addresses violence, complex intergenerational pain, and particularly class-based trauma. Please take care when reading.

With our love,
QC

CHAPTER ONE

VERY MAY, CASSIE LOCKED UP THE OLD DOUBLE-WIDE for the season and instead slept in her RV with the windows open, listening for the busy summer hum of honeybees. Their lullaby was not the only gift that came with the heat: there was also the smell of rain and blue moon hailstorms on the wind, black-eyed Susans spooling over her kitchen sink. Sometimes she dreamed about them carpeting her bed, the Agatha Christies on her built-in shelves, the '80s green plastic breakfast booth, the flowered curtains, the shower.

On especially hot nights like tonight, when the air was bathtub steam, she dreamed beautyberries, just like the ones on Grandad's old china, bloomed purple over the bed and Solomon's seal gathered in the shade under the unused driver's seat. She dreamed azaleas settled on her pillow and grew down to the floor until everything was soft, living green.

The RV—a big, beige crouched cat—hadn't been moved in years; weeds poked out between the tires and tickled the exhaust pipe on the front lawn of Cassie's childhood home.

The double-wide, the family home, was all right. But if she stayed there too long, Cassie felt herself aging backward.

She'd become a child again in her childhood bedroom and hear Grandad humming down the hall. She'd forget how to read and wait for Mom to appear in her nicotine clouds, hair crimped and bleached with lemon juice because Mom never quite left the '80s. *Cassie girl, what are you doing, staring like that?* she'd say. *Are you dumb? Go swim in the lake. Go, be a kid. Shoo.*

So most nights, Cassie chose to sleep in the RV and listen to summer. Summer meant the hives would wake up. After so long spent cultivating her ten small hives, she'd learned honey vintages could be as variable as wine. It was the second day of June after a wild, rainy spring, and the taste of the latest batch was as rich as blood oranges, the usual gold laced through with burgundy.

Summer had kicked off with a helter-skelter storm that washed treasure onto the shore of Lake Prosper. Cassie hadn't gone to the shore at all but had lain out, freckling on the hot RV roof, the commotion bouncing off the water to her. For an entire Saturday, the fishermen pulled up nothing but reed-tangled necklaces, soggy husks that had once been books, glass bottles. Before handing over their finder's fees, she'd asked anyone who found anything—locals were used to her quirks—to lay the wet things out in the sun outside her antique shop, guarded by the statuary: a one-winged lion and a flock of metal lawn flamingos. The treasure had dried for two full days before she took it into her shop to be looked after.

Cassie turned on the electric kettle, one of the few birthday gifts Mom had ever gotten right. This evening, hot tea was in order. When she turned back around, the cutlery drawer had opened itself. Odd. She plucked one of the spoons and nudged it closed with her hip. The kettle made its angry snake hiss. Behind her, the bed sighed. Cassie paused. Nothing but readjustment. Air, settling where her body had been.

She took her tea out under the vine-laden eaves. Her little plot of land was peaceful, the trees cut back in a rough rectangle to let the sun shine down, and there were only two breaks in the mossy green walls: the gravel road up to the highway and the dirt path down to the lake. She let knee-high weeds have that one, let them bleed over the beaten path. If the Grand Destiny—the resort owned by Valerie and her son, Mitch—weren't down that way, Cassie would have stitched it up with saplings until it was grown over and she couldn't see the shallow prism of water anymore.

It was now after Memorial Day. Minivans were rolling lakeside, kids tumbling out wearing their bathing suits under their clothes, unwilling to sit still for sunscreen. The cicadas had known it first. They sang their June hymns; the weather was changing, and people were coming back to the shores of Lake Prosper.

Soon the air, which had been steadily heating, would burst, as if the whole of the South sat on a massive hot plate. At the turn of June, heat raged up from the ground, like it wasn't the sun's doing at all but the work of shifting tectonics and magma currents under a thin crust. Cassie wiggled her toes in the grass to feel that heat as she picked her way through the hives to the double-wide.

Soon as well, Mom would arrive to drop Bolt off for a summer at the lake with Cassie. Bolt never quite felt like her younger brother; they were separated by ten whole years in age, which might as well have been an ocean. He wouldn't even be staying if Mom's rich best friend, Gladys, hadn't invited her on a post-divorce girls' cruise down South America, which promised to be a two-month affair. In preparation, Cassie had almost entirely cleaned out Bolt's old room in the double-wide; only a few knick-knacks remained, along with some of Grandad's softest sweaters and a few pieces of furniture she thought she might refurbish and sell in the antique shop someday, though someday had not yet come. She'd found some of Bolt's old toys too. He was seventeen now, probably too old for the stuffed tiger and plastic slingshot, but she'd charged his Nintendo DS just in case and left it on his bedside table. She still needed to get fresh sheets.

A splash and a girl's laugh peeled through the air. Cassie nearly sloshed her coffee over her fingers.

The laughter rang out again, along with big playful splashes, the rhythmic slap of an enthusiastic swimmer. In a flash, Cassie was a child again racing toward the dock, water wings constricting her pale, freckled upper arms. And there without fail was her friend, waving at her from the shadow of the shallows. Her wet curls framing her tanned face, her smile, her *come on, Cassie, jump, and I'll catch you—*

This late in the evening, who would be swimming? Cassie started down the path, stomach swooping like a too-long fall off a tire swing over hungry water. She had been enamored with the light dancing on the surface back then, with the lullaby of waves against the ankles of the dock, lured by a voice as thin as air. "*Cassie, jump and I'll catch you.*"

"Catfish?" Cassie murmured, throat dry and weak.

She crept to the edge of her land, where the clearing began to race down, down, down to the water. Below her, there was Valerie's sea-green sign: GRAND DESTINY RESORT AND MARINA. There was the postcard-pretty pool and a few paddleboats tied to the dock under a passion fruit sunset.

Cassie drank in the Destiny's safety before dragging her gaze to the lake. Once, the lake had been smaller, shallower, but it had been engorged with the building of the Damnation—Grandad's name for Prosper's large industrial dam. Once, Lake Prosper had been manageable. But ever since the dam, it sprawled into every valley, every creek, every crevice like blood pooling from an opened vein. It washed away crops that had swayed in the wind, grew fingery canals and swamped the boundaries anticipated by the dam surveyors. When the rains fell every year, the lake rose, crawling higher and higher up Cassie's hill, desperate to eat.

It was quiet. The water was empty. Not even a ripple. The only sound was her own fast pained breathing.

Cassie rushed back until the lake shrank, hidden by her land with every step she took. She retreated all the way into the double-wide and closed the door behind her, then slammed the windows into their sills, letting no sound—no watery calls— inside. Only sunshine.

ᘓᗩ

The highway ran in a swift dark current away from her, and Lark searched for the only radio station that might reach her out in nowhere. It was an oldies channel with a Southern angle, one that played a lot of Tom Petty, a lot of the Band. When they had traveled this way together, Daddy used to twiddle the dial like this, twist and turn through static, when he forgot to charge his iPod. Lark snorted at that thought even as she listened to the AM stations, a thief picking the lock of a high-security safe. That old iPod was a fossil nowadays, with its supposed three days of shuffle that always seemed to exclusively play "Hurdy Gurdy Man" by Donovan.

It was blackest night beyond the milky wash of her headlights. This old road wasn't used to company so long past sunset, and it bucked nervously beneath her, took unexpected curves, plunged between the inky shadows of trees, and then curled back on itself like a wilting petal. Lark gave up on the radio and clutched the wheel with both hands, feeling increasingly like a passenger as the highway tossed her onward, cranked her up, spat her out, drove her ever closer to an inevitable sickening drop.

When things at home were at their hardest after the incident, Mom had delayed, set this chore aside for weeks, until she'd admitted she just couldn't do it. And then, still, Lark had put this journey off for more than a month and then all day.

Hours before, as the beloved, slightly decrepit silhouette of Memphis had disappeared in her mirrors and she'd cruised through the endless horizontals of the Arkansas Delta, it had really, honestly felt as if Lark would never actually arrive. Thirty minutes from the scatterings of docks and houses that made up undefined, unincorporated Prosper, the cozy downtown and charming tourist stops of Charlene hadn't wanted to let her go. The NOW LEAVING CHARLENE. BE SEEIN' Y'ALL! sign took on a skeptical ring, as if to say, *Come on back. Nothing to see down that way.* But now the speed limit slowed, the woodsy curtains drawing back on familiar sights: the little gas station with its chubby pumps, the junk shop and its associated sculpture park of scrap metal, the stores selling Arkansas quartz. And then she was out of highway, and she turned, her right front wheel growling over gravel. The car, her rusted-out old Explorer, got its teeth into the loose paving and roared down the familiar path, rocking, like Lark was voyaging out into a vast shifting sea.

She passed the riding stables, the crumbling mobile homes, the turnoff for the marina. The eyes of five ever-startled deer flashed iridescent in her lights. Her heart cracked quietly with each bump in this back road. There had been so many happier trips down to Lake Prosper. Her skin, the color of faded white linen from her indoor job and her city life, had once glowed all year round with a healthy summer tan from days in the sun out here. Boat rides, fireworks, lunches out at Aunt Valerie's restaurant.

Never once had Lark come this way alone.

As much as Lark wanted to be self-sufficient at twenty-four, having Mom there would have steadied her. They could have found some way to laugh, to break up the cement heaviness that hardened around them when they were apart, that imprisoned them in solitary horror when Mom was caring for Daddy in Hot Springs and Lark was working at Goner Records in Memphis. Together, they might have paused for cheeseburgers at Stella's drive-in, jalapeños raging on their tongues as they cackled over the latest hijinks of the family's dopey brown poodle, Doris Ann. Doris Ann's nickname was Methuselah; she was about a thousand years old in dog years. Deaf and nearly blind, she was content to stagger merrily through the woods around their house, roaming like some woolly donkey, Mom chasing after her, shouting her name at top volume for absolutely zero response.

Yeah, Lark would've felt braver with Mom there. But Mom had everything on her plate right now, not just the grind of her forty-hour weeks but also making sure Dad somehow made it out of the long shadows of his own mind. She was doing her best; she was doing everything. Lark could take this one burden on. She could settle the boat and the collection. She could make sure no one had this dark hole to fall back into.

The road opened into the familiar grassy lot. Lark parked the Explorer. The air was warm and heady. It tasted like midnight, and closely set trees, and damp pavement. With one strap of her backpack over her shoulder, Lark took the long, steep walk down to Echo.

The path tripped down toward the water through dense woods. Lark's steps, short and careful, sounded loud, unwelcome in her own ears. An owl cried curiously at her from somewhere above. And then the ramp came into view. The lake was low, so the ramp connecting Echo to solid ground was at a violent diagonal. In the distance, looming like a cloud, the bridge above the massive dam hung, the dam that had expanded the lake all those years ago. Lark paused, looking over the sunken nighttime vista. Toward Echo, or E Dock, where Lark's family had kept their houseboat, the *Big Dipper*, for more than twenty years.

Hefting her pack, clutching the rough rail, she eased down the gangplank, through the silent neighborhood of floating homes, and toward Slip 23, where the *Big Dipper* was docked. Her chest fluttered with the leftover thrill of childhood to reach it, but there was something else too—the flat clap of dread to see them, for them to see her. Throughout her childhood, the collection had always ogled Daddy, joints squeaking as they turned on their own, adjusted their myopic focuses to fix on him. But now he wasn't here, and Lark, the next best thing, would enter their lair alone for the first time.

Besides the carved mallards on Jerry Mason's boat, who watched her peacefully from their perch in the front window, there was no one to notice her so late, not yet. No one was out; not a curtain rustled. There was lots of peeling paint, yards of faded canvases. The Snyder boat, where Lark had her first ever sip of prosecco one New Year's Eve, had a FOR SALE sign on it. Everything looked older. Duke's GONE FISHING welcome mat seemed to speak for the whole dock, as if everyone were out, tucked into quiet coves, listening through their cast lines for bass stirring far below.

Just as she'd expected, Lark's houseboat saw her coming, its hundreds of eyes turning their glass lenses on her in tandem. Propped on tripods, or any conceivable surface, really, the collection littered the entryway, crowded the side stairs, and jutted up from the top like a miniature skyline. The dread in her rose. It was pitch-dark, yet light seemed to catch in them, to pool in their fishbowl eyes. Lark stopped a few yards away, stunned at their number. Mom had warned her, her neck splotchy red with anxiety. *The collection got totally out of hand. I just—nobody knew what being down here on his own would do to him.*

Inside was just as bad, maybe worse. Aunt Valerie had felt so guilty. *He always came to the Destiny, never had me over.* She'd been over once after the intervention, cleaned the worst of it. Even so, there was no free surface, no place for Lark to put her feet or lay her pack. The boat was hot and musky from months of being shut, slightly sour with loneliness and the things that had spoiled there.

Lark didn't bother turning on a light. Thrusting open every window she could manage to reach through the clutter, she battled her way to the guest bedroom, and then she threw herself straight on the dusty coverlet of the bed.

It was very quiet. As if she were the last person left anywhere. Daddy must've felt that, in endless cycles, constantly before the audience of these things. She'd always been too much like him. Overimaginative, her teachers had said. Out in la-la land, said Aunt Valerie. Even as a child, as she'd dozed in her bed here, glow-in-the-dark stars twinkling above her, that quiet from below had been immense, a presence more than an absence. It seemed to come from the deep cold of the water. This would've been near the town once, almost a hundred years ago, when Old Prosper had still stood in this valley that was now a lake basin. Then the dam. And now that huddle of ruins—church, churchyard, town hall, even train tracks—was buried in the deepest parts of the lake, covered in sediment and far from the sun.

"Damnation and hellfire," Lark groaned, turning over to face the wall. She'd always slept best here, out on the water. She would try to sleep now. Though this time it probably wouldn't be so easy. These days, ghost stories of the town under the lake were the least of it.

Because like strange googly-eyed voyeurs, her father's collection of telescopes—hundreds of them, strewn through the boat in every size, design, age, material—had been waiting for her. Now Lark was caught in their unblinking gaze.

CHAPTER TWO

ATERY LIGHT SHIMMERED ON THE CEILING ABOVE
the guest bed. *Angel choir*, Lark thought sleepily.
Country dance. Bright reflections like that, the lake's
morning jig, were a sure sign that Lark had slept in. She should
smell bacon now, hear a deep roar as Daddy tested the engines
or the low skid of the swim ladder being pulled out. But there
was nothing. Lark lay in a dusty silence. One small spyglass, no
larger than a pendant and made of milky jade, perched on the
windowsill, its tiny lens fixed on her. Lark resisted the urge to
snatch it up and smash it against the pale wood of the floor. She
might've, had there been even a square foot of free floor where
she could hurl it. *Never look through them*, she hummed to herself.
Never look, or they'll get you like they got him. As if she would. As
if she'd even be tempted.

Carefully, so carefully, she lifted herself down from the bed
and tiptoed from the guest room. Houseboats on Lake Prosper
came in every shape and size: from tiny shoeboxes with little
more than a couch and a sink inside; to tall sailboats and cruisers
with cavernous cabins; to the three-bedroom Suncoasters, like
the *Big Dipper*, with cheery canvases and wide decks. Most of the

boats were old and a little cobwebby, fishing boats roped up at the rear, swim towels drying on the backs of lounge chairs. Over at Charlene Marina, there were one or two half-a-million-dollar behemoths docked, with five bedrooms and luxury kitchens, Jacuzzis and saunas. But Prosper was almost allergic to fancy. Year after year, it was just the same old families in their same old slips. If a boat was put up for sale, it was big news.

Lark crept down the houseboat's main hallway. This narrow artery connected the *Big Dipper*'s front room, where the cooking and the living were meant to happen, to the three bedrooms. The large(ish) master bedroom—her parents' room—was at the back, with a view of the cove and the islands opposite. From the back deck, they would swim or read; they'd watch for turtles or for herons. Between the guest room and the master bedroom was the cuddy down a short flight of steps. There were two beds there, and high windows just above the waterline. The cuddy had been Lark's kid space, full of her books and stuffed animals—perfect for sleepovers. She'd filled it with her dreams since she was four years old, when they'd bought this boat from one of Daddy's uncles. Now the cuddy, like the rest of the boat, was crammed with telescopes. All the living space they'd once shared had been appropriated, serving merely as a great floating warehouse for the collection, for Daddy's daydream made real.

Lark sidestepped a heavy modern telescope that could've been the Hubble's little brother and inched her way toward the kitchen. Huge cobalt and emerald blossoms adorned every curtain, every chair, the sofa, and the place settings on the table. It was a big bold pattern that remembered the 1980s shoulder pads, a kind of loud American optimism that was difficult for Lark to wrap her mind around now.

Prosper was abuzz with summer, and outside, Echo was lively. It was early in the season, and people were either spraying down their old things, trying to make them like new again, or showing off a latest purchase: shining new tubes from the marina shop, new (to them) Jet Skis, any variety of watercraft available to the Arkansas boater. A loud, jovial voice she didn't recognize boomed from the end of the dock. Somewhere, children whooped and splashed, leaping from the top of boats into the chilly water. Jerry passed the *Big Dipper* with fishing poles and coolers and a box of crickets as he went to meet Duke, his longtime fishing buddy. A boat down, one of the Pickle sisters—the one whose name wasn't Margaret— was painting her toenails, her dog racing from one end of her deck to the other. Doris Ann had been like that in her youth, falling into the lake every other day and then splashing mournfully until she was rescued. Out back, speedboats and party barges putted out toward the wider lake with tubes, wakeboards, and skis, their cruising playlists booming. Lark recognized many of the families who chugged by from lunches at the Grand Destiny, holiday dock parties, even a few from her school in Hot Springs.

It wouldn't take long for the neighbors to realize somebody was back on the *Big Dipper*. If the whispering wasn't rustling between bows and sterns yet, it would be soon.

Lark knocked over an antique spyglass and nearly upset several wavering boxes of unopened telescopes as she scrounged through the kitchen. She got the coffeepot going with some slightly stale dark roast from the pantry, then laboriously cleared off a chair at the table. She sat with a faded mug, one she'd hand painted as a child, clutched between her hands, gazing at the absolute wreck piled around her on every side.

She'd assured Mom she could inventory the telescopes and prepare the *Big Dipper* for sale. *Sure, Mom. Of course. No problem.*

There was a massive splash outside as a nearby child cannon-balled into the lake. One of the telescopes closest to the window teetered ominously.

So where the hell did she start?

ↁ

Early in the morning, Cassie coaxed her blue El Camino to a grumbling start. The car knew the winding, wooded back roads from her land so well, it practically drove itself. Tourism on their side of the lake depended on that single strip of road, a loop that ran around the lake before charging off toward Little Rock. The basin road curved straight down into the marina, where it sprouted houseboat docks. Cassie parked where the forest crowded close to the gravel lot of the antique shop, then crunched across to the locked door and dark windows.

Grandad was a Prosperite from way back, old enough to remember the days before the Damnation, old enough to have lived in the town when there was one. He used to tell her stories about Prosper, about the church bell you could hear clear across the water, and his nights spent sneaking out to lie in switchgrass and count stars, where he first discovered he wanted to fly among them. Grown up, Grandad had indeed flown a Dauntless in the Pacific during World War II, and throughout Cassie's childhood, they'd made models together. He'd taught her the different types of fighter planes. English Spitfires, Japanese Zeroes, Thunderbolts.

In 1964, Grandad had seen the burgeoning marina, the incoming flock of summer visitors, and bought himself some land, starting at the basin road's turnoff from Route 380. There, he had built Fairchild's Treasures, a one-story rectangle with a slanted roof and slightly wonky gutters. The expansive bay windows were almost too big for it, dwarfing the door between them. Dreaming windows, he'd called them sometimes. They showed you a nice, big slice of the world. When he'd died, he'd left the deed to the four acres and the title of the shop in Cassie's name. She hadn't changed a thing. Even the sign was the same, simple white paint on blue wood: FAIRCHILD'S TREASURES. Sometimes when she opened the door, her heart still expected Grandad to be sitting at the worktable, tinkering away in the lamplight.

Cassie jiggled the lock open and let herself into cool air. The shop was home for the tired, the poor, the antique, the broken, the rusted. Lit almost entirely by sunlight, the front had some locally made furniture and even some kitchenware: cow-shaped salt and pepper shakers, succulents that needed loving care, her own mason jars of honey: dark, light, and honeycomb.

Of course, only some things could stand that much sunlight; many of the antiques, all the things fished from the lake, lived near the back, where shadows ran deep. Paintings, photographs, furs, books, old sifters, and vintage dresses, including a high-collar wedding dress with a row of pink pearl buttons from nape to tailbone. China cabinets and tired dining room tables and chairs; a whole section of Remington typewriters. Ancient cameras, faded dolls and chess sets, a gleaming Tiffany tea set missing only the sugar bowl. A rosy-cheeked family of Hummels, a tiny carved ivory mermaid, jewelry that wanted badly to tarnish. She wrote tags for each one, pricing it all, every drawer of copper forks and every glass lamp that collected so much dust, it needed cleaning every day. The sprigs of lavender and jasmine she hid around the shop kept it smelling more like the ghost of perfume than mothballs or the dust of previous owners' lives.

Tourists liked to come, browsing for the most interesting souvenirs—better than boogie boards and pictures of themselves holding foot-long bass. Dads with sunburned necks liked to riffle through the lawn furniture and statuary. As children, Cassie and Bolt hadn't had a dad like that. All Cassie ever knew about hers was that she had his pale Irish skin and narrow feet. But she'd had Grandad. He was the real reason Mom had moved back to Lake Prosper after getting pregnant with Cassie. As a young girl, Cassie had spent hours at Fairchild's Treasures. When Mom picked up a day job cleaning houses or waiting tables, Grandad had acted as babysitter and teacher. He would sit at his counter with the cash register and beckon Cassie over to watch him work.

"If you can't fix it, give it a new start," Grandad would rasp as he stuffed a blackened nail into his pocket. "We can make something out of this." They made lots of little creatures, automobiles, and planes. Dauntlesses, Spitfires, Zeroes, and Thunderbolts hung from the shop ceiling, strung on fishing line, soldered together from rusted keys, screws, and shells from Old Prosper. Doodad frogs, crawdads, dragonflies, and birds were sold next to the houseplants.

Cassie brushed her hand over the counter, where he used to sit. Once, after Bolt had come along when Cassie was ten, she and Grandad had carved their names, one after the other, into the top of the worktable. Tobias. Cassandra. They'd added Bolt for good measure.

Grandad hadn't just run a good shop; he had built a legendary one. Everyone in fifty miles knew Tobias Fairchild. Charlene had its share of antique shops and consignment stores, but when something needed fixing or a rare piece of the past needed finding, it was a known fact: go to the Syrian man on the older side of the lake. Strangers would bring him their microwaves, their fishing poles, rusty jewelry, once even a grand old cuckoo clock. Bolt had been in diapers and pacifiers, so he didn't remember it, but Cassie had spent hours watching Grandad's hands as he fiddled with this gear and that spring. They had a shared fixation, an inability to stop fixing and tweaking, even those pieces that were never going to sell.

Cassie never felt time passing at Grandad's worktable, only now she spent those hours fiddling with trinkets herself. Today her project was robbing an antique piggy bank, which had been fished from the water's depths. It smiled up at her with a blank, muddy leer and faded china eyes. The moldy cork in the piglet's rotund belly had already proved unwilling to be dislodged. She was battling the lake gunk glued around it when a burly shadow crossed her work space, casting the ceramic face in sinister darkness.

"Okay. I hate that thing." It was Mitch, his laugh a low, pleasant growl that filled her with warmth. He leaned his elbows on the table, peering at her project. His eyes were turned down at the corners and eternally sleepy. A few smile lines already collected around them from the sun, and his skin had a warm, deep tan. In looks, he took much more after his father than his mother, Valerie, with his dark hair, expansive face, and broad, bearish shoulders. "There can be nothing good in that."

"I won't know until I get it out." Cassie held it up—and slightly left of Mitch—to the light and turned it to catch the groove she'd been aiming at, to wriggle her screwdriver in and force the old cork out. She tried again. "If this doesn't work, I suppose I'll let you smash it."

"It'll work," Mitch said, setting a bottle of root beer down for her. He must've brought it over from his market. "Just throwing this out there: I hope it's full of gold."

Even for him, it was a little difficult to put down her screwdriver, but the root beer fizzed hopefully. She'd always liked root beer best, ever since Grandad had showed her an *hoja santa* and its perfume had been just the same. She took an earthy, freezer-chilled sip. "Thank you."

"Cheers," Mitch said, gently tapping her root beer with his own chunky Yoo-hoo bottle. He was the closest thing Cassie had ever had to a next-door neighbor. His mom's motel and restaurant, the Grand Destiny Resort, was just through the woods from her house. So, growing up, he'd always been right there, a little boy with a serious face, tromping through poison ivy and catching crickets for bait. He'd enjoyed Grandad's shop as a kid, perhaps because it was quiet. He would skulk through the aisles in total silence, touching old ruins with gentle fingers, choosing oddities from their shelves to ask for when his birthday rolled around. He'd given an engagement ring from the shop to a girl he'd met in college, Farha Banerjee, and they'd lived together in Little Rock for a few years.

Cassie had never met the girl, but she remembered the ring. Gold band, an oval diamond inset with three tiny rubies. She remembered the day he'd bought it and the tight, breathless feeling in her stomach, like a spider trapped under a glass.

But now he was home again, making some room for himself at the resort, including taking over the newly renovated Grand Destiny Market, where weekenders and locals could pick up a few bare necessities if they didn't feel like making the drive to Charlene. But he didn't look at the jewelry case anymore: maybe he was afraid he might see the empty space where Farha's ring had lived before it was hers, when it had meant something else to someone else.

With a frank mewl, Smoky appeared from the shadows, jumping up onto the desk to lick condensation from Mitch's Yoo-hoo. Years ago, Smoky, an ancient charcoal-gray cat with a smoker's meow, had adopted the shop as her territory. She didn't always come out for Cassie, but she always appeared for Mitch. He gave her a luxurious scratch behind the ears and then up her back to the sweet spot at the arch of her spine. He yawned, and Smoky yawned back at him in a drowsy afternoon chorus.

"The summer crowd is stocking their refrigerators," Mitch said mildly as Cassie returned to scraping at the piggy bank. "We're out of *everything* at the market. No bacon. No eggs. No milk. Nothing. Only VCR tapes, Tic Tacs, and those bags of premade bagels. We're all going to starve," he continued, glum. "More business for Mom at least."

The thought of food—of Valerie's divine fried catfish, the perfect crunch of her fried chicken, her seasoned rice with broccoli and almond slivers, her slow-cooked, oven-browned pot roast, and even Valerie's Achilles' heel, the slightly soggy steak fries— made Cassie's stomach rumble. Was it lunchtime? Had she given the entire morning to this piggy bank? The screwdriver finally caught. She passed her root beer to Mitch to hold for safety.

He took it with bated breath, bending low so his chin rested on the table for optimal view. It was quite a lean for such a tall man. "Be gold, be gold," he muttered. "Or pearls? Or at least not something poisonous."

It felt like a warm roof had settled over her. He smelled like he'd been out on the lake all day, muddy and green. She took a deep breath, and the cork finally budged a little, then a little more, then—then it shot across the floor, Smoky on its tail, claws scrabbling madly. Mud pooled out, bubbly and black with age.

Mitch winced at the foul smell of the bog forming in a dark ooze around the piggy bank. He grabbed the nearest dried herb to prod at it. "Sick. This sludge must be almost a century old."

From the depths, she pulled several things, one lumpy shape, one very rusted key that wouldn't fit anything larger than a diary, and a hard knob the size of a spitball. With one of the old dishrags, she wiped them off. The bits were two very old green pennies. The lump turned out to be an ancient toy soldier. "How about copper, instead of gold?" She bit at the pearl. "This is fake."

Mitch groaned, forehead hitting the table. "That—don't—in your mouth."

"It's just how you test if they're real. It's too smooth to be natural." She pushed the coins across the desk. "But the pennies were made with real copper back then. They're worth more than a penny each."

Mitch caressed each penny with a large fingertip, just as he had with things he admired in the shop as a boy. "Hey…" He smiled at her, his shy, particular smile, one not everyone saw; he didn't like exposing the charming little gap in his teeth. "I'll put one penny in my pocket, and you put the other in yours. Luck to share."

It was a sweet idea, so Cassie couldn't help but stop her tinkering to smile up at him and open her palm. He plopped one penny in her hand, then straightened up with a sigh. "I need to go back and help Mom fight off the disgruntled customers..."

"Here," Cassie said, screeching her chair back and darting for the front. Dark or light? No. Honeycomb for complexity. She found the best jar, with the biggest comb floating in its heart, and brought it to him. "For you and Valerie, if she needs the strength."

Mitch's whole face opened, light catching in his eyes like sun through the honey. It was his first jar of the season. "Thanks, Cassie," he rumbled. "Looks like honey pie is back on the menu." Cassie was submerged in a hug she felt all over. Then, humming, he backed out through her shop door.

The penny was up on heads. Cassie slipped it into her pocket and went to the window as Mitch jogged to his car and waved before he drove onto the road. Warm, Cassie waved back.

Smoky appeared again, wafting through her legs, and deposited the mangled cork at her feet.

℘

There was no place on earth as depressing as the belly of a Greyhound bus. It was the wrong side of midnight, when time halted and the road blurred. June was never able to sleep in transit. The movement of the wheels, the hiss whenever the bus stopped, the bump of her temple against the window all night long, her need to use the bathroom for fifty miles coupled with absolute refusal to use the dingy one on the bus: she was in a traveling purgatory. And out the window, rain fell so heavy that the panes were too slick and fogged to know if the rest of the world was still there at all.

The temperature was never right. She felt like a badly cooked casserole: half-freezing, too cold to take off her jacket; half-burning, the back of her neck all sweaty under her hair. She'd woken up with it long and wild, rebelling after a year of being cooped up under the paper triangle hats All Night Diner had made every employee wear. The one bright spot was remembering she would never return to All Night Diner, or Chicago, again.

As far as themed nightclubs went, All Night Diner—with its seersucker shorts, red plastic stools, ironic suspenders, and Signature Short Order Martinis—was among the worst. June had lasted almost a year there trying to find her post-college path, mostly providing table service in the VIP section. But there had been problems. Every night she'd worked, the faux-wholesome atmosphere had become full moon at a biker bar. The other servers had jokingly called it the June Curse. But a week ago, a few of the regulars had smashed up the bar after she served them a round of Jell-O Salad Shots, and Jasmine, the owner, decided enough was finally enough. It wasn't her fault, June had argued. She hadn't overserved, and she'd barely spoken to them. But that dead-end job wasn't worth the fight, so she'd handed in her clip-on bow tie and HI, MY NAME IS JUNE! name tag. She wouldn't miss serving up Burger and Ryes or Ketchup Collins. Lemon Pie Limoncellos. Jukebox Mojitos. Grease Trap Margaritas.

Hurricane June, Mom had called her sometimes. *Hurricane June blowing through.*

June folded her feet up onto the seat and rested her cheek on her knees as the endless nowhere flashed by. She was running out of somewhere elses to go—and that wasn't a pleasant thought. But she only needed a couple of weeks, maybe a month. Just until her part of the lease on that stupid two-bedroom in Hyde Park ran out. Just until she caught her breath. Then she'd know what to do again. She'd formulate a plan of action. She'd settle somewhere entirely new and make a real go of it. A better go of it. One that included no cocktails named after condiments.

Her nail polish had worn off from being picked at, maroon flecks drifting down, catching in her shoelaces, by the time the bus wheezed to a halt. "Hey. Seat five," the bus driver snapped after a moment of silence. "Sweetheart."

No one replied. A man in ragged fatigues had been sleeping on one of the benches since Tunica. They were the only two left. Wait a second. Surely he didn't—June lifted her head. "Do you mean me?"

"Yeah, you, señorita." June would never understand how people saw her, a product of a Black mother and white father, and decided Latina. He sat back, scratching at his stubble. "You said that church with the lady pastor, right? You're about half a mile down this side road. I can't go any farther off route, unless you've got a few more bucks on you."

"It's pouring rain," June pointed out.

"I'll drive you to the doorstep for a hundred bucks."

"Fine. Fine," June said before scooping up her backpack and dashing into the deluge. Rain fell in a silver curtain, catching in her hair, running grooves down her jacket like the little rivers on either side of the road, and it rained so thick that she could barely make them out. The trees stood sentry, blind giants along the one-way street.

Her walk quickly became a stagger. Distantly, she heard the rain hitting water, flat and hollow, and wind whipping up waves.

The downpour tasted like salt water. There was a lake here, and as she walked, she couldn't shake the sensation that she was about to walk straight into it, led there blindly by the screaming wind. This was no cultivated paradise. It wouldn't be the sedate body of water hemmed in by glossy Spanish villas where movie stars made their summer homes. *No, this is a wild lake*, the rain seemed to say.

What was this place anyway? June had stolen the address off an Easter card, but she hadn't imagined it would be like this—anti-civilization, solitary houses buried so far from the road, they were invisible except for glints of yellow light from windows, like the eyes of wild and lonely beasts. Even so, she didn't want to go to distant California, where Dad and his new wife, a breeder of Persian cats, now lived. Mom would never turn her away, but her apartment was so small, and she'd let June intrude forever out of love, even if it was too much. Instead, there was Aunt Eliza, loving and kind enough to take in a wayward niece on the fly, with a guest room in the historic house that came with her job. Assuming June didn't get lost in the woods on the way there.

June felt Chicago being washed off her, water sluicing down to her bones, but it was a relief because even that was better than the horrendous, consuming boredom that had gripped her before.

That boredom. That restless, anxious twitch that came from too long spent standing still, too long without change. The feeling always found her. It ruined the tiny, stuffy apartment she had so recently shared with Delilah. The place had been a creaking shoebox, but her true home had been the soles of Delilah's feet poking out from blankets, how cool her eyes could be in the evenings, the way her hair—originally dyed platinum—had faded into dirty gold, dry and split at the ends: an elderly lion's mane. They had been isolated too, in their cubic space, suspended in the clouds above Chicago, the noise of the L train far below, and June had thought maybe this time she could find peace.

But June had spun against the walls. No number of nights out or spontaneous road trips had put off the inevitable. "Let's go," she'd begged on too many nights. She lived nocturnally, on a stray cat's schedule. "Let's just go."

"Go where?" Delilah finally asked at the end. "Why do you always want to go? Can't you ever just—"

"What?" June coaxed, draping her arms around her neck in the way that usually got her to soften.

"Stop," Delilah replied. "Just stop."

Later, she told June through pursed lips and teary eyes that the lease was under Delilah's name and that she cared for June but couldn't live with her, not an hour before June went in for her final shift at the All Night Diner.

Her hands shook, so pent up that the cocktails all shivered, splashing grenadine and vodka onto the tables. Then the punches had been thrown around her, the liquor shelves had shattered like applause, and frankly, June had known she would be fired for it because when the universe gave June signs it was time to move on, it wasn't exactly subtle.

June's jeans were muddy, calves burning, when the church appeared like a lighthouse out of the gloom. It was a white craftsman-style building surrounded by flower beds. It was no Saint Peter's Basilica, no grand bells or marble columns that could reach heaven. Here, apparently, God's house was much like anyone else's, only with a steeple. June had never seen the church in person.

It took two bobby pins and the better part of five minutes before the locked door clicked open for her, and she dripped into the church. When the door closed behind her, the rain quieted.

In the gray darkness, just in front of her, a table was stacked high with welcome brochures and some orchids, robbed of all color. Then came a few long pews, fewer than twenty, each lined with red faux velvet and identical black King James Bibles placed at regular intervals. A weathered but kindly piano sat on the stage to the left of the pulpit, dinged up but polished all the same. In an alcove above the pulpit, and the bleachers where the dinky Sunday choir must have gathered earlier that day, was a single large stained glass window bearing the image of the cross against a brilliant sunrise.

June wandered down the aisle aimlessly before picking a pew at random. She pushed the Bibles out of their order, dropped her bag at the end of it, and flopped over the armrest, letting her muddy feet dangle. She kicked off one shoe, and it took a bedraggled sock with it.

She was asleep before she managed the second.

CHAPTER THREE

 VOICE REACHED JUNE FUZZILY IN SLEEP, AND THOUGH she jerked awake, the pew under her and the face above her were incomprehensible at first. Her neck was sore after sleeping on her leather jacket—its old rock star smell comforting, if not particularly pillowy—and her hair had the mussed feeling that came from air-drying, her mouth ashy with dehydration. She had the colorless, driftless feeling of someone who'd been traveling too long, until she was strung out on miles: a junkie for a diesel and gas fix.

"June? Honey?" Now the face above her resolved itself into Aunt Eliza, shocked with an amused twist. She held June's squashed backpack in one hand and one of her beat-up sneakers with once-white laces and Sharpie sketches in the other. Every square inch of the shoe—and June herself—was caked in dried mud.

June had vague toddler memories of a teenage Aunt Eliza, a kind of second mom who had taken her trick-or-treating dressed as a pumpkin and held her in vain during her inconsolable moods. June had been a lively kid, from the terrible twos all the way into her fours. But Aunt Eliza had always been patient with her before leaving for college. She'd loved singing hymns to June, sitting with her at the tiny electric organ Eliza practiced on at home while June hammered all the keys at once and Mom hummed.

Eliza had always been a bit of a dork about church. Apparently they'd had a preacher in the family a few generations ago. In the old house in Texarkana, Eliza kept a framed picture of him on the organ, one of the very few tattered relics they had of family history: a tall dark-skinned man, his Sunday best almost lost in the muddy shades of the ancient photo, the thick stem of a sunflower the size of a hubcap in his hands.

When Mom had heard Eliza was going to some random church in the middle of nowhere, serving a handful of broken-down old locals plus whatever tourist poked their head in, she cried first, then laughed and said, "Good luck."

But Aunt Eliza had simply ignored the sarcasm and smiled. "You know we have roots there, right? Great-Granddaddy's church is somewhere under that lake. Nobody else wants that appointment. Most everybody moved away, but—that's his flock."

Now June smiled at her from the pew. "Hi, Aunt Eliza. Nice church you've got here. I like the..." She gestured vaguely at nothing.

"Why in the world didn't you knock on the rectory door? Come here. It's so good to see you." Aunt Eliza pulled her up into a hasty hug. Aunt Eliza was a particularly tall, stately woman with very dark skin, and she was grounded in a way June could admire. She was wearing neon running shoes and looked more like a college professor on her day off than a pastor. She smelled like cinnamon and soft earth, a hint of hard work. June only came up to her cheek.

"Is that where you live? The rectory?" June asked. "Sounds like the back end of something. No thanks."

"Well, girl, you look like the back end of something." Eliza chuckled, swaying them a moment before letting go. Her gaze was so fully on June's face that June was tempted to slide on her sunglasses. "Come on. What are you doing here?"

"Vacation," June said and sniffed her shirt. "Most urgently, shower?"

"Seems like you've already been through one," Eliza said mildly, glancing at the mud.

"Oh, this? Mud bath. Supposed to be very healthy." She wiggled dusty fingers. "Good for the skin." It had been years since she had seen Aunt Eliza. Too many years for this to be normal, showing up out of the thin air, sleeping in a pew like a girl without a home. "I wondered if I could crash here for a bit. A couple of weeks, maybe."

"Of course you can," Eliza said, without a blink, without a thought, and June relaxed out of the defensive stance she'd unknowingly taken. "I've got plenty of room for you here." There might've been a hint of a challenge in her voice. *You can't shock me, girl. I've seen everything.*

She offered June her backpack and shoe, and June took her few possessions, which were still damp from the rain. "Cool. Show me to the rectum."

Eliza hooked an arm around her. "Right this way."

છ૭

Fairchild's was quiet around Cassie as she spread out a blue-and-white-striped swimsuit on the worktable. It looked just like Catfish's. It had come from an estate sale, one piece of many locked in an old steamer trunk. Cassie had pulled it out, and instantly, she was five again, swimming near the dock in Catfish's care.

When Cassie was a little girl, long before Bolt was born, she would have lived in the water if Mom let her. She'd play at the shallow, muddy shore all day, the lemon-pie sun smiling above her, Mom opining on the phone from the porch while her painted toenails dried in the summer breeze, both waiting to hear Grandad's car rumble up the road so they could walk down to Valerie's for dinner. Cassie was never supposed to go past the dock, but that was where the water glittered the bluest. Blueberry blue.

The first time she met Catfish, she felt a spray of water hit her on the back of the head, and she turned around. And there was a girl in her faded blue-and-white suit, treading water like it was air, wet ringlets framing her face. She was a teenager, maybe one of the beautiful ones who sunbathed on boats, mature enough to no longer need life jackets.

"Hi," she said. She was almost under the dock, paddling in its shadow. "I hope you're not swimming alone. Are you lost?"

"No." Cassie kicked a bit closer. "I live here."

Some of the concern in the girl's expression soothed, and she glided closer, into the sun. "Good. It's easy to swim too far, especially on a day this lovely."

In the face of this girl's wiry arms, Cassie wished she could hide her yellow water wings. But Mom wouldn't let her swim without them, just like how Cassie couldn't go past the dock and had to stay where she could see Mom and Mom could see her. Cassie was too young. Other people lived on the lake, and a lot of kids were near the marina. But the marina was a whole world away. The girl must have swum far to get there. She must be a very good swimmer.

"What's your name, honey?" she asked, flipping onto her back and looking at Cassie upside down. The girl made a silly face, and Cassie laughed.

"Cassandra—but Grandad says it's too big a name for me, so he calls me 'Cassie.'"

"Catfish," she replied, tapping her chest. "That's what my dad calls me."

"That's a funny name."

"Isn't it?" Catfish smiled, indulgent. "It's because I can swim really far underwater without taking a breath. Want me to show you?" When Cassie nodded, Catfish dove before pushing through murky water to the other side of the dock and popping up in the vague blue distance. She waved and then dipped back. When she reappeared, panting hard, Cassie could only smile at her, too shy and starstruck to know what to say.

"Where's your mommy?" Catfish asked gently. Cassie pointed to the house, where she could see Mom's feet propped up on the patio table. Catfish nodded. "That's okay. I can watch you for a while."

And from then, every day of summer and spring when Cassie went swimming, she was no longer alone. Catfish had been there with her, teaching her to dunk her head without getting water in her nose, guiding her through careful somersaults, and demonstrating how to pinwheel her arms like a paddleboat.

"Stay in sight," Cassie murmured now, fingering the stretched, used lining of the waistband of the swimsuit. "Don't swim past the dock. Don't swim. Don't swim…"

The bell over the door jingled. "Hello, hello," a man called, too backlit by the blistering sun streaming through the door for Cassie to immediately know him. Then her customer turned enough to reveal the boyish face of Jeff Daley. It was well-known from the new billboards and from the newspaper, which had done a big article when he bought the Prosper marina a few months back. He took off his hat and fanned his flushed, clean-shaven neck with its wide brim. "Whew." He let out his breath, chuckling. "It's hotter than the fires of hell out there, even this early in June. How are you, Miss Fairchild?"

Jeff Daley, with his cherub cheeks and his Bill Clinton hair, came from Charlene. He'd moved his half-a-million-dollar houseboat over to E Dock when he bought the marina, and now he reigned over them all from there. He'd been a butcher once and still aged his own steaks, but he'd made his fortune opening convenience stores across the state. Now here he was, pouring that money into the Prosper side of the lake with such gusto, it was a wonder nobody heard the splash. His houseboat was twice as big as any other out on the water. His life was as large and loud as the speedboat in which he often roared across the water.

"Mr. Daley, hi," Cassie replied, brushing off her jeans. They were covered in hand shapes from absentminded swipes when she was elbow deep in tarnished precious metal. "Call me Cassie."

"Cassie, then." She had a sense of him committing it to memory. Three months into his life in Prosper, and apparently he wouldn't be content until he knew everybody. He leaned on her counter, grinning his lopsided schoolboy grin. His was a mercantile kind of affability—networking that led to exchanges of favors, box seats, shortcuts, and handshake deals, a foreign language of brotherhood with nuances that had always escaped her. "Mind if I look around?"

"Of course not," Cassie replied, hands fluttering back to her pockets. "Take your time."

Jeff took a stroll through her wares. He nodded enthusiastically around the store, eyes fixing on no particular piece. It was more a gesture of approval than of interest. After a few minutes, he returned, pulling a packet of Bazooka bubble gum from the breast pocket of his button-down before he stuck a piece in his mouth. The pink strip was just a shade or two lighter than his tongue. "Gum?" he offered.

Cassie took the wax-wrapped square and unfolded it. "You know, we've got a lovely Queen Anne wardrobe in right now," she tried. It had come from Charlene, just like him. There was nothing else here she could imagine him wanting. "If you'd like to take a look."

His eager nod returned, but he didn't pursue it. "I've been wanting to discuss something with you, Miss Cassie. A little business talk."

"Oh. All right," Cassie said, but it didn't make much sense. She dealt in the old, the forgotten, and Daley liked his trappings shiny and new.

"It's—well, I'd rather sit down with some materials. Don't want to just spring it on you. Why don't you come over for supper?" he suggested. "Let's see… How's next Wednesday? Then you won't have to dodge tourists on the way down the dock—just you, me, and my son. I've got some great filets right now."

"That's kind of you," she replied. Jeff Daley might have known her name, but he didn't know anything else about her. "But I don't like to go out on the water. Sort of a phobia."

"Oh no." He gave her a folksy sort of pout. "That so? Well. Let's go out, then. We can go into Charlene. Ranalli's has the best lasagna around, or—"

"The Grand Destiny has fried green tomatoes on Wednesdays."

"Wonderful. That's wonderful. I'll sure be looking forward to it." He withdrew a battered leather wallet and shimmied a business card free. "There's my number, if you don't happen to already have it." He smiled at her again—a charming, bubble gum–scented grin—as he pushed open the door and let a gust of summer heat inside. "Bye now. Keep cool, huh? Gracious."

He got into a big white Jeep, so new that the license plate was temporary paper, and with a last jovial wave, he whipped out of her parking lot, kicking up a wake of gravel, and zoomed down the road toward the marina.

Cassie leaned her back on the door. Airy and blushing with afternoon light, her shop seemed to expand back into place in his absence, filling the space he had taken up. She popped the gum in her mouth, then chewed until her tongue tingled with artificial pink flavor. But even as a child, she'd never had the taste for bubble gum, so she spit it back into the wrapper and rolled it into a ball.

"Smoky," she murmured and tossed it. In a blur, Smoky was out from under a chest of drawers and after it, batting it between the legs of a dining room table. If she were small enough, Cassie might have hidden under the furniture when she heard that man coming too. Whatever business proposition he intended to serve her at dinner, she suspected she wouldn't like it.

ঙ৹

Lark kept her back to the dock, ignoring neighbors chatting as they strolled by and dock-rat kids chasing between spotlights where the sun leaked through spaces in the tin roof. Besides the out-of-control telescope collection, their houseboat had remained in an odd expectant stasis, like it was waiting for the family to come back and get started with summer festivities. Her family's charcoal grill still perched on their dock box, a memory of rib eye smoke, rich char, and heady July evenings reaching Lark across the gap. Mom's chimes, roofed with cobwebs, bonged in their corner. Around her, everyone else's weekend was a distant joyful roar.

She'd started her labors with the part of the collection Daddy had left on the front porch. The three dozen or so telescopes out there were in rough shape. Some were in cases, and those were only damp, but the spyglasses watching her from tripods had rusted necks and watery eyes, all cracks and cataracts. Even these junkers would have to be measured and then photographed if she stood a chance of unloading some of this and selling the boat. With gentle hands, Lark loosened tacky screws, lowered stand legs, measured lens diameters and extendable shafts. Anything engraved on their pocked green hulls, a brand or anything, she noted. All in all, it wasn't that different from inventorying the vinyl that came into Goner Records from estate and yard sales, their labels rumpled and stained, long fallen from collective musical memory.

For two nights, she'd had strange, fish-eyed dreams, loud and too bright, and woke up tired. Daddy was close in those nightmares, like an indecipherable mutter that lined her sleep. It was that—the closeness or kinship she felt when she woke—that left her gasping and afraid.

Damnation and hellfire. She needed to get out of this dusty mausoleum. Lark only stubbed her toe once as she pulled free of the *Big Dipper* and set off down the dock. She passed some familiar faces: Joe, a bald eccentric who drove down from Magnolia every weekend to his minuscule canal barge near the gangplank, sauntered by with one of his snow-white ferrets draped around his neck. Allen and Josh, the twins from Slip 17, were on top of their squatty cruiser, doing chores for money. Lark had babysat them years ago when their parents went for dinner at Aunt Valerie's, but now they were shamefaced preteens with identical acne. Allen peered at Lark over his broom handle.

"Hey, Lark." It was Mable, sitting regally up on her front porch, her bunioned feet resting in a basin of cucumber water. She'd had her little boat with lilac canvases down here since before Lark was born, and Mable always had some snack or another ready to hand out to passing kids. Lark had eaten many of her crispy oatmeal cookies over the years. "Your daddy doing any better?"

Lark didn't quite stop, ducking her head a bit as she passed. "Um—no, ma'am, not really." She meant well, but it was an impossible kind of question to answer.

"My granddaughter Sammy's here for the summer, sugar," Mable called after her. "Maybe she can help you with all that business down there. Keep her out of trouble."

"Ha. Right," Lark called back, already jogging up the ramp. *When hell freezes over.*

It wasn't a long drive to the Grand Destiny Resort, which had been in the family since the 1940s. Daddy had grown up at the Destiny, and his favorite stories to tell were about what it was like to be a boy there. In 1960, the resort was in the middle of a growth spurt, a new generation's ambition ballooning it from its humble postwar footprint. Lark's great-uncle had built some of the cabins nearest to the water, the smell of fresh paint and varnish mingling with fish batter and chlorine from the brand-new swimming pool. Back then, Daddy's job—a very important one, his mother had insisted—was to make sure each table had its own glass ketchup bottle in between two shiny salt and pepper shakers. *Boy, did those summer folks sure go through some ketchup*, he'd tell her, chuckling. Later, when he was a teenager, Daddy would sit behind the motel desk and check in guests over the pages of his *Astronomer's Monthly*.

As Lark pulled into the gravel lot, the green-and-white-striped awning over the restaurant waved to her. The high season perched on the horizon, and Aunt Valerie was notoriously a terror trying to get everything ready. The place had the scrubbed, rebellious look of a little boy in church clothes. The grass down to the lake and docks was perfect, the pool freshly cleaned. A fresh coat of green paint gleamed around the restaurant windows.

"Oh, behave!" Aunt Valerie stomped a warped floorboard back into place on her way to greet Lark at the door of the restaurant. "Honestly, this place is just like Dennis the Menace."

"Up to your usual tricks, then?" Lark ran a hand over the old wood paneling. The whole family knew it was a lazy old motel. The place loved for things to go wrong. Back in the forties, they'd built the motel from every stick they had managed to carry out of their timber yard. That green wood—salvaged, orphaned, and damp from the lake water that had buried its hewn stumps—was full of mischief. But Daddy's older sister was perfectly capable of keeping the place in line.

Aunt Valerie looked happy to see Lark in her distracted, slightly prickly way. She couldn't be more different than Daddy, with her direct, no-nonsense face. "Hey, honey." The hug Aunt Valerie gave Lark was firm: sure knots tied by confident hands. She smelled like her grandmother Destiny's world-famous piecrust. "I just got off the phone with your mama a little bit ago."

"Hey." Lark held on to the bony hug. "This place is really looking summer ready." Mom had already called and explained everything. Aunt Valerie didn't have to ask Lark how Daddy was, and she didn't have to tell her.

Valerie pulled back to give her a hard looking-over. As usual, Aunt Valerie's bangs were carefully blown out, the rest of her hair tied up with a purple rubber band. It was a blond-gray blend, a sort of oatmeal color. Oatmeal with all the fixings. The tan she'd cultivated in her youth was now permanent and leathery. She was so down-to-earth, visitors sometimes found her rude. A dustrag hung from one of the belt loops of her work jeans. "Mitch! Your cousin is here."

Mitch poked his head out of the office, which connected the motel and restaurant to his little grocery. "Lark!" he bellowed, replacing Valerie's tight embrace with a huge solid one of his own. "We've been looking for you, kiddo. Diego nearly drove over this morning to check on you."

Lark had had a massive crush on Mitch when he was a teenager and she was a squirmy little kid in her polka-dot swimsuit. He'd only gotten taller and brawnier since, but the days of her mooning after her cousin were long over. Now Lark just felt a little like a garden gnome next to him.

"Lordy. What did you do to your hair?" Valerie cringed at the faded cotton candy pink, and Lark swiped at it, smiling.

"I just needed a change. But it was pinker at first. More Pepto-Bismol." She had to laugh at Valerie's expression. It had been an ill-conceived coping mechanism, maybe, but she was still feeling it. Though her punky hair had fit in better during nights out on Beale Street than it did out here in the boonies.

Aunt Valerie scoffed. "You look like a flamingo."

"Come see the market," Mitch said, guiding her through to the grocery. Started by his father before his sudden disappearance sometime during Lark's childhood, the Grand Destiny Market had been under Mitch's management since he broke off his engagement in Little Rock a little while back. "We've just done a big renovation in here to try to keep up with the new swindler over at the marina. You won't believe it. Whole new ceiling and everything."

"Really?" Lark gazed around at the familiar space. There was the same old faded welcome mat Mitch laid out every morning, the fishing section with the tackle and line and poles, the floaties. There was the little case of hot pizzas and chicken strips and hot dogs Lark used to rummage in after a swim. The creaky old swivel chair with its fraying seat still sat behind the horseshoe counter; one side faced the lobby so guests could be checked in, and the other side faced the market, where hungry weekenders stocked up.

Weekenders always descended on this place like the seven plagues of Egypt. As teenagers, she and Mitch had stayed plenty busy stocking their minuscule dairy section with milk and eggs and bacon from the farms a few miles west of them. Lark loved the plates of baked goods Mitch picked up each day from the local old ladies: Mrs. Freemire's pistachio brownies, Sadie Simpson's Rice Krispies treats, Linda's meringues, Mable's giant oatmeal pecan cookies, not to mention the Fairchild honey. They were friends, all those little treats in their plastic wrap. Thanks to the family sweet tooth—the Destiny was known foremost for pie, after all—nobody could complain that the market candy section was subpar. They had everything from horehound candy to Charleston Chews, nutty nougats and rainbow sticks, hubcap-sized lollipops, Hershey's and Cadbury and Nestle, plus special extras: homemade chocolate speedboats with caramel stripes, marzipan houseboats (mostly for display because those things took hours), rock-candy Arkansas quartz, and chocolate-marshmallow life preservers.

All these things were sewn into the lining of the shop, and so it was precious. Even the video rental section, a small room behind the wall of bread and cereal and canned goods, stayed as unchanged as Mitch could keep it. That had originally been his dad's idea too, back in the day. Lark peeped around the corner. The smell of the moldering VCR boxes was comforting. Those old tapes—*Jurassic Park II*, *Air Force One*, *Titanic*—still made up most of the library, though Aunt Valerie had apparently forced Mitch to surrender a back corner to a few DVDs, plus one or two video games.

This little world was built on routine. The shelves were dusted, the glass dome of the gumball machine shiny and stocked. The tiny customer bathroom was spick-and-span. But Lark could discern no change whatsoever from this so-called "renovation." Mitch watched expectantly for her reaction.

"It looks absolutely perfect," she told him, giving him another quick squeeze.

They moved into the heart of the Destiny, the ancient icy

window unit shuddering to life as if in greeting. Huge rotating fans sent breezes all through the place to form a dozen competing wind tunnels. Aunt Valerie said, "We aren't open today, but I just put some peas on. And I'm fixing pie with some of our neighbor Cassie's honey. Remember her? I bet you're starving to death."

"Yes, ma'am. Food please." Lark slid onto one of the red vinyl barstools at the restaurant counter, the gleaming pie case rotating enticingly behind it. "Cassie. She runs Fairchild's Treasures, doesn't she?" Cassie had long been a presence Lark was aware of without truly knowing, a neighbor girl with an oddball young mom and a mild look of panic at any social gathering.

"Yeah." Mitch was straightening the stand of pamphlets featuring local attractions. "You should see the old stuff she repairs over there. Stuff most people'd just throw away. Makes good money too."

"Oh really?" Lark took a slow spin on the stool, taking in the restaurant that belonged on a 1950s road trip postcard. Down the hill, Valerie's business partner, Diego, crouched at the back end of the old swan paddleboats, giving them their annual coat of paint. Lark had always loved those swans bobbing along the lake like a bevy of puff pastries. She rotated back to Mitch. "You think she might be able to help me out with Daddy's telescopes?"

Mitch and Valerie exchanged an unmissable glance. "I'll call and ask her," Mitch said. "I'm sure she'd at least have some advice. Who knows? Maybe she'd want to buy some for the shop."

"There, now. That's a good idea." Valerie plunked a huge glass of sweet tea in front of Lark, hands on her hips. A turkey club complete with pickle spear had already appeared on the counter in front of her. "Now sit still and eat something." She was already halfway back to the kitchen to check on her peas. "Just like your daddy, too busy thinking to eat anything."

Lark winced, half the sandwich already crammed into her mouth. But Valerie was right: Lark's mind was already down the road, knocking on the door of Fairchild's Treasures.

CHAPTER FOUR

ASSIE WAS NAPPING, HER BOOK OVER HER EYES AS A sun shield, when the bees roused her. She felt them circling above her like a little cyclone, and she lifted herself out of gauzy dreams, no more than brief flashes of color, sound, and familiar laughter coming from the water. Three bees had settled on the end of her braid; from a distance, they might have looked like a decorative flower. Cassie stretched, back bowed against the warm roof of the RV, and rolled toward the edge. She caught the railing and shimmied down until her feet found first the open windowsill and then the cinderblock she had propped on its head as a makeshift step stool, and she hopped to the ground.

She wandered into the space between the hives. Perhaps this year, she would split another to keep combating her losses. It was a hard world for bees. Every year, the air smelled more like ozone, and fewer returned. They got lost in attics, mistook blouses for blossoms, ran afoul of fly swatters, were poisoned en masse by insecticides. Bees knew as well as humans about the dead. They appointed their own undertakers, who towed their bodies away from the hive, away from the new life trying to grow.

No one was around, so Cassie didn't bother with her apiarist suit as she pulled a frame from the nearest hive. It was the first home she'd tried to build for them, gleaming white with ten frames inside. A couple of bees settled on her fingers, another tickling her wrist in its search for pollen or perhaps stray drops of honey. Even in the beginning—when that first hive came home with her from the blind auction of a storage unit, a gift she had not asked for or expected— she didn't use a suit. All these years, and never once had one of her bees stung her. Some people never saw more than the stingers.

She scraped her fingernail along the corner of the frame to check on the bounty underneath. They immediately scuttled over to clean and patch it. She dipped her finger and came away with a few drops. Tasted it. Wildflowers—clover too.

She gave jars of honey to Valerie for pies, to Diego to send his children down in Houston, and sent at least a dozen jars to Mom every year, to serve the members of her book club. The day Mitch had returned from Little Rock in shambles from his broken relationship, she'd given him honey too. She still remembered the electric thrum she had felt, seeing him slumped on a lawn chair on Destiny's dock as if he'd never left at all. But she hadn't known what to say to him. There had been no way to tell him how she'd felt seeing him leave and how elated yet how sad she was to see him again in that state. He probably didn't even remember, but she had snuck over, early in the morning, and left a basket with two jars of honey and a fresh loaf of bread still warm from the oven wrapped in cotton cloth. When she couldn't find the words for what she felt, the language of bees sufficed.

There was no sound of lapping water, boat motors, or laughing children. Bees wove sensible tight harmonies that she could wrap herself in until it was all she heard.

Usually. She heard the heavy pull of tires on gravel in the distance, and then Mom's huge station wagon pulled into her driveway and sprawled on the grass.

Cassie slipped the frame back into place and hurried across the lawn as the car shut off. The passenger door opened, and Bolt loped out. He'd grown a little even since Christmas, lankier and blonder than ever. He approached and tossed an arm around her, already smelling of sunscreen. He was sandy and good-looking, a little like a golden retriever, with limbs too long and feet too big for the rest of him.

"Hey, Cassie," he said.

"You're getting so tall." Cassie patted his back. They didn't look very similar; he was tan where she was pale, and she was dark-haired where he was blond, but there was some reflection of each other in their bones. She had been ten when he was born, and her preteen years had been consumed by learning how diapers worked and how to bottle-feed a child, watching Bolt growing at lightning speeds. He'd been quick to speak, quick to walk, quick to run.

Mom followed, kissing Cassie's cheek. "You're looking very freckled. Are you wearing your sunscreen?"

"You're early," Cassie said, moving into her embrace. "I thought you'd call when you were close."

"And where's your phone, huh?" Mom smelled faintly like her nicotine gum.

"It's right over..." The phone wasn't in her direct sight line, and Cassie couldn't remember the last time she'd charged it. Oh well. It was somewhere. Unless she'd accidentally sold it at the shop.

"I don't know why you're not glued to it like everyone else these days." Mom had been a hollerin', smokin', beerin', fightin' Katharine Hepburn. Cassie didn't holler, smoke, beer (much), or fight, and she had never resembled any movie stars. She'd never had the curves that now had expanded like sand filling the bottom of Mom's hourglass.

She patted Cassie's back and pushed her toward the door and through to the kitchen breakfast table. Behind them, Bolt jogged in with Mom's cheetah-patterned overnight bag.

"I got your room ready," Cassie said to him. "If you want to drop your things."

Bolt paused and cut his gaze across to Mom. And there came a familiar feeling, of the two of them communicating over her head, silent words in a secret code she didn't know.

"Right. Cassie girl, Bolt and I were talking on the ride up," Mom began. She picked up Cassie's quilt from the back of the loveseat and dusted it off. "And *I* thought it might be a good idea if he stayed down at Valerie's."

"Oh," was all Cassie could reply.

Bolt was still smiling, but there was a worried tinge turning it sour now.

"She's got one of the unrenovated rooms available; I just called," Mom went on. "He'll be working there in the mornings and at the marina in the afternoon, so it would just be easier. And she's got an internet connection all set up for the guests now, which would help him get ahead in school, and that way you wouldn't have to clean up after a teenage boy all summer."

"It's really no trouble for me. I was expecting him to stay," Cassie said and again felt their silent line of communication burn.

"I'll basically be staying with you," Bolt added in a hurry. "Just down the hill a little ways." The Grand Destiny's glowing sign was visible from the top of the path.

All at once, Cassie understood and felt like a fool. The two of them were always very careful about her feelings. Cassie had been branded as strange and fragile before Bolt was even born, a freak child who threw tantrums when her mother tried to get her on a boat and fought night terrors that glistened blue and tasted like mud in her throat.

It must have been decided in the car. She could picture it almost as if she'd been there, Bolt's cheek pressed against a window, arguing with a mixture of guilt and resolve, Mom's frustrated hands clamped on the wheel as she relented and made a frantic, last-minute call to Valerie for new accommodations. They were painting over the truth: Bolt didn't want to spend all summer with no company but his odd older sister. Cassie sometimes wondered where he had gone, the sweet little boy who used to run to her instead of Mom to read him a story at bedtime.

Cassie felt a wild urge to tell them they could spare her the charade; she wasn't a child. But she would play along, or else Bolt would feel guilty all summer.

So instead she nodded. "That's a good idea. I didn't remember to get new sheets for the bed anyway."

It was the right thing to say. Now everyone looked relieved.

"Can I go to the marina?" Bolt asked, turning to Mom. "I think Rig's down there, and he said to find him when I got here."

"Yes, but only if you're back for lunch. That means two hours and no more," Mom cautioned him, and in a flash, with a final grin at Cassie, Bolt was off, chasing his way down to the water.

"Now," Mom said. "We've got to straighten up a little, Cassie girl; I don't know how you live like this."

"Sure," Cassie sighed and stood to get a broom while Mom dug out the all-purpose cleaner and a few rags. It was easier to give in to Mom's wild hares. She knew from experience: with Mom in the house, everything was much tidier, and in comparison, Cassie got younger, dirtier, and clumsier. She'd been a bad child, Mom often said, one who'd cried and screamed and threw tantrums like no one's business. It was unconscious regression; with Mom in the house, even Cassie's dreams grew stark and sharp as winter branches. She always had the worst dreams in the double-wide. It made her small again, crying in her damp swimsuit, with scratches on her arms all cold and hot, while Mom paced frantically. They'd never quite gotten the muddy stain out of the carpet and couch cushions.

Mom was happy now, though, eager to relay compliments her friends had given Cassie's last batch of honey, tell her about Bolt's ACT scores, and describe a Japanese vase she saw at a store that she thought Cassie would like. So Cassie never said much about it. The thought of Mom's stricken expression if she ever got the impression Cassie didn't want her around—no. It was unbearable. Besides, she had missed her, and it had been a few months, so Cassie felt more charitably toward her.

Soon, Mom scrubbed the counters, Cassie swept the floors for the second time in two days, and Mom unearthed boxes from the storage closet, a surreptitious hint that Cassie needed to organize. Mom had cleaned the refrigerator, the floors were freshly mopped, and the fixings for lunchtime sandwiches were out on the counter when they took a break because Mom could only go so long without caffeine.

The silence was companionable as the perfume of coffee permeated the entire house, which was so long and narrow that smells had nowhere to go. Noise had nowhere to go, people had nowhere to go in that long shotgun barrel, bedroom leading to bedroom leading to bathroom leading to kitchen.

Cassie made the cups while Mom sliced tomatoes and laid lettuce out to dry. Bolt's two hours would be up relatively soon. They talked very little during the process.

"Cream?"

"Only if it's nonfat."

"I don't have that. Sorry."

"Well…just a smidge."

When she'd moved out, Mom had taken the strings of plastic peppers Cassie hadn't liked, the decorative porcelain bowls of fruit, the strange dancing half goat half men that once had been on the windowsills. Cassie had replaced them with homemade candles, and her favorite antiques—not ones from the lake but from estate sales, the things that had seemed to be especially loved. A child's huggable, sagging teddy. A music box, hand-carved wood with the inner mechanism showing. The crudely formed yet smooth-worn horse.

Putting down her soggy rag, Mom stood in the window, steam from the coffee curling up from the mug like a cat's tail. Her skin looked translucent and fragile, bathed in that light. The roots of her hair were like dandelion fuzz.

Cassie curled her legs under her at the kitchen table. Then she realized Mom wasn't looking out the window but at the yellow paint Cassie had spread on the lower pane, painted so thick, nothing below the sky was visible. Specifically, Lake Prosper wasn't visible. Embarrassment pricked up her spine.

"You used to love that water," Mom said finally. "So why would you do a thing like this?" She tapped the painted glass. "And if you have to ruin your window to avoid looking at it, why don't you just move? You can't be keeping this place for my sake or Bolt's."

It was always like this. The more Mom said, the more Cassie's tongue swelled, until words were impossible.

Mom scratched at it with one fingernail. It flaked, but Cassie had painted it on thick. There was only more yellow underneath. "What did you used to call your little friend? That little made-up playmate?"

Cassie swallowed around her tongue, which spasmed in her mouth, choking her on songs from a sunbaked homeland that wasn't hers, with Italian words the older girl knew by heart but barely understood. She envisioned strong arms, that confident laugh, and skin so tanned, it seemed like the sun would never burn it, only make it glow.

"Catfish," Mom recalled. "You used to make yourself so happy with your imagination. I moved us here, and you loved it so much, I thought that once, finally, I'd done the right thing..." Mom cut herself off, turning to look at her, with a frank sip of coffee. "What did you say happened to her? Most kids just outgrow imaginary friends, but it was so horrible what you imagined happened to yours."

The back of her neck felt cold, and she took a sip of coffee to wash down the muddy taste in her mouth. "I don't remember."

"You had such a lively little mind." Mom's face was set now, her gaze steady. This would not be a conversation Cassie could escape. The fish trap had closed around her. "But I have to say something. It's soured. That bright thing in your head. It just went bad somehow, sometime when you were growing up, and it scares me for you."

Not this again, Cassie wished, though wishes had never proved particularly helpful to her before. Of course, Mom couldn't just let it be. Of course, she had to get her two cents in before Bolt came back. She had twelve hours here, barely enough time to scrub and needle her daughter into shape. And Cassie had been so careful not to blab about the antiques and the bees past the point of interest and hadn't complained about the reorganizing— "I'm fine," she said.

"You don't date. Your only friend is Valerie, a woman older than your mother. You live in your childhood home, barely making a profit, when you could be out there making something of yourself. I don't think it's good for you to be here alone anymore."

Cassie curled her hands too tight around her coffee cup. It scraped along the table.

"If you're staying because of the land, or me, or Grandad, don't—"

"I'm not staying for *you*," Cassie cut over her and bit her lip. She hated the way confrontation made her feel, sensitive and wounded. "I'm not staying for you. I like it here."

"You hate it here, Cassie!" Mom exclaimed. "You painted over your window so you couldn't see the lake!"

"You don't know what I want, Mom," Cassie replied, and that exposed-nerve feeling grew.

"I know what I see," Mom countered, crowding over to the table and reaching for her, capturing Cassie's hands and pulling them toward her. "Your life is so small, and I know you don't like it when I say it, but you're too old to be coddled."

Coddled? Mom had never coddled her. Mom didn't know how to coddle anyone; she valued toughness too much. Cassie pressed her teeth together.

"Didn't I offer to send you to college? Only you said no."

Outside, the bees were swarming into a black storm cloud.

Mom was well into her stride now, a train clamped onto its track, and Cassie was younger than ever in the face of it. She was six again, tantrums boiling up from her gut and into her throat. "I didn't work to give you and Bolt a future that was better than mine to watch you sit around here like I did at your age, wasting your youth the way I wasted mine—"

"Stop it!"

The bees outside went silent. For a moment, even the wind stilled. Mom caught her breath, ruffled, and before she collected herself, Cassie pressed a hand to her forehead.

"Stop it," Cassie repeated softly. "Mom, I don't want to fight. Please."

Mom let go of her hands and folded her arms, sitting back. Her eyes shuttered, lights out, doors locked, keys thrown away. Cassie had shocked her into bewildered muteness.

"I'm fine," Cassie tried out. "I'm happy here. I'm happy. I'm an adult. I like my life." It sounded flimsy. But it was the truth. It wasn't a town, the collection of people who lived here, and hers wasn't a fancy home. The crusty retirees who had earned their relaxation, the regional antique dealers who were always happy to consult, Valerie and Mitch, the shop and its treasures. Maybe, just maybe, Grandad would be proud to know she hadn't let it all rust.

"I don't want to fight," Cassie said again, instead of explaining. "I want to have a nice day. I thought maybe we should drive into Charlene for dinner, go to the Hotel Saint Germain, and have those burgers Bolt likes, and maybe go to an estate sale."

It wasn't an answer, nor an end to the fight, but it made the corners of Mom's mouth soften. It was enough, just barely, to get them through the rest of the day.

❧

Patient as the second damn coming, Lark waited for Mitch to get back to her about his antique-store friend. Like the universe itself, her task on the *Big Dipper* showed every sign of continuously expanding. The telescopes were definitely spawning. Several times, Lark found a batch of minuscule kaleidoscopes or a wicker basket full of jeweler's magnifiers that could only have come about through some bizarre spyglass reproduction.

She went over to the Grand Destiny for dinner some nights or to pick up groceries from the market. The dock was quiet, though on a twilight walk down its length, Lark had spotted a new boat, the Monstro of houseboats, docked at the very end. The lights were on inside, and she saw the glow of an enormous TV before she turned and walked back to the *Big Dipper*.

It took three days to organize the telescopes on the front porch, and that didn't count those up the side steps to the houseboat top. At first, she wiped each of them down before they went in the box, but then, anxious that this treatment might damage them, she gave up on cleaning at all. One she did break, a wobbly stargazer perched on the narrow window ledge. This accident shook her badly, the shame of the error radiating through her body with the sharp ache of a bruised rib. Still clutching her side, she'd scrapped the pieces mercilessly on the dock box along with the one rusted beyond recognition.

Lark put them in numbered boxes that corresponded to the inventory she was writing out on graph paper, but she didn't seal them, in case Cassie over at Fairchild's Treasures wanted to appraise any of them. Finally, she couldn't stand waiting a second longer, and Lark just marched right over to the antique shop without invitation, but the place was shut up with a sign that said closed for family. The sulking gray cat in the window wouldn't tell her any different.

She called Mom on the drive back to Echo, very briefly, just because she missed her, but she'd spared her the details. Dad didn't get on to talk, and Mom had chatted weakly about home and work and a piece they'd both happened to catch on NPR. Mom hadn't mentioned medical bills or health insurance battles even once. Lark had promised that everything was fine, that she had it in hand, and got off the phone. It was the extent of what they were capable of just then.

After her attempt, Lark looked out over the lake on the walk back down to the dock. Her eyes lingered on the horizon, where the dam hovered. As she approached the boat, the telescopes turned to ogle her as usual—

A pair of eyes glared out at her from among the collection. Lark paused at the gate and watched the girl lurking on the side steps in a striped tank top and jean shorts. One of the spyglasses turned back and forth on its stand, as if shaking its head in disapproval.

"Who are you?" Lark managed, taken aback.

The girl was probably about fourteen, tall and gangly, her tanned legs sprawling down the steps. Her narrowed eyes were the shade of sea glass, dark hair curling close to her head. Between her fingers was a vape pen, which accounted for the vague scent of cherry vanilla smoke. There was something familiar about this intruder. She had the shocked look of someone who'd grown very quickly. That was it. It could only be Mable's granddaughter, Sammy. There was Mable's mischievous glint, here in miniature. Lark caught sight of a tube of Life Savers, half unfurled into rainbow ribbon, shoved in her pocket. One of her hands was wrapped around the nearest tripod.

Lark knew even before she actually did it. "Don't—"

The teenager shoved the tripod at her, and it plummeted to the deck with a horrible crack. Sammy leaped off the houseboat's side and cut the corner onto the dock. The tripod had hooked the leg of another stand, and after a moment of hazardous wobble, there was a second smash. Lark dropped, her heart giving a painful spasm—and Sammy was running off down the dock, her eyes flashing back only once.

Lark sprinted off the front of the boat. She was still holding one of the cases, and tears burned hot behind her eyes. Suddenly, what she'd been resisting, what she couldn't even admit to herself she'd been avoiding, was no longer resistible. She had to look. Just to catch the girl's face again, maybe see something there to explain the act. Jerking the case open, she ripped the telescope from its spotted silk lining. She hesitated another instant—she really shouldn't—but then held the old device up to her eye, the smell of the polish on its soft leather grip and the lacquer of its fine rosewood shaft filling her nostrils. For a moment she searched in the fuzzy dimness, adjusting to the magnification. But it was as effortless as focusing her own eye. She seized her gaze onto the vandal again. There she was, sprinting through shafts of light between the dock's wooden slats, the vape pen still clutched in her hand. And also—

Lark's breath caught. She tore the telescope from her face, blinking, as if to clear the stardust out of her vision. *No more. Don't look again.* But it was like cautioning herself against taking a breath. She pulled the eyepiece back against her face.

Sammy raced between shadows down the dock. And behind her, nearly overtaking her, was…

Lark jerked the spyglass down, shaking. No. It wasn't real.

But there it was. As solid and corporeal as Sammy herself through the lens of the spyglass.

A massive hurling wave. The form was as dark and dense as an oil spill, reaching for the girl, threatening at any moment to devour her, to swipe her off into the inky water under the dock. It boomed into the dock piers, forcing itself through narrow gaps as it surged in pursuit. Lark gasped, clutching hard at her chest, frozen in place as she watched the wave roar over the girl. Lark felt the spray, the secondary tug of a riptide around her own ankles.

But when she lowered the spyglass and looked again, there was nothing there at all. Mable's granddaughter was out of sight, and Lark was left in a wreck of broken glass. She crouched amid the glittering spray, staring down at it. Her eyes were tired, the world fuzzing at the edges. There was a panicked quake in her legs. She shook her head once. Again.

Wake up. Lark rested her open palm on the deck to steady herself and felt the tender pricks of the glass shards. With a shivering breath, she ground her hand into the debris. *Real. This sensation is real.* Distantly, the sharp grit burying itself in her skin reached her.

But the afterimage of the wave still roared behind her eyelids.

ↂ

"Welcome home," Aunt Eliza had said, when she showed June her little gabled guest room, where the air-conditioning was optimistic at best. The rectory was cozy, a white clapboard house that was half porch. Eliza's scuffed-up bike was tucked beside the door, helmet dangling from a handlebar. The laundry/storage room had a definite church smell of hymnals and candle wax. Eliza still kept essential oil diffusers in every room, dispensing gentle florals. There was the picture of Great-Granddaddy holding the giant sunflower, preserved in his customary place of honor on her organ. This place—or close to it, at least—had been his home until the dam.

Aunt Eliza never grilled June about why she was there, but she did immediately give her various odd jobs. Visit the market attached to the motel and buy granola, plus chia seeds, steel-cut oats, and Greek yogurt from the scruffy half giant who manned the counter. Jostle the Wi-Fi router. Drive into the nearest idyllic little town—Charlene, an aging debutante tourist trap—and print a batch of next Sunday's welcome pamphlets. On Friday night, they dusted the inside of the chapel and laid Bibles in the pews for the upcoming service, and Aunt Eliza sang B. B. King—some Howlin' Wolf too. Just a hint of contemporary hip-hop. She had an untaught, yet rich, real kind of a voice that rang when she sang the solo parts of "Open the Window, Noah." *Open the window, let the dove fly in.* Like Mom's.

They hadn't talked about June's midnight ride into town. They giggled at reality TV, throwing Red Hots across the couch at each other, and set a mason jar of tea bags on the porch for sun tea. Apparently, there was no rush to talk because the talk was somehow inevitable. Aunt Eliza trusted the truth would appear when it was needed. It didn't seem to be her job to pull it out hand over fist.

"That art museum up in Chicago is really something, isn't it?" she asked wistfully, sitting at the kitchen table with the fan blowing straight at her face after her morning yoga. "Did you ever get over there?" The coffeepot burbled, filling the kitchen with the warm scent of chicory.

"Once or twice," June replied. "I spent most of my time working."

Eliza grinned, stretching her shoulder out. "Weren't you on the radio for a little while?"

College radio—early morning coffee and shooting the breeze with the stoner kids, who played Fleet Foxes and Vampire Weekend and practically worshipped Arcade Fire.

"Yes," June replied, delayed by surprise. She lifted her head from where she'd been resting her cheek on the table. She brushed a single bread crumb off her skin. "How did you know that?"

"Are you kidding?" Aunt Eliza chuckled as she got up, scooping a yellow coffee cup from a peg. "If somebody in our family is on the radio, you can bet I know about it. You think I don't ever talk to your mom?"

June grabbed a mug too. "Is this place what you'd thought it would be?"

"I'm not sure," Eliza said levelly, cream clouding her coffee. "Great-Granddaddy was pastor for the Black folks' church, a very popular speaker." She was thoughtful. "I've met a few from his flock over the years. He just had this shine on him, they say. Never stopped moving for a second. He did something for people, woke up their hearts. People'd come in from all over the county to bask in his words and enjoy the vegetable patch he kept." Eliza sighed. "Of course, it was swamped along with the church when they built the dam." She took a sip. "This is a sleepy little parish these days; the congregation's tiny and mixed now. Weird combo of poor locals and rich tourists. I'm not sure if it was God's will pulling me back here or...just me, looking for roots."

"I never knew all that about him," June said, staring into the mug. "I mean, I know on my dad's side, they can trace their lineage back a long way. But Mom never told me much, just that we were from here."

"That's because your mom likes to think about the present, not the past," Aunt Eliza said with a warm smile.

Still, there was a quaintness to it all. Change was always diverting, which was close enough to fun to keep June occupied. But it wasn't long before she went in search of what nightlife might exist for twentysomethings and fireflies on the lakefront. She tried to move quietly, avoiding the pool of light from the living room, where Eliza was reading with a cup of tea, and avoid all those questions. *Where are you going? When will you be back? Why are you like this—*

"Try the Mosquito Bite," Aunt Eliza called when June creaked the door open.

Caught, June paused and backtracked rather sheepishly. "Where's that?"

Eliza's smile was knowing. "Straight down the road along the lake. About a fifteen-minute walk."

June jogged past the church, then pushed through tangled undergrowth and short, stubby plants that looked a bit like cacti but weren't. Occasionally, she came upon a stray flat bicycle tire or detached bumper—something scraggly and forgotten. She passed shabby houses behind chain-link fences, built far back from the road. In one yard, a Doberman perked its sharp, tiny ears and charged the fence with low, loud woofs. His owner, a skinny, browbeaten man, didn't look up from the guitar he was refinishing on the porch. On another, a woman smoked, a can of Pepsi between her knees, and she watched June, her eyes unmoving until June curved along the road and out of sight. It was all a line of solitary individuals weathering life.

Distantly, boat wakes hushed against the shore. The road turned a slow, cruising corner, and up ahead, a faint orange glow came through the trees. A shabby dark building lay between the road and water, with a rickety dock that looked one storm away from crumbling, a few houseboats tied off there. The sign over the door read THE MOSQUITO BITE. It had the faint grungy smell of a very cheap bar. If she licked the wood, she'd probably taste decades of spilled Bud Light.

Curious, she went inside, and a cheesy motion-activated bass over the door started a tinny song above her. Tables and barstools gathered in low greenish light. A cluster of older men held beers in sun-spotted hands at one of the tables, and a few more were at the bar. There were fish instead of deer heads on the walls, tails pointed to the nets on the ceiling. June had the distinct disquieting impression that she and everyone else within were underwater, that perhaps the roof was truly a surface, dotted with fishing boats that dipped their nets in, hoping to pull wriggling treasure back up. As if they had all already drowned, only none of them knew it.

June picked her way to the bar and chose a stool under the biggest catfish, though it was more of a skeleton than a fish. If she was noticed, no one said anything, just shuffled to make room for the new girl. The bartender, who was the type of wizened and dried out that came from years of hard knocks and toughening up, just looked at her expectantly.

"Guinness," she said.

"Good order."

She twisted to face the man who had spoken. Sitting next to her, he was one of four in a line, all with sunburned faces and scraggly beards; the nearest wore one of those fishing hats, floppy and dotted with tackle and bait hooks like dangling earrings. He bent over the bar, picking at a peanut shell with scarred fingertips. "You new here?"

"Where's here?" June replied. A Guinness appeared silently at her elbow, already sweating. "It's not technically a town, is it?"

He didn't look offended—if anything, he was amused. "Good question. It used to be a town, did you know?" He had the ambiguous, ageless quality of a man who could be forty or sixty, all salty hair and beard scruff.

"Oh yeah?"

"Yeah," the next one down the line said, lifting his dusty bottle to his lips. His Hawaiian shirt was faded from red to sunburnt pink. "The dam got built in… When was that?"

"1920," one of the others murmured around a mouthful of pretzels. Even they looked slightly green in the low light. "Remember?"

"No, no, it was 1930—you're always about twenty years off. During that big sickness." Behind her, someone paced the floor to the pool table, their footsteps strangely muted on the scratched wood floor.

The fisherman nearest to June offered a small wry smile. His right canine was cracked and browned from an old injury. "Everybody moved out of town a long time ago. It's under the water now."

"Why?" In the quiet, June felt compelled to inch closer to hear better, and she fought it off, scratching at the label on her bottle. "Who floods a perfectly good town?"

"A *perfectly good* town." He scoffed. "You ever heard of yellow fever?" The crow's-feet around his eyes were white, like he smiled a lot out in the sun, enough to have tanned that way, and a pocket of burst veins flowed across his forehead. "Prosper got hit real bad with it back in the day. Men, women, kids, little babies, all with jaundiced skin in the end, bleeding, crying, their livers and hearts dying. Nasty way to go. Took out the whole town." He gestured at her with his beer. "You aren't from here."

"I'm not, technically," she replied.

Behind him, two of the fishermen wandered off to settle their differences at the dart board so old, it was missing most of its felt. The bartender kept cleaning glasses, either oblivious to June and her company or a very subtle eavesdropper. But this man looked at her with a glint of knowing in his eyes. "You ever been to a place without hope? A place just so out of luck that there's no saving it?"

The beer label shredded, caking under her fingernails. She wiped hurriedly at her jeans. "I don't know. Yes."

"It became a place like that. Old Prosper, right before they engorged the lake. It's hard to love a town on borrowed time. Even the dead had to be rehoused after the dam—all those graves flooded," he replied. "Funny, isn't it, that we built a new grave-yard for the dead and didn't build a new town for the living?"

June leaned closer. "So everyone just left?"

"Most did," he mused. Behind him, the two bickering fisher-men agreed that they were both wrong—the dam must have been built in '37. They were getting up to go now, floating on the dark current of whiskey and beer and ready to close their eyes on the night. "It's heavy. Things might have felt different, life might have picked back up if it hadn't been for the fever. You got to understand the kind of fear that lived here back then."

"Fear of death?" June guessed.

"Even worse," he said with a jerk of his head. "Fear of a *bad* death. That fever was a bad death. Wouldn't you do anything to save your kin from that?"

June only stared at him.

He stood, brushing off weathered pants. "It's been years since the town was given over to the lake and years since the lake took it. But sometimes it doesn't feel all that long ago." He drifted out of sight. "Only thing heavier than fear is the weight of all that water."

June's throat was dry, fingers locked around the bottle. Distantly, she felt a creak and sway, like houseboats slumbering on a dock, like families sailing above her without any thought to her existence, silent and present underneath. If the fisherman had meant to scare her, it hadn't worked. She wasn't afraid but awake and itching for a swim.

Thwack—something cold and compact slapped down on her head. June cursed, beer sloshing over her hands, and distantly, she felt the thing plop on her lap, where it winked. It was a small irregular pearl. She picked it up. The ceiling above her had no secret mother-of-pearl stash. All she saw was that huge, monster catfish, mounted above her, mouth agape.

CHAPTER FIVE

NCE HER MOM LEFT, CASSIE CLIMBED ONTO HER tiny built-in table, braced one foot on the paisley-green-and-orange booth and carefully unscrewed the light bulb from the overhead lamp.

She was exhausted from the visit, from the work of hosting, and it was a shameful secret relief to have her home back, ready to be restored. The plants on her sill seemed to stretch taller, the morning light gleam a little kinder. Even the bees, which had seemed to pause their work, were singing through the flowers again.

Mom had put light bulbs in all the RV's fixtures before she'd even moved on to cleaning everything and rearranging Cassie's things into places they did not belong. Cassie would fix it all. She couldn't sleep with the electric drone in her home, hooked into the walls of the RV, not when she had her collection of carefully chosen lamps, including one Grandad had built out of a single piece of steel. Of all the lights, the worst offender was the four-bulb fixture over the breakfast table because the third bulb flickered. Mom never listened to Cassie about the lights, especially the fluorescents. It was dark inside the RV at night, but God help her, Cassie could live there with her eyes closed without bumping her knees. It was all just as she knew it. She'd thought about remodeling before, replacing the paisley green and orange of the booths with royal blue, the Formica with soft, nice-smelling wood. She thought sometimes she might like copper fixtures, white walls, and big windows.

But she never did it. It would mean removing traces of Grandad and the way he had lived when it was his.

"What are you going to do with those? Is it an art project?" A lanky blond shadow appeared in the door. Bolt, bearing a root beer for her and an orange soda for him, both fresh from Valerie's icebox. "Oh. Mom put those in?"

Cassie nodded. "I don't really need them. How's Valerie treating you?"

Bolt grinned. "Like a long-lost son, finally returned to mow the lawn. So many chores."

"That's how she shows her love."

He brought her the drink and wandered, poking at the honey and wax slowly separating themselves in a pot on the windowsill. "What are you going to do with them?"

"Maybe Mitch can sell them." The bulb came loose, and Cassie let it tumble into a paper bag where all the others would soon be banished.

He'd probably try to tell her he couldn't sell the random loose light bulbs Mom had bought from him just days ago, but he would still take them off her hands, and then they'd be done haunting Cassie's home. He wouldn't begrudge her the trouble or comment on its oddness. Mitch took that kind of thing at face value.

"I can take them over to Mitch's store if you want," Bolt offered.

"No," Cassie assured him. "No, I don't mind it."

"Really?" She could hear Bolt smiling, turning his words into mischief. "Why should you walk all the way down that hill when I live there? Unless there's another reason you want to visit Mitch's store? Besides the light bulbs."

Cassie yanked the next bulb out from the fixture so hard, her knuckles almost collided with her face. "Why not? He's my friend."

"Uh-huh." He tapped his fingers on the edge of the sink before he hopped up, then bent backward to jimmy the cover off the ceiling bulb there. "We should go down for dinner. What was that thing Grandad liked to get? Valerie always rolled her eyes about it."

"Beer?" Cassie snorted.

"Do you remember the last time we all went there?" Bolt laughed. "He got in that fistfight with that old dude, Duke Something. It usually took him ten minutes just to get up from his rocking chair, but he was throwing punches like Jermain Taylor."

Cassie smiled. "Grandad used to box, actually. He learned in the army." Bolt had been young then, seven at the most, but it had been the kind of day a person remembers, a cherry-pie Fourth of July, and Duke had said something sour to Grandad on the way into Valerie's. Right there, amid the picnic benches and kids playing on the lawn, the chlorine splashes from the pool, Grandad had socked him in the jaw. They'd both gone down, brawling in the grass until Mitch and Valerie stormed out to break them apart then help them stand, the old men no longer hot-blooded and invincible. Mom and Cassie half carried Grandad home.

It was a funny thing about Grandad—he had lived all but his

war years in Prosper, and yet he had few friends among the people there. He liked the tourists best. That night, Cassie had lingered in the hall while Mom and Grandad split a finger of whiskey, a rare ritual reserved for only the worst days.

"Shit town with some shit people, that's what it is," he spat as Mom held a bag of frozen corn to his eye. He had a quiet voice that often seemed to get lost on the way out of his mouth, but on occasions like that, hot words could come booming up from his stomach. He was as he had been in the fight, an old dragon, saving up what remained of his once-great fire. "I guess I'm shit too, since I'm still here."

Cassie had never gotten the chance to ask him what he meant; he was gone about a month later. But they all knew Grandad couldn't have lived away from the water. He loved it too much. If it had made him sad when Cassie stopped swimming, started avoiding the lake, she didn't know. He'd never said a word about it.

Bolt tore his light bulb free with a whoop and dropped it in the bag.

"Chicken gizzards," Cassie said, working on the final bulb in the kitchen fixture. "Grandad liked chicken gizzards. They're a real pain to make. You've got to boil them before you fry them if you want them to be tender, so they take a while, and Valerie hated going to all the trouble."

After a brief confused pause, Bolt caught on to her train of thought again. "She always complained," he remembered.

"But she made them every Sunday for him."

"Maybe that's what I want for dinner," Bolt decided.

"She'll probably tell you to make them yourself."

Bolt laughed.

Two more light bulbs joined the others. One more, in the ceiling over the bed. Cassie stepped around a pile of books to hop onto the old springy mattress and fish for it.

"He must have been sleepwalking by then," Bolt said, voice carefully light. Cassie stopped her fiddling and looked at him. He'd followed her over to the bed, shuffling his feet, his face a half-cracked door. "Mom doesn't ever want to talk about it," he said in his own defense.

"I know," she assured him. Mom had no qualms about saying how she felt, but this topic had always been closed, even to Cassie until she trembled from holding back the urge to shake her mom and shout, *This is mine too. This happened to me just as much as it did to you.* "I don't mind," she added.

Bolt looked a little relieved. "I can't remember when it started, that's all."

It hadn't occurred to Cassie that his experience might have been so different, but of course it was. He was a child, and she had been almost an adult when Grandad died. "The sleepwalking wasn't new. As long as I can remember, Grandad would sleepwalk."

Bolt raised his eyebrows; this likely wasn't the story Mom would have told anyone. It wasn't the one she knew.

"I used to hear him outside at night because the RV door squeaked," Cassie admitted. "He'd go, and then later, after maybe an hour, he'd come back. But about a year before he died, he stopped bringing himself back."

He had to be moved to the double-wide then. So many nights were cut with the loud, confused bawling, like an infant's, blind and deaf to everything outside itself. So many nights, Cassie and Mom would be roused to stumble out of bed and rush outside.

"Come back," he would call distantly over the water. "Don't leave me, come back..." Grandad was physically strong even then, and it took the two of them to wrestle him back. Though she was a teenager, Cassie couldn't get in the water, not even for him. She could only kneel on the dock, pleading, waiting for Mom to wade mulishly in and drag him, stumbling, close enough that Cassie could hook on his collar or wrap her arms around his shoulders, and the two of them together would urge him back onshore then up the steep hill toward home. Once, when he'd been almost waist deep, Mom hooking her arms around his stomach like a linebacker, her feet tangled in the underwater weed, and they both went under. Cassie was nailed to the dock in horror, too petrified of the water to jump in, splinters piercing her fingertips until, finally, they'd come back up and she grabbed Mom's hand and helped pull them both to safety. Afterward, Mom had screamed at Cassie on the lawn so loud and so long, Valerie had rushed outside with her shotgun, convinced someone was being murdered.

"It's a miracle he never killed himself, walking into the water like that," Bolt said softly.

"We couldn't get him to stop." Cassie freed the last light bulb and dropped it in the bag. "He never remembered it in the morning either."

Bolt frowned at the floor.

He was less comfortable with silence than she was, so Cassie broke it. "If you want chicken gizzards, you'd better tell Valerie now."

Just like that, he perked up. "Want me to tell her to make enough for two?"

"Sure." Cassie smiled at him. On his way out, he plucked one of her black-eyed Susans and tucked it behind his ear. He batted his eyelashes at her before jogging down the hill.

All in all, she exorcised ten bulbs from her RV before her lungs unspooled in relief. For a moment, Cassie stood out in the sunlight. A pair of bees returned to sit on her sill and tickle the air inside her home with fragile wings, a benevolent sign of the natural state restored. Cassie let out a long slow breath and tried not to think anymore.

Before Mom had gone back to Louisiana, she'd cupped Cassie's cheeks with firm hands and gazed at her for a long time.

"What is it?" Cassie asked.

"You hold your whole heart in your eyes sometimes," Mom replied. One of her thumbs followed the high end of Cassie's cheekbone. Mom had said that before, when Cassie had been young. Hearing it again now had felt funny in her gut, in her chest, even in her elbows and wrists. "You know that, out of the whole wide world, you and Bolt are what I've got, right?"

It was as close to an apology as Mom could speak. Sometimes, Cassie thought maybe the two of them weren't so different. It was hard for Cassie to say the most important words too.

☙

Lark had seen something through the telescope. A vision. A hallucination? Something.

She lay on one of the fraying deck chairs atop the *Big Dipper*. It'd taken half an hour with the tweezers to get all the glass out of her palm, and even a few days later her hand felt raw. The night stretched around her, a hand grabbing the docks, the distant bank, and the green trees beyond. It was all air out here, a free fall. She took a deep breath.

Lark remembered the storybook summers of her childhood, drowned in daydreams, hours flowing by and ignored like they'd last forever. Endless games of Skip-Bo huddled around the table in still-damp swimsuits, homemade ice cream on the deck, sunset boat rides to watch the fireworks. Magical temporary moments that had felt completely normal. Mom opening a bag of Cheetos. Doris Ann lumbering across the dock to tumble into the speedboat for a ride. Now, afloat here, looking through the lenses Daddy had left behind, Lark felt life transforming into a fragile waterlogged fantasy of a different kind.

She was on her father's path.

Since Sammy smashed the telescope, Lark's dreams had gone haywire. She stayed up late to avoid the wild crush of indecipherable images, the blur of color and sound that seemed to travel through murky water. She woke to find the telescopes spinning out of control on their stands. She'd sat up in the bed, shivering, stomach turned to acid. And yet—

She couldn't leave. There was still so much to do, so many more boxes to fill before they could sell the boat. This summer daydream turned nightmare was an asset they just couldn't hold on to anymore. And she hadn't solved it yet, any of it. What had this place done to Daddy?

What was it trying to do to her?

She couldn't shut the door on this. Every staring match she had with these spyglasses had something to tell her. Some secret to share. Terrifying as that was, Lark couldn't walk away. Did that mean her aunt and cousin and mom would be down here in a few weeks carrying her out like Daddy?

Lark hadn't seen it. She'd been in Memphis when they came to get him, after his radio silence had scared them all. But she and Mom were too close for her not to know all the details. Dried blood had striped his cheeks like tears. They still couldn't get a straight answer from him about what had happened to his eyes.

Lark held a pair of mother-of-pearl binoculars, which had gleamed knowingly at her earlier in the day. A smarter woman would throw it in the lake, leave this boat to rot, and never look back.

But maybe Lark really did have too much of her father in her. What if he hadn't been driven mad out here? What if he really had been under attack?

She stared up at the stars, and they trembled, tiny water droplets on a dark window, barely there, like they might slide off at any moment and disappear under the horizon line in glistening trails. Most of her telescope companions were sleeping, their shafts drooping, not bothering to track her. The ones up here on the top were some of the largest, some of the most science-fictional. The longest was much bigger than Lark, its bronze stand glinting with an elaborate tarnished pattern of filigree. The lens at its end was probably two feet wide, at least. Dad had loved that one. He and Lark would look through it together at any kind of eclipse, planetary phenomenon, or comet. On a clear night, the telescope made the craters on the moon as big as soup bowls.

They were on the wrong side of Echo to see the dam from

the top of their boat; concealed by the dock's tin roof, it was ever present and yet hidden from view. They kept their eyes fastened on other things.

The collection was different now than in her childhood. She'd looked once, and now the can was open and the worms were out. Maybe a more grounded person, like Aunt Valerie or Mitch, could have caught a taste of this dream and then abandoned it. But Lark couldn't just leave it there after what she'd seen. Hands trembling, her bandaged hand still stinging, she took the small mother-of-pearl binoculars from between her knees and held them up to her eyes.

The first thing she noticed wasn't the image, which was a fuzzy and abstracted view of one of the houseboat's navy tarps. It was the smell. The binoculars had soft leather grips around their shining shell inlay.

She lifted her head, shoving the binoculars up at the Big Dipper in the sky. Through their low magnification, the constellation set in the darkness wasn't a void but a close embroidered presence. White stars reached for one another with delicate frilling arms, a drapery of white lace. Doilies as big as galaxies, gentle as a whispered word. Mother-of-pearl, as if made from the shells of mussels that had lived in this water.

Lark set the binoculars down a moment, waiting for her pulse to slow a little. She checked herself over and stared at her hands. She could still stop, couldn't she? That could be the end of it. She shifted, crisscrossing her legs, bracing herself. Then she lifted the binoculars again.

Now they pointed at the dock across the way—D Dock. At first, there was nothing but the still night. The wind seemed to kick up. She scanned the line of boats, the fanning dock lights in the water. She was losing her nerves under that lacy starscape. She needed to go in, go to bed. But then—

Lark started, nearly dropping the delicate instrument in her hands. Figures—there were people trudging along the roof of D Dock. She leaned forward, pulse hammering through her eye socket. They hung suspended, feet dipping near the tin without quite touching it. A dozen or so, in old-fashioned rags, torn and faded overalls, molding linen, skirts stained at their base. The desiccated forms hunched under the weight of a small dingy coffin. It was black and distended, as if it had already spent a long time submerged in some primordial bog. The pallbearers moved at the rhythm of a funeral dirge until they reached the end of D Dock. Pallid faces slack, eyes dead, they handed their small charge down into the darkness below.

There was a splash from the nearest shore, and it took everything in Lark not to scream. "Damnation and hellfire," she snapped, clutching her chest. She threw the binoculars down on the deck chair and shot up. It was late; no one should be out now. Any ghost who came this way would get a telescope to the skull, that was for sure—

There was a ripple out past the docks, in the cool open, in the bear-paw swipe of shallows that curved around the deepest, bluest part of the lake. Lark had begun to think she'd imagined it, the shadows and the spyglasses playing tricks, when in the distance, someone rocketed out of the water with a huff for breath and pushed long seaweed strands of hair out of her face. She bobbed in the water once, twice, and then dived again, vanishing with a tiny flip of her ankles.

Who was swimming in the middle of the night? Lark peered through the nearest telescope, but the lens was as yellow and opaque as a mud puddle. Quietly, she climbed down from the top of the *Big Dipper* and onto the back deck, still squinting through the darkness.

The woman appeared again, swirling around in the water. She slapped it with a loud, carrying curse and then dived again.

Lark couldn't know if she was real or not, but that flat-handed smack against the surface of the water had *sounded* real. What was she doing out there anyway? The vision in the binoculars' stare had ended right there at the water, right where the woman dove. Lark had to find out for herself. Because she had to know. Because she wanted to know. Because her Daddy wasn't just some traumatized old man who'd hurt himself. She would go deeper here, dive in. Maybe there was some truth he'd left for her. Quietly, Lark hopped into her shabby little dinghy tied up beside the houseboat and rowed the hundred yards or so into the water to check it out. It had a small motor too, but she didn't want to disturb the night.

Soon she could draw up beside this diving expedition. "Hey," she said, when the woman surfaced yet again. Lark's boat sent moonlit ripples out toward the rocky beach and smelled strongly of rotting rope. "Are you okay?"

The stranger looked a little surprised to see her, swimming close enough to grip the edge of the boat. She was naked, bare shoulders in the water and totally unconcerned with it. "Hi." She swiped water droplets out of her eyes.

Lark almost laughed but ended up just gaping at her, mouth slightly open as if the laugh might escape at any moment. She didn't recognize her from among the lake's old familiar faces. "What are you doing out here?"

She had a rich, lively gaze, focused as a spotlight. "Diving. I'm actually getting tired, so you came at the perfect time. Hold on." And with that, she vanished again.

"Wait, why are you—" But there was no point. The skinny-dipper had already slipped out of sight again. Lark waited.

This time, the ripples started to fade, as if she'd been a mermaid, not a person at all, another spyglass dream in the nighttime. Then the woman rocketed up, heaving something dark and huge over the side of the boat with a clatter. She sank back against the side, clinging with her fingertips, panting for air. The boat rocked, swooping toward her. She rested her forehead on her wrist, recovering.

"That was pushing it." She flashed an obscured grin at Lark, a single dark eye and half of her smile. "I thought I might not be able to get it. It was lodged pretty deeply in the mud."

"How did you even—" Lark was too struck to even fix her eyes on the discovery for a few moments. She just stared at the girl resting against the boat. "What is it?"

"I don't know. But I banged it with my knee when I was swimming along the bottom. Wanted to know what it was." The girl offered her hand. "June. Help me in?"

"I'm Lark." She took June's hand but hesitated. This time she did manage to laugh. The tension built around her by solitude and psychosis had eased as soon as June spoke. "Any sailor worth half her mettle knows you shouldn't bring a mermaid aboard," she said and June smiled, wide and surprised.

"Excuse you, I'm not a mermaid!" June protested, then

looked down at herself with a flash of self-consciousness for the first time. "Actually, that's not a bad idea. I left my seashell bra over…" She waved at the dock. "Yonder."

Lark cleared her throat. "I'll pull the boat up at the shore and let you in that way." She gently paddled into the shallows, a dark heap of clothes coming into sight on the rocky beach.

June hung on the boat until they were near enough for her to slip off and to her clothes, pulling an overlarge maroon shirt over her head with a wince. She shrugged into jean shorts that seemed unforgiving on wet skin. She'd barely been out of the water for two seconds, and already, the ends of her hair had begun to curl as she pulled it in layers through the collar of her shirt. "Have you ever gone night swimming?"

"Oh yeah. But it's been a long time." Lark prodded the heavy thing June had thrown in the boat. In the darkness, it looked almost like a pirate's treasure chest, lost in some legendary shipwreck. "I can't believe you dragged this thing up."

June clambered onto the boat, stuffing her underwear in her back pocket, and knelt beside the thing again before lifting it. It was solid when she plunked it on the bench next to her. The box was beyond soaked, goopy with mud and weeds as thick as yarn. Underneath, it seemed to be wood. June pressed her fingers against the seam of the lid. It didn't budge. "This is better than I expected," she said, grinning up at Lark as if they were co-conspirators. "I wonder what's in it."

Lark wondered too, a flash of real summertime hijinks in her gut. Not like the sick dread combined with hopeless curiosity that had moored her here. The telescopes waiting on the dock were probably gossiping about it all, winking to one another and whirling their screws. "I have a tool kit on the houseboat," she offered, ears buzzing. This dream, which had started with the binoculars, was getting away from her, and Lark loosened her grip on all the reasons why that was a bad thing. "Maybe we can get it open in some better light."

"Good idea, sailor." June sat back in the boat and winked at Lark. "Full steam ahead or whatever."

With her new cargo on board, skin prickling, Lark headed home.

CHAPTER SIX

HEN SHE WAS YOUNG, JUNE WOKE UP SOMETIMES with petals strewn across her pillow. Red, pink, a dusty desert blue. They smelled like cardamom and silk, like faraway places where June wanted to be.

"Where did you get these?" Mom would grumble, playful and anxious, sweeping them off her sheets, crumpling them in her rich brown hands. "Are you leaving the windows open again?"

June never opened the windows. She knew, of course, and Mom knew where they really came from, but neither of them ever talked about it. They played their pretend game, that silly June had left her fifth-story apartment window open again, that the flowers had blown in from the balcony. But she knew it scared Mom.

Sometimes Mom's eyes would catch and worry on the back of June's head, where petals were tangled so thick at the nape of her neck that a comb couldn't get through it. She would quietly get the gleaming pair of silver barber's scissors, pull June's hair over her shoulders and—*Snip. Snip. Snip.* Always careful not to cut June's hair but thoroughly slicing every blossom out. Mom would kiss her head, praying, "All I want is for you to be safe." And June would sweep it up and throw it out the window. Watching the petals drift would make something in her heart thrum and her fingers itch. *I*, she would think, *I am alive. I am so alive that it hurts. I am so alive that it's growing out of me.*

June hadn't intended to go skinny-dipping at all that night. But she'd woken up in the darkest heart of the morning and found bloodred petals tipped with black all over her pillow for the first time in over two years.

She'd only gone to the water intending to wash them away, but then she'd remembered her conversation with the fisherman, and it had sounded like an adventure. June wandered the shoreline, and the rest of the world was black, lined sterling by the moon, and everything except for her, the bugs, and the owls was asleep. The church was near a marina, where houseboats full of sleeping people rocked against the dock. Everyone and everything were dead to the world. Except for June. The water had called to her, dared her to test it, and June never could resist a dare—

Then a box. Then a boat. Then a girl.

June wasn't the only one awake and alive after all. Dressed in wet clothes, the box at her feet, June watched the flex of the girl's arms as she maneuvered her shabby boat with care. Lark's eyes—gray as a tarnished mirror—were sharp on the docks, chipped black polish glinting on her nails as she steered. She knew what she was doing in a boat, but she didn't look like one of the water people June had seen at the bar or around the church, tanned and casual, with something of the South in their voices and their footsteps. Lark was different.

She'd appeared out of the gloom shyly at first, but it must take a kind person to venture into the night for a stranger. Maybe she was lonely. She seemed a little lonely.

"Careful," Lark warned as she tied her dinghy on the back of a hulking shadow of a houseboat, painted in a past-midnight monochrome untouched by the buzzing yellow dock lights. "It's a little..." But that sentence sputtered out.

"It's fine," June said. "I've never been on a houseboat before." From what she could tell, it was basically an RV on water instead of wheels, a nightmare for people who were easily seasick. "I have no expectations."

But when June stepped foot on Lark's houseboat, it felt a little like walking into the middle of a surprise party poised to reveal itself. The space was pitch-black but full of something, presences that might as well have been nudging one another, shushing this one or that one as they jostled together, waiting for the perfect moment to jump out and shout, *Surprise!*

Instead, Lark flicked the light on to reveal an antiquarian's mechanical paradise. Spindly shapes—telescopes and spyglasses, even a couple of astrolabes—littered every surface. There was no room to live and barely enough room to breathe. And, even more bizarrely, every glass seemed trained on June like a crowd of unblinking eyes.

"Don't be rude," Lark scolded, and it took a moment for June to realize she wasn't talking to her. She was having a staring contest with some of the fish-eyed lenses nearby. And maybe she won, because after a moment Lark let her breath out, shooting June another of her shy, humorous smiles. "Sorry about the, uh—clutter. Come in."

What kind of person accumulated this many telescopes? Was she trying to own one telescope per star in the sky? June tapped the nearest one experimentally, and it spun slowly away from her on its swivel neck. What kind of person *talked* to their telescopes?

At first glance out on the lake, where her every pore had seemed to absorb moonlight, Lark had looked blond. But her hair was fading in sunset streaks of peach and pink, a fun decision losing its steam. June couldn't help but picture her as a barefoot and tangle-haired wild child or a pink-haired ballerina-punk teenager. But now, everything about this girl had a fading quality, like life was wearing her down.

"Interesting hobby you've got here," June said.

"Not me," Lark replied, to June's relief. "These are all my dad's. I'm just trying to get out from under them."

June followed Lark's path step by step down the hallway and into the houseboat's large front room. It was equally stuffed. Lark switched on a huge—almost surgical—reading lamp over the table and cleared a space for the chest.

"I guess collecting stuff is a dad thing. For my dad and his wife, it's these fluffy white cats they breed," June said, rambling while Lark dug around in the piles of debris and lenses, looking for something. "Persians. He sews them little bow ties."

"Really? Do they look happier with the bow ties on?" Lark found what she wanted and ducked for it, nearly toppling a pile of books. She returned, triumphant, and clunked a huge jeweler's tool kit onto the table. "There we go."

"You seem awfully prepared." June heaved her treasure down beside it. It was heavy, but not solidly like iron. Instead it was a kind of heavy like a Maine coon cat, a weight that shifted and might rear around and lunge for the ground. A towel lay nearby, and she co-opted it, wiping away at the surface. The box was too big to hold in one arm; two were required. There was a subtle bump on the top and metal bits, hinges, and a latch, perhaps. A faintly reedy, mucky smell hung around it.

"Welcome to the dragon's hoard." Lark leaned against the table, arms crossed, as she supervised. "Try those pliers." She brushed one of the hinges. "I can't believe these haven't completely rusted out." She sniffed the air, frowning. "It's sort of rank, isn't it?"

Of course it was. June shook it. It made no sound. But there was something in there, something besides water. She was sure. June put it back down. "I'm not intruding, am I?"

"Not at all." Lark readjusted the light for her. She seemed as interested in the find as June was, examining it through a tiny lens like jewelers used.

"Good, because I'd love to intrude a little more. Do you have spare clothes?" June gestured to her still-damp outfit. Out of the water, she was getting goose bumps. "Or maybe some coffee?"

"Absolutely! Sorry, bad host." Lark danced around the spy-glasses, and June heard her rummaging around in one of the other rooms. "Damnation and...oh good." She appeared a moment later with a pair of sweatpants and a T-shirt that said *GRAND DESTINY Resort and Marina* in curling, 1960s script. She looked a little proud of herself about scavenging through the mess so fast. "How's this?"

"Did you just say 'damnation'?" June asked, shoving out of damp, scratchy jean shorts. No use in modesty now. Lark had seen it all out in the moonlight.

But she was very polite, busying herself in the little kitchen alcove. "You mean you don't swear like an old Western prospec-tor?" she asked, laughing a sweet, sort of rusty laugh. "Here." She brought June a friendly glass of brandy she'd poured from a dusty decanter and took a little sip of her own.

June took a small burning drink. Maybe it was her natural inclination to seed trouble, to find beehives to poke, to start fights. But June wanted to pry open this girl's secrets too. "Is this your boat?" She thwapped her wet shirt gently Lark's way. The Grand Destiny one was warm and overlarge.

Lark tilted her head back and forth, almost in a shrug, as if she were listening to some song that June couldn't hear. "No," she said. One of the long-necked telescopes had somehow loosened on its stand and now drooped onto her shoulder as if to stare at June. "Or sort of. I grew up out here." She swirled her brandy and sat beside June at the table, smiling. "So are you splitting your finder's fee or what? Half the mud for you, half for me?"

"It's really cute that you think I'd go half and half." June poked tweezers and something else—a dentist's toothpick?—at the lock, scraping gunk out of the grooves. It did not want to be scraped. It clearly liked where it was. "You can have 10 percent of the mud."

Lark laughed around a swallow of her drink, shy and a little stifled. "Tell you what," she offered. "I've got to take a bunch of these telescopes over to this antique shop. Fairchild's, just up the road from here. We can take that chest too. Maybe she'll be able to tell us what it is."

"Tempting," June admitted and ducked her head, returning to the chest. "But I'm not ready to split my treasure with any other dashing strangers."

Color crept into Lark's face. The flush was good for her. "Well—that's fair enough."

"Tell *you* what." June clinked their drinks. "This is heavy. I'll call my aunt and get her to pick me up so I can get out of your hair—also so she doesn't worry—but I'll leave you my number. That way, when I get this box open, you can track me down for your share of the loot." Eliza was a bit of an insomniac herself and stayed up late reading most nights. It should be fine.

Lark raised an eyebrow at her, mouth twisting. "Awfully confident, aren't you? What if it won't open?"

"Of course it'll open. It's just wood." With the box tucked in her arms, June dug for her phone, her heart thrumming with mystery, with the unexpected gift of the night. Her blood was rushing, high on the scent of cardamon and those faraway places. *I*, she thought, *I am alive.*

೪

"You're a real hard worker, kiddo." Valerie locked up the restaurant, and Bolt followed her out. They'd had to stay an hour past closing because the Destiny had decided to try to explode the kitchen right before their last customer went home. Luckily the feisty old motel had not succeeded. This kind of thing happened often enough that it never worried anyone much. With the grease fire now extinguished, Valerie was even humming. "It's so nice to have you back here at home where you belong." She fixed Bolt with a squinty look. "Except those gizzards. That was the last damn time I am *ever* fussing around with those things."

Diego chuckled behind her. Mitch might take off after the grocery was shut and the motel office light was out for the night, but Diego never left Valerie on her own to close.

"I've got a taste for them now," Bolt joked. Just like Grandad. He'd have laughed at that. Cassie remembered Grandad much better; most of what Bolt remembered were contained flashes. His rusty laugh. The way he used to help Bolt make his bed, every sheet precise and without wrinkles. His hummus recipe, which no one else could replicate. The little dog figurine he'd made for Bolt out of broken watch parts.

Who knows what he'd think of Bolt working at the marina, for a man from Charlene, no less.

It had been a long day. He felt so pleasantly lulled by hours of sun and the smell of marina gas filling up his head, his ears, his chest. He'd gotten a job there filling gas tanks and polishing boats because he knew Mr. Daley, the new owner, through his son, Rig. Before Bolt moved away with Mom, Rig had been his best friend at his school in Charlene. Mr. Daley was a boisterous and generous boss, much easier in some ways than Valerie.

Crickets croaked over the lawn as Bolt let himself into his little motel room. He was full and greasy from eating a platter of chicken gizzards with Cassie that were just as crisp and hot as he remembered. Between the two of them, they had reduced a full plate to crumbs and crumpled napkins.

"Gizzards are a little muscle in the chicken's throat. Chickens swallow a stone to grind things up in it. Sometimes you still get bits of pebble when you chew them up," Grandad had told them over a similar plate, years before, the Destiny unchanged down to the ketchup bottles. "Around here, a girl once found a pearl in a plate of gizzards."

Cassie was like the Destiny: unchanged. Stubbornly, quietly herself. She was resilient. A tidal wave could wash them all away, and Cassie would likely be there in the morning, picking through the wreckage for something to save.

Bolt was the same too, though. He was still working two jobs to pay for his choice in colleges, still struggling to keep his English grade up, still browsing colleges out of state and far and away out of pocket. Trying to make something of himself was like trying to climb up a steep and muddy lake bank and sliding down as often as he gained any ground. He was still tied to Lake Prosper, as if it didn't want him to succeed anywhere else in the world.

Bolt closed his mint-green curtains and lay down on his squeaky mattress, drifting off and cataloging the aches in his body: his lower back from bending over fuel tanks, his finger from a burn on the morning stove.

But he snapped awake under the glint of cold stars, swaying on his feet and up to his thighs in freezing dark water.

Where was he?

Bolt's throat tightened like the sharp return of his childhood asthma, and he crumpled, plunging under the surface. Water swallowed him whole, black as oil. He couldn't breathe. He couldn't see.

He was so lost, beating for the surface—

Was he dead? Alone in endless cold, endless dark—it must be death.

Bolt's feet found muddy purchase, and he wrestled back up into an unfamiliar world, gasping in air, blinking water out of his eyes.

"Help!" he screamed.

Only no one came to fish him out.

But the blurry world began to resolve itself in front of him into a familiar long dock. The Destiny's dock, gray in the moonlight and pointing like a finger to the horizon. And Bolt was so grateful to see it, to recognize something, that he clambered over to the nearest mooring pole and clung on it with both arms, shivering. The metal pole was scuzzy with biofilm, gunk, moss animals, decaying reeds—but Bolt didn't care. The lake. He was in Lake Prosper, wheezing for breath, and his legs felt so weak, if he didn't hold on, he'd slip under the surface.

How had he gotten here? Had he been sleepwalking?

Tonight, the lake he'd grown up with, grown up smelling and swimming and sunbathing beside, was unfamiliar. The surface trembled like a cowed dog. The swan boat flock jostled against the shore, waves crashing under them—rushing out, sucked back in—and the moon above him was a hole in black paper. Bolt had never wandered in his sleep before. How had he come so far into the water without waking? He'd even put on shoes; when he moved, the lake bed tried to suck them off his feet.

And then came the sound. Bolt knew it had been what woke him. A voice, somewhere, bouncing off the water. He couldn't see anyone, no sign of a boat, no figure on the shore, but somewhere, someone was making a horrible cry. A furious, desperate sound, between a sob and a scream. It bounced off the water, one moment carried on a bitter-cold, distant wind. The next, startlingly close, whipping around him until—

"Stop!" Bolt snapped, and to his shock, it cut off abruptly, a pulled switch in the fabric of the universe, the water's mouth clamped shut.

This late, no shore in sight, the lake didn't look like a lake at all. It was nothing tamed, nothing that could be dammed. Hungry water—that was what Grandad had said before. It was hungry water.

In an instant he was not alone under the dock. Bolt felt someone else's tearful breathing fluttering in his ear. He flinched back, still wrapped around the pole. And the presence began to let out a soft keen.

"Stop," Bolt whispered. But the wordless, syllable-less sound— that guttural moan—grew. His ears rang as the whisper became a wail. A cold, distant-shore wind battered him, bitter with salt— tears; was he the one crying?—rushed around him.

I'm dreaming, he realized. *It's just a dream.* The presence moaned louder, a volume dial turning up too fast. As it pushed against his body, the edges of that formless howl tightened and fluctuated, and he knew with perfect clarity that it was about to become words.

"Stop." Bolt clung tighter, squeezing his eyes shut. "Stop!"

And it did.

Bolt dreaded opening his eyes. He waited, huddled in the lake. All he heard was the hush of water and his own panicked breathing.

When he finally unpeeled himself and waded out of the shallows, he still couldn't feel his legs. Finally, his sneakers squelched on dry grass—

And Bolt woke up under his blankets to pale morning light in the motel window. He gave in to the fuzzy confusion for a second before he sat up, relief blooming in his chest because the dream was over. He pulled the bedspread over him, fabric scratching fabric. The fan turned above him, casting shades of blue across the ceiling. He breathed in the motel's powdery '70s scent.

Bolt threw off the covers and planted his feet on the

floorboards—heavy wet clunks. He looked down. He was wearing his shoes.

They were damp.

ও৯

"You're a lifesaver, Cuz," Lark told Mitch fervently from the passenger seat of his truck. Twelve boxes of telescopes were bundled into his truck bed—only half of what she'd packed so far in the leftover cardboard boxes she'd gotten from Bud over at the Mosquito Bite. They jostled restlessly with each bump in the road. Lark couldn't resist glancing back to check on them.

"It's about time I did something to help you," Mitch grumbled as they took the loop away from Echo toward Fairchild's Treasures. The lake glittered out the window. "Least I can do. Cassie said she'd be happy to take a look."

"I just really appreciate it." They passed the church, where June's aunt was the pastor. Lark turned in her seat to look at the little plot, but there was no sign of June out on the rectory's porch swing. Eliza had been cool about picking June up so late after their surprise treasure hunt the other night.

Mitch followed her gaze. It was noon, and the modest steeple clock was chiming the hour. "Diego and I did some roof work for Eliza a few months back, and the bells up in that steeple are gnarly. All green and brittle," he told her. "They're much older than the building itself. Mom told me the Old Prosper church folk carried those bells out with the silver candlesticks and the altar cloth right before the dam."

"Seriously?" Lark cracked the window to hear them. They rang out across the gravel parking lot and the churchyard, and their sound was, she realized, somewhat hollow. They were small bells, and their tolling was tinny, rather muffled, as if, despite their escape, they still had to sing from beneath the water.

"Have you talked to Uncle Stu since you've been down here?" Mitch asked as they pulled into the antique shop lot. "Mom told me he hasn't been saying much."

Lark winced. The effort it took for Mitch to bring up this difficult topic was almost a physical presence in the car. "No," she admitted, her voice low. "He's still pretty—upset. I haven't wanted to worry him with boat stuff when he's…trying to get better."

Mitch parked the truck, letting out a breath. He cut the ignition, and they sat there as the cab started to heat up. "I'm really proud of you," he said gently. "I know this isn't easy."

Lark nodded at him quickly. "Thanks, Mitch," she managed, vision blurring right at the edges. Her eyes felt hot. There was so much she couldn't say about her time on the boat, the things she'd seen in the spyglasses.

They sat there together for another moment or two. Lark's T-shirt started to stick to her back from sweat, but it wasn't a moment she wanted to rush away from. Mitch, Valerie—they were the steady side of the family. She needed them, even if she couldn't tell them everything. "Okay, then," Mitch said at last, smiling at her. "Ready?"

They walked toward the shop together. Fairchild's looked as old as the antiques it sold, its wood exterior and sign shabby from time and lake weather, but the windows were clean and cheery, lit from the inside by lamps that once must have rested on bedside tables and beside sofas and loveseats. The lamps were an eclectic mix of pottery and mosaics, one delicately painted with a dogwood flower. Several small mason jars of honey glinted in the sun, each topped with cheesecloth and wrapped tightly with twine. The sign was tilted on open.

Mitch held the door and called, "Knock, knock."

At first, the young woman behind the counter blended in with her stock, another relic from the past. Pale and intensely freckled, she was surprised and then pleased when her gaze flowed from Lark to her cousin. Her hair and eyes were the color of lake-bed mud, and a braid as thick as a rope hung over her shoulder, nearly grazing her waist.

"Mitch," she said.

"Hey, Cass." Mitch grinned at her. "Mom used those light bulbs you brought over in the lobby." He set the two telescope boxes he was holding on one of the tables. "This is my cousin, Lark. Lark, remember Cassie? We've been friends for..." He shrugged helplessly. "I don't even know how long."

"Hey." Lark thunked her own box beside his, giving Cassie a breathless smile. "I used to come in here with my dad sometimes."

Tell that little crawdad I say hello, Valerie had said when they left. Lark could sort of imagine what she meant by it; Cassie was thin and spindly, and she dressed like she spent her days in a canoe drifting nowhere on the water. She wore a soft men's linen shirt and baggy overalls, the butter-soft kind designer stores were always trying to mimic. Only these were real, flecked with whitewash.

"Right. Of course." Cassie offered her a hesitant smile. "What have you got for me?"

Lark showed her the box. *BOX 8,* she'd scrawled on its side.

Taped to its lid was the little chicken-scratch inventory she'd made for it. "I don't really know very much about them," she confessed. "I've been doing my best, but there are about a hundred more where these came from."

Mitch laughed, a little nervously. "I'll go unload the rest of what we brought."

The box opened, silent as a cat's yawn. Inside, treasure glinted. Cassie pulled out the first telescope, which was enclosed in a beautiful leather container. It smelled like polish and age. It was a spyglass, proud and brassy with a black leather exterior worn away in bronze streaks from being opened and closed. Lark knew it was heavier than it looked. She'd held it when it went into the box, and it had had a firm, real feeling in her hands. Cassie pressed it against her eye.

She pulled, and it expanded, growing four rings. "Leather case doesn't match. Brass. Handheld," she murmured to herself and rubbed her thumb over the inscription: "Bardou & Son Paris. John P. Lovell Arms Co. in Boston…circa early 1900s." Cassie nodded. "It's a rifle-range telescope. Lovely piece. It was from here in the shop." She looked up. "The man who bought it also bought a beautiful pair of 1920s binoculars with a working stand the same day. I remember. That was your father?"

Lark couldn't pull her eyes from the spyglass. She nodded. "He was in here a lot." This shop was exactly the kind of place where Lark's dad would have loved to search. She could imagine him so easily here, a proud connoisseur browsing the store, peering in the cases like a little kid at the zoo, eagerly talking about objects on display with his familiar enthusiasm.

Cassie hummed without looking at her. She retrieved another

telescope, this one small, made of burnished brass, with a clam-shell clasp protecting the lens. "This one was from our shop too. But not all of these. He must have been to every shop in the state if this is only one box."

"Oh yeah." Lark had to laugh. There had been weekend getaways, years ago, roaring down Arkansas back roads in Dad's classic car, a 1969 Austin-Healey Sprite, taking detours to waterfalls, weaving up through the Ozarks, testing the car's upper registers on the open yellowed land of the Delta. They'd found new telescopes, new ways of seeing, all over the place. But that had been years ago. "He found a lot online too." She swallowed. "But we just need them gone now. If you're able to help, I can pay you. For consulting, or—"

"No, this is interesting," Cassie said. "Besides, you're Mitch's cousin." The rifle-range telescope had absorbed her again. "I'll buy some off you. This one, if I can. It's a lovely piece."

"Absolutely." Something in Lark's heart yanked to part with it, but that was absurd. "Thank you so much. I've been sort of up a creek."

Mitch returned with another load of telescope boxes. "Cass, Mom said you're having dinner over at the Destiny tomorrow with *Jeff Daley*? What's that about?"

"Is the *Godfather* his boat?" Lark asked. That was the name painted across the side of the behemoth parked in the very last slip on Echo.

"Yes." Cassie put down the telescope before brushing her hair back over one shoulder to jot down notes—an offer on paper for Lark to consider. "He says he has a business proposition, and the Destiny is better than his houseboat."

"He's a snake. Thinks he can sneak over here from Charlene

and take everything over." Mitch scowled. "I'll tell him what he can do with his business propositions."

"Whoa, whoa, whoa." Lark chuckled, patting him on the shoulder. It was quite a reach. "Simmer down, why don't you."

Cassie only smiled. "I'll hear what he has to say. But I can't imagine there's much we'll have to talk about."

"Well, then." Lark thunked another box down between them, its content shifting. This shop, this woman, soothed something in her. Her spirits were lighter than they'd been in days, and the visions out on the water felt far away. "I guess it's lucky that you and I have so much to talk about."

CHAPTER SEVEN

ASSIE LINGERED IN THE SHOP PAST CLOSING TIME
the next day. Customers had come in surprising num-
bers that afternoon, most drawn to the front, with the
honey, candles, clay mugs, and oiled wood serving bowls. These
were all the new things. Not everyone wandered into the back,
where she kept the true treasures and curiosities rescued from the
water. Photographs. Old mirrors. Pieces of silver.

After the tourists were gone, heading out for early dinners or to
snatch a good spot in the coves to watch the sunset, Cassie lingered,
enjoying the emptiness and silence. She'd spent some time with the
spyglasses from Lark's boxes, taking careful notes. Many of them
were quite valuable. Now she sat behind her desk in the light of a
beautiful Handel Company lamp with yellow glass flowers glowing
on its bowed shade, polishing a silver clasp with a single pearl. It
came from a mink stole fished out of the lake so heavy with weeds,
Mitch had needed to lumber down from the grocery and haul it to
Cassie's antique shop for her. The silver mink, rich with charcoal
stripes, had been almost entirely ruined. It needed fresh stitching,
deep cleaning, hours and hours of brushing and oiling, and time
in a vinyl garment bag. She'd had to call in a fur expert from the

original Neiman Marcus storefront in Dallas to guide her through the process of saving it. Now it sat on the old dressmaker's dummy in the front window, waiting for its clasp to be returned to it.

She didn't dread her dinner with Daley; in fact, she felt a stirring of curiosity. Everyone who lived around the lake knew Cassie Fairchild, mostly by Grandad's reputation, but she was rarely sought out. She was quiet, and odd, and most of her talents were with objects rather than people. Once, she'd expressed this idea to Mitch, and he'd grumbled around and said maybe other people were the problem. She'd cling to that thought if the dinner with Mr. Daley grew awkward.

Before she left, Cassie picked a couple of jars of honey, both light gold, easily digested, the kind Valerie preferred for honey pie. With the jars clinking in her passenger seat, she drove home and paused there long enough to change her shirt, then took the short path down her hill and onto Valerie's property.

The lights of the resort twinkled through the leaves like fireflies. Mitch's grocery was already shut up. It was always quieter on weekdays, but a few people were on the benches outside motel rooms or lounging beside the pool. One of the swan boats, rented for the day, was paddling home now over a blood-orange lake. Daley's Jeep sprawled in the lot outside the restaurant.

Valerie waved as Cassie came in, a quick flap as she rang somebody up on the register. On a Wednesday, most of the diners were locals, but they kept her busy.

"Cassie." Jeff Daley was at one of the tables by the big windows, the lake glinting behind him. He stood to give her hand a warm shake. "So good to see you!"

"I hope you weren't waiting long," she said, sliding in across from him. There was already a glass of sweating sweet tea in front of her place at the table.

"Not at all, not at all." Daley looked crisp as the golf course in his sports polo, and he smelled like money, like dry cleaning and small expensive bottles of cologne. For someone who worked down at a marina all day, he smelled nothing like bait. He pushed one of Valerie's well-worn menus over to Cassie. "I tell you what. Your brother has been such a great addition to the marina team. That boy works so hard. Everybody loves him."

Bolt was an easy topic, a safe one to start with. "He's always been a hard worker, even when he was young. Isn't your son there too? They were friends, I thought."

"Oh yeah, they're thick as thieves again." Daley chuckled. "He's always been such a good influence on my boy. I'm counting on Bolt to guide him down the straight and narrow." Daley raised his eyes heavenward as if this might be an impossible task, then went on. "He told me he has his heart set on Vanderbilt. I know someone in the dean's office, so I told him I'd put a good word in for him just as soon as he has his application in order."

Vanderbilt? No one had told Cassie about Vanderbilt. As far as Mom expressed, Bolt would be going to the University of Arkansas, hopefully with at least some scholarship money. Vanderbilt.

"That's generous of you," Cassie managed.

Valerie came to the table to get their orders. Bolt wasn't working that night, so she was just a little shorthanded. Even so, she seemed especially gruff with Daley.

"What can I get you, Jeff?" she asked shortly.

Daley gave his menu a friendly once-over. "I'll have the

special." It was chicken-fried steak that night. "Side salad, Italian dressing. And how about an order of those fried green tomatoes I've heard so much about?"

Valerie's pen swiped aggressively over her pad. "What about you, honey?" Her eyes softened as they landed on Cassie.

"My usual," Cassie asked. "I brought this as well." She produced the two jars of honey. One, she pushed across the table to Valerie. Then, though it felt as natural as a stage play, she pushed the other across at Mr. Daley. "For your tables."

Valerie thawed out a degree or two as she took the nectar. "You are just too sweet," she said, heading back to the kitchen with the slightest shake of her head.

"My, my. So kind of you to think of me. Thank you." Daley patted the top of the honey, fingers drumming some rhythm Cassie didn't recognize, maybe from a song on the radio. "Well, I won't leave you in suspense, Miss Cassie. You're a successful business owner in the area. I'd love to tell you some of my plans for the marina."

"I wouldn't say 'successful,'" Cassie admitted, twisting her hem in her fingers, unable to quite take her eyes off the honey. Bringing Daley a jar had felt like the polite thing to do, and it was her habit to bring gifts of honey to people; now she wished she hadn't. "It's a small antique shop, and if you mean the honey, that's just a hobby."

"You're being too modest. You've managed to make a living in a humble little place like this," he said, smiling at her. "And I've been speaking to the surveyor. Your property holdings around the lake are not insignificant."

Cassie couldn't speak while he took a sip of his iced tea—he'd looked into her land. Into *Grandad's* land.

There wasn't enough time for Cassie to figure out how to reply. "Any idea why your grandad had the deed under his old name? Except those four acres, where your shop sits. Those are under T. Fairchild," Mr. Daley continued. "Took me finding your name on both papers to realize Taft Farhi and Tobias Fairchild were one and the same."

In those times, Grandad once told Cassie many recent immigrants were changing their names to sound more American, the Farhis becoming the Fairchilds, the Pescatores becoming the Fischers. These were deep family roots, and Daley must have scavenged to find them.

"Why were you looking into our property?" Cassie asked.

"Well, I didn't know it was yours until I looked," he explained with that same twinkle in his eye. "Don't be modest. Amassing what he did was quite an accomplishment. I always respected Tobias. He was a good man. I think he saw in this place the same thing I do." He leaned forward on his tan forearms, a bulky watch glinting at her across the Formica table. "Have you ever been over to the Charlene marina, Cassie? I grew up right over near there—got a business or two in the area nowadays. They expanded about ten years ago, and it's just beautiful now. They've got houseboat rentals, state-of-the-art marine services and repair shop, at least a dozen brand-new docks...even a Starbucks. Can you believe that?" He chuckled, unrolling the paper napkin from around his silverware. "What I'm looking to do is make Prosper a real competitor in Arkansas leisure. I've already hired a pyrotechnics company to do a massive Fourth of July fireworks show over at the dam. This guy is world-class, seriously." He gave her a conspiratorial look. "Given that you have so much of your personal capital invested in this land, I wanted to discuss some potential opportunities with you."

Personal capital. Invested. These were not words Cassie had ever used. The land didn't even feel like hers. It was Grandad, who worked on the Great Damnation, who must have foreseen the growth of Charlene and how the developers would one day move in to claim chunks of Prosper. He'd bought it up when no one cared. Grandad never did anything with it, just left it wild and free, so Cassie only had a vague idea how much it was. Grandad himself never talked about it, other than to say he hoped the shores where their home stood and the shore across from it would stay exactly as they were for as long as a Fairchild held the deeds. Most of it was untouched.

"What kind of opportunities?" she asked, and now she ached to take the honey back. Perhaps it was simply good business to do his research, but she couldn't shake the feeling that she'd been spied upon.

"Oh, there's amazing potential for development in your land," Daley told her, face full of boyish eagerness. "I'm sure you know. Condos, new docks, commercial space. With your land and my experience, a whole new town could rise from the ashes." He glanced quickly at the surrounding tables. "I'd be delighted to be a partner with you—an investor—for that kind of economic progress."

One of Valerie's summer hires brought their salads over, which gave Cassie an excuse to duck her head to drip dressing onto it.

Daley, spearing lettuce onto his fork, was caught in his own pitch. "There's interesting history on this side of the lake, you know that? The president himself came to see construction at the dam site a few months before it was completed. Not to mention that pearl rush—you ever hear about that?"

Prosper's rumored gold mine. Of course she knew. Anyone from Prosper, *really* from Prosper, with roots that went deep underwater to the flooded town beneath, knew about the pearl rush of 1936.

Grandad used to keep a piece of weathered cotton-soft newsprint in a frame on his bookshelf, and Cassie had gazed at it many times, fascinated by the all-caps headline: PEARLS! PEARLS! PEARLS! She especially remembered the tiny photo of a man, beaming and crouched over two full pails of mussels, holding what appeared to be a ball of light in his palm. She'd read the first sentence to herself before, whispering it like a magic spell, because it had seemed so wonderful, and she had wanted so much for it to be part of her life. "*The pearl rush of 1936 began when Italian sharecropper Benigno Fischer (pictured) says his daughter discovered a faintly pink pearl the size of a grape inside of a freshwater mussel she dug out of the shallow north end of Lake Prosper.*" A pearl the size of a grape.

"Magic pre-Damnation days," Grandad had said when he first showed it to her. "Those *were* magic days. Some will tell you it's not real, but it was. I saw them with my own eyes. The Fischers found so many, you wouldn't believe it if you didn't see it. They filled their entire house, until pearls were spilling out of cabinets and poking like pebbles in the bottoms of all their shoes."

"I know the pearl rush," Cassie said to Daley. "It was before the Damnat—before the dam."

"Exactly." He took this as positive encouragement and went on. "I think any kind of expansion around the lake should highlight the fascinating local history. Don't you?"

"How?" Cassie asked, poking her salad around her plate. "What do you have in mind?"

"The sky's the limit. Actually, do you know what happened to any of those pearls?" His eyes were bright. "Any ever turn up in the shop?"

The muddy piggy bank and the fake pearl she'd found inside flashed through her mind.

"No, other than the odd string. Nothing definitive," she replied. "We don't often get pearls. They're heirlooms the family usually wants to keep."

Cassie had long ago realized the pearls were gone. Pearls, out in the world, became anonymous and didn't need to be tracked like diamonds and other jewels. Pearls joined a string, became parts of another whole, and there was no telling where they were now.

Still, the idea of the pearls was their Sam Bass treasure, their private El Dorado that could be strung into a hundred necklaces. Some people lived in hope. *Hope*, Grandad had said, *never hurt.* Every time something locked came through the shop—music box, jewelry box, hatbox, cigar box, lunch box, shoebox, steamer trunk, safe—Grandad used to save it and wait for Cassie to join him so they could investigate it together. *You never know what'll come through this place*, he'd say in his sandpaper voice, propping her on his knee so they could lift each lid together. *Maybe it'll be diamonds. Pirate treasure. How would you like a box brimming with chocolate?*

Jeff Daley's gaze was filled with the same treasure-seeking zeal. "It's such a good story, though, isn't it?"

A shadow fell on him, and he looked up. Mitch was standing behind Cassie with their dinners on a tray. He almost never worked in the restaurant these days, but he was now, arching an eyebrow over Daley's hostage chicken-fried steak. "Jeff," he growled, in the polite, irritated voice he used when he had to answer the phone. "Thought I'd come over and say hello."

"Mitch. Great to see you." There was some tension behind Daley's jovial smile now. It made sense that Jeff Daley wouldn't go to Valerie and Mitch with this scheme. For one thing, it had only been a few years since Diego came on as a full partner in the Grand Destiny. They didn't need him. For another, they didn't have more land than the resort's footprint. And there was no way Daley didn't know how they felt about him throwing the marina shop into direct competition with Mitch's market.

Mitch settled a large hand on Cassie's shoulder. It just caught the underside of her braid, and she nearly shivered. "You need anything, Cassie?"

"No, thanks," she said.

"Okay. Well, I'm doing some fixes for Mom in the kitchen, so I'll be around." Mitch twitched his lip at Daley and set down her usual plate, two of Valerie's buttermilk biscuits with cream cheese and a layer of whatever jam they had on hand. Fig jam. Apple butter. Today it looked like raspberry preserves.

Once Mitch disappeared again—out of sight but still watchful, she knew—Daley sighed happily at his plate. "This is a special place, Cassie," he said as he sawed into it. Aficionado of choice cuts of meat or not, he seemed delighted by this gravy-smothered, breaded sirloin. "Ever since I moved here, I can't help but feel like the water is speaking to me. There's more to this little patch than we can see now. I'm in a position to help realize that."

In her experience, following voices from the lake brought nothing but pain. But then, no one believed her when she said so. Perhaps it was different when you were Jeff Daley. Maybe his wealth afforded him immunity as well as status and credibility. Or perhaps a man like him, with a life made of achievement and old-fashioned American entrepreneurial spirit, couldn't be lured. His mind was already occupied. A man like him wouldn't find himself wandering into the water when the night was darkest.

"I appreciate your offer," Cassie said, folding her hands in her lap. "But I'm not interested."

"You know it's funny, but—" He stopped, a spoonful of mashed potatoes halfway to his mouth. "What?"

"I'm not interested. I can't think of much that I would like less or that I would be less suited for," Cassie said. Likely, Mom would have called this kind of statement "abrasive" and "overly blunt," but surely a businessman would appreciate not having his time wasted. "I mean no disrespect, but my grandfather didn't buy the land for condos, and I tend to trust his judgment."

Mr. Daley's expression froze solid, the astonished smile turning as gray and blank as the lake in February. "I'm sorry to hear that," he said faintly. "I—Cassie, surely you want to sleep on this offer I'm making. It would help everyone who lives around here. It would only expand your grandfather's legacy—"

"He already has the legacy he wanted," Cassie replied. "I'm sorry if that's not what you were hoping for."

It was an uncomfortable moment. Daley gazed into the amber glow of the honey, tapping a finger on its top again. "I can understand it," he said gently. "You enjoy the peace of your life. You don't need much. But—at least consider selling me the land nearest the marina. Give me some growing space for my own business. And I'll pay top dollar, of course. Get Bolt that Vandy money." He sighed, digging for his wallet to pay. "Just think about it, huh? For the town."

Cassie wasn't particularly hungry after all. Maybe Mitch would find her a to-go box. "I'll think about it." She wouldn't, but it was a kinder note to end on. Besides, the only town she knew was already underwater.

ల౨

It was late when Bolt, Rig, Sammy, and Woody passed the NO TRESPASSING signs meant to block off the houseboat graveyard. Bolt was in the lead because he knew the way best. They'd spent the day absorbing sun, filling gas tanks, and buffing prows, but it was a different world under the rising moon, the air heavy with the green scent of dampness.

When Bolt had come back to town, venturing down to the marina, Rig had been the one waiting for him. The Daleys used to have a speedboat in a Charlene dock slip, but now they could lounge on the back of their truly spectacular whale of a houseboat, just a short walk from the Grand Destiny—on Bolt's side of town for once.

He found Rig sitting behind the marina counter, reading a worn-out old paperback with the cover folded over, listening to music that wasn't on the radio, and only kind of paying attention to the goings-on he was likely meant to be overseeing.

"You look like you need a smoke," Rig said, as if it hadn't been a couple of years and was in fact only yesterday that they had last seen each other. He'd grabbed a couple of small bills from the register and waved Bolt outside with an idle gesture. It hadn't taken

Rig long to get the measure of their side of the lake. In the time since his dad had bought them a marina, Rig had proclaimed himself king and chosen his small circle of court jesters carefully. He only did the work he wanted and delegated the rest, usually the cleaning, to lesser employees.

But he would never know it the way Bolt did, which meant there were some places only Bolt could introduce them to. One of them, Rig's favorite, was the houseboat graveyard. He visited often on his own now.

It was a little over a mile down from the marina, past Cassie's RV, over bad roads and through backwoods, brush, and mud as thick as a blanket. It was the place broken or abandoned boats went to waste, a junk heap and scavenger's paradise. When boat ownership became too expensive or someone's beloved vessel broke beyond repair, they paid to have it hauled here, turned their back, and tried to forget.

The houseboat graveyard was a vast ancient lot banking the lake, grass shooting up through the craters in the old paving. Boats that could no longer float, were no longer useful, or weren't wanted, sat out there like dry bones, well-picked by buzzards. These were mummified husks at various stages of decay. The smell of mildew hung across the entire graveyard, and everywhere, there were wriggles of fraying moldy rope, broken glass, gasoline cans, and fishing line.

Occasionally a new geriatric reject would appear in one corner or another, ready to be explored. A cruiser with a small cabin haunted the southern edge, its portholes totally obscured by caked-on, long-dry sludge. One speedboat nearby was overturned like a bath toy; it was easy to crawl under it, into the close, hot space within.

At the far edge, where the cement disappeared into the water, lay an old dock, and the grounded boats were stuck carelessly beneath its rusted-out tin roof. Someone had laid out a big sheet of metal across the mud there, once the hood of a car, to bridge the small gap to the remains of the dock. It bowed when they stepped across. When Bolt was two beers in, it felt as if at any moment the planks might crumble underneath him.

The land here was marshy. In the moonlight, water puddled under the dock, gleaming in the yawning gaps where the wood had moldered. The first boat crushed up into the wood supports was an ancient tugboat, its name long since bitten away by rust. It had been red once. The lake seemed to draw closer with every visit, testing the dock's old foam supports, ready to sweep it out on a devouring current.

Embalmed in the distant dock lights, the houseboats wedged in the beached structure and those bleaching in the lot, as many as twenty, watched with broken-window eyes. They dribbled decade-old oil and peeled paint. Forever landlocked now, they jumbled against each other like shopping carts abandoned in a grocery store parking lot. Anything soft—cushions, life jackets—had grown soggy and miserable, puffy with water, and then dried out, cracked, desiccated.

Rig's favorite boat was near the center of the wasted dock. It was the tallest, in part because it was propped nearly on top of another, tilted up at an angle. The door didn't lock, and could be wriggled until it slid half-open, where it stuck. It was mostly dry there, and they'd taken it over, littering the corners with chip wrappers and discarded Ring Pops, broken bottles, pocketknives, empty wallets.

Sammy had been humming the same snatch of a song for at least half an hour, even louder once she realized how much it irritated Rig.

"Go to hell, Samantha," he complained, even as he gave her a boost onto the dock.

She hoisted herself up, jeering at him. "Make me, dickhead."

Bolt followed, leaping up on his own. Sammy had quickly charmed Bolt with her perfect memory for disturbing trivia. They'd tell each other the bad jokes printed on the rainbow Popsicle sticks and laugh.

Rig touched one of the decomposing drainage pipes, and his hand came away orange with rust. He stuck it in Sammy's face, and she snarled at him, catching his wrist in a steel grip.

Woody clambered after them, caught sight of the fun, and— snickering—grabbed the same pipe and followed suit. He was Rig's friend. Though he always wore faded clothes, he was another Charlene kid, and Bolt knew Woody's parents had money. He had slightly pathological tendencies and an eternal case of mono, and whenever the mono was bad, he blew them off.

Woody shoved his palm at Bolt, and Bolt stepped around him with a sharp elbow, dodging an old Shiner bottle. "You guys are gross."

An owl hooted forbiddingly from somewhere close as Sammy pressed her thumb into the rust and drew red strokes onto her cheeks. Rig tested a dangling flagpole by swinging on it. It snapped, and he just avoided twisting an ankle between rickety beams. Bolt laughed at him, loud and clear. Woody only laughed *with* Rig; even now, his eyes naturally darted themselves away.

"So what's on the agenda?" Bolt asked Rig, folding his chilled hands into his sleeves. Rig was moving with unusual purpose. Normally they just rolled joints and shot at cans with Woody's old BB gun.

"Funny you ask," Rig said. "Catch." He nearly smacked Bolt in the face with a can of spray paint resting beside the unhinged gate of one of the dinky mud-choked boats. "Art project."

Bolt shook the can experimentally and pushed a red line along the faint shadow of a windowpane on the opposite wall. It was hard to push, sticky and acrylic. "Glad to see you still like art."

Rig ignored him. He'd carried around a sketch pad in their middle school days, a more innocent time. He liked to doodle guitars and lightning bolts. Once he'd done a really good sketch of a lion. But that felt like a long time ago out here in the damp night.

"Let me try," Woody said, snatching for it.

"Wait your turn, Woody Willy." Bolt evaded, tossing it into his other hand. Woody's shoulders tensed, and he swiped for it again, managing to snatch it this time and then spraying it close enough to Bolt's face that his eyes watered.

"Spray this up there. Everywhere." Rig drew one of his ratty paperbacks from the inner pocket of his jacket and flipped to a folded page. "It's the—" He paused, checking the caption. "The eye of the chaos bringer." He flashed the graying page at them in the darkness.

"Is that like a satanic thing?" Sammy squinted at it with interest through fading moonlight.

Rig scoffed at her, pulling out more cans. "Satan is so nineties."

"Why can't we just spray whatever we want?" Bolt asked, tracing the ink and paper stare. "I had my heart set on a unicorn."

Rig snorted, revving his black paint up. It rattled in his hand.

"Because this is badass." He checked the image again and then got to work on the side of the boat. "Maybe it'll make something happen in this shit place." Rig was always saying that kind of thing about Prosper; he missed his house in Charlene.

Bolt grabbed a can of his own and pressed down. Fuzzy paint spattered on the starboard wall over the remains of a window seat. "Where'd you find that book?" Woody asked, rifling through Rig's bag for lukewarm beer.

"It was stuffed in one of the seat pockets on that ancient Stingray speedboat across the lot," Rig said. "Never know what'll turn up out here, man. Just have to keep your eyes open." He flipped the cap of his flask off and took a swig. "Keep spraying."

Sammy had slipped off her sneakers and was clambering down the rails of the boat, lowering herself into the shallows. However much she dogged him, wheedled him, tripped along in his wake, she was impervious to Rig's commands.

After a few minutes, the hull of the boat was staring back at them, eyes pimpling every angle of scarred and rusting metal. The houseboats creaked on the occasional low wakes, still dying down from the day's traffic. The four trespassers rode the gentle movement of the geriatric boats rubbing shoulders.

Past the staring eyes, Bolt couldn't make out the far furry line of the opposite tree-lined shore. Under the cold angular stare of the chaos bringer, he remembered the dream—formless moaning in his ear, the chill of the water in his shoes when he woke up wearing them in bed—and shivered. He hadn't felt quite right on the water since that night, cold in a way he couldn't shake, even in the summer heat. He needed to get a grip. The only person who felt that way about the lake was Cassie.

"You know what?" Sammy poked her head up over the edge. There was a large irregular pebble in her palm. "This isn't far from the mass graves."

"The what?" Rig scoffed at her, annoyed at this distraction from his vision.

"From when Yellow Jack came to town." She waggled her eyebrows. "That means yellow fever. They were in such a rush to get rid of the bodies that they just threw them in a big pit. But Nonnie told me it's close to here. That's why people avoid this place."

Rig was staring at her, open-mouthed. Then he remembered to be cool. He shook his head and went back to his work. "Bullshit."

"No, she's right," Bolt murmured. "It was bad. Really bad. A lot of people died, and so Prosper, back when it was a town, was basically decimated. I used to hate those stories." They'd kept him up at night as a small child; he'd dream of jaundiced, rotting skin, of finding yellow sores and barnacles on his face. For a while, every cold, every fever was terrifying, and he'd washed his hands so often that Mom finally yelled at Grandad until he sat Bolt down again and explained it was unlikely he'd ever have to worry about contracting yellow fever—astronomical, even. *Do you know that word, kiddo? Astronomical?*

"You know what I heard?" Woody said eagerly. He shook his paint can. "There were people in town when they flooded it. All these people, sleeping in their beds. They did it to kill the yellow fever. Drown it out."

Bolt shook his head. "My grandfather worked on the dam, dipshit. He says he had already been moved out of Prosper before they flooded it."

"That's a wild story, man." Rig tossed an arm around him.

They were all quiet for a moment, staring at their handiwork. Eyes now watched them from every angle.

Then Rig gave Woody a sudden kick in the ass. With a yelp of pain, he smashed face-first into the prow, then crashed off the rotted timbers into the sludge between boat and dock carcass. Rig chuckled, ducking inside the boat itself. "Enough ghost stories. Let's get drunk."

Somehow, the hard stares of all those painted eyes seemed to follow them inside.

CHAPTER EIGHT

"I SHOULD CALL THE COPS ON THOSE KIDS," MITCH growled to Cassie a couple of days after he'd heard the teenagers shouting drunkenly in the woods and busting bottles right behind the Destiny. "Cops" was a bit of an exaggeration. The law enforcement of Prosper was essentially a feckless sheriff's deputy whose wife ran one of the Arkansas quartz shops. Cyril had recently read an article about the ill effects of radio waves on the human brain, so he usually kept his scanner off these days. Mitch rubbed another glob of wax sheen over the warm cherry tabletop, grumbling. "Somebody's gonna end up dead if they keep going out to that junkyard. I just don't want it to be Bolt."

They were in the shop, laying a coat of finish on an antique table that had come in from Charlene. The boxes of Uncle Stu's telescopes sat piled in the corner, where Cassie and Lark had been slowly going through them the day before, but today, the table took precedence. Cassie had already sanded it, applied new varnish.

Sometimes Cassie gave the impression that she was deep underwater in her own head, but she was one of the best listeners in the world. She didn't always reply right away. Sometimes she didn't reply for days. But she never forgot a word Mitch spoke to her either; she simply absorbed what she was told, marinated in it, and returned it in her own time, annotated with her careful, precise thoughts. Some people liked to battle for their share of conversation, for the pleasure of hearing their own voice. Not Cassie. A conversation with Cassie was writing a letter and sending it off with hope.

"They shouldn't be out on the lake at night. It isn't safe. I'll tell Bolt not to go, but he won't listen to me." The news of her brother's antics had alarmed her; Mitch could tell by the faint line of strain appearing between her thin, wood stain–dark eyebrows. "Kids only like danger until danger likes them back. Then it isn't so fun." She brushed aside a strand of her hair. The wood was starting to preen under her attention. Soon it would be fresh and stately again. "Sometimes I think I don't know Bolt at all."

"Cassie…" Mitch frowned, bending down to watch her buzz around her task.

"Bolt wants to go to Vanderbilt," she went on. "Daley told me." She finally moved on to another table leg. He watched her face. It was a foreign language to most people, but Mitch had started studying when they were in school together, and he was fluent now in the subtle shift of her expressions. Though her voice gave nothing away, her eyes told all: distress and preoccupation, the nerves that came with a break in her regularly scheduled life.

Mitch stuck his brush back in the warm beeswax and caught an edge he'd missed. Vanderbilt was one of the best universities in the South. But it was pricey, way beyond the dreams of most people Mitch knew. "I wonder why Bolt wouldn't tell you."

"It's expensive. He also didn't want to stay with me," Cassie added with her usual unassuming frankness. "He and Mom didn't want me to know that, though."

Mitch had witnessed when Dorothy had brought Bolt into the Destiny to ask Mom for room. He hadn't put the pieces together at the time. "He's just a teenager," he said, more gently. "He doesn't know what's important yet."

"I know we're different. I just don't want him to get hurt."

"I'll tell Mom and Diego to keep him as busy as possible over at the Destiny." Everything in him wanted to reassure her. "He'll be all right. He's smart."

Cassie smiled. "Maybe. But he's still a teenage boy." She stood and put the lid on the wax.

The beeswax on the tabletop was already drying. She touched the surface with loving hands. That tenderness tugged Mitch in, and suddenly he wanted to touch her hand, those pretty, calloused fingers against the dark grain.

"So you're sure about telling Daley no?" Mitch had already heard Cassie's frustrating abbreviated story of the dinner. "That land by the marina?" It would be a big step toward a fancy college for Bolt. Still, it would hurt. Daley was a Charlener, and they loved nothing more than sucking the marrow out of this side of the lake. There had been a small uproar when Ludwig sold Daley the marina, but no one else in Prosper had the free funds to take the place over.

"I can't give him land so close to my house and the Destiny," she said. "The noise from the tourists would keep me up all night." She dipped her hand into her pocket and withdrew with a glint of copper in her palm. Mitch looked at it a moment before he realized what it was. Then he drew his own lucky coin, the one she'd rescued from the old piggy bank, from the back pocket of his jeans. The two pennies made a soft clink when they met.

⁊

Summer in the South was very different from summers in Chicago. There, heat was metallic, as if the skyscrapers were sweating along with everyone else. Here the air churned with wind and bugs, birdsong from somewhere on the horizon, and sunshine so bright that when June woke in the late morning, she had no choice but to cart her treasure from the dinky sink in the laundry room, the safest place for its lake grime, outside onto the grass and flop down in front of it.

Eliza had snorted when she'd seen June lugging the thing into the car at 2:00 a.m., waving the smell of mud away, and she laughed when she wandered outside onto the porch with another of her many brews of morning coffee and saw June lying on the grass and digging into the chest's lock with a screwdriver.

"I want to know what's inside," June said, smiling at her. "What if it's treasure?"

"It probably was, for somebody." Eliza had her sermon notebook in her hands. She usually waited until the last minute to get all her thoughts down for the coming Sunday. "Doesn't mean it's treasure for you." She shrugged, settling in on the porch swing. "It's probably a bunch of rotten papers. Or a picture of that naked white lady in *Titanic*."

"How could it not be a treasure for me?" June asked, pushing again on an inner mechanism without success. "I found it."

Eliza only shook her head as she slipped her Airpods in and opened her notebook.

June had rarely met a lock she couldn't hack, but this one was proving to be difficult. When her screwdriver found some invisible cog and tried to cajole it, playing at being a key, nothing would budge.

And sometimes, when she paused to wipe sweat from her brow or readjust her grip, she'd poke the end of the screwdriver back in and wouldn't scrape up against a thing. She couldn't find any purchase, as if she'd poked a hole through a blanket into empty space and the lock was just decoration.

Cracking this particular beast would require surgery rather than piracy.

There was a dull roar as a truck turned into the church parking lot. It was an ancient rust bucket, with bulbous headlights and a bed covered in jewel-toned canvases. BAG OF TRICKS TRAVELING PYROTECHNICS CO.! it read in lurid letters that spilled from the end of a painted magician's wand. The man at the helm was scrawny and crow-like, his bristled face pinched as he threw the thing into reverse. His tires roared over the corner of the church's lawn.

Eliza frowned, slipping an earbud out as she watched him. "Guess he got lost?" she muttered.

June sat up, caught on the truck's painted sides, suddenly full of the taste and smell of fire. "He's not one of your flock?"

The man in the truck raised a hand to Aunt Eliza, and she nodded to him, face impassive. "Never seen him before."

"Fireworks. That should be fun," June said as he nearly clipped a flower bed on the way out. There was something about the truck, its grumbling engine and the hulking shape of the canvases on its back, that gave the illusion they weren't covering up simple sparklers but something big and cohesive, like the slender sharp back of a dragon. She stood, watching it go. On the truck's tarnished chrome rear end was a wide black rectangle: a bumper sticker. Emblazoned in white was a circle caught in a diamond, glaring out like an abstracted eye. The sticker seemed to watch June until the truck's tail vanished through the trees.

"Should be," Eliza repeated, though she didn't sound quite sure. The phone rang from inside the house, and she went in to answer it, glancing back only once.

The truck left scuffed grass behind and a strange whiff of cigarette smoke. June kneeled again beside the chest, frustrated and too hot. She shoved it, and despite its weight, it tipped over onto its back, the lock too tarnished to shine in the sun. She picked up her screwdriver again and slammed the handle down onto the lock.

Finally, some piece of her she hadn't even known was coiled tight now relaxed. After so much careful tinkering, holding herself back, it was fun, so she hit it again; a shard of plastic grip glinted off through the air. The lock itself, and the chest as a whole, remained unscathed.

June's fingers burned from holding the thin metal end of the tool, but it was a good burn now. She hit it again.

❦

By the time the marina closed on Sunday, and Bolt, Rig, and the others ended their shifts, the sun was already gilding the edges of the lake, and Bolt was starving for a break. The four of them gathered at the Daley slip, where Rig lowered the Jet Skis into the water with a fancy mechanized lever; they hummed on their way to the water like racehorses chomping at the bit.

It felt like the whole *world* was chomping at the bit for something. The water was choppy from a day of activity, delighted shrieks and boat engines still echoing from shore to shore, and Bolt himself was loopy from the smell of gas tanks. He'd always liked Jet Skis, even if Mom worried when he went out with friends on them. *Motorcycles on water*, she grumbled. *Only you aren't wearing a helmet.*

The summer before ninth grade, a girl a few grades above him had died in a Jet Ski collision. *Going too fast*, people murmured at the memorial service over iced tea, blaming the kids rather than facing the actual legal problem with this. Mom had made him attend, and he'd stood in a corner trying to swallow down a dry chicken salad sandwich. *What a tragedy. Her poor mother.*

Bolt shook himself and hooked an arm around Sammy's shoulder. It was getting too quiet. "Do you want the pink life jacket? Or can I wear it?"

She snickered. "I'll take the tie-dye."

Woody was watching open-mouthed as the Jet Skis dipped into the water.

Rig slung a life jacket over his shoulders, the Jet Ski key clipped to its chest. The idea was that if you were thrown off the back of this bucking bronco of a water raft, the key would disengage and kill the power.

"Looks like most of the boomers are off the water now," he noted, shading his eyes to look past the no-wake zone. He leaped onto the nearest Jet Ski. "Ready for a night out?"

"Very." Bolt took a long, lunging step from the dock to the Jet Ski, and it rocked under his weight.

"I wanted that one. I wanted to drive," Woody snapped; Bolt ignored him.

Rig snorted. "As if, Wood."

"Sam, with me?" Bolt offered. She hopped aboard behind him, zipping her life jacket. Her grandma Mable had second sight about boat safety.

"Hey, you know where you want to go?" Bolt hit the ignition, and the Jet Ski purred to life under them. "I know some kick-ass channels that boats can't go in." The Snake was the most famous, a thin, winding waterway where the lake's chop never touched. You could punch the accelerator on a Jet Ski and move like quicksilver down those aquatic back roads.

"Actually." Rig was already revving his engine, putting enough distance between himself and the boat that Woody had to hurl himself across the breach. "I want to see it."

"See what?" Bolt called, but it was lost to the wind; Rig was already off, wake splashing them as he burst out of the slip, curving in a sharp arch west into the setting sun. He never followed the rules.

Bolt sighed. "Hold on," he said, then turned their nose to the sun. Sammy's thin fingers dug into the straps of his life jacket as they kicked off the water and revved across the lake.

Rig had always been a reckless driver, zooming as fast as he could over the wakes, chasing them down. Once Bolt had been riding behind him and bit his tongue so hard, he tasted blood. It had hurt to talk for a week.

Bolt skated through his turbulence, smooth and fast, avoiding the bumpy ride Rig seemed to crave. Not all wakes looked as dangerous as they were. Some mountains, stirred by powerful engines and wind, hid themselves in shades of blue, pretending to be ripples until they surged under the hull of your craft.

The lake felt endlessly big from the back of a Jet Ski. Grandad had said it was probably about two hundred feet at its deepest. They crossed into the deepest parts of the water, away from the prettiest part of the lake. Bolt felt them leave the summery warmth and tall trees of the lake he knew best. It was about ten minutes before the edge of the lake resolved itself into a thick charcoal line, and their destination became clear.

The Damnation, Bolt heard Grandad's whisper across years. The dam loomed ahead of them, a black wall holding up all that water, keeping it from the riverbed where it once used to flow toward a far-off ocean. It was what powered much of the state, what made the lake, accounting for every visit from every weekender. A silent, man-made backbone everything was built upon.

"No wonder we haven't come out here before," Rig shouted over the water as he ripped toward the shore. He only ever cut the engine at the very last second. "This is a fucking long way." Though the ride must've been twice as far from Charlene, miles and miles away, down at the other end of the lake.

It should've been pitch-black out there, but lights twinkled on top of the dam.

"What's that thing?" Sammy murmured as they cruised onto pebbles. Rig was already loitering on land, tapping a cigarette against his pack. His lighter gave several false starts.

"I don't know. A guardhouse? Maybe?" Bolt suggested. Sammy squinted through deep twilight, scraping her way onto dry land. "It doesn't really belong."

"That's a tent, you idiots," Woody said. He hopped up the bank, rocks falling in his wake. "Pyrotechnics," he read, and his face lit up. "*Fireworks*."

Rig, who'd gotten his smoke lit at last, exhaled softly.

They climbed onto the dam, hiking up the grassy hill until they crested the top. A tent like the center ring of a grand circus glowed golden ahead of them. Paisleys, painted faces, dancers, and mythical beasts veiled by the night waved faintly on the surface of the canvases. The yellow light lit Sammy's face as she stared at it. "This is bizarre," she hissed. The firecracker tent had an element of storybook wonder in its seams.

"I can't imagine he gets many customers looking to buy fireworks here," Bolt said. "It's too remote."

There were no cars anywhere. Not even a parking lot. The tent floated above the lake, standing right on the precipice. It might as well have been conjured out of the shadows. Bolt walked to the edge of the dam, heels on the ground, toes in open air. It was just high enough to be uncomfortable. Far below, a trickling, unfed creek wound away from him.

The construction had held since Grandad was about his age. He'd worked there when he was barely eighteen, carting gravel and supplies across the gorge as it was built. Once he told Bolt about an early test of the lock system. The river had allowed them to corral it through the locks. They could siphon energy off its back as it raced through the dam, he said, but when it came time to cut off the flow entirely, Grandad privately expected the mechanism to fail. The locks had slowly activated for the first time, and he'd watched the river narrow to an angry trickle, white water frothing as the gates pushed through its current. It was like watching God close his fist, Grandad had thought, and the river, not the dam, gave way.

Bolt could almost see him there now, crouched on top of the dam, hat pressed to his chest in honor of the river's death.

"We've got to go inside," Rig said.

"Don't you have to be over eighteen to buy fireworks?" Bolt asked, kicking a stone over the edge.

"In Arkansas, you only have to be twelve," Woody said, finally catching up. He knocked Sammy hard in the shoulder so roughly, she nearly tripped. "Didn't there used to be a fireworks tent outside Charlene, with a different guy? Marty, you know?"

"I used to score pot off Marty," Rig said regretfully. "Hope this joker makes up for that loss."

"What are you kids doing loitering out here?" rasped a voice, and then a man ducked out of the tent to greet them. Where the twin flaps of the opening met was a gilded, diamond-shaped eye. The familiarity of the shape gave Bolt a lurch. He remembered the eye more in the muscles of his arm, the five sprays of the paint can nozzle it took to put it on that abandoned boat. A shooting-range smell accompanied him. He scratched a weathered cheek, surveying them with a gleam. "Welcome, one and all."

Rig glanced past him into the tent. "You open even after dark, old man? All the way out here?"

The fireworks man's lip curved as he examined Rig. "I keep long hours in the high season. Come on in."

In threadbare clothes, with a tent that appeared older than the dam, the man looked like a vagrant by choice, someone who lived beyond the corners of the rest of the world. No wonder Rig was drawn here. He liked to peel up the corners of the world too. Bolt nudged Sammy, and she gave him a swift elbow in the side.

The fireworks man drew back the curtain. The interior was dim, the low light catching on glittering boxes. Firecrackers lined four wide shelves, high piles against the tent edges, threatening to overflow from cracked whiskey barrels. The gang was immediately drawn in, each eye catching on different mystical names. THUNDER-BRINGER mines, BATTLE OF THE BULGE shells, something called THE KRACKEN, and a hundred more in boxes with no brand names on them. Some boxes were dusty and venerable, others were so new that the ink appeared barely dry.

Woody and Rig immediately went off together to browse, talking in low tones as they turned firecrackers over, peeped under lids.

"Hey. Where are the ingredients?" Woody asked, waving a golden pyramid labeled THE MAGIC TORCH at the owner. He considered himself some kind of expert in explosives. Bolt had watched him blow up a wasp's nest earlier that week using an old car battery. The thing had been obliterated, popping open, the shell as dry and dusty as a mummy in a tomb. The wasps had been enraged, wings sizzling, a smell of something roasting in the air as everyone watching got stung.

The fireworks man had returned to his wide desk, where he was fiddling with colored powders and silver twine. "Unlisted," he said dryly. "I can answer some questions."

The group browsed, and Sammy towed Bolt through the shop, only marginally interested.

"Dude, look at this one!" Woody exclaimed, holding something that looked like a tiny red dragon, pushing between them to get to Rig.

Bolt wandered closer to the desk, where some of the most interesting, oldest ones rested. He touched one wrapped in plain black paper with FIVE GOLDEN RINGS emblazoned on the sides. The packaging was too beautiful for something crafted only to be destroyed. He glanced back at the fireworks man. "How long have you been selling these?"

"Oh. An age and a half." The fireworks man gave the stars on the tent's top a long, kindled glance, full of humor. "Since gunpowder, kid. That's how it feels." He stood. "I've been out here, a long time ago, but I'm working on a few new things, need testing. Y'all want a demonstration?"

Bolt followed his gaze to the ceiling. "Sure. Why not?"

Woody chuckled appreciatively, holding a firecracker shaped like a space shuttle on a launchpad. An astronaut was tied to its exterior. "This is so demented." Rig dragged him along through the tent and back onto the dam. It was the perfect stage, all concrete and open air.

The fireworks man faced them, visage illuminated in the flickering shadows cast by the lit match between his sooty fingers. Here—amid a chorus of cicadas, his bag of tricks on the ground beside him—he looked like some sleazy roadside magician. "Whipped this up today," he said, laying the match flame against the fuse of a cardboard disk in his hand. "I call it the UFO." For a moment, it only whistled, but then—and Sammy gasped—the disk rose gracefully off his palm, whirling in place. It hovered, in perfect balance, the golden lettering blurring into a ribbon in the darkness, before shooting up and bursting into a hundred green sparks. They rained down in emerald trickles, reflected in every transfixed eye.

The next one was round and scaled, like a giant roly-poly. The fireworks man laid it on the asphalt, lighting its end, and it rolled between their ankles, popping, sending out puffs of colored smoke before skidding to a stop and erupting in a torrent of rainbow sparklers. Bolt felt the smoke getting in his head, tangling his thoughts as the demonstration grew larger, louder, more elaborate. Golden canaries of fire alighted on shoulders; flying fish jumped between them in a heady whirl. The fireworks man lit four, each in the shape of a miniature cardboard instrument and at once there was a quartet playing in fire around them, leaving a coda of afterburn imprinted on the air.

"How—Who made these?" Bolt breathed at one point, drunk on dancing fire.

"I did," the fireworks man said, as spinning wheels crashed like comets through the air. "I make just about everything I sell."

Light cracked above them, and for a brief second, the shadows on top of the dam lost their shapelessness. Bolt could have sworn he saw a cluster of men sitting shoulder to shoulder, draping fishing poles down into the creek side of the dam. But the image was gone with the next loud boom.

Time singed at the edges, minutes bleeding into one another, the world melting into a backdrop for the fireworks' dance. The night stretched like taffy. After a dream so rich and strange it should've brought on dawn, they stumbled away with their pockets full of free samples. The pebbled shore was an avalanche beneath their feet. Slow to waking, they were lost for words as they shoved the Jet Skis free of the bank. The fireworks man had assured them in his ragged, amused way that he'd be around until the Fourth and that he'd have any number of new tricks for them each visit.

As they roared out into the water, Woody started babbling again, full of ideas for Rig, where to launch the firecrackers, whether they could sink one of the old cruisers—did Rig like that idea? Didn't he think it sounded so friggin' cool?

Bolt gripped the Jet Ski handlebars, the shadows of the dam looming like they might swallow the group whole. Outside the range of colored fire, he felt cold.

CHAPTER NINE

OW OPEN YOUR HAND," DADDY SAID, EYES WIDE with Christmas-morning glee. Every day that a new telescope arrived was filled with the same energy. Daddy was springy and green despite his age and not much taller than she was. Thin like Aunt Valerie but distracted, with the shaggy gray of his hair and beard hiding his face like some desert ascetic. Mom was flipping pancakes on their griddle, and the stereo was playing.

Lark uncurled her fingers, staring in wonder at the tiny spyglass resting in her palm. Its stubby turquoise body gleamed. "This thing is minuscule." She laughed, his wonder contagious. It caught and warmed in her chest like a candle. "How could you see anything with it?"

"Eyes are small too," he pointed out, an arm around her as he showed her how to adjust the focus with a brass gear the size of a nickel. "Tiny rooms you can hold the whole world in."

And another time: "Telescopes can catch fog inside them. If they crack. Did you know that, Little Bird? They never see things clearly after that."

Lark stirred. Now she had seen the shadows caught in the

fog, the visions that lurked between the lenses. The wave that chased the girl down the dock. The pallbearers, hurling the coffin into the water.

She saw Daddy the way she'd seen him last—the bright windows of his eyes were dark holes, shut-up cellars, the flat pits of stone fruit.

Lark opened her eyes.

"Bag of Tricks, yes, sir. He's setting up an artisanal firecracker tent here in the meantime." Jeff Daley was strolling down the dock. She'd met him with Mitch the other day. He had his phone at his ear, life jacket hanging open like they were about to go out on the lake. "It's gonna be the best show in Arkansas!" He noticed Lark eyeing him and mouthed a boisterous "hello!"

Lark stood to stretch. There was actually room to do that now on the front deck: the first real evidence of her labors. Even at dusk, it was too hot; napping had been a mistake, even if she still wasn't sleeping much at night. Her hair clung to her neck. Maybe she'd take an evening swim.

She went inside for a drink of water, shedding her clothes in the dark hall. She applied a quick layer of sunscreen, then pulled on her suit. Her shorts ended up on a tripod, her best red bra dangling from the end of a refractor's mount. The telescopes turned politely away.

She was about to pull the swim ladder down when she heard the gentle thud of someone hopping aboard. Mitch? Mable's granddaughter, back for another smoke? Lark ducked her way back through the boat.

"Who's the mermaid now, sailor?" A voice echoed down the hall. June stood on the porch, the door cracked, grinning down at Lark. Her visitor was wearing shorts over a new swimsuit, nostalgic blue-and-white stripes that reminded her of pastel yogurt shops and doo-wop songs. In her arms, she carried a big shape Lark recognized as the chest she'd heaved from the water, and a grocery bag draped from her wrist. "I came to return the clothes I borrowed, washed and dried," June said. Her thick hair was practically springing out from the bun on top of her head. Any moment, if June wasn't careful, it would burst free of the band.

"Oh, hey." Lark grinned at her, feeling a wash of purest relief. She hadn't stopped thinking about her since the night of their discovery. "I thought you were a bandit."

"You get bandits around here?" June lifted her eyebrows.

Lark shrugged. "Only some of the dock rats. They like to smoke where their parents can't see them."

"I have so much to learn about the native flora and fauna. Give me a hand?" She offered the grocery bag.

Lark took the bag of her clothes. She quirked an eyebrow at the moldy box June had her arms around. "You're getting pretty attached to that."

"It's my fortune. I don't want it to be stolen." June stepped inside and set the box on the ground, where it squatted between inquisitive telescopes. She leaned forward as if sharing a secret. "I want an adventure."

"What did you have in mind?" Lark laughed, though inside she thrilled at this confidential tone. It felt as if they were already on one, an adventure that had begun the night they met and now bound them together.

June chuckled. "Something tells me you have some ideas."

They took the dinghy out, the chest stored safely beneath

their feet. Lark had really had to search the banks of her memory, back to adolescent jaunts after hours, bending rules on the high tides of summers past. Evening was on, grills firing and house-boaters enjoying cocktails on the dock, so the lake was quiet enough not to capsize their little expedition. "It's a little out of bounds," Lark warned as she revved the dinghy's go-kart motor. She only bothered with it for longer journeys. "Up for it?"

"Out of bounds. Does that mean I'm getting a peek into your rebellious, pink-haired childhood?" June crossed her legs and propped her chin on her hand. "Tell me more."

A wide-eyed stargazer rolled in the bottom of the boat, and Lark hefted it into her lap for a gentler ride. "Those teenagers running around this lake had to learn from somebody, didn't they?" Lark had grown up with her own posse of dock rats, and they'd roved through these woods like Robin Hood, letting the heat stir their blood and turn their heads. The spyglass had a dis-tressed leather strap she wrapped around her hand. She smirked at June, feeling her face warm. "My aunt Valerie would kill me if she knew I ever went out here."

"Sounds fun," June said, turning to watch the bank, which had become ridged, craggy, and undeveloped, more suitable for wildlife than people. Water moccasins might come slithering out of weedy crevices in search of sunshine, and trees grew thick and close all the way down to the water. "I thought there was nowhere to go here," she admitted. Her skin had that sun-warmed, cleansed look that came from long summer days. "It seems like a dead end to me. But this doesn't sound half bad."

"Oh, trust me." Lark had to raise her voice over the grouchy rumble of the engine. "This is the deadest end of the lake."

They skimmed over darkening water. Lark had never navigated there in the boat, so it took a little guesswork and a glance or two at the sky, where Polaris already twinkled. After fifteen minutes or so, the half-sunken dock came into view, silhouetted against a fading sunset. "Here we are," she announced as they chugged toward the silty water's edge.

From the lake, the houseboat graveyard looked like either a forgotten shanty or some bizarre art installation. Boats tipped and teetered, rusted hulls intact through prayer alone. Lark pointed at the farthest corner of the lot, where a massive cruiser loomed over the graveyard, a mighty obelisk. "That's the *Captain Morgan*. I climbed it once. Drunk, with some friends." All her asshole friends had agreed it was a truly heroic feat. She remembered Layla Pearson smashing a bottle of André against the cruiser's speckled side, a ceremonial launch for its departure to the underworld.

"This is wild." June laughed, delighted, and was the first to hop out of the boat. Box on her hip, she scrambled onto the rickety dock that seemed one tug away from being ripped from the bank entirely. Some vandals had been around recently: the boats here were dotted with spray-painted eyes and weird comic book symbols that struck her as somewhat familiar. Where had she seen that eye before? "Where are those friends now? We could have a party." She looked over her shoulder at Lark with a wide grin. June always seemed to be clocking Lark's position, sharing every moment, every flitter of emotion she felt without reservation. Being around her required full participation and total engagement.

Was this a bad idea? Maybe. But that glance was a powder keg in her gut, and with a rueful shake of her head, Lark found herself grinning back. She hopped out before dragging the dinghy a little farther ashore. She brought the telescope along. "Long gone." That sort of friend, the groups you found and fell in with when the days were long and sweltering and your hormones were volcanic, evaporated like summer rain on pavement when the season ended. After what happened with Dad, Lark definitely hadn't heard a word from the old crew. She jogged to catch up, angling them toward the *Captain Morgan*. "Who needs them? We'll have our own party."

"Cool." June finally put the box down, eyeing the *Captain Morgan* and how it slanted against the sky. She shot Lark a dangerous wink and darted forward, hooking her arms in the railing, rusty with time, and hoisting herself up. "If you can do this drunk, I can do this sober," she said, clambering onto the deck. "I used to climb the balconies at our apartment. Irritated my mom to death doing it."

Lark chuckled, throwing the telescope's strap over her shoulder. "Why does this not surprise me?" She gave June a head start, steeling herself. Her first handhold was the base of the cruiser's battered flagpole. It twisted in her hand, letting out a metallic shriek. A mouse-eaten buoy hung loose over a scummy porthole. "What—floor did you live on?" she grunted. Night came on thick over the tree line now. They might have to wait for the moon to get home.

"All over." June huffed, shoes scrabbling for purchase on the lip of the clouded, cataracted window. She pushed up onto the roof and kicked her feet at Lark. "When we lived on the fifth floor, the neighbor on the next-door balcony had flowers and a cat. Don Gato. He was grumpy."

"There's a really grumpy cat at Cassie's antique shop." Lark glanced down. They were high. Far below, all those graffiti eyes were a watchful audience, as unblinking as the telescopes back on the *Dipper*. The cruiser sat on its stern, nose in the air like the *Titanic* right before it sank into the Atlantic. Even on the roof, the cruiser's prow loomed over them like that one vaguely threatening bro at a party. After the climb, June's hair was closer to springing free of its tie than ever. A loose tendril tickled the back of her neck. "There are rungs on the deck. See?" Lark almost couldn't make out their tarnished shine. Still, she crept down the windshield, fumbling for a handhold for the final climb. "We are definitely gonna break our necks."

"No, we won't. I've never fallen yet." June was probably one of those people who liked leaning out over the Grand Canyon and went cliff diving. "I wish one of those telescopes could show me inside the box. Then I could make sure it's worth all this anticipation."

"You could try it," Lark huffed over her shoulder as she hauled herself toward the top. Her hands felt raw from pricks on the rough metal. "You never know what you'll see through those things."

Lark could hear her shoes on the deck as June followed in her wake. "Do you see a lot of things out here?" she teased. "Ghosts and mermaids?"

A cool breeze rustled Lark's hair, and she shivered. The laugh she attempted to summon didn't quite materialize. "Honestly?" Her slick palms slipped on the last rung, but she scrambled up. "I don't even know." She settled in at the precarious top of the boat, half sitting, her foot braced on a porthole. She slid the telescope strap off her shoulder and looked down at it. "Maybe it's just my imagination. Fantasy kind of runs in the family."

June settled next to her and gently leaned their shoulders together. "Who gets to say, anyway? If you told me you'd seen some things, I'd believe you."

Lark felt like a kettle, ready to sing. When she reached up to tuck a hunk of hair away from her face, she swore she felt warm steam drifting from her ears. Suddenly the terrifying distance between their feet and the gravel lot was nothing more than a skip. The chest was just a dark shape, a square on a game board, far below. "So. We didn't die. Do you want to hunt for stars?" She tapped the telescope. "I don't know a ton, but…Saturn is really bright this month."

"This must be the best stargazing in the area." June gazed up at the sky. "The night has a thousand eyes and the day but one," she recited. She hadn't leaned away, remaining propped against Lark. It felt like they were alone in the world, on top of their capsized mountain. It was very quiet. "I don't know much about the stars," she added after a moment and turned her soft eyes to Lark. "Show me."

☙

When June returned to the rectory, she was buzzing with starlight.

Lark had driven her back in her little boat, drifting up a shallow canal until she could drop June off in the trees behind the church. The silence between them had felt luxurious, as pleasantly heavy as caramel, until June started humming "Walking in Memphis" to make Lark, the Memphian that she was, laugh and roll her eyes. Once she started, she couldn't stop busting up, her whole body bending over the side as she choked through a story about her family's dopey dog eating all the hot dogs off their neighbor's grill while his back was turned. Their voices carried far across the water, skimming over the surface like skipping stones.

The boat silently bumped against the shore, as close as Lark could get, and June stepped out, wrapped around the treasure chest. She'd sacrificed the cleanliness of shoes—Eliza's old sneakers—to the muddy bank. Lark watched until she was safely on dry land.

"See you next time," Lark called, giving the spotlight on the front of her dinghy a swift smack as it flickered. That got her laughing again, and she wiped at her eyes. There on the water, face flushed with evening and adventures, she nearly glowed.

June turned back and sang a last bar of "Blue Suede Shoes" to Lark in lieu of a goodbye.

As she crept through thick grass and weeds toward the back of the church and the steeple that poked through the trees, something of the night, the song, the stars stayed with her.

A spotlight shined on the steeple during the night, one of the cheap ones that people put in their yards at Christmas, and it led June with misty yellow-white light that broke through the trees. It was her only guide. She stumbled over something hard, a flat rock perhaps, and dropped the box once, tangling her hair in some grasping branches.

But eventually, June emerged in the clearing, where Eliza's Accord was parked. For once, Eliza's bedroom was already dark, though the porch light shone expectantly for her. A silver ladder still stood against the side of the church, where workmen were replacing shingles. She crossed the lawn, the box on her hip, and as she turned to the front of the church, it became apparent that the little spotlight on the lawn wasn't on at all. It was not shining on the steeple. The light that had guided June came from the headlights of a beat-up old truck. June stopped for a better look. The truck's wizened hood was open, a slack-jawed gape, and a man bent over it, fiddling with the wires.

The truck was hitched to the shabbiest trailer June had ever seen, with a canvas over the contents that read PYROTECHNICS—

Of course. She'd seen him driving around, selling fireworks. He'd done a U-turn in the church's lot.

June stepped as close as the corner of the church where the ladder was, keeping the building between them.

"Car trouble?" she called across the pool of light.

"Sweetheart, this truck is nothing but." The tip of his cigarette glowed orange, hovering over his truck's gas line. His voice was like tires on gravel. "All temper, this one." He shot her an appraising glance, a soiled rag thrown over one bony shoulder. His eyes, she realized, were on the box. "Looks like you've got your own fair share of trouble right there."

"What, this old thing?" The attention made her hold it a little closer. "What makes you think so?" She rested her arms, propping the box against the ladder, hooking an arm through a rung. The back of her neck felt flushed, overheated, as if he knew she'd carted it down to the marina for the most helplessly selfish reason: to have a secret to share with Lark once again.

The fireworks man glanced at her face for a moment, then went back to his work under the hood. "It won't open easy. Bet you know that by now." He wiped his hands on the oily rag. "I might have a solution for you, though. Controlled explosions are sort of my life."

Controlled explosions. Maybe he had the same burn under

his skin that kept him moving as June did. "How would your solution work?"

The fireworks man had many pockets in his ashy-black coat. He dug around in one of them, and after a moment, a small parcel appeared. It looked like a Tootsie Roll wrapped in shimmering foil. "This might get it open," he suggested, stretching his gloved hand out for her to take it. "Light it in the lock."

June set down the box and crossed the lawn. The air around his truck smelled rich as cigar smoke. She took the little parcel before turning it over in her fingers; it was light and tightly coiled. Holding it was like holding a dare. "I don't know. That lock is tough, but it's made of wood."

He shrugged and returned to rummaging in the truck. He pulled a duct tape cap off something, and smoke gushed. The headlights blared. "So what's your idea?" he coughed.

"I don't know," she said, turning it over in her fingers. "I've tried to pick it, and it didn't work. I hit it with a rock, and it didn't work. I actually dropped it on a rock, and it doesn't leave a mark." If it contained gold, jewels, pearls, money, her wildest dreams, then shattering the wood wouldn't hurt it. After she'd dropped it, she did it again, off the porch. It had tumbled, crushing grass and flowers, but hadn't been hurt at all. "How'd you know I was trying to open it?"

He was quiet for a moment, caught up in his repairs. He waved his hand, trying to disperse the ugly black smoke. "Well—what the hell else would you do?" he managed, lungs still under attack.

"Good point." June's head was swimming with smoke and hints of sparks. "Well, I'd thought about... You know the lock wouldn't really be a problem if I could get the wood cracked. But the wood is still really tough. I just want to crack it open, really. Just look inside. Then I'll know."

It only took one tilt of his chin. One look up. "So crack it open."

June followed his gaze up the spotlit steeple, glowing in the headlights, until it pierced the dark sky. The steeple had never looked so tall or so tempting. And the ladder was waiting for her. June had always been a climber. "It's worth a shot."

She walked back to the corner of the church, where the box sat at the foot of the ladder, close enough to pick up the scent of the flowers Aunt Eliza struggled to keep from wilting whenever the noon sun hit. June lifted it, used to its weight now, and propped it up against the rung above her head, stepping from grass onto metal still warm from the light absorbed throughout the day. "Keep the light on," she called back, and she began to climb.

The light was unwavering on the church, so bright that every handhold stood out in stark relief. The fireworks man was whistling.

The only challenge was keeping the box moving, bracing it on one rung at a time to keep it steady. But she'd done worse. It was much more dangerous to be braced on a balcony railing, gripping the bottom of a hanging planter with one hand, a potted succulent in the other, and step across a yawning gap back to her own balcony, gravity pulling at her ankles. The air had felt so still and thin up there, when she had climbed at age ten. A ladder provided much more stability. But her burden was heavy, and by the time she was close enough to grip the gritty, rubbered edges of a shingle, the wind felt strong, and her arm, clutching the bottom of the box, was on fire. She pushed it onto the roof and followed with one knee so it didn't slide back down.

"Oh, Señor Don Gato jumped with glee—he fell off the roof and broke his knee…" came the kindling voice from far below. He wasn't much of a singer, but the tune was an old one, well worn, and he carried it well enough.

June had farther to go. She pushed the box ahead of her, feet braced against the gutter, lying almost flat to get it as high and stable as she could manage. The box was rough, and the roof was rougher, potholed from the repairs. It was serendipitous; the box wouldn't slide, and she could hook her fingers into the edges of the grooves where new shingles had not yet been laid to pull herself up.

"But in spite of everything they tried, poor Señor Don Gato up and died…"

Finally, she could sit right in front of the steeple, feet braced on either side of the rooftop, and haul the box onto her lap. Sweat prickled over her limbs, and a stitch ached in her side. June grinned down at the fireworks man.

He was standing straight, looking up at her now with an unmoving gaze. A cigarette dangled from his fingertips. "Oh, it wasn't very merry, going to the cemetery." His voice creeped up to her ear despite the breeze, close as a whisper. "And though the burial was slated, he became reanimated…"

The box's lock didn't even glint in the light. A closed eye, it gave her nothing.

The chest was still in need of a clean; her focus had been on the lock, and what mud she hadn't been able to clean off had dried long ago.

"Bon voyage," she murmured to herself and it, her blood singing like hummingbird wings, as if she too were about to make a grand swan dive.

June pushed the box forward, and it tipped wildly—

And then came a small, strange sound, so sudden that she could have imagined it.

There, high up, in the moment gravity took hold of the chest, June heard a small rattle. Not from the shingles, not the flicker of a moth burning itself on light or the tap of a falling acorn. It came from inside the chest, a delicate sound, like the clink of china plates. Something small, something breakable. It was the first hint the chest had given her that it wasn't empty after all.

June lunged, but it was too late. The box tumbled while hot-blooded instinct yanked her back, and down below, there was an almighty slam.

And then silence.

June inched forward, heart pounding an alarm. She lay flat again, clutched the edge of the roof with fingers that felt snappable as flower stems, and looked down. The box was on its side, and it trembled once, then slapped down onto its face. The headlights were bright enough that even from there, she knew it hadn't cracked at all. Not on the outside.

The fireworks man hovered near it but made no move to approach. Like a lantern and a moth, something about the chest both tempted him and kept him at bay. "It was a good idea," he allowed as he wandered back to the driver's door of his truck. The engine now purred like a contented cat. He climbed inside, shrugging. His next words came through the window. "Maybe next time you'll try it my way, huh?" He reversed, headlights roaming away now that the action had ended. The steeple fell into darkness like a curtain had abruptly dropped. "Be seeing you," he called, just as he left her in darkness.

_cᴐ_

Cassie hadn't had the dream in a long, long time. It had taken many sessions of talking with the nice lady doctor who let Cassie play with blocks and draw to make the dream stop.

"Do you know who Cassandra was in Greek mythology?" the nice lady doctor had said once. Cassie stacked a red block on a blue one. "Have you learned about Greek mythology in school yet?" The blue blocks were nice to spread on the carpet. "She was someone very smart. She knew when bad things would happen, but when she told people, they didn't always hear her." And green, green blocks, hills that could become mountains if she built them tall enough. "Cassie, when you tell stories, are you heard?"

It had taken a year of these sessions, of blocks and talks, but the dream stopped coming to her.

Until tonight.

Cassie was a child again, floating in the water, a pair of strong, wiry arms under her. She opened her eyes, and Catfish smiled down at her. "See? You're doing it. You're floating."

Cassie patted the surface of the water, so happy that she forgot to keep her lungs full of air, and her bottom sank, followed by the rest of her. Catfish caught her and scooped her up.

"There, you almost got it. My family came from another place where hills met water. But, _mio dio_, my mamma got so seasick on the way here, she never wants to touch the water again!" Catfish laughed.

Cassie liked that she never had to talk much to Catfish to be understood. She only had to listen and watch her, and Catfish could keep the conversation going as long as she wanted. Cassie's mom was barely visible on the porch, painting her toenails. Cassie talked about her new friend to Mom all the time, and Mom just smiled and said maybe Cassie would make a real friend one day.

But Cassie didn't want a real friend. Catfish was an older girl, practically an adult. She could do tricks, and she'd taught Cassie how to get a mouthful of lake water and spit it up in a beautiful arc. Even the way she said goodbye was wonderful.

"I'll be seeing you," she said, so quickly that it all blurred into one word: "Abyssinia." Like a far-off kingdom. The kind that only existed for children, for dreamers.

"Hey," Catfish said. "We can pretend you're my baby."

"Okay," Cassie said, shy all over.

Catfish was happy, and she crouched, rocketing them both out of the water until they fell back in, and she paddled them gently around the dock. Cassie wasn't allowed to go past the dock, but maybe with Catfish it was allowed. Catfish was a very strong swimmer. She could swim the length of the dock and back without coming up for air.

"When I have a baby, I'll take good care of her," she said. "I'll teach her to love the water too. To dive. To fish. I hope she's just like you."

It was all so kind, so warm, and Cassie hung on her neck, unconcerned about if her water wings got in the way.

"You don't have a baby yet?" Cassie ventured.

For a moment, Catfish didn't answer. The silence felt very odd, very stilted. "Let's float again."

Cassie unwound and obligingly lay on her back again, filling her belly with as much air as she could hold. Catfish smiled down at her. She was so lovely. She didn't freckle like Cassie did. The sun just made her glow.

Cassie shut her eyes, concentrating as hard as she could, keeping her toes and chin above water. She was floating (on her own!).

"Will you bring your baby to play too?" Cassie asked, hoping to get her talking again.

There was no reply. Then, suddenly, there were no arms underneath her, cradling her in case she sank.

Catfish's voice came from farther away than Cassie expected. "It's rising too fast."

Cassie struggled for a breath so she could answer, but the water was already pulling her down. She clawed at the water desperately before her water wings buoyed her back up as she gasped for air, flailing. Catfish had drifted away from her, far enough that she was under the dock.

Cassie frowned. Her toes strayed into a cold spot below her as she stared across the water.

Catfish was facedown, the soles of her feet pale, jutting out into the sunlight. Was it a new game? She didn't know the rules. A spasm ripped across the strong muscles of her back, but she didn't roll over, didn't wink at Cassie. One of her hands spread spider legs-wide, twitching.

Cassie paddled over to the fishing dock and tapped Catfish's foot. "I floated. Did you see me?"

The only response was water slapping the wood, a current from a far-off boat. It must have been a game. Mom said there was no going under the fishing dock where she couldn't see her. But Cassie grasped the top of the dock and kicked, pulling herself up enough to peek up the shoreline where she could still see Mom, her bright pink shirt, a bloom of color inside the open kitchen window. Her sunny laughter echoed down the hill. And she wasn't looking. Maybe Cassie could be quick.

"I'm coming," she told Catfish. "Hold on."

With a deep breath, she pushed herself down under the water, wood scraping her forehead as she ducked under the dock and popped up underneath. The air smelled funny and damp, like the inside of an armoire that hadn't been opened in years. Every breath was louder, the world outside more distant. Cassie might have been inside a box.

Cassie kicked once toward Catfish—then there was a painful tug on her hair, yanking her back.

"Ow!" She was caught, held fast, barely able to twist enough to see the problem: a whole hank of her hair was caught, tangled in a metal clamp that held the underside to its pole. Her fingers couldn't reach the place, not trapped in her water wings. When she wriggled, it hurt. "Catfish," she tried. Now it seemed very dark and cold under the dock, out of the sun. "I'm stuck." She remembered why Mom didn't want her under there; there might be old fishing lines and forgotten hooks tangled in the green lake weeds around her feet. She curled her feet against her chest, but it only made her body roll off balance with another sharp tug on her hair. Tears blurred over her vision. "Catfish," she called again, grasping her leg to pull her closer, to wake her up.

And then Catfish responded, but not with words. She had started to choke, faint and weak, bubbles trailing from her mouth. The sound of sloshing grew in power, followed by a close growl of thunder, and water rolled over Cassie's mouth and nose.

"Mom," Cassie tried to shout. "Mom. Mommy!"

Catfish's grasping hand flinched around Cassie's ankle. Her eyes were desperate and milky under the water. And she pulled.

Lapping water swallowed Cassie's head once—she popped up gasping—twice. There was water in her eyes and ears. Everything was blurry, Catfish's hand a panicked vise. Cassie didn't see the underside of the dock anymore or the lake bed. She was someplace deeply dark and underwater.

A series of pale forms floated in the water. Too big to be the pebbly jellied blobs of moss animals. They were people, a row of sleeping people shrouded in identical white sheets that drifted on unseen currents. They—and Cassie, blinking rapidly—seemed to be enclosed in wooden walls. A room. A flooded room. The place looked like a cross between a school and a hospital, beds in the middle and old gray wood and iron desks shoved against the walls, with matching chairs that folded up like bats in sleep. These were too heavy to float and huddled far beneath the sleeping people who hovered just under the surface of the water with Cassie.

And Catfish. She was still at Cassie's side, only now, like everyone else, she was wrapped in a white sheet, and she slumped against a door. Now her hand clung weakly not on Cassie but on the doorknob, like she'd been trying to wrest it open. Somehow, in her panic, in her confusion, she'd sought to pull open the unbudging door and instead tugged Cassie into the deep with her. Her eyes were closed, her face tinged sickly yellow, her lips cracked.

"Wake up," Cassie pleaded. She swallowed water, then air, then water again. She coughed and spluttered. "I can't move, Catfish. Wake up."

Catfish's hair floated in clouds around her head, and Cassie sank. And finally, Catfish opened her eyes. They were no longer the warm color of Mom's morning coffee. They were milky pale all over with faint blueish veins.

Cassie scrabbled against the hold on her hair but couldn't rip free, only jerked above water and banged her head again against the slick underside of the dock. She beat her hands against the wall of the building, against the confines of the dock, and screamed.

Suddenly, something sliced through her hair—she was free and warm. Firm hands pulled her out of the flooded room, out from under the dock. Mom.

"What have I told you—don't go under the dock!" Mom shouted. The sun was as bright as a peeled lemon in the sky, high above the deep reeds and the darting water bugs. Mom must have heard her scream from the inside of their double-wide and left their phone swinging on the cord, Aunt Babs in Kentucky, concerned in curlers, still on the line. Mom had rushed out, kicking off her house slippers, and charged into the water. She'd sawed away at the tangle with her pocketknife, Grandad's gift, to pull Cassie out, leaving a hunk of hair shorn from her temple behind. She was covered in mud and draped seaweed like lace sleeves. Mom hoisted her up, and Cassie only screamed harder and struggled. She peed in her skirted pink bathing suit bottoms.

"What did I tell you—stop it—what did I tell you?" Mom murmured soft words, but Cassie thrashed in her arms, hard enough that she bruised Mom's jaw. "Stop it!" Mom screamed. She heaved her back into the little house, with its yellow kitchen and the smell of wax and balsam, where Mom had been making candles, and tumbled Cassie into the bathtub, turning on the shower. And Cassie stood there on an aching ankle, shorn hair straggling and dark as the mud sticking to her face. She'd kept on crying, wailing wordlessly. Mom had turned on the hot tap, wiping mud off her face, checking for injuries. Some of her fingernails were broken, and there were scratches on her ankles and her arms.

Mom pulled her out, her hair still a mess, and wrapped her bathing suit and all in a thick, robin's-egg-blue towel, before sitting her on the couch. "Stop it!" Mom pleaded again. "Stop it! Stop it!"

But Cassie had yet to look at her.

And finally, as if her hands had moved without permission, Mom slapped her. For a moment Cassie stopped, eyes red and stunned, tears still trembling off her eyelashes.

"Stop," Mom told her, her mouth huge and horrified. "What happened? I told you not to go under the dock, I told you."

Cassie didn't speak a word but opened her mouth and screamed louder.

Now Cassie wrenched herself awake, her mouth dry. She sat up in her narrow bed, and though she didn't look out the window—wouldn't look at Lake Prosper—she listened. Just in case there was someone still in the water, waiting for her.

CHAPTER TEN

HE PHONE RINGING WAS LIKE A SHRIEK, VIBRATING between the wall and bed so that Lark had to scrabble. She never left her sound on; the service was so poor at E Dock that her phone had spent most of the past few weeks charging beside the coffeepot.

"Hello?" she mumbled, still clambering out of a swiftly receding dream.

"Lark?" The voice was strained, escaping from a locked jaw. That youthful tenor, so fond of waxing on about this or that cosmic event, cracked with anxiety. She hadn't heard it in weeks; while in the hospital, he'd barely spoken at all. "Are you there?"

"Daddy." Lark sat up, hot and then cold. Nausea ran down her body. She didn't let any of the telescopes stay in the bedroom with her, but she heard them rocking all through the boat. "I'm here. How are you? Mom didn't tell me—"

His voice scraped over her through the phone. "You can't stay there now. Not now. Not *now*, Little Bird. Something's broken— broken glass. That whole place is broken glass on the *floor*."

Lark was numb. She stared at the blankness of the wall, only lit by a timid dawn. "I swept up the glass, Daddy. You don't have to worry about this anymore. I'm fixing everything."

"You can't fix what's wrong there." He sounded thick, groggy with medication. But it didn't stop the frantic flow of his words. "It gets in you. Smell it and smell it and see it and touch it and drink it—that water gets in you and wrings you out—"

"Where's Mom—" Lark tried, but his words rushed over her.

"I know what you've seen. I know because I saw. I saw—" He sobbed. "You'll see more."

Lark shifted onto her knees, containing herself. Steady. "What did you see? Where should I look?"

He was too agitated to answer her, crying on the line. Mornings were bad, Mom had told her. He didn't sleep well, waking up far away in orbit. "It gets in you," he repeated. "You can't stay there now."

"It's okay, Daddy." Lark wiped at her face, shivering. "Everything's okay. Put Mom on the phone."

"Get out," he urged. "Don't even look at it. Just get out."

"I love you," Lark tried, though her voice was a wreck by then. "Daddy? I love—"

The line went dead.

Lark listened a moment longer, chest thundering. The phone was like putting her ear to a shell. She hung on it, hooked by a dull suction of need. Did Mom have him now? Would he be okay? She couldn't breathe. She gasped, stumbling out of the bed, shoving her hands into her hair. Her phone hit the floor. The air felt close and too hot as she tripped through the boat before wrenching open the back door. Fresh air, fresh air would—

She flinched back inside, almost falling as her heel caught on the floor rail of the sliding door.

"What am I seeing?" she demanded of the spyglasses huddled around her. But this was no vision. She saw it with her naked eye.

It must have been sometime during the night, in the hours after Lark had giddily tied up her dinghy. June's song had still hung in her ears as she hopped onto the *Big Dipper* and whistled her way to bed. Too dark to notice. Too happy.

Around her, she heard the shocked murmurings of her neighbors, the early risers just taking morning coffee out for their quiet porch time. But the air buzzed, hot as high noon, still and fetid as a slaughterhouse. She wasn't imagining it? She leaned out again, screwing her eyes shut to confirm it. But nothing changed the hazy 6:00 a.m. panorama.

Don't even look at it. Just get out.

Lark sank into one of the porch chairs, squeezing her eyes shut again.

"Jeff!" Ferret-fanatic Joe called a boat over. "You have to see this!"

"Should we call the sheriff?" Margaret Pickle hollered.

Lark couldn't say a word. The image burned behind her lids.

The lake had been distorted, its odor sticky and metallic. Sometime in the night, the gray-green water had curdled. It lapped at the shore, dark, glistening red.

∙

Everything was all wrong. Even down at the Destiny, Bolt could almost hear Cassie's bees roaring their panic up the hill. Her feelings about the water had always been hard to wrap his mind around. But what if she'd been right? Mitch had gone up to see her the minute they all saw the lake that morning, and he hadn't returned.

In the shadow of the bank, the water looked black—solid, mineralized. It was only farther out, where light struck it obliquely that the lake sparkled crimson. Against the loud blue of the June sky, the tender green of new summer leaves, the lake water stung, sharp opposites, a spider bite sting of wrong. And it was almost beautiful too, like staring at the deep, fractured interior of his mother's garnet earrings, the heavy scarlet teardrops Grandad had given her for her fortieth birthday. That almost beauty, the moments when Bolt caught himself staring, made it that much more horrible.

After his shift in the restaurant, trying to shake the crawling of his skin, Bolt grabbed a Coke from the icebox and propped it on his navel out by the pool, watching the liquid inside the glass wobble every time he took a breath. Diego had tugged the swan boats up to the roost on the lawn so their white tail feathers wouldn't be ruined. Rig would be coming by any moment now after dinner with his dad.

Usually, the Grand Destiny would have been buzzing, but the red water had left a pall over everything. The motel wasn't taking it well—some appliance or another seemed to start smoking every hour. The toilet in Room 4 had exploded with such energy that the bowl had nearly blown a hole in the roof.

Bolt stared at the powder-blue deep end of the pool. At least *this* water was behaving like it was supposed to. Diego was on the opposite side, capturing leaves with his wide square net. Every so often, Bolt glanced over at the Grand Destiny restaurant, watching the golden clouds reflected in the windows. The grocery was shut; Mitch had gone with Cassie to Charlene, but Valerie was inside the restaurant, serving slices of lemon meringue pie to a couple of dinner regulars. She'd sent her waitstaff home. There were only three cars in the lot, and one of them was Mitch's beat-up green pickup.

"When there's no lake, the pool is king," Diego murmured, with surprising cheer, and it wasn't totally clear if he was talking to Bolt or to himself.

Bolt sipped his Coke and settled back again. "All hail the pool."

Diego chuckled, dumping some of his debris over the fence. He glanced over his shoulder, tracking Valerie as she marched across the lawn to sit with them. The last of her paltry dinner crowd had trickled away.

"Well, I can die," Valerie exclaimed, plopping down beside Bolt on one of the pool chairs. "I have truly seen it all now." Her eyes were fixed on the sunset licking Lake Prosper's still surface, which glowed a fevered carnelian. There wasn't a breath of wind, the water thick and quiet ahead of them. In that fading light, it looked almost like the surface of Mars.

"You should make a menu based off it," Bolt suggested. "Tomato pie. Bloody Marys. Red pepper dip. Mr. Daley told us today that 'anything can turn into a business opportunity if you think outside the box.'"

"Oh, phooey on Jeff Daley." Valerie swatted the air like she had a damp rag in her hand. "Did he leave any more messages today, Diego?"

Diego was checking the filters, but he nodded. "Deleted them."

She snorted. "You doing all right?" She gave Bolt a gentle nudge. "Where are your mean friends, huh?"

"Rig's on his way, Woody's got mono, and Sammy's with her grandma. And they're not mean," Bolt added, a little late. "Sam's pretty cool actually. And Rig just gets bored. He can also be... different. What's Mr. Daley calling you about?"

"Oh, he thinks everybody needs his money and expertise." Valerie rolled her eyes. Diego was smiling into the filter at her tone. "He should try throwing that cash straight into the water. Maybe then it'll turn green."

"Did he offer you guys money or something?" Bolt put down his bottle. "When? You guys aren't struggling, are you?"

"Don't you worry." Valerie put one of her bony hands on his shoulder, rocking him back and forth. "We don't need any more investors around here. Honestly, honey, you can't take everything on all the time." Which was a little rich, coming from the busiest bee in the hive.

"Good, because if you sold the Destiny, who would make me pie and gizzards?" Bolt asked, catching her hand with a grin. "How would we all go on without you?"

"Well." She patted his head a few times, grumbling in the happy way she did when she couldn't take a compliment. "You and Rig have big plans tonight? Be careful with that boy. Mitch doesn't like him one bit."

"I won't be out late," Bolt promised.

Valerie shrugged, standing. "Okay. I'll get up to check on you too. Your mama is trusting me to look after you. Diego, you about done? Nightcap?"

The sun cast a lurid glow across the water, pooling at the base of the Grand Destiny dock, and there was a slight rugged shadow coming toward them—Rig, hands in his pockets, schlepping down in his headphones. He leaned against the walkway, checking his phone.

It was a familiar image, the freshest of Rig in Bolt's life. It was an old friendship. They'd met in school, one day at indoor recess, rain slashing against the windows outside. When Bolt had left a battered, ancient game of Sorry! and gone to investigate the kid in the corner, he'd found Rig bent over a piece of graph paper.

"What are you doing?" Bolt had asked.

Rig had grinned and lifted his arm to reveal a half-done sketch of their teacher, Mr. Fox, recognizable by his thick beard and the large spectacles perched on his birdlike nose. "What do you think? Does he need more hair?" he'd asked, shy but sly. Mr. Fox had discovered the doodle at the end of recess. It had pleased him so much, he'd given it a permanent place of honor on the blackboard.

A few days ago, when they were alone, Bolt had asked Rig if he still drew. "Not much. But sometimes," Rig replied, and without Woody, without beer, without the nighttime air, he'd looked almost shy again.

The Grand Destiny had a broad dock—a parking lot of a dock—made for a lunch rush's worth of boats. For once, there were no firecrackers in sight, though Rig was staring into the pale flame perched on top of his cheap marina lighter. Lately everything was about the fireworks tent and the mysterious products the crew carried away from it. Tonight, Rig was on his own, wearing one of the Under Armour tanks he wakeboarded in. He glanced up at Bolt, smirking over the little fire. "Thought they'd never leave."

"You could have said hello." They ambled down the dock, the flinty click of the lighter sounding every half a minute or so. "I was surprised you wanted to come all the way out here. Usually you make me come to you."

"I needed to get away from Dad." Rig was really better looking in profile, with a fine, almost sculpted silhouette, whereas he was almost serpentine head-on. "I swear he's losing it. Calls twenty-four seven. Always staring at the water." They stood at the very end of the dock, and he hooked an arm around Bolt's neck. As casual as the move had been, the arm was full of some buried tension; around Bolt's neck it felt like bundled wire. "I set off a firecracker on top of the boat last night. There are still sparks floating around in the dock rafters. It was fucking amazing."

Bolt could envision it, light arcing into the sky. Maybe last night he'd even heard it. "The fireworks dude definitely isn't selling legal stuff. It's too..."

"They're too good," Rig agreed. His laugh was special or at least very characteristic—a raw, cynical sound. Tonight it had some extra edge. "I've got a few more, just looking for the right thing to do with them."

"I heard your dad wants to invest in this place," Bolt said. "Is that true?"

"Where do you think that old coot will set up next?" Rig asked, heedless. There was a strange catch to his voice when they were on this topic—a rush, like every minute dwelling on the firecrackers gave him a tiny high. "Listen, you remember that night at the graveyard? What we painted? I think this is the answer. *We* are the chaos bringers. The fireworks are the key."

"What?" Bolt could only laugh; even Rig's veneer of cool seemed to crack under this manic enthusiasm. "Seriously?"

"Seriously." Rig's lighter animated again, and he ran his finger, ever so slowly, over the heat. "I have really fucking weird dreams here. Do you?" He stared into the flame, the skin of his finger growing angry. "The fireworks are the only things that make any sense."

Bolt snorted. "Woody must've gotten you the good shit this week. Listen—your dad. Why would he invest in the Destiny?"

Rig sobered. He looked annoyed as he stuffed the lighter in his pocket again. There was something off with him tonight, some pissed-off agitation. "He wants to pour money into all these run-down mudholes. Red water won't stop him. Seems like it's inspiring him. He, like, never sleeps." Rig snorted. "That's the whole reason we're here. To clean up this side of the lake."

"I didn't know," Bolt said. "Why does he want to do that?"

"Guess he likes to solve everyone else's problems. And be the boss." Rig sat on the dock, dragging a toe in the water.

"Don't touch it." Repulsed by the way the surface rippled, Bolt tugged at Rig's collar. "Come on. Get up."

Rig rolled his eyes but stood back up. He glanced back at the motel. "They should let him invest. This dump needs a few coats of paint." Rig grinned lazily at him, a challenge. "Wouldn't hurt that junk shop either."

Bolt elbowed him in the ribs. "Don't be an ass."

Rig barked a laugh, loud and harsh enough that Bolt stared into his face.

There were his dark eyes, still full of firework sparks and some ill humor. They stared at each other, for too long, at too close a range. Bolt searched for something else to say, found nothing, just watched as that deep-down thing, that rage, grew starker in Rig's look. Maybe he felt challenged, that Bolt never blinked, that he didn't look away like Woody would have. Maybe it was something else, something he'd brought out here from home, that was nothing to do with Bolt or this impromptu staring contest. Whatever it was—

Rig gave Bolt a sudden hard shove.

The loss of purchase, the heartless tug of gravity. There was the disbelief too, the dull whoosh of empty air. It was like on TV, when the air lock on some sci-fi space station is released and someone gets sucked out into open, silent space. There was no chance for a final gasp of air.

Bolt plummeted into the muddy red lake.

Then came cold, ugly shock; water rushing up his nose. And Bolt sank, too far, too deep, too quickly. He flailed, losing one flip-flop then the other, kicking to bump up against a muddy bottom that didn't come. Blind and breathless. Pressure pounded in his temples. Green dock light flickered through the water. Too far up. It was his only guide toward the surface.

Bolt kicked up through nothingness. But the lake didn't want to let him out.

It was cold, so heavy and soundless. Hungry water. It wasn't red under here. It was blackness, nothingness.

Bolt lost half the breath he had left, pushing up. Reaching for air that wasn't coming. *Don't go past the dock*, Mom always insisted to him, holding him back while trying to drag Cassie into the water. But now Bolt was past the dock, long past.

He heard it again, the formless howl of someone somewhere in the water screaming with rage.

Bolt fought against the water that dragged him down, pulled until the pressure broke, and suddenly, he was rising, racing up toward the surface again. He burst into the air, coughing, and grabbed the slimy dock pole before the water changed its mind.

"Help me out, you shit," Bolt rasped.

Rig was doubled over laughing from his place on the dock, which he somehow managed to occupy like it was a throne. Whatever Bolt had seen for that instant was veiled again, curtain drawn. "Did you forget how to swim, loser?"

Bolt heaved himself over the edge of the dock, stumbled to his feet, and launched himself at Rig, knocking him onto the wood slats.

"Fuck—c'mon—" Rig tried to jolt him off, kneeing him in the gut. "It was a joke, dude."

Bolt shoved him back, fists balled in his collar. "You're the worst sometimes, you know that? Is it fun for you?"

His bones were rubber. Rig rolled them, and in an instant, Bolt was pinned. There was a gentle click, and then something cool tickled his throat. Pocketknife. "I mean..." He snickered. "Sort of."

Bolt's throat ached under the knife. Water licked at the dock. He should have been scared by the cool playfulness, the curiosity, in Rig's eyes. He should have put his hands out, not just tightened his grip on his collar, fists pressing into his chest. "You're a psycho."

Rig drew the flat of the knife over his cheek, eyes bright like black light lamps. "And yet I'm your only friend."

It wasn't true, Bolt wanted to say. He might have been his *oldest* friend, but Bolt was getting out, getting away from Lake Prosper, and going to bigger places. "What are you going to do, cut me and dump me back in the water?" Bolt snorted. "Or get up so we can find beer?"

Rig chuckled. Then the pocketknife disappeared. He got up, offering Bolt his hand. "Let's get out of here."

Bolt gave him the smile he wanted but didn't take his hand. It felt safer standing alone.

എ

When night fell, June left the church. She hiked through long grass, the night air buzzing around her with the kind of heat that raised swarms of circling gnats. The moon was low and enormous, casting cinema silhouettes in the grass. Eliza had been fielding calls from her flock, all convinced the red water was a sign from God. June knew better. The problem wasn't one from the heavens. It was from the water. The box. It sat, a bad omen, on the rug in her borrowed bedroom, leaking mud into the fibers.

The chest had survived its long fall off the roof. June had nearly killed herself, fumbling on the ladder in the darkness as she descended, and she'd scooped the box up and carted it inside. In her room, she'd pored over it for cracks and shaken it gently to see if she heard that sound from inside again.

But nothing. The chest was unmoved, unbroken, and closed to her. The next day, she'd woken to water the color of blood, of vengeance and violence. It was like she was living in a locked box, someplace hot and close and inescapable. Maybe that was why she'd been so determined to yank it out of the grip of the lake bed. She empathized too keenly with trapped things. She knew why they yearned to lash out.

Maybe it was texting Lark that did it; the thought of her drew June behind the church, through the trees, seeking the edge of the water where she'd last seen her, where Lark had dropped her off in the shallows. Outside, the world was as awake as she was—insects buzzing, wind whispering, owls screeching. June wouldn't find peace in her room, with the box there. Dropping it from the church had caused all this. June didn't usually bother to lie to herself—her uncontrollable heart, her stomach, knew the truth. She was desperate for comfort.

The path down to the water from the church was easily lost, gone one moment, there the next. It wasn't much of a path, too skinny, clogged with mossy logs and a thin branch that bowed over it, and difficult to see in the dark. She was blind until she stumbled into the familiar moonlit clearing, bordered on one side by dark water. Sinking back into damp grass, June rested her head against something hard and ivy covered. Aimless, she brushed her fingers over it, rock that faintly reflected silver moonlight. Rock that looked deliberately carved.

June straightened, turning to examine the thing she'd been leaning against. She brushed ivy and dirty leaves away.

It read: *1900–1931.*

For the first time, not caught on the memory of cotton candy hair, not subsumed in the mystery of a box, June realized where she was.

The land at the edge of the church, bordering the red water, wasn't just a clearing. It was a graveyard. It was old, barely recognizable. But the jagged dark shapes resolved themselves into headstones and, occasionally, weathered, cracked statues whose forms she couldn't make out. A cross, here and there, so swamped in overgrowth, it was difficult to make out. Once upon a time, their rows must have been straight and their plots orderly. There were probably others too covered in growth to be seen. Now the rows were gone, most of the graves barely more than broken stones, forgotten by the living. Red water encroached on its territory. Someone had left a rusted trowel dug into the ground, a monument to someone's attempt to clear the weeds. They had been upended along half of one row and piled there, but they had already grown back, a little smaller but just as ambitious.

"Well," June said hoarsely into the silence. "You've all let yourselves go a little, huh?" She picked up the trowel; the wooden handle was warm and worn in her palm, like a hopeful silent question in the night. Like possibility.

And then someone else spoke. "It ain't the only thing that let go."

June jumped.

On the other side of the cove sat five lawn chairs and five men with five fishing rods. One of them lifted a hand and waved, but he was too far away for June to discern whether he was familiar or just a polite stranger. She couldn't imagine how she hadn't seen them before; she'd felt so alone in such a large quiet space.

"What brings you out, missy?" one of the old fishermen hollered. His voice was a bullfrog's croak across the distance, loud, rough, but somehow allowed. It didn't disrupt the song of the evening. The man beside him checked his line, whistling along with the wind.

June dropped the trowel and walked to the shore, standing near a headstone barely holding its chin over the water. "Wanted to see the Red Sea," she called over. "You guys?"

"Full moon," growled the fisherman farthest from her. He had a skullcap pulled low over his brow. Somehow, in this light, it looked like he had only one large eye glittering from beneath it. "Best time to catch trout. If any are left."

"I've seen you before," she replied. "You hang out at the Mosquito Bite, don't you?"

"Sometimes," agreed another of them, and this voice she recognized from the bar. She could hear the smile lines in his voice. "You're the girl with all the questions. You come here for a story?"

No. She hadn't. "Do you have one?" June asked. The night air was so hot, and the men looked wrong, off-color in a way they hadn't in the harmless light of the Mosquito Bite.

The posse exchanged looks.

She recognized the one who spoke. At the bar, he'd had a cap pulled down over half his face. Now, with midnight hanging between them, she could still only see that one glimmering eye. "One of the oldest stories there is." The cyclops rummaged in his tackle box. "It was a long time ago, near Memphis. The original Memphis, you know, down in Egypt." He pulled something out, inspected it, rummaged again. "Pharaoh's heart was hard, and Moses turned the Nile to blood to teach him."

Maybe they went to Eliza's church. Only she'd never seen them filing in and out after a service, not even one, much less all of them. But the night was morphing around her, taking on the fevered unreality of a dream. Or a bad mushroom trip.

"Not that Moses's trick worked. Pharaoh had sorcerers too, ones who'd discovered red food coloring a few millennia early, I guess," the cyclops grunted as he reeled his line in to add the new bait. It rested in his palm, like a peeled egg, round and dewy under the moon. "He'd believe anything not to have to let those people go. Pharaoh wanted them there to build his great monuments of stone. Every day, they toiled on those pyramids, and the Egyptians reaped their own destruction."

"People'll do anything to keep the lights on," his neighbor, the Cajun, recast. "Even build a dam to flood their own town."

June shifted her weight. "Even deny an act of God."

The red lake certainly looked like one. Random, monstrous nature. Algae. The water had been blue, sweet and summery when she'd been diving that day she kicked the top of her foot against the blunt corner of the mysterious box. She'd ripped it out of the mud, reeds clinging then breaking when she pushed up from the bottom. She'd thrown it off the roof, and though the chest hadn't cracked, she couldn't shake the thought that something else, something in the world around her, had. Hurricane June striking again, breaking precious things in her wake.

"God sent those plagues to smite Egypt, one after the other," the sunburned one sighed, shaking his head. "You know what's the worst of 'em, girl?"

"Locusts," June guessed. She edged back from the water. It wasn't fun anymore. She wanted to dig, to clean those weathered stones, not to speak of red water and pharaohs. Why couldn't she be that person instead, one who made the things she touched better?

"I'll tell ya." The Cajun scratched his chin with the grip of his fishing pole. "Pestilence. Nothing makes folk stir up like pestilence."

She shook off the urge to shudder. "Right. I have to go..."

The whistler laughed at that, his weathered, ruddy face cracking. "Sickness came, and Pharaoh didn't do a single thing. Didn't lift one finger." He nodded to June. "Times like that, we do what needs done to save our kin. We let them other people go."

June swallowed, fear building. "Cool story," she said, cutting as she could make it. "But the pharaoh sounds like a dick."

"We let them other people go," the cyclops repeated as he

threw his line, the hook and its new bait hitting the surface with a wet plop. June could hardly see their chairs now through the fog. She could imagine them standing in it as it rolled over the town. How could she get out of here? His words smothered her. "The dead have a tight grip on this place. Making them let go of you, that's the trick."

One sunny autumn day when she was seven and riding her bike home from school, a car had slipped behind her, prowled after her, slow and deliberate. She was too petrified to look at it, sure if she did, the standoff would end and some terrible unknown would happen. For three blocks, tears filming her vision, she pedaled with that shadow hunting before she'd dared to veer down a narrow alley and finally escape. June wanted to go now too, but she was rooted to the spot, more and more unable to move too suddenly because of that terrible unknown, the violent question mark of what they might do. She would wait until she found her alley.

The whistler's strange fluttering song took a sudden dip, and with a splash, a fish flew into his grip. It wriggled there, eyes huge and stunned. He shoved it in the cooler.

The fishermen looked older than she had imagined, sunburned with gray stubble, huddled among their coolers, their heads bent together, laughing, and she was pretty sure she was the joke. But she wouldn't be their joke.

She followed their lines down to the water, imagining dark shadows, catfish sliding through the mud. There was debris down there—bottles, sodden towels—and five fishing lines that gleamed like strands of silver hair, drifting just under the surface.

At the end of the cyclops's line, something pale floated on

the surface, the size of a golf ball. But it wasn't a golf ball. It was marbled with veins and had a dark iris in the center, the hook buried like an optic nerve somewhere in the back, thankfully out of her sight.

The eye, the human eye, bobbed. The cyclops was staring at her, his mouth a gross expectant smile.

Fury and revulsion mingled, rising all the way up her body until June broke. She stormed into the bloody water and hurled her only weapon, the trowel, at them.

"Fuck off!" she roared.

Silence.

The trowel plunked down in shallows, kept company by nothing but the ferns and bending old trees.

As suddenly as she had been visited, June was alone again.

CHAPTER ELEVEN

I N ALL HER NIGHTMARES ABOUT LAKE PROSPER, CASSIE had never imagined this. She'd spent the first hours of the unholy water's appearance crouched in her RV, the bees a roaring cloud all around her property. She couldn't calm them into their hives when she wasn't calm herself. But Mitch had assuaged the worst of her fear. He saw the red water too. It wasn't her imagination. For once, Cassie wasn't the only one repulsed by the water. They'd spent the day firmly on land, Cassie and Mitch, finding a blackberry farm outside Charlene, somewhere far enough away that she couldn't smell the water. And she had felt better.

Still, she hid from the water in the shop. Today was not a day for helping antiques find new homes, or watching tourists browse the shelf of honey from her hives, or restocking her homemade candles and the novelty oven mitts and aprons that kept tourists coming in. Today, the door was locked, and the sign read CLOSED. A new box of telescopes from Lark, Box 15, had been waiting on her porch with a page of careful notes written in Lark's deliberate hand. Cassie didn't need Lark to make notes, but she hadn't said. It was a kind effort to make her life easier, and reading analysis in another person's writing fetched back the memory of warm days in the shop with Grandad. Cassie had been the scribe then, learning her letters with words like "Victrola," "second-edition," "curio," while Grandad sorted through old silverware, lamps from the '60s, and Grecian-style vases.

Yes, he would murmur, running spidering hands over faded labels. *Are you ready, bug? I think I know where this was made.* Sometimes she wondered what he was looking for in all those washed-up trinkets, the junk piles he divided into trash and treasure. Cassie lifted out a newer telescope, one fit for amateur stargazing, examining its sleek white curves, when there was a knock on the window. There stood a lean, familiar shadow with messy blond hair. Bolt. He pressed his face to the window, trying to see in. He had a half-eaten breakfast sandwich in one hand, a grocery bag dangling from his wrist.

She put down the telescope and went to unlock the door, nearly stepping on Smoky, who streaked to hide under a wardrobe. He pushed it open, letting a wash of warm sunlight into the shop with the jingle of the doorway bell.

"Hungry?" He unearthed a small wrapped parcel from his bag, and even before she took it, Cassie knew what it would be. A freshly buttered biscuit sandwich, cheese and egg melting into one creature in the middle. "Valerie told me not to come back until you ate. Mitch says 'please.'"

She took it. It was still warm, and someone had drawn a smiley face on the paper in one of Valerie's green markers. "Thank you."

He'd brought the smell of the Grand Destiny with him: baking apples and cinnamon, lemon meringue, potatoes frying in oil, the whisper of Mitch's paperback pages.

"Haven't seen you in a while. Aren't you supposed to be

watching me?" he asked so lightly that Cassie could practically smell how hard he was trying. Trying to sound normal, trying to sound like *she* was normal. "You okay?"

"I'm fine," she said. His smile dimmed. Cassie's heart twinged. She'd been terse. "Really," she added. "I'm no worse than usual, even if the lake is." It was sweet of him to come. She knew he loved her. But he didn't understand her, and wasn't understanding the work of love?

Bolt sobered. "It looks really freaky out there. I keep wondering what Grandad would say if he could see it."

"Probably that this is a shit place full of shit people." Cassie sighed, unwrapping her sandwich and tearing off a corner. "Or that it's karma. Somehow."

He nodded. "I'm fine too. By the way. If you care."

That didn't sound fine. Cassie raised her head. Bolt scratched aimlessly at the back of his neck.

"Are you?" she asked. Now that she looked, there was something worn about him, a lankness. "Did you get enough sleep last night?"

Bolt snorted, a sharp, cross sound. "No. I had a crappy night. Don't want to talk about it."

Silence sank between them. Cassie peeled off another piece of her sandwich, letting it crumble. Bolt glared out the window. "Okay," Cassie offered. What else was she meant to say?

"I heard you had dinner with Mr. Daley."

"Yes." Grateful, she grasped the new topic. "A business proposition, buying up land, developing it. I wasn't interested—"

"Yeah. I heard that too. You should consider it. He's a good businessman. He likes me, so he'd do right by you," Bolt added and then waited. For what, she wasn't sure. For her to agree? Run out and call Daley? Wasn't Cassie supposed to be the older one, the more responsible one? When had Bolt grown up so much, enough to give her unwanted advice?

"He does like you," she managed, the only agreement she could offer. "I've got…" She gestured vaguely to her workstation, the unfinished mending to be done.

"Of course. Right. Don't want to interrupt." Bolt backed up, swiping a hand through his hair and over his clothes like he was trying to wipe off mud she couldn't see.

The bell above the door chimed once, and so Cassie bent her head over the box of telescopes again, putting the sandwich aside on her worktable for later. She was already spinning with lenses and tripods, when from above her, someone spoke.

"Uh, hi. Antique shop girl?"

Cassie wasn't alone after all. A girl stood at her counter, her face caught in a tense, nervous smile. She must have come in as Bolt was going, and knowing him, he had held the door, because she had not come empty-handed. In her arms, she held a huge, ugly beast of a chest. What a heavy burden.

"Oh. Hello." Cassie stood and gestured to the counter.

Gratefully, the girl put the box down. "You run this place? You're helping Lark, right? With the tele…" Her gaze darted to the cardboard box. "Yeah. Okay. There's my answer."

"Cassie," Cassie said, tapping her chest with a finger. "This is my shop."

The girl nodded and pursed her lips. "Okay, so look," she said, voice loud as fanfare in the quiet. "I dug this out of the lake a few days ago, and Lark told me to bring it in. I've been trying to get it open with no luck. I thought, hey, maybe there's treasure inside. Or maybe just trash. Or mud." The longer she talked, the wider her eyes became. She was a person of motion—shifting feet, hands raking through her thick dark curls, as if any second standing still were a second wasted. She turned her head, and Cassie caught a glimpse of red peeking out from under the shell of her ear. "But the thing is, I'm not—I can't open it. Maybe you could. Or maybe you could, I don't know, fix it up?"

She paused for breath, pressed her lips together, and gazed at Cassie for answers. So Cassie bent over the box to look for some. The chest was large and dark, made of old wood and mottled metal fixings. It looked calcified, caked in black mud and under-water moss, but with a gentle clean, she could help. She could ease the grip of the lake bed, pull water out of the grain, restore it to something like what it had been before.

"I'm June. By the way," the girl said, much more softly, and tucked her hair behind her ear, revealing again the flash of red. This time, Cassie felt a jolt of recognition.

It was the red flare of poppies. But not fully blooming, rich blossoms. These were fresh buds, furled crimson petals that seemed fused into her hair, as if...

You've got flowers, Cassie wanted to say. *You've got flowers, you've got flowers in your hair.* But she didn't. "You have no idea what's inside it?" Cassie asked for clarification. She rested a hand on the box. It was cool as if it had never seen a moment of sunlight.

"No. It's not mine. Or, I guess, it wasn't. I just wanted to know what's inside," June said softly. "I don't think I can open it without breaking it. I don't—I don't want to break it. I'm not much of a fixer."

Cassie nodded. "And Lark referred you to me?"

"Yeah. Lark actually helped me bring it out of the water." June's voice smoothed around her name as if she could taste it, like it turned from a word into a lemon gumdrop on her tongue.

"And it's from…"

"Red Sea Lake." June swallowed. She wore an expression startlingly close to guilt. "Yeah. Can you help? Fix it up, maybe? I don't know how to fix it." She pressed her lips together. "I don't know how to fix it," she said again softly.

For so many years, Cassie had rescued so many things, cleaned them from the water, baptized them in wax and oil and polish.

Are you ready, bug? Grandad whispered from somewhere inside her heart. *You know where this is from.*

I don't. She touched the scalloped edge of a black, heavy lock. *I don't know if I want to.*

☙

Late at night, Cassie pulled the box out of the trunk and heaved it into the double-wide. A few curious bees followed, floating on top of her head like helmet lamps, as if they were helping her see. She set herself down on the floor in the kitchen on a pile of old newspaper with candles and a lamp to work on cleaning the gunk off.

Cassie worked with her own cleaner, Grandad's recipe, which was effective on lake gunk and gentle on wood underneath. Starting at the top, she rubbed it into the surface.

Ooze melted onto the newspaper, clinging to the edges of the lock. The smell of sandalwood and lemon was heady all around. Here, there wasn't a trace of that coppery stench of the—

No.

What would Mom think, now that the lake terrified everyone, not just Cassie?

By the time Cassie put down the cleaner, it was late. Just past eleven.

While she took several deep breaths, she examined the lock for the first time. It was less bulky now, freed from its muddy prison. Grandad had loved trying keys in locks; a myriad of them always came through a shop like theirs, and he loved locked cabinets, chests, and boxes. He'd gather Cassie and Bolt and try his favorite keys in new locks. *You never know when something might find its home,* he'd said.

Perhaps it was too late for Cassie to save this box. Maybe no matter what she did, the lock would never open. Too long in the water, rust and barnacles winding like lovers inside the metal workings, freezing it in a solid, immovable embrace. Once, maybe fifty years ago, the box might have recognized its key. Maybe it wanted to keep its secrets to itself now.

The top of the box was almost visible now. The edges were worn smoother than any varnish ever could have made them. Nothing stripped a surface bare like water. But the top had been brutally muddy.

Cassie leaned over the box to rub at the thin shell of mud that remained. Under gentle pressure, the last layer began to crack and soften.

The work was delicate, like those special days when Mom would sit Cassie down and comb her homemade deep conditioner through her hair, her own grandmother's recipe, written in a mixture of Arabic and half-learned English. Mom didn't identify much with Grandad's Syrian heritage—preferring the Southern food learned at Grandmama's table and coiffed dyed-blond hair—but she'd kept that at least. They'd have their best talks at the kitchen sink, with Mom's fingers buried in her hair, tender on tangles, the air smelling of blackseed, ghergir leaves, and almond oil.

Cassie kept at it until she could run her hand over it and feel—wood. But it wasn't the smooth plateau she had expected. The top of the chest was scarred with slender wavy grooves. Curious, she wiped the debris off, hefted the box, and tilted it toward the light to see what it was.

Long ago, presumably, someone had carved an inscription into the chest. Water had weathered it, but it was still visible, even legible. It had likely been done with a fishing knife, the slender kind used for cutting hooks out of fish and other delicate work. It looked as if the lettering had been made with an inexperienced but careful hand, one that stopped often to readjust or rest.

"Pearl…" Cassie read aloud, dragging a finger along it as if, like braille, it could be read through her hands. All capital letters. One word. "Pearl."

The air around her shivered, and what little light her candles offered flickered, faded, turning the words back into shadow.

As if in response, from across the water came a scream—not a child's playful shout, but a wordless, instinctual sound that ripped out of a throat against a person's will. It was a gut-punch scream, a childbirth scream, full of pain and terror and blood. A formless howl.

Cassie scrambled to her feet before racing to the window, heart jackrabbiting in her chest. But just like that, the air was silent again. For a moment.

Outside her window, smoke rose from two of her hives, five and seven, where just that morning, she had left the bees a gift of a grape—sweet, rare nectar. Through it, twin shadows, boys, raced out of her clearing and into the cover of trees. Distantly, they were laughing, the crazed laughter of hyenas that sounded like many instead of just two.

Still, her first thought was that smoke would make her bees drowsy; they would pause their work, docile and heavy.

Three pops crackled through the air, rapid-fire. Light flashed from inside the two hives—

Boom.

The sound was close and powerful, and Cassie flinched for cover. It busted free from the hives, exploding out of them, and light raced up above the trees. Phoenixes, Cassie thought, terrible and on fire, roaring for the sky. They exploded there, showers of red light. But Cassie's gaze was fixed on the ground, on the wreckage of wood and dust and wax.

Little flames danced on the grass around her bare feet, around her home, her sanctuary. The rest of the hives rose in a terrified fury, swarming in panicked defense until the air vibrated.

Through the trees, the two boys raced away.

છ

Nothing good usually came to the door after midnight, but someone pounded on the door again, urgently, and Mitch staggered to it. He heaved at the knob. Cassie looked ready to set fire to the world, her dark eyes wide and wild like two screaming mouths. She must have stumbled through their woods to get here, crashing down the hill from the RV to the Grand Destiny and his small

house behind it. "What is it?" he asked anxiously. Her hair billowed around her in fretful, undone ribbons. Her pale nightgown
glowed under the lights from the Destiny sign, rippling around her
knees. She wore a pair of unlaced boots underneath. "Your mother?
Or—" Bolt? What brought a bee from her hive in the darkness?

She braced a hand on the doorframe. "I don't know what to
do," she managed.

Mitch wrapped an arm around her. She felt as hard and brittle
as quartz. "Here." He led her inside before pausing to watch the
night for a moment. The dim lights of the closed motel shone in
front of him, but the air around his house was still. He went in
after her, locking the door carefully.

She shook her head and stared at him, eyes welling with
sudden tears. She'd carried a whiff of smoke inside with her.
"My bees."

"Your bees?" Mitch forced himself still. "Tell me."

"I don't know why I live here," she snapped, stumbling into
the kitchen. "I don't know why anyone lives here." She crumpled
at the tiny rickety table that never wanted to stop wobbling, no
matter how many times he fixed it. The light overhead barely
reached beyond her.

Mitch joined her at the table he miniaturized with his presence.
There was a reason he always had his coffee standing in front of his
linoleum counter. Cassie dug her hands in the grain of the table,
her shoulders trembling minutely. He felt his hands tremble in
time. "Cassie…" Bees grew sick; hives fell to disease all the time.
But somehow, he knew that wasn't it. "What happened?"

"Two of my hives were destroyed." She wrapped her arms
around herself, face raw with pain. "Blown up."

Fury blew through him. "It was those teenagers," he growled. He didn't recognize the sound of his own voice. They'd been dancing with fire all summer, and now the red water had got in them somehow and driven them to it. "The lake does this to people. These damned *kids*. *Damn* it!" He braced himself against the refrigerator, trying to rein his emotions in. Chiding himself. This was selfish. This anger was easier than feeling the devastation rolling off Cassie in waves. He took several long, slow breaths.

Cassie covered her face, shoulders heaving when she breathed. "I spent so many years trying to make something good here, and I don't know why. It's not a good place, nothing good can grow here."

Mitch couldn't quite speak. She had seen something when she was young. What Cassie hadn't told him herself, Mitch had heard from the circle of mothers gossiping in the school office all those years ago. *No, Dorothy called her in sick again—girl's still babbling, out of her head—called a psychiatrist?* "I believe you," he murmured. He walked to his bed and tugged the mussed quilt off it to drape over her shoulders. "I'll always believe you." He watched the blanket pool around her shoulders.

Cassie let herself get wrapped up. Now the panic was bleeding away, and she was dropping in its wake without fear giving her strength. She leaned ever so softly against him. "They kept me quiet. The bees. I felt like part of something, part of them. I don't fit anywhere else. I'm—I know I'm weird."

"You are not." Mitch took her hands and held tight to them, fearful.

"Everyone else seems to live here and be fine. I'm the only one who"—she swallowed—"paints my windowpanes so I can't see the lake. I don't swim. I needed bees just to—breathe. But I'm the only one. Which means either I'm weird or everyone else is, Mitch."

"Hush, sweetheart." Mitch pulled her against him. "There's nothing wrong with you. It's the psychos who would *blow up a beehive.*"

Cassie sighed, nearly silent. This close, he could feel her heartbeat. Though tinged by destruction, there was still the faint scent of honey that followed her everywhere, caught in the threads of her clothes, sticky under her fingernails, lingering on the corner of her mouth. Her hair was close enough for him to bury his nose in. "I'm tired of feeling this way." She glanced up again, nervous. Then her eyes darkened, and long confident fingers slipped around his.

He tried to keep himself on track, to say something Mom might've said, like *everything feels manageable come morning...*but he couldn't get past that tender glimpse of her throat, her collarbone peeping out of her nightgown, framed by soft tendrils of her hair. "There's nothing wrong with you," he repeated, thumb brushing her palm. "You're wonderful."

She tightened her grip on him. Their faces were close. Though she could seem so delicate, fingers gentle when she ticked around in the belly of a watch or rubbed shine back into old wood, she wasn't fragile. Her grip was calloused and her nails dull, and she wore boots with her nightgown. Tonight was the first time since he'd known her that she had ever hinted that it mattered to her what others thought of her, and already she was back to looking at him as if she only cared about what the two of them thought. And what he thought, despite himself, was that she would be a lovely swimmer—fluid, exact strokes, water beading like more freckles on her shoulders. She had swum, once. A long time ago. Now whatever kept her from the lake had driven her here, to him.

Mitch's free hand slipped around her, between nightgown and quilt. They watched each other. Cassie shifted, falling into his gravitational orbit and pressing her forehead to his cheek. And then—it only took a tilt of his head and hers and they were kissing. Soft, insistent. It was almost too much, too intense in this tiny, overheated, charcoal-dark space, to be here with her after so long, so many years that they'd skirted each other's lives. She'd always been his mystery, and here, now, suddenly given this chance to unravel her, to discover her—Mitch was almost afraid.

It wasn't the right time. She'd just been through—Mitch began to pull back, to check on her, but Cassie opened her eyes and caught him. "Come back," she murmured.

Kissing Cassie was like living inside the hive itself—sweet, stinging, hypnotic. Her body hummed in his arms as they moved from the table to the couch, where they both sank. Cassie had always been a haven for him, a friendship he'd doled out carefully for himself, taken only what was offered, tiptoed to protect. Because hers was a guarded goodness, and few people were welcome. Now, suddenly, Mitch was here with her, fingers buried in her hair, discovering freckle constellations on her skin, tracing these new star charts with his mouth. He was allowed.

Cassie had always had her own rules; she abided by no one else's. There was no kind of etiquette here but her own. She wasn't shy about telling Mitch how she wanted to be kissed, touched, more— slower, there, like this, like that. Her hair smelled like good earth underfoot, and flowers, and honey, and for a perfect moment, Mitch—who'd avoided the bottle all his life—was drunk.

Suddenly, outside, an avalanche of noise broke over the front step. A chaos of gunshot bangs, the hoot of the truck's testy alarm. Shattering glass. Mitch hurled himself to his feet, ripping toward the door. Thoughtless, with absolutely no plan, he wrenched the door out of the way. The cacophony crescendoed: cracks, bangs, footsteps, retreating laughter. Harsh chemical smoke met him. Sparks flew into his face. He coughed, cursing.

Cassie didn't scream, didn't make a sound, but she'd gone stiff and scared again, ready to shatter. Still, she joined him; he felt her hand on his shoulder.

There were ghosts in the smoke, running young figures beyond the veil of firecrackers.

"He's fucking the freak. Figures." The voice was like exploding ammunition and full of laughter. There were at least two of them. A splinter of fire bit into Mitch's arm.

Cassie threw the quilt on Mitch's smoldering front step before it could catch. She smothered the fire, glaring out at the figures. Mitch knew without asking that they had been the ones to desecrate her land.

"I'm calling the police," Mitch snarled uselessly. The firecrackers fizzled, leaving a haze of green-and-red smoke in their wake. The laughter was fading, plunging into the darkness toward the houseboat graveyard. Mitch stamped on cinders, fuming.

"It's no use. The damage is done." Cassie gathered the quilt back up. There was soot smudged on her wrists, the heels of her hands. He felt just as marked, every place where she'd touched him.

"They're out of control." He glared through the fumes. Across the highway, a few hundred yards down, the firecracker tent glowed. Growling, Mitch checked Cassie over. He thumbed a streak of ash from her cheek. "Christ."

Her eyes were haunted and somehow very far away. "It's going to get worse."

An exultant whoop echoed back to them through the night. Though they were well away now, Mitch could still see them sparking out there, their fuses lit, whizzing between dangers like bottle rockets. *Y'all go home*, he thought, the fury suddenly tinged with a jab of fear for them.

Don't let the deep dark catch you out there.

CHAPTER TWELVE

HE PORCELAIN WHITE PROW OF MR. DALEY'S SPEED-
boat was stained brown where it cut through the lake
water. It was a magnificent racehorse of a boat, only
months old, almost as large as one of the humbler houseboats.
Its double engines guzzled an eighteen-wheeler's worth of gas.
But the shining sides were now spattered with mud-red spray.
Apparently Daley hadn't been keeping it on its motorized lifts
since the algae bloom.

Bolt's hands burned from the leather polish he'd massaged
into the seats. Now he stood on the dock below the lifted boat,
scrubbing red scum off its bottom. The red-water smell made his
head swim, and he ducked to wipe at his nose. Rusty, soapy water
ran down his arms.

Daley liked Bolt because he was good with his hands, an
education learned in Grandad's shop before he'd passed. Even as
a kid, the smells of polish had made him feel queasy.

"You shouldn't have him around all those fumes. Just because
Cassie hangs on your every word doesn't mean Bolt will too,"
Mom scolded once.

Grandad hadn't reacted to that, other than with the wrinkles around his mouth and beetle-dark eyes, which pulled taut like a tightening line.

"He's all right, Dory," he said, using the special name no one else got to call Mom. But he'd knelt beside Bolt and handed him a root beer. "Buck up, son," Grandad said, not unkindly. "There are worse things."

So many nights, Grandad had been drawn to the lake, sobbing and sleep-blind as a newborn puppy, stumbling down their sloping lawn.

Would he have gone into the red water? Would he have been dragged up by Mom and Cassie with his pajamas stained? Bolt had wrung his clothes out in his motel room sink after Rig pushed him in. He locked his door, then propped a chair against it in case the water called him while he slept and he couldn't resist any more than Grandad had.

He'd spent the whole night sinking in that stink coming from his drying clothes.

"Mr. Daley," Bolt called up. "Do you need a gas up?"

Daley had been on his phone most of that morning, speaking into his Bluetooth headphones like he was an announcer at a ball game. He was speaking about the water with university experts, who had shut down his plans to market it as a long-term tourist attraction. Apparently the water would return to normal with time; already the shade was turning from garnet to the warm brown of Mississippi River silt. All the businesses he ran or consulted for in Charlene and the rest of the state bombarded him with calls at all hours, but the advice Bolt had overheard him giving that day shared a certain tenor, a loose-ends energy that had left Bolt antsy.

"What was that?" Daley swept his gray hair back with a fretful hand, leaning over the side. His collar was folded up on one side. "Oh—yeah, go ahead, son. Great—yeah, great work." He climbed down while Bolt was watching the nozzle burble in the tank. "It's hot out here," Daley announced, loitering, his hands retreating into the pockets of his golf pants. "This summer's gonna make it into the record books, that's for sure."

"I think my mom says that every year." Bolt was done, as done as he could be, considering the boat was going back in the water as soon as he finished gassing it. "Hey, Mr. Daley, I'm going for some college scholarships with early deadlines. Would I be able to get that rec letter from you a few months early?"

"Oh, absolutely. Absolutely. I have a good start on my computer at home." Daley leaned against his boat as Bolt knelt there holding the gas nozzle. "You know, I think we're a lot alike, Bolt. I understand you, how you tick." He laughed, wiping at his face. "Sometimes better than my own son. You know what you want."

The first time Rig had brought him over, Mr. Daley taught him that the lake wasn't just cruising estate sales. It could be speed boats and waterskiing, steaks on the charcoal grill, and video games in the TV room until it was bedtime.

He was so scared to try skiing at first, but Mr. Daley hadn't let Rig tease him. "Have a little courage, son. The worst that'll happen is that you might fall and get some water up your nose." He was patient for half an hour as Bolt learned to stop fearing the gravity of water pulling at his limbs and let the rope tug him out of its hold to glide on top. He'd been the one to tell Bolt not to settle for a state college, that the world was changed by men who dared to want more.

"Never lose that drive," Mr. Daley urged, giving his shoulder a pat. "You know, when Steph and I split, I just wanted to make it all right for Richie. I wanted to fill our lives with new people. Help people who needed help. You know? Like this town. But...I've lost it somehow. I can't...make it all come together. I just wish your—" He stopped himself, taking several swats at the air like he was batting the topic away.

Bolt listened to the pump disengage under his hand. "What was that?"

"Oh, nothing, nothing." Daley squeezed his eyes shut, like he'd gotten sweat in them. As he'd spoken, his speech had slowed, halting. "Aren't you thirsty in this heat?" He nodded at the water cooler they kept near the dock in offer.

"I am, actually. Thanks," Bolt said, standing, wiping his hands off, and heading for it.

"I've got it." Daley smiled benevolently, even as sweat poured down his face. He had a ruddy sheen, like he was wearing makeup not quite the right color for him. He pulled one of the paper cones from the water cooler and—before Bolt could open his mouth—bent to scoop some of the lake into it. He passed Bolt the cone, where sediment swam, the white paper already staining rosy. Bolt's lunch rose in his throat. Still, if this was some joke, he didn't want to leave his benefactor waiting for a laugh. "Ha," he tried, a bit lamely. "Good—yeah..." But to his horror, Mr. Daley was filling a second paper cone with the lake.

"To a job well done," Daley said, tapping his muddy share against Bolt's before raising it to his parched lips. Dead skin was flaking off them, as if he were peeling from a bad sunburn.

Without quite deciding to do it, he slapped the lake water

from Mr. Daley's hand. It slopped once against the dock before landing in the water. The cup saturated red, then sank.

Daley stared at his own empty hand, an almost comical—and deeply horrible—look on his face. Of disbelief, a genuine, rather fragile hurt that something he would offer someone would be unwanted. The slap of rejection. He turned his gaze on Bolt, and the look shifted, for one instant, to rage. It was the same look Bolt had seen on Rig's face that moment before the hard shove into the dark water below the Grand Destiny dock.

"Nice job," came a shout from the shop door, where Rig had just appeared, grinning. He wandered over, squinting at the speedboat. He gestured with a languid finger. "Might've missed a spot. Right there." Bolt and Mr. Daley looked up, and before Bolt could search for something to say to him—maybe *are you okay?* or, bizarrely, *I'm so sorry for being ungrateful*—Daley strode away.

Rig glared over his shoulder at his dad's retreating back. "What was that all about?"

"I don't know. He's your dad. If that was a joke, it was messed up," Bolt said, tossing the water back into the lake where it belonged and the empty cup toward Rig's feet. It didn't feel like a joke. "Where have you been? Blowing things up with Woody all day?" he asked, just to shake the moment off, to reclaim the summer day.

Rig hopped onto the side of the speedboat, legs dangling. Up there, leaning lazily on his throne, there was something of Daley's strange energy in the flick of his feet. "You missed a real show last night," he said lightly, leaning back on his hands. "Can't stop thinking about it." He snorted. "Burning bees kind of smell like peanut brittle."

Bolt had stooped to gather his bottles and rags. He rose slowly. "Bees?" A sick red feeling crawled up his back like sunburn. "What did you do?"

Rig just shrugged, his face twisted with a sick humor. "Woody dared me. I had no idea all the stuff in those beehouses would break apart like that. Dude. It was like putting a bomb in a mummy."

Even with Woody's influence, Rig wouldn't. He wouldn't breach the lines built over years of friendship. "One of Cassie's?" Bolt asked. "One of my sister's?"

"Huh?" Rig pushed up to frown down at him. There was a brief falter in the humor, though his legs still kicked without tempo. "Didn't even think of that, bro. You're like never over there. I thought you said she's super weird."

"Like hell you didn't think. Was she there?" Bolt straightened. Cassie would have been home. Of course, she would have been home, close enough to hear the attack, to see the wreckage while it still smoked. He could see her face, cracked like a plate. "Why the hell would you do that?"

"For fun," Rig snapped, though all the mirth had drained from his face. "Anyway, my dad's losing his mind. The whole thing with your sister is driving him up the wall."

"What *thing* with my sister?" Bolt started toward him before skidding to a barely controlled stop.

Rig hung forward, mouth twisting and ugly. "You're sweating over this boat, saving pennies and begging my dad for scholarship letters, when your sister could take care of everything if she'd just get her head out of her ass."

"You don't know what you're talking about. My sister lives in a trailer and sells antiques," Bolt replied, humiliation choking him. "You had no right to do that to her." How would he ever make it up to her?

"Are you—" Rig shook his head at Bolt in disbelief. "Shit. You don't know?"

Bolt's face must have given him away, because with a pitying look, Rig continued. "She owns like half the lakefront on the Prosper side. Your grandad bought it all up, and now my dad is basically screwed cause she's a crazy hermit."

To that, Bolt had no response. Of course, he knew that Cassie owned the land around their home, buttressed on one side by the Destiny, and the land where the antique shop stood, and a few other vague green acres. They blended, without a landmark. But half the lake? Could that be possible? Did Mom even know, or had it been left directly to Cassie, only Cassie? "You're lying to me," Bolt tried. How had Grandad, whose biggest expense had been the RV, had that kind of money?

Cassie had never said a word.

"Maybe a few burned bees will bring her to her senses," Rig suggested, stretching across the gleaming leather hide of the boat. "For both your sakes."

Bolt didn't stay to hear anything more. He stormed down the dock and found his bike, which Cassie had fixed up for him when he was ten with her gentle hands. He'd been such a needy child; he'd clung to her side, buzzing around her all day, because he hated being alone, and he ran to her as much as to Mom when he had nightmares. *Cassie, read to me. Cassie, I'm not tired yet. Cassie, can I stay with you tonight?* And now...

He jerked his bike onto the road. Rage and betrayal fueled

him, carried him up the narrow curving country roads to his childhood home.

ᏋᏗ

When Cassie slipped out of Mitch's bed, she sensed he was awake, but he didn't try to stop her when she left him without a look or a word. He knew her, knew that sometimes she got exhausted with people. He knew, without her telling, that she had her own rites to conduct. She had dead hives to set to rights. She had built these hives until bees came and their hum was as thick as a forest, and she had thought maybe it was enough to block out the sights and sounds that came from the water, the ones no one else ever seemed to notice. She climbed the hill, dreading the sight that awaited her.

When she crested the hill, it was in perfect, eerie silence. No rustling in the wildflowers. The surviving hives were quiet. And two were just broken. Charred husks littered the yard, wooden frames scattered. A third hive, the nearest to the two, was marred with scorch marks. But that wasn't the only anomaly, and something cold squeezed Cassie's heart.

The chest June had pulled from the water stared at her from the center of the hives. Only Cassie was sure she had left it on a protective layer of old newspapers in the middle of the double-wide. She would never leave it there in the middle of the wreckage. No, she'd run to Mitch's, desolate and anguished. Had the boys moved it? Had they stayed after she fled? Had they touched her things? Cassie rushed up the hill before heaving the box out of the grass and carrying it to the double-wide. The newspaper where she had been sure she left it was still on the floor; a torn piece of an old Sunday crossword, half-done, still clung under one corner of the box. Thirty-four across: *Banquo*, Mom had written, daring in pen.

Cassie put it down there and stepped back, keeping her eyes on it as she crossed the lawn to return to her work. She knelt in the grass, her head full of the smell of burned honey. A few dazed survivors floated around her head. Some had fled. They might not come back.

Cassie unfolded a paper bag to collect everything too burned to be salvaged. She sifted through charred, melted wax and the blackened bodies of bees caught in it like amber. The rest— frames, honey that wasn't too badly burned—perhaps could be saved. The bees were masters of reusing what they could.

Cassie stood when the bag was full and immediately tripped over something hard and unmoving. She gritted out a curse, catching herself on her palms. Her forearms ached, scraped to hell but too shocked to bleed just yet. Her eyes were watery, but she didn't shed tears. The box was back. It was in her path and caught her shins, the lock as fixed as a scowl. She wanted to scream, so badly that holding it back made her jaw ache. Cassie stormed over and dropped the bag of ruined hive on top of it, an anchor to keep it down, keep it away. She rushed to the double-wide, her breath trembling out of her.

The newspapers were still there. A muddy rectangle framed the open space where the chest should have been. Where she had left it. Cassie yanked that door closed and locked it too, then turned. Now the blood came. She felt it pooling on her skin, saw a couple of drops fall, slipping down her thighs.

Cassie wiped at her eyes to clear them. She had tried—when

she was very young—to tell her family about what was wrong with the lake, to put words to the horror that people sunbathed beside. But there was no way for a child to explain they lived on the lips of ravenous water. No one believed her. She'd stopped with her futile warnings and stayed, trying desperately to keep her home from being swallowed.

She took a deep calming breath.

And then Bolt shot around the corner on his bike, his expression thunderous through the window.

She swiped at her eyes, trying to compose herself before he skidded to a stop on the doublewide's porch. Cassie unlocked the door, and stepped out to meet him. "Bolt. Hi."

He didn't say anything. Letting the handlebars hit the grass, he stomped to the steps and then sat heavily in the shade. His eyes skated between her and the hives. "You look like hell," he said.

"I feel like it," Cassie admitted.

For a moment, the only sound between them was the distracted buzz of a honeybee landing on Cassie's shoulder. Crickets roared away in the trees, never sensitive to human silences. Bolt had a fresh crop of freckles on both cheeks from days in the summer sun, though his dwindled during the school year, and Cassie's never faded. She paused, a hard truth lodged in her throat beside an even more unbearable fear: *Did you know?* "This was done by your friends. Rip and the other one." She gestured to the char on her grass, to scattered wood pieces and honeycomb burned black and curled.

"Rig. He's an asshole." Bolt's Adam's apple bobbed. He ducked his head. "It won't happen again." His voice faltered, anger heavy and embarrassed. "But he told me why he did it."

Cassie stiffened. "There was a why?"

Bolt pushed a hand into his hair, pressing it down against his scalp. "He said we're rich." The pieces began to slot into place. Rig Daley. Was that why this had happened? Because Cassie refused a business proposal? Bolt watched her. "Rig says Grandad left you enough land on the lake that, by my guess, neither of us should have to work. That I could go to ten colleges if I wanted to."

Cassie sighed. "It isn't that simple."

She approached, meaning to sit on the porch with him in the warm, darkening night, but he shot to his feet and wheeled around to pace the short length of it. "Either it's true or it's not."

His anger didn't make sense. Cassie couldn't fathom why he would care except—*I could go to ten colleges*, he'd said. She put up her hands. "Then yes. It's true that he left land in a trust and true that I became executor when he died. But it's not that simple. There's no money on hand. It's all in property, and I don't really know how much."

"Figures," he spat out, shoulders and neck tense and red. "That's just like Grandad. Selfish bastard. Leaves it with you, not Mom. Doesn't even tell me."

He was lit from within. "Why are you angry?" Cassie interjected. "Because I didn't tell you?"

"No." He scoffed and twisted away from her. "You don't get it."

"Okay." It was easy to accept that she didn't "get" many things. "Because he put me in charge."

Bolt shot her a narrow, almost suspicious glance. "I work all the time." One hand drummed on the porch railing. "Every weekend. After school. During the summer, it's two jobs." There were particles of wax and firework casing on the grass below his feet. "Because in my head, I've got to get into college, and one day, I'll probably be the only one able to support Mom when she gets old because you're not going to do it. Then I'll have to take care of you when you get old. But now I find out that you could have done all that."

"I've never asked you to take care of me," Cassie said, and that familiar anger reared. It was his worst quality, Mom's judgment and dismissiveness reincarnated in her once-sweet little brother.

"You didn't have to, Cassie!" Bolt said, red creeping up to his ears. "Damn it—you live on this piece of nothing in the middle of nowhere. Mom still picks up weekend shifts at the grocery store, I'm working my ass off, and all this time, you could have helped, and you didn't."

It was hit after hit, and she fought to keep herself calm, though her resolve trembled. "Grandad bought it so people like Daley didn't get it," Cassie said through a sawdust throat. "He wouldn't want me to sell it to him—"

"Grandad's dead! Don't you get that?" Bolt's voice smothered the evening cricket song. "Or is your head too far up in the clouds? He's dead, and it doesn't matter what dead people want." He stared at her like she was a muddy child, something small and misbehaving, and it felt all wrong. Cassie felt the thin, glass calm inside her crack and that wild-child scream rising.

"I'm alive, Mom is alive," he said. She couldn't control the way her heart started racing. "How selfish—how oblivious are you? You don't even care about us."

And she shattered. "It's not about you!" Cassie shouted.

Eyes wide, Bolt darted back, physically recoiling because Cassie had never, not once in all his life, shouted at him.

She had been a loud child, had screamed at Mom, thrown

tantrums when she had nightmares, but not with Bolt. Even at ten, when she had first seen the little pink-as-ham face wrapped in one of her old baby blankets, she had recognized it was Bolt's turn to be the one with tantrums, his turn to be the one with feelings bigger than his whole body, and she had never begrudged him for it. Until now.

"You couldn't even stay with me for a couple of months," she said, harsher than she'd ever been, and Bolt's face turned stricken. "I'm not stupid. I'm not oblivious. I know the reason you're staying down the hill instead of having the double-wide to yourself. You didn't want to be stuck with me. You look down on me. You love me, but you don't understand me. You don't even try."

"You're right," Bolt snapped. "I'll never understand you. You don't even like it here—you hate the lake—so what do you care if it gets developed?" His eyes were welling up now, but she didn't think he would cry. He would fight. "Why are you protecting it?"

But Cassie had never been good at explaining things. Like how Grandad had despised the residents but loved the water, loved the trees and the land as a part of him. Bolt should have known already how Grandad's mother died before Grandad turned six, the last one who remembered their homeland. That time had washed the memory of the old country out of his bones—even their old family name was discarded for a more American one—and Prosper had been his new homeland and history. Bolt didn't know yet how complex an instrument the human heart was, the many ways it could love and resent and despise and cherish all in perfect symphony. So how was Cassie meant to explain it to him? All he heard—all he cared to hear—was that Grandad had left a wild, prodigious inheritance in the care of his favorite grandchild and nothing but old war medals and a pocketknife for Bolt.

But Cassie was so tired of fighting to be understood, of explaining herself. And Bolt was like Mom: happy to fight forever.

"I don't want to sell to Mr. Daley, Bolt," Cassie said finally. "The thought makes me feel—I can't—" She shook herself. "But tell me what you'd like me to do."

Bolt's face had turned to stone. He pushed past her and off the porch without a word and rushed down the hill into the dying light. It left Cassie winded. She retreated across the lawn, trudging toward the RV. The sun was falling quickly now, and shock was blooming into shame before she even unlocked the door and slumped inside.

Flowers coiled in the windows again, and the RV reeked of vanilla and rosemary from the candle wax cooling on the counter. And there, planted in her rumpled bedclothes like a headstone in loose earth, the chest waited.

౭ఌ

That evening, the sunset turned garnet depths to onyx, flat as a countertop. The water still caught the moon, which gazed wide-eyed up at itself from the dark ripples. Sitting on the back deck of the *Big Dipper*, Lark stared at it through the oculus of a telescope from the box she'd labeled with a large number sixteen. Even with all the things determined to distract her in Prosper—Dad's terrifying warning, her worried family over at the Grand Destiny, the red lake, June—Lark was still doing what she'd come here to do.

June. Lark pulled out her phone and snapped a quick picture of a telescope bravely inspecting the shallows at the end of her slip. She captioned it, water may be a little more brown now? and hit send.

Many of these telescopes showed her the same old world, with varying degrees of magnification, warped only by yellowed lenses and wavy, convex glass. No elaboration, no explanation. But what was she expecting? Lark sighed, tucking another spyglass back into the box in its protective tissue. The breeze ricocheting off the fading red of the lake had a mineral smell. She shut her eyes, breathing in. It still stung her nose.

Lark's phone dinged with June's response. Let's go out tomorrow. She stared at it, the metronome of her heart speeding. Her fingers hovered over the keyboard.

Aunt Valerie had come by that morning to check on her. She brought along enough food to cater a party. "You should come stay at the Destiny for a little while," she suggested as she deep cleaned the *Big Dipper* kitchen. "Lord knows we have the room with the tourists run off." Apparently Jeff Daley's plans to remarket the red water as a major summer destination hadn't quite come together yet, and most people were pretty put off.

"Really?" It touched her, for her family to want her at the motel.

Aunt Valerie's shoulders were tense; her head hung as they worked on the countertops. "I let Stu down. I waited way too long to come over here. What I saw once I did…" Aunt Valerie was very still for a moment, hands braced on the stove. Lark might have heard one impatient sniff. Finally, Aunt Valerie leaned back against the stove top to study Lark. Her aunt's eyes watered. "This place got to your daddy. I don't want it to get to you too."

Lark swiftly gave her prickly aunt a quick squeeze. It was like hugging an eagle: Aunt Valerie was bony, all talons and hard work.

"Don't worry about me," Lark reassured her, though she felt something like panic when Aunt Valerie suggested she leave.

Her aunt was definitely right—living on this ecological war zone couldn't be healthy. At its most concentrated, the color had been gruesome. Even with the floral curtains pulled shut, sleeping on the bloodred lake in the houseboat disturbed Lark's dreams, destabilizing her sea legs. There was the constant threat that the hull of the boat might dissolve and cast her into the slurry. "Honestly, I'm afraid if I leave, I won't be able to finish this."

They'd gone back and forth a few more times, and Aunt Valerie had stayed most of the morning. Now the kitchen was spotless, and Lark was on her own again.

There was a gentle splash somewhere close, a turtle breaching the surface. Lark laid the phone down and pulled the next telescope free. She hesitated with it in her hands. Dad's call had been a warning not to do this; he wanted her to stop. But how could she, really? It still felt important. Time was running out. The telescope seemed to hum, warm temptation, an invitation only for her. Sighing, a soft surrender, Lark pushed it immediately against her eye to search for the source of the sound.

Nothing at first, only the dim, fuzzy darkness of magnified space. She scanned the water near the deck's edge for a disappearing turtle shell, saw nothing, and scooted closer. The seat of her jeans was damp with the mist collected in the rough deck carpet.

Straight down, from far, far below her, there was a dull glint of gold. Lark lowered the lens, and instantly the hard wall of dark water obscured it again. The telescope thinned the lake's veil, revealing something lost beneath it, under at least forty feet of water and ten years of sediment. She recognized it, of course. It had been hers.

The golden houseboat with a tiny pearl on the prow had been a gift on her thirteenth birthday. Her first real piece of jewelry, Daddy had said. He'd been proud of it, a tiny *Big Dipper*, the soft surface of the gold pressed with every detail of the canvases, the windows, the painted stripes. The pearl, he claimed, had been spit from the mouth of the catfish in the Mosquito Bite. Full of magic. Except the latch on the chain inexplicably failed one afternoon a few months later, as Lark sat reading at the lake's edge. Down the golden houseboat sank, fluttering on invisible currents, a descent much faster than *Titanic*'s. Lark had spent the rest of the summer diving, diving, searching for the magical gift, while her father shook his head regretfully at the loss. Now she could see it down there, winking at her, its chain flowing around it like shimmering, untethered rope. Just another lost thing in the deep.

Lark's fingertips paused inches above the surface of the water, far above the lost necklace. It called to her in a low, coaxing voice from below. But she somehow knew, if she dove, if her head went below the water's surface, even for a moment, she'd never come up again.

Quickly, she took up her phone instead, June's text still waiting for her there. Okay sure, she tapped, her hands still shaking. Where?

CHAPTER THIRTEEN

THE MOSQUITO BITE'S BARSTOOLS SAGGED, HALF-stuffed, compressed from the many rear ends they'd borne over the years. Lark wheeled in slow motion on hers, just two rotations, to take the place in—she spun, and there went Bud, pouring Jäger for an expectant tourist; the old jukebox, its neon arches flickering as one of those old fishermen prodded through hits; the mummified catfish, who supposedly spat up pearls. It was Saturday, the water was much less red, and the place was heating up. The bar was small, and soon there wouldn't be an inch to breathe in. A band was just setting up on the low stage, a ragtag skiffle group with a washboard player and a big upright bass.

It had still taken everything in her to drag herself out of that boat, escape the dream state that hung over the twilit lake. But as soon as Lark had gotten away, hauled herself into her Explorer, the night had bloomed with promise. The air itched like new clothes, slightly too tight, unbroken around her. Soon June would appear in the doorway, scanning over heads, and Lark would be the one she was searching for. The back of her neck tingled.

"Y'all got any Wiseacre?" Lark called, catching Bud as he scuttled by.

Bud grinned his stubbly grin. He was missing a tooth or two, but he'd never relinquished his roguish charm, polished and smooth from years behind that old bar. "People get real loyal to those Memphis beers, don't they?" He ducked for a frosty mug, then turned to pour from one of the taps.

Another glance at the door. Lark bent over her phone to check the time and found a rare text from Mitch waiting for her. He wrote messages like he hadn't participated in very much online communication since his AOL instant messenger days. Saw ur friend Trayce in grocery little bit ago. Said hey and ppl r havin a bonfire 2night.

Lark had a sip of her IPA, snickering over the message. Thnx cuz snds kewl g2g ttyl, she typed back. She hadn't been out to the bonfire pit in a long time. Trayce had been one of her weekender gang. Last Lark had heard, he was in law school down in Dallas. Probably just here for a quick visit.

The legs of the stool beside her creaked against the floor, and a cloud of flower scent filled the air—not perfume, with its perfectly crafted chemistry, but new blossoms too fresh to be bottled. "Hey, sailor. Hope you weren't waiting long." June had joined her, hair loose and effortless, wearing dark red lipstick, bold and peppery.

Lark's heart kicked into warp drive. She patted the barstool she'd been staunchly defending. "How's it going? You seem..."

June radiated pure energy, a rocket leaking fuel. "I've been gardening actually. Just a little. There's this graveyard out behind the church—not important." June's beer arrived, and she took it before tilting it Lark's way. "Cheers." The glasses clinked pleasantly when they met, Lark's already half defrosted.

"Every time I don't see you for a few days, I figure you skipped town," Lark admitted, their knees brushing. "On to the next adventure. But now you're *gardening*? I'm impressed, city girl."

June glanced away with a shrug, the corner of her mouth turned up. She bumped their ankles together.

"Hey," Lark said, nudging her ankle right back. "I heard there's gonna to be a bonfire out in the woods tonight."

"A bonfire?" June perked up, a dangerous light sparking in her eye, the kind that drew moths to ecstatic deaths. "Here I thought we were the only two youngsters out here. Can we go?"

Lark snickered, tugged into the deadly flicker. "Bud?" She rapped her knuckles on the bar, catching his attention by a miracle. Everyone else was absorbed in the band's wild hoopla. "Can I get a couple of shots of the special?"

The "special" turned out to be some nefarious moonshine brew that had Lark doubled over with laughter, her head whirling. They closed their tabs, leaving Bud a good tip—June, introducing herself as a former bartender, insisted loudly and proudly. And then they were tripping their way down the worn path to the usual place.

June took her hand, spinning them until they nearly got lost in the trees. "That stuff is poison." June tugged Lark on as if she knew the way. "City bars water down their drinks."

"Right?" Lark could already smell the crackle of dry brush. The orange glow of the blaze reflected on nearby trunks. Music drifted out to meet them on the breeze. "Just hope these people don't ask me about Dad or anything."

"Ask about his telescopes? Why not? My dad collects Persian cats. That's way more out there." June braided their fingers into a loose hold.

"Not that." Lark snorted, squeezing her hand so hard, she probably cut off the circulation. "About how he…" But June didn't know about any of that. Even now, Lark hadn't said a word. She might have never said the words aloud to anyone. Pine needles tickled her skin.

"Go on," June said, nudging their shoulders together. Her eyes were kind and open, campfire warm. They staggered to a halt under the low boughs. Cicadas hammered the air around them.

There was no humor now. Why had she ever said a word? But she'd held her breath for months and said nothing. She planted her feet, kept them there in the pause. June's warmth was thawing her out, and Lark, suddenly, impetuously, wanted to speak. "Can I really tell you?" she asked. "It might be too much."

"I like 'too much,'" June said.

Lark took a breath. It was a big risk. She thought of them scaling that boat out in the junkyard, rung by rung, then perching aloft beneath the constellations together. That fearlessness. That piercing sting of joy.

She plunged.

"My dad broke down out here on the lake," she murmured. Even now, Daddy's face swam before her eyes. She could hear the echo of his panic over the phone a few days ago. "It was a few months ago. He was on sabbatical, alone on the boat, just him and the collection…"

Lark forged ahead, speaking low and fast. "When he looked through the telescopes, he started to see…more. Not just magnified but hidden things. Secrets." Lark stared so hard at June, it was almost a glare. "And I see them too. When I look through his spyglasses, I see the world differently. And at first I thought it was just us being, like, sick or something. But I don't believe that anymore. I believe Daddy."

June didn't look skeptical, only serious. "What do you see?"

"It's hard to explain... Memories?" That wasn't quite it. She charged on. "You know when you're listening to an old record and it's warped or scratched, and the needle will skip? And—this sounds so stupid."

"No." June's voice was steady. "Go on."

"It's like this place is the battered record, playing the same old song," Lark forced out. "And the telescopes...with the telescopes, I can see the skips. The left-out bits."

"And the left-out bits aren't gone," June murmured. "Just passed over."

Lark nodded. "With my dad..." Her throat tightened, and her voice betrayed her raw, nervy tears. "I guess they showed him too much. The telescopes. There are bad things to see out here." She searched June's face there in the darkness. "He went too far and just couldn't stop. I think—" Hospital bed. Fluorescent light. Weathered hands worrying sheets. Lark's voice didn't make it past a whisper. "Because he hurt his eyes. On purpose. I think by then it was the only way to escape."

June shivered, pulling them to a stop. Cloaked by trees, she watched Lark and waited.

Lark hadn't been there. She hadn't seen him for another week, until he was safe and sound in the hospital, his face carefully bandaged. But the telescopes had all seen it. And Aunt Valerie had found him. She'd seen the blood that flaked off the wall in the hallway, that was still dried in the corner of one frame, the picture where Lark peeked over the back of the houseboat from the water, pink goggles strapped on her forehead.

Lark took an unsteady step backward, her back scraping tree bark. "But he was right, damn it," she snapped. "He didn't make it up. Something real is going on."

"Hey. Come here." But it was June who moved, wrapping her arms around Lark, guiding her head to rest against her neck. "And you're here alone, taking care of it so your mom doesn't have to," June read in her silence, in her unsteady breath. "I believe you, sweetheart."

Lark hid there against her skin, shivering from somewhere deep within. "It's like a glue trap down there. It caught Dad. It—"

"Yo! Is there somebody hiding over there in the woods?" called somebody brandishing a Solo cup. "What's up, y'all?" Scattered laughter. There were probably a dozen or so people out there. When Lark and June didn't respond, no second call came.

"We can ignore them." June retreated just enough for the bonfire light to catch in her hair and glow on her collarbone. "We can get another drink. Dance. Leave. Catch a bus. Whatever you want."

Someone was playing a guitar now, quietly strumming beside the bonfire, but it soothed her. Lark thought again of the boat waiting for her, ready to swallow her whole. "No," she said, steadying herself. She smiled feebly. "Let's just hang out for a little while. Being with you...helps."

June watched her, and whatever conclusions she came to seemed to settle somewhere deep inside her bones, making vital changes so that when she curled her hand against the back of Lark's neck, it was more like a beloved habit than the first time. "Then let me help."

Many bonfires had burned in the usual place, for a long time before Lark had started hanging around out there as a teenager. Aunt Valerie and Daddy had definitely come out here when they were young, and Lark could almost see their spectral selves in that clearing among the crowd of locals and weekenders mingling in the fire's glow. Aunt Valerie would be eternally gathering brush, eyes never leaving Diego, quietly lounging with the older kids. Daddy would've stood where the part between treetops was widest, eager to tell any newfound and short-lived friend about the planet Jupiter. It burned above her now with a stubborn brightness, a beauty mark next to the broad white face of the moon.

Lark took June's cool hand again in hers.

"Hey, Lark!" Trayce called from across the firepit, broad and ashy from decades of use. He was the one with the guitar, long legs tossed out toward the flames. "Great to see you." A chorus followed him, and Lark waved at half-forgotten old friends. People sat on stumps, groups absorbed in late-night summertime talk. Others chatted around the keg, distributing Solo cups to anyone who wandered over to them. A group whooped over a game of cornhole, palm-sized bean bags flying. Nearest to the heat, a few dancers flowed with Trayce's guitar, their soles stirring the pine needles. There was the occasional bang and crackle of firecrackers somewhere in the darkness beyond the party.

The night was too warm for the fire, but the uncomfortable burn against Lark's shins was nice somehow. Logs fizzled, occasionally shooting sparks out at them, igniting into lightning bugs in the air around June's curls. Trayce was fingerpicking now, humming a James Taylor cover to himself. He'd gotten pretty good in the years since he'd plucked brokenly through "Stairway to Heaven" on the front of his houseboat twenty-four seven. The reality of the things Lark had said aloud still stung, but the melody of Trayce's idle strumming was soothing. Behind a truck where a few people were smoking weed, the fireworks man sold cinders and sparks from his beat-up trailer.

Lark tugged June's hand, tugging her into the circle of light before slipping an arm around her waist. They swayed into each other along with the rest, the moon throwing light on them like a stage set.

June pressed her cheek against Lark's. "I'm serious about that bus, you know."

Lark stilled, lost in the heady cloud of June's hair. "I don't know how you persuaded even one bus to come down this back road." She pulled back just an inch to catch June's eye. "I can't leave."

"Sure you can." June's eyes were full of eager unspoken words. "You're too good to waste away here. You could come with me."

Lark kept a tight hold on her, in case she suddenly took flight or melted away. "Come with you where?"

June's smile bloomed in the firelight. "Wherever you want." She ran her hands down her arms. "Memphis. Austin. Atlanta. If this place is a sinkhole, why go down with it? Come with me."

June was so beautiful, so charming; she was temptation itself. Lark imagined the two of them in Memphis, posing with the giant animals outside the zoo, ranking barbecue spots, walking along the Mississippi as the sun sank behind Arkansas on the opposite bank, the M bridge gleaming. "I'd like to go with you anywhere," Lark admitted. "But—this is really important. My family's been here forever, and they're still here. What my dad went through…maybe it could mean something if I don't give up on it." She tried to laugh. "I can't just—give up on it." It wasn't the kind of pain you walked away from.

"You're not giving up." June shrugged. "You've been here for, like, a month. You tried." She pressed her lips together, drunken singing filling the brief thick pause. "I was never planning to stay this long. You get that, right?" Her eyes skated, a dusky flush rising on her cheeks. Someone jostled them, and beer foam splashed over Lark's foot. "Don't stay here and let this place destroy you too. Let this stuff go. It doesn't have to be your problem." She tugged Lark's hands, her smile flitting and nervous. "Run away with me already."

Lark gaped at her for a moment. There was a hot stroke of something in her gut at June's words. "Goddamn it, June." She jerked one of her hands away, frustrated. "Can't you hear what I'm— It's like you're not listening to me at all." Her hand strayed back to June's face, her thumb brushing that tender skin next to her eye, huge and burning with that stupid invitation to just go, get out of here, forget this load of bullshit and just...

Lark pushed against her, crashing their mouths together. They hurtled back a step or two, nearly tripping headlong over a stump, almost toppling into the bonfire. They were bound in a private world now, the party receding into blank noise.

June kissed back without a beat, catching her hips, holding her closer. She was still poised to fly, but for the moment, for the kiss, June was letting Lark ground her. It was hard to breathe, especially with the burn of the fire at her back and beer in her throat. Lark felt awakened, the rest of the party, the people, the lake, the telescopes were all a fading dream compared to June's full, bright—fleeting—attention. June's quick hands, her breath, the pinch of her fingernails through cotton. Lark was heatstruck, moonstruck, claustrophobic.

June broke away first, lips skimming her jaw. "Eureka Springs first. Then Memphis. Then wherever you want. It's just stuff, Lark."

Lark didn't want it to end, wanted to seize that moment in both fists and never let go. Something in her promised that if June flew, the cage door would slam behind her and leave Lark trapped within. "Can't you wait?" she asked, trying not to sound as desperate as she felt. "Anywhere we could go, this will follow me."

"If we wait, what happens then?" June slipped back, and Lark heard that telltale whisper of wings. "There's something wrong about this place. If we wait, it eats at you and then it beats you. That's all there is to wait for. If you're so scared, why won't you just come now?"

"I'm scared," Lark confessed, the words catching. She dropped June's hand. Let the cage door shut, then. "But I'm not scared enough to just forget it."

June's face was raw.

"What about your garden?" Lark attempted. That conversation at the bar felt like a distant echo after all this. "Your aunt. You have things here too that matter. It's not just stuff."

June faced the fire, watching logs crack in the glow. "I had stuff in Chicago too, sailor. It all mattered. Until it didn't." Her smile was a pale flicker of what it had been. There was nothing else to say as June gathered herself before leaving the drunken circle to trip her way through the trees toward the distant light of the parking lot.

Lark didn't watch her go. Though her face was scorched by the fire, all she could feel was the lake's chill at her back.

ℰℬ

June walked into trees as dark and inscrutable as inkblots. "Why are you like this?" she murmured to herself.

No noise but crickets filled her body, and there was nowhere to escape from it. June never should have mentioned the idea burgeoning in her head, her little Thelma and Louise gasoline fantasy. A bus ride into the sunset. She should have kept it to herself, wrapped up her hope in good feelings, in firelight and heated skin. Lark would still be with her, and June—

But June had never seen a land mine she wouldn't set off, dirt she wouldn't dig up, a lock she wouldn't pick, a chest she wouldn't toss off a roof. A question she wouldn't ask too soon, a line she wouldn't draw in the sand. She was drunk, and it was too hot all the time and—

And Lark hadn't wanted to go with her.

June found her way to the road out of sheer drunk luck and kicked a rock down the pavement. It glittered very faintly in the moonlight. Flecks of something caught faint starlight. She kicked it, once, and again. Hopefully Cassie was fixing the box, undoing the damage June had caused.

Maybe it ran in the family. Maybe Dad poured his relentless love and attention into raising cats because when June had grown up so distantly from him, he hadn't known where else to put all that energy. Or maybe Mom had it, driving her to work so far past the point of burnout that she turned a little more into ash every day. Maybe even Eliza, who seemed, so far, to draw her life force from an endless well, had something burning in her core.

Or maybe it really was just June.

The light glimmering on the road glowed warmly. At first it

had been silver as slate when June kicked her rock across it, but now it turned buttery yellow.

Interesting.

June kicked the rock again and chased after it. Now the road glittered orange, like the heating rods inside a toaster.

She kicked it again. The rock clattered and rolled—and stopped, cradled in soft, sooty fabric folds.

June looked up, woozy and curious. The pyrotechnics tent was planted in the middle of the road, waiting for her. Its painted sides, fluttering in a warm breeze, seemed to hover and swirl like smoke. As she watched, a scarecrow in a long dusty coat appeared through the flap and walked to a familiar canvas-covered truck. Closing time. He stowed a box in the bed of his truck, then, as if she'd called out to him, turned to wave.

June passed him, drawn to the tent. She pulled back one of the folds with a whisper and stepped in, moonshine still lighting up her veins. This new world smelled sharp and full of ozone. The nearest firework had a ghostly wolf on the wrapping, baring its teeth and charging, with flames blazing in its footsteps. "I guess being a traffic hazard is one way to get customers," she said.

"All roads dead-end somewhere." His raspy voice met her before he did as he ducked inside his carnival. "You came just in time. Haven't had anybody in but those teenagers all night." The fireworks man stepped around her to the checkout, where baskets of trifles gleamed on the countertop. He went about his work, hands always busy, eyes on his inventory. "You ever get that box open?"

"I gave up on that particular pet project," June said, picking up a few crackers that resembled bright red lollipops. "Letting a professional handle it now."

The fireworks man seemed to let it go. He pointed at what she held with a scarred hand. "Those look small, don't they? But they're packed with trouble." He arched an eyebrow. "Want to see?"

"Sure," June said. She felt oddly charitable toward him, grateful he provided the distraction she'd been so desperate for. "I'm June, by the way."

"Jack," he said, grabbing another small sample from a jar. "These ones I named after myself." They were striped in black and bright gold. YELLOW JACKETS.

He led the way outside onto the road, digging for a pack of matches.

"Yellow Jackets. Yellow Jack. Jack. Funny. I get it." June chuckled, following him into the buzzing night air. "Must be difficult to drive around with a bunch of bombs in your truck."

"I think about that sometimes." He cackled, splitting the plaster wrappers around the firecrackers. "What would happen if my gas tank lit. Wouldn't it be amazing." He struck a match, and it blazed to life, fizzling like a Coke when it touched the fuses. The firecrackers on the ground lay quiet, but the air buzzed in anticipation.

"You don't seem scared of it. Dying and…stuff. Driving with death in your trailer."

"I guess you could say I've been carrying death around for a long time, kid." He lit the fuses, bending carefully on early arthritic knees. The fuses skittered, energy rushing as they jumped to life. The lollipops spun and squealed skyward in tight, dizzying spirals. Just above the tree line, they popped, zinging to glittering pieces. It happened so quickly that June barely had time to draw breath before it was over. Their shadows remained, smoky cobwebs imprinted against the sky.

"Oh," she breathed.

Jack watched with a satisfied look on his haggard face. "One town to the next. Place to place. Always on the move." He scratched his chin, eyeing her. "You may be the same."

June's thirst nagged. It wasn't water she craved but fire. This expertly wielded chaos, bound up and tamed but still vibrant. No, not tamed, maybe. Channeled. "Do you move because you get bored? Or do you get kicked out?"

"Depends." He scuffed the firecracker rubbish into the grass. "Sometimes there just ain't anybody left." Jack nodded to his truck. "You need a ride home?"

"Sure," June said and dragged a hand through the knots in her hair. "Sure. I'm not far. Probably."

Jack's truck smelled like the inside of a cannon. June sat on the edge of the ripped passenger seat, coils digging into the backs of her thighs. His headlights struck the road, blanching the night as they ground their way toward the church. Jack was quiet, tucking a stick of gum between his jaws and offering her own piece from the crumpled pack.

Wasn't that what they always said—don't get in a car with strangers? Don't go to a second location? Don't. Don't.

June didn't take the gum but rolled the window down so she could feel the sobering breeze. "Why'd you tell me to throw that box off the roof? Pretty dangerous thing to do."

"That was your idea, kid." The evergreen tang of his gum mingled with the truck's peculiar chemistry as he chewed. He nodded at a familiar Tootsie Roll firecracker poised on his dash. "I said you should blast it open."

"Right. Yeah. Even more dangerous." She stuck her arm out

the window, where her flat palm caught the wind and became a sail. "Why?"

"I told you already." They rounded the corner, his headlights hitting the church grounds. Somewhere beyond their illumination lay her cemetery. But caught in that white glare stood Eliza, her hands on her hips as she gazed across the road at them. Jack pulled over to let her out, not bothering to turn into the church lot. He faced her. "You've got a spark about you. A little like me. You could burn what's left of this ruin down if you wanted." He tossed the truck into Park.

Eliza took a step or two off the porch, shielding her eyes against the brightness.

"I don't know what you mean," June said boldly, but she was caught in the memory of feeling so cooped up, of holding herself in until she trembled, trying so hard to be good. She tried so hard to squeeze that feeling down inside her, to contain it, that flowers grew at the ends of her hair. That thought made her relent. "For me, it's like this buzzing in my head," she said finally. "I swear, once it got so bad, my coffeepot boiled itself dry. I got fired from my last job because it started a bar fight." Confessing this felt like being reduced to a newborn thing that had crawled out of the dirt into the sun, oversensitive and saturated, easily scoffed at, easily mocked—easily blown off as the antics of a lifelong troublemaker.

He nodded. "Life is never boring for you. But never easy."

"I keep trying to find ways to control it," June admitted. "How do *you* control it?"

"You don't control it." He shoved his thumb back at his bed of firecrackers behind them. "Only one thing to do. You gotta let it out."

June nodded. She had the half-drunk, half-hungover feeling that came with moonshine wearing off. She opened the door. "Thanks for the ride."

"Sure, kid."

Eliza had given up on waiting and was marching toward the truck, the muscles around her mouth tensing.

"Bye," June said and hopped down from the truck before crossing the lawn toward her. "Hey. Sorry I'm late."

Eliza watched as Jack's old rust bucket pulled back onto the road. "Who was that man, honey?"

"Guy who sells fireworks. He's a weirdo, but he's harmless," June said. "He was just giving me a ride." She pushed her hands in her pockets.

"Hm." Aunt Eliza put her arm around June's shoulders, but she didn't turn, didn't even blink, until the Bag of Tricks Traveling Pyrotechnics Co.! truck rumbled out of sight.

❦

Woody's brother might have had the choicest weed, but it was Sammy who rolled the best joints, as exact as the wings of a folded crane. After the fight with Cassie, Bolt found her. She didn't ask questions. She and Bolt lay down in the houseboat graveyard and passed a joint back and forth. Even through the tie-dye marina T-shirt, the pavement scraped at Bolt's back. Complex avenues of grassy fissures crisscrossed the ground, so he could at least rest his head on a pillow of ragweed and damp, fragrant moss. Above them, the corroded hull of a beached houseboat curved down so close, Sammy could skim her long, tan fingers over the pocked surface. With each herbal puff, the burned battery hull expanded, its dome more like a coppered starscape. The blocks at the four corners that held their sky up seemed rooted in the asphalt, growing up, up, .pushing the ruined houseboat higher, like the arms of Atlas.

He'd never fought with Cassie before. No one really fought with Cassie. He'd seen Mom scold her, even shout at her before, but Cassie became still and quiet when confronted like that, retreated deep inside herself. She turned to stone. How did someone get through to stone? This fight had felt different. Charged. Cassie hadn't retreated. She'd been there the whole time, meeting him with fire in her eyes and money, unprecedented money, in the bank.

"Ever seen an alligator gar?" Sammy asked, blowing smoke in his face. She'd soared along beside him on the way out here; happy too, maybe, to be away from the bullies for once. Why the hell she bothered hanging out with any of them was anybody's guess.

"You mean those freaky fish with teeth? Yes." Once, Grandad had flicked on the dock lights, and they'd gathered, pushing their toothed reptilian bills up at the surface. Little monsters, with huge flat eyes, desperately seeking moonlight in the dock lamps.

"Jodie—you know her from the marina—she's convinced one ate her puppy."

"What?" Bolt glanced at her, disgusted, and snatched the reefer.

"Yeah, really. Some horrible Chihuahua thing. It, like, loved the water. She let it swim by the boat, but she swore a gar came up and grabbed it right in front of her." Sammy dug around in her pocket for a key. "She's such a liar. Gars don't do that. They eat fish. They're endangered, you know? I read about it in *National Geographic*. They get seriously overfished."

Bolt watched the water, stomach churning vaguely. "But the dog is gone?"

"Huh?" Sammy used the key she'd found to scratch a new constellation into the bottom of the houseboat. "Yeah. But it probably just swam away or got lost. It'll turn up in a few days."

"Weird."

"Alligator gar can get up to ninety pounds. They break fishing rods."

Sammy chatted on, and Bolt stared at the rusted-out star patterns above, brooding. "Hey. Rig ever pull a knife on you?" Bolt murmured at last.

"A knife? No." Sammy was intense when she listened. She didn't seem to blink very much. A lot like Mom. "He doesn't like me as much as he likes you."

"Still." Bolt's nerves pricked at the memory of the blade's sting. "You probably shouldn't be alone with him." There was something about Sammy that really brought the bully out in Rig.

Sammy smashed the butt of the reefer into their canopy. "Sounds like you need to follow your own advice."

"Maybe." Bolt army crawled out between the timber supports and stood on the edge of the water, black and oily. The boats sighed, knocking softly against each other. "He's been strange lately. Everyone has. I wish I hadn't come this summer." He kicked a stone into the water.

And something pale and round glistened under the lake weed.

Bolt froze, heat flashing over his skin, then, just as fast, chilled air.

Footsteps joined him at the edge. "What now?"

The thing in the water was bloated like a marshmallow, visible because of the full moon only, catching the light. Moonlight swelled in an unmoving milky eye.

"What—is that?" Sammy leaned in too, picking up a stick to give it a prod. "Oh my God—"

And Bolt stared. From below the surface of the water, half obscured under the dock, a dead man stared back.

CHAPTER FOURTEEN

ITCH SLIPPED FRESH LOAVES ONTO THE BREAD shelf in the market. Their neat rows, the scent of recently baked wheat and rye, was comforting. He sipped his coffee, flipping an inventory page on his clipboard. With the water shifting from shades of red clay to more natural greens and blues, business was in a modest uptick. Monday mornings were quiet at the resort, the restaurant closed, the market restocking. A perfect opportunity to reorient for a new week. Mitch hefted the box of new baked goods he had spent the early hours gathering from his regular circuit of local grandmas. Betty Martin's blueberry muffins had been so warm when she packed them up for him that they'd broken a sweat in their individual plastic wraps. Mitch liberated one, half of it disappearing in one enormous bite. A figure darted through the market from the motel, moving quickly for the door.

"Morning, Bolt," Mitch called, waving. "Hungry? I—"

But before he had an opportunity to offer anything, Bolt was gone.

Strange.

Mitch went back to work. He was peaceably fitting ground

beef and pork chops into the market's refrigerators when the bell chimed again. He turned to find Cassie standing in the doorway.

She was flushed with late-June heat, rosy under her freckles. Her braid was bunchy on one side, and one of the buttons on her linen shirt had been fastened wrong, but the fabric looked soft from across the counter. "Mitch," she said, resting a familiar steadying hand on the counter. No one said his name like she did; no one else could gentle all those hard letters the way she could. "Is Bolt here?"

He hadn't seen her since that night, since she'd appeared at his house after midnight, when those jackals destroyed her hives. In the moments he'd lain in bed since then, he'd closed his eyes and felt the force of her face, its warmth, the hard insistence of her forehead against his cheek. "No," he managed, stuffing a package of 80 percent lean ground chuck onto a chilled shelf. "I saw him a few minutes ago, but he didn't say a word to me." He hesitated a moment. "How are you?"

"I've been better." She tapped her fingers on the counter. "Where could he be?" They wore anxiety similarly, Cassie and Bolt. It stirred their thoughts, made their jaws tight, and blinded them to the rest of the world. It sat like a layer of grease over everything else.

Mitch raised his shoulders, helpless. "Restaurant's closed Mondays, so I bet he's down at the marina." That was the brilliance of Bolt's summer plans—there was no one person who was explicitly responsible for knowing where he was, what he was doing. The privilege of being generally well-behaved. But at seventeen, that kind of free range came with risks.

Cassie nodded, staring at the whorls in the countertop. "He

found out about the land and Daley's offer. And now he's mad. And I don't know how to fix it."

Mitch rested a hand on her back. "He was going to find out about the land eventually, Cass. That's a lot for a kid to take in." Her braid tickled his thumb. "He has to learn what it means."

She leaned against him. "I don't think he cares. And I can't blame him for it. For wanting to escape. When I was young—" She pressed her lips together. "I'm tired of fighting him and this place."

"He cares," Mitch said gently. "He cares about you. It'll work out." He racked his brain for something more to say, to breach the subject of that night. The way she'd looked up at him—but it wasn't an easy thing to capture in words.

"Hey." He loped to one of the boxes waiting to be unpacked and rifled through it. Out came the little package, all wrapped in parchment paper. It had to be ordered special, and he never bought enough to sell. He took it to her. "Remember? None better." The goat cheese came from a couple of counties over, soft and creamy, massaged with home-grown herbs. Cassie enjoyed so few luxuries imported from outside their little plot that each was special.

Cassie took it, folded her hands around it. "Thank you," she said, and this time, when she looked at him, she looked a little less troubled. Her eyes were brimming, full of silent thoughts he couldn't interpret. "You remember what I like."

She was so burdened, always had been, by things she couldn't seem to share. Even as a little girl, she'd looked out at the world with those huge serious eyes. When Mitch used to browse in Mr. Fairchild's rusty toy shelves, her rare smiles were always the best treasure to be found. They were like a silver shimmer beneath tarnish—the light had to be just right to catch it.

"We could cook something together," he suggested, as casually as he could. "On the Fourth of July. Maybe…watch those fireworks they keep talking about."

Cassie gazed at him, and then he saw it, the beginnings of a silver-shimmer smile. "All right."

The door opened again, letting in a blast of hot air.

"Good morning, good morning!" blustered the man in the doorway. It took Mitch a moment or two to recognize him as Jeff Daley. He was in desperate need of a shave, and the collar of his polo shirt was half flipped over itself against his neck. In the quiet morning, his voice rang loud.

"Morning," Mitch replied, dragging his gaze away from Cassie's. He sounded impatient to himself. "You're sure out early."

Daley stared at his wrist, where, normally, a Rolex nestled. "Early riser," he put in, a jovial smile setting like Jell-O in a mold.

Mitch sniffed, almost wincing. There was a rank smell heavy in the air around them. Even worse, maybe, a palpable tension, as if every muscle in Daley's body were pulled taut.

"Mr. Daley, have you seen Bolt at the marina?" Cassie asked, leaning an elbow on the counter, closer to Mitch. "I was hoping to catch him this morning."

He glanced at her, just a quick flash. "My ex-wife is coming down this evening. Been planning it for a month. I'm making dinner. And I—did the strangest thing." He laughed a bit. "I like to age my own steaks, you know. That's just a little thing I like to do. I enjoy it, you know."

Mitch raised an eyebrow, catching Cassie's eye.

Daley went on. "But this time. This time…" He dug around in a back pocket and withdrew a large graying mass. It looked like an organ, something pulled out during a delayed autopsy, until he flopped it onto the counter. Cassie heaved and pressed a hand to her mouth, pushing back a step in revulsion. The rib eye was mottled, the meat stinking and slick, covered with mold and maggots. "I left them too long," he murmured, the undercurrent of cheer not totally eclipsed at the sight of it. "Would you just look at that." His voice had shifted, a low growl now beneath it.

There was a long pause. Mitch searched for something to say. The audacity of tossing rotting meat on his freshly buffed countertop was stunning. But Daley's expression, that unhooked stare, made it difficult to know how to respond. "So, uh, you're looking to buy some replacements?" Mitch gestured at the meat shelf. "I just got in some choice cuts from the butcher on the highway. Really…nice."

Daley nodded distantly, steak already forgotten, because his eyes were now clamped on Cassie.

They all stood there for a moment in silence.

"*Have you changed your mind yet, Miss Cassie?*" Daley barked out suddenly. "We could make Prosper a good, good place. Otherwise we're all going under."

"No," Cassie said, nothing but hard refusal in her voice. Her face was very white. "I won't change my mind."

"All of us. Right under." Daley's hand seized up and out, like he wanted to grab her. But he stopped. He blinked too deliberately. He blinked again. Mitch watched the flutter of his fingertips, dreading how they might, in an instant, wrap around Cassie's throat. Was he drunk? Was there some essential medication he'd forgotten to take? His other hand rested on the fetid meat. Slumping, slack-shouldered, so all his force was in that resting arm, he ground the steak into the counter. It squelched with roadkill wetness. "It'll all. Be. Because of you."

"Go home, Jeff," Mitch said.

Jeff Daley opened his mouth, then closed it. Whatever words he seemed to want to say, they didn't make it out. But his eyes never left Cassie's face.

Mitch crossed his arms, taking a single step in. He had a full four inches of height on Daley and thirty or more pounds. "Just go on home."

Finally, the rotten meat forgotten where it lay, Jeff Daley went out the way he'd come.

ᘒ

"Blueberry," Lark bellowed into the Grand Destiny kitchen. On the other side of the kitchen window, Aunt Valerie shot her a stern look. After drying her hands, Aunt Valerie marched into the restaurant.

"Child. You cannot eat three pieces of pie," she huffed. "Where are you putting it?"

Lark thunked her head on the counter.

Aunt Valerie surrendered and stomped over to the case and then dragged a slice of blueberry pie out. It was comforting to be here at the Destiny, with the familiar hum of the freezers, the faded maps of the lake lining the wood-paneled walls. Somewhere, the industrial dishwasher chugged. It was a dead shift at the restaurant, a Monday night just before closing. Diego had dropped in during pie number two to deliver an industrial

bag of flour, sugar, cornstarch, and the last of the summer figs
sold from the fruit stand by the highway, which the same feather-
haired old woman had been running since Lark was a toddler.
He'd looked from Lark to her pie and given her shoulder a sturdy
pat on his way back out the door.

Aunt Valerie clunked the pie on the counter in front of Lark.
"You want ice cream on it?"

Lark nodded without lifting her head.

"There now." Aunt Valerie cleared her throat. "I'll just go heat
this up for you."

This place had always been a part of her life. Lark remembered
being lifted into a high chair, her legs kicking, her wormy fingers
catching carrot sticks. Aunt Valerie had made special pies for her
birthdays, and packed fried chicken into to-go boxes for her, and
changed the channel on the TV in the lobby so she could watch
the Disney Channel with Mitch while Dad and Diego caught up.
This was a safe place for her, now much safer than the *Big Dipper.*
The whole day prior, she'd nursed a hangover on the houseboat,
packing the telescopes wedged into corners of the cuddy, her
head pounding, her heart broken. The walls around her seemed
to swell and sag, bending in, the pressure of the water too much
for them. She half expected the hull to buckle in and trap her.

Chocolate cream and then Dutch apple hadn't quite solved the
weight of June's words, her heady invitation and its sharp with-
drawal. God, Lark had been this close. Maybe June had offered,
if carelessly, Lark's last chance at escape. But Lark had said no,
and it had opened an incredible chasm between them. And the
thought of that distance, a breach June might not bother to leap,
filled Lark with a gut-deep misery. June might be gone already.

"Has Cassie been helping you with the telescopes?" Aunt Valerie called, and Lark heard the microwave whirring behind her.

"Yes, ma'am," Lark replied dully. She had received a rather rushed but exacting appraisal for the latest box of telescopes that morning. Cassie had offered to buy more than half of them for the shop. "Haven't seen her much, but...don't know how I'd do any of this without her."

"Well." Aunt Valerie delivered this offer with the pie à la mode. She paused. "Anything else you want to talk about?"

Lark sat up, arming herself once again with her fork. She nudged the ice cream scoop and wiped at her face. "Pie is better than people," she said. She sounded hoarse to herself. "People just let you down. They leave. They—get lost in things and pick that over you." Daddy had looked too deeply at the very least. He hadn't protected her from this. "And then it's...just you again."

Aunt Valerie sighed and went to pour herself a glass of tea. Her anxiety over Lark's unhappiness was making the resort anxious; the ceiling fans, clearly trying to be helpful, were whirling so quickly that they swung and bucked.

Valerie scraped her kitchen stool over and sat opposite Lark with her tea. "People leave," she agreed heavily, and Lark saw Mitch's dad in her eyes, in the delicate nest of lines around them. No one knew about absence better than Aunt Valerie and this rickety old motel. This had been a family business, generations, and now they weren't here. All loved, all temporary. "Lord knows they make mistakes. They slip up. Your daddy...struggled. Maybe he forgot he was loved." She had a long drink of her tea. "Maybe we let him forget."

Lark held an enormous bite in her mouth, her eyes shut.

Maybe she could just disappear into the sensations of hot and cold, tart and sweet, crust and berry. She had forgotten him, a little, when she was in Memphis, flitting between the self-centered musical world of the record shop to her apartment, where she and her friends stayed up late, drank, laughed, went out on Beale. Wrapped up in her life, it had been easy to excuse not calling him as much, not pressing him when he sounded distant or lonely. Dad was always dreaming, bubbling over with his own ideas, his private musings that sailed over other people's heads. She thought his magnificent imagination insulated him, made him safe. She'd misunderstood how vulnerable he really was.

Aunt Valerie's voice shook slightly when she continued, "But we go on. We have to."

"How?" Lark managed, her voice thick with pastry.

Valerie had already nearly exhausted her capacity to sit, so she grabbed the cleaner and rag to wipe the counter. "How what?" she asked gruffly. "Going on just happens, honey. It's happening right now."

"Is it?" Even outside it, Lark felt the weight of the houseboat anchoring her. She felt the bonfire's treacherous heat. "I feel like I'm just stuck in it. All of it."

Valerie scrubbed rings and crumbs down the well-worn surface. How many hundreds, thousands, of times had she done it? "It can feel that way." The dishwasher hummed through yet another cycle of dishes. Surely even Aunt Valerie got caught in a rut sometimes. "But you're going to be okay."

Lark had no answer for her, words concealed behind a chewed lip. She had another bite of pie, mostly ice cream. Here Lark was constantly in the rich gumbo of her own feelings, hard to untangle now that they stewed together in the pot. June... Daddy...all set to simmer.

"Now where's Bolt gone to? I think he's avoiding me." With her usual helper MIA, Valerie put Lark to work cleaning the tables, lifting the chairs, collecting the ketchup bottles. An evening routine that had lasted decades. When the floor was mopped and the crust prepped for morning, Valerie walked Lark out, roast beef and turnip greens wrapped up for her.

"You know," Aunt Valerie said at last, as they stood on the threshold, "you're not your daddy, honey." She hit the lights, rustling her keys. "People are always gonna hurt you, let you down. Hell, you'll let them down. But...keep the door open."

છ૭

Bolt woke up sick inside, lake water damp on his sheets again. In his dreams, he saw the dead man's eyes, their glassy, marbled plea.

He would forever remember last night in sick jolts. The taste of bile in his mouth. Being so cold that no amount of sun could ever warm him. Hissing at Sammy to "cover it up, throw some leaves over it—" before grabbing her arm and towing her away. They'd run all the way back to the marina, Sammy peeling off there with a darting dragonfly glance at him. Bolt had stumbled into his room to vomit again in the toilet.

He needed to tell someone, but his immediate urge had been to hide, and he still felt it. He didn't even know why he couldn't say a word, except for how wrong it felt. How much it felt like another bad dream. And the choking fear that he might lead someone out there only to discover it had been a trick of the lake. The fear that whatever was getting to Rig, to Mr. Daley, to

Grandad, even to Cassie all these years, was finally coming for him too.

Yesterday, Sunday, he'd missed getting up early to make pies with Val. The thought of her egg-custard pie, as yellow and bright as a full moon, of uncooked dough dotted through with butter—he couldn't face it. He wished he'd never seen it.

Bolt had never been brave, not really. Being adventurous or outgoing didn't count. He was a coward in the ways that counted.

The sun burned on his shoulders all day, yet inside, some part of him was still just as frozen, just as immobile and cold as the body.

Sammy had wandered into the marina but hadn't spoken to him, instead going to hang around Rig at the register. He felt her eyes from time to time. They should have gone to the police, Bolt had thought wildly, at the melting of afternoon into evening, as he clocked out of his shift. Why hadn't they just gone to the police? He should have woken Diego up or Valerie, even Cassie.

"What are you, hungover?" Bolt startled as Rig's fingertip scanned his ribs. Now he was grinning at Bolt as he tipped one of his earbuds out. Rig's eyebrows had a way of knitting when he smiled, making the expression ever skeptical; his was a deep, sly humor, constantly testing itself and everything else. "I heard you've got a big secret for me." Sammy was watching from her spot restocking T-shirts from a large cardboard box.

Disappointment rose in his throat. "What did she tell you?" Bolt asked. He didn't have the energy to meet Rig at his usual sardonic level. He didn't want to laugh at the world today, and his shift was almost over anyway. He hung his whistle on the wall with all the others.

"Just that: you two have a secret." Rig spun the earbud idly, searching Bolt's face. "So what is it? Give me something good. My dad's been a real lunatic lately. He let these steaks go rotten and then, like, carried them around with him."

Those last details were sickening enough that he relented. Rig wouldn't give up. He pushed a hand into his hair. "We found something last night while you were off with Woody."

"Oh yeah?" Rig's eyes seemed to darken, his interest piqued. "Something out in the graveyard?"

"I don't want to talk about it here," Bolt hissed, as a couple of kids passed, running for the fake arrowhead key chains. Sammy shrugged at him across the room.

"Fine." Rig checked the time on his phone. "After work. My mom was coming down, but she canceled."

Bolt didn't want to go, didn't want to see those eyes or know if the sun and fish had taken their share. But there was no arguing with Rig when he set his mind to it, and if Bolt didn't meet Rig after his shift, Rig would just come to the resort and bug him until he broke down.

The four of them gathered in the rich purple dusk. Woody—stringy, unshowered, and excited—had his Swiss army knife out, tossing it and spinning it between his fingers. Bag slung over his shoulder, Rig had picked up a stick as they walked along the highway, and now its tip bucked and skidded across the uneven surface of the road.

"He read my mind," Sammy muttered, ambling along beside Bolt on her roller skates. "What were we supposed to do, anyway? They're our—friends." He caught that moment of hesitation, one that matched the strange cognitive leap he had to make to arrive at the word "friends."

Bolt's skin remembered the chill of being pushed into the red lake, Rig laughing when he tried to clamber out. In his bones he remembered the secret Rig had spilled about Cassie's land, the havoc he'd wreaked in her yard as punishment. "Are they?" he murmured.

They looked at each other, and for a moment, they might as well have been alone. They *were* alone, somehow. But now the prows of abandoned boats peeked at them through the trees. It was too late to keep their secret.

"Holy shit," Rig breathed, kneeling beside the bloating mass in the shallows.

The body lay like a heap of sodden rags in the reeds, the face distended into a topography of grayish mounds. Nose blurred into swollen cheekbones, which seemed to run in waxy rivulets around parted bulging lips. The leaves and debris they'd tossed hastily over it in the darkness clung to rough, homespun clothes, and tangled in the tongue of a moldering boot.

"This is sick." Rig drew his stick up and gave the mounded gut of the corpse a sharp jab. The body had the soft give of a fish belly. The slackened mouth fell as far open as the ruined jaw would allow, an icy stench of bile issuing from it. Woody leaped back.

"It looks old," he said, fingers twitching. Rig snapped a couple of photos with his phone. "I don't recognize him. But, hell, bloated up like that, it could be anyone. Is there anyone who's been missing around the docks?"

Sammy rested her hands on her knees, leaning in. She didn't seem to fear the corpse either, squinting at it with the same arrested disgust she'd had the night before. "It does look old. And yellow." She glanced at Bolt, the only one she was speaking to. "I bet he's from the churchyard down there. Under the water. Just like Nonnie told me, remember? There were a bunch of people who died from yellow fever, and they left some bodies and stuff when the town sank."

"Bullshit." Rig straightened, giving one of the floating work boots a light kick. "You mean from a hundred years ago? This asshole is fresh."

"No," Sammy insisted. "My nonnie was around then. She says there were still—"

"It does look yellow," Woody added. "Yellow fever sounds like a bad way to go."

Bolt's throat went dry. Grandad had talked about it so rarely, but Bolt remembered. "Mosquitos did it," Grandad had said. They'd been on the porch, and Bolt had felt one whine at his ear. He had sat still, terrified it might bite him. "There were so many around the water. No matter how early you went fishing or farming, there were mosquitos, clouds of them shimmering like heat waves in the air. About a week later, you'd know because you'd get chills, deep in your bones. Fever. You'd ache. Like your whole body had turned against you. And some—when the jaundice set in, you knew a person didn't have long. Do you know what jaundice means, Bolt? It means the skin turned yellow. That's when the body gets toxic. Not much a doctor could do, not then. When it got bad in Prosper, they got all the healthy people out and turned the old schoolhouse into a makeshift hospital."

He shook his head, tilting back his beer. "Only we didn't have a doctor back then, and the Charlene doctor never went. Even he was too scared. The man who was supposed to have the answers was too scared. And if most everyone who had it was either poor or an immigrant or Black, he wasn't risking his life."

Bolt shivered and shivered, and later, when he saw a mosquito bite on his arm, he burst into tears and ran to Mom, sure he had been infected. Mom had yelled at Grandad for scaring him, and Grandad's face had pinched up with guilt.

Yellow fever had a vaccine, and people around here didn't get it anymore. He was safe. Everyone was safe.

But as they stood there, Woody and Rig performing their own personal autopsy, Bolt began to believe Sammy. The clothes didn't look modern and were almost worn to shreds. The boots, still crammed around swollen ankles, were so different from the soft sandals weekenders wore around the marina. These were boots built for hard work, patched in the heel and sole. The laces were gone, stolen by fish perhaps, leaving only torn leather eyelets behind. But it was no mummy, no dried-out husk or prehistoric man from deep in a peat bog. This was all mass, all tender layers, grocery store poultry left on a kitchen counter. And that skin, yellowed like old linen.

"Why would it still be here?" Bolt asked, as the sun was making its definitive exit beyond the tree line. "If it's that old?"

"Same as the rest of the stuff that washes up." Sammy touched a button on a stained and rotting shirt cuff, avoiding the mottled flesh beneath. Something clung in shimmering clusters to the roots of his fingers. "It's probably cold down there, you know?"

After his investigation of the corpse's wrecked pockets, Rig pulled back, rummaging through the bag he'd brought along in the darkness. The air was warm and fetid. "I have the best fucking idea I've ever had."

"What's on his skin?" Woody asked, pressing the end of his stick against the cheek. Bolt saw it too, shining like fish eggs at the corner of the dead mouth. More, larger, tucked into the coils of an ear. He imagined there were great swells of them under those stretched eyelids, precious blight growing in the warm caverns of the empty sockets. Maybe inside too, the skull a stinking treasure chest of them, clustering in that distended belly.

"They're pearls," Bolt said. Poor son of a bitch. The lake rippled, and when it touched Bolt's ankles, it was cold. "Woody, don't. Come on. Let's go."

"Hey, get back," Rig commanded, moving past Woody with something in his hand. He stooped over the body, working, his back blocking Bolt's view. "Toss me your light."

"What are you doing?" A wariness crept into Sammy's voice.

"Sick!" Woody crowed and scrambled back, eyes gleaming, and staggered up the bank, pulling his shirt over his mouth.

The blue night briefly warmed with the lighter in Rig's hand, and then there was a sharp crackle of ammunition. The whistle of a lit firecracker fuse. Rig ducked back, laughing. "Somebody record this!"

The fuse hung from the corpse's mouth like some kind of demented cigarette, lighting his face in ghoulish relief. For a moment he was animated, living, his face full of vivified horror. The invasive pearls were illuminated in sickly shades by the sinking, sparkling lit fuse. Bolt staggered forward—it wasn't too late to rip it away, throw the cracker as far as he could into the lake—

"C'mon." Sammy wrenched Bolt back a few yards, sucking in a haggard breath.

In the space of a second, the firecracker went dark. Then it flashed, a strike of lightning bursting from the water and clawing up at the sky.

Bang. Bang. Bangpopopopop—

"Sick!" Woody screamed in his ear. He and Rig leaped around them, hands up in praise at the arc of white fire in the sky, the streams of smoke and chaos. Sammy and Bolt had both fallen, and she had a gravel scrape on her cheek. They scrambled up. The firecrackers burst again as if they just couldn't help it, lighting up the roadkill form—or what was left of it. Now it was pieces, legs and most of a torso, an arm here, and a mouth that was nothing now, a throat that was gone entirely. Charred, seared edges and teeth popped like popcorn, and then there were those boots, still perfectly intact.

Sick, Bolt leaned over and heaved, but nothing came out. The lake had been disturbed, churning against the spoiled shoreline.

When Rig turned away from his masterpiece, his eyes crackled, like the munitions had caught in them, embers burrowed deep. He swept his hair back, breathless, flushed. Ecstatic. "Well, gents," he managed. "Looks like our work here is done."

CHAPTER FIFTEEN

UNE WOKE UP ON THE FIRST OF JULY IN A HAZE OF florals, her white pillow bleeding pink with petals. Begonias. For a moment, she expected to find Mom standing over her bed, worry creased in her face, scissors already in hand. When she raked a hand through her hair, she felt a few worn buds tangled at her temples. She tugged. They resisted. Her arms felt heavy when she flopped for the bedside table and the kitchen shears she kept within.

After Lark and the bonfire, June hadn't left the church grounds for days. She stayed in the church's cool air-conditioning, ostensibly cleaning for Sunday and staying busy enough that Aunt Eliza wouldn't worry. Much. She was too discerning not to worry at all, and she asked several probing questions about Jack, but June dodged them.

Instead, she cleaned the church. She wandered the grounds. She taught herself to play the yellowed piano keys. Every so often, like missing a step on a staircase, a confident press of her finger yielded no music, just a long, breathy exhale where a note used to be.

Despite herself, she thought of the box in Cassie's care, even considered dropping by to check. But she wouldn't do any good.

The buzzing inside her didn't stop. No one had ever known what it was like until Jack told her he knew how to *make* it stop. The cicadas droned in the evenings and followed her into her dreams, where they loomed, flexing their tymbals in chorus, blinking black marble eyes. They made her whole body thrum in concert.

So she'd started to spend hours, long hot hours, outside in the cemetery. It was barely dawn, and there she was, tramping into the blueish light with her shirt wrapped around some old primrose bulbs she'd rescued from Aunt Eliza's shed.

June stopped at the edge of the clearing, upturned dirt and new flowers sprouting between gravestones. She had half of them cleared off now, the names becoming visible again. But there were beautiful flowering vines clinging to the trees and up the wings of a single weatherworn angel statue. Sunflowers peeked through on the edge, and spiky purple flowers, each an individual trumpet. None of it had been there the day before. Just like that, all the frustration, all her cramped anger—it dissipated like mist facing the sun.

She knelt beside the angel, touching gentle silk petals. "You don't look like the picture of milkweed on those seeds I bought," she said. "What are you?" The smell was familiar, like warm summer evenings, like lingerie. "Jasmine," she realized. "Jasmine. What are you doing here, gorgeous?"

The angel offered no answers. June stood again. There was no true order to the new growth. It wasn't clean or in sensible rows, but mixed, blending, swirling, all the roots tangled under the earth. It was as wild and random as a bar fight. It wasn't a garden planted among the gravestones. This unexpected upshooting was something else.

It was chaos.

"What are any of us doing here?" she asked. At the edge of the cemetery, the tributary of the lake shrugged with the far-off passing of a Jet Ski, ruffling lily pads the size of dinner plates, and maybe it was her imagination, but the jasmine seemed to shiver.

Surrounded by new growth, June picked a spot for the primroses. She imagined them, little patches in the shade around a lion statue she'd found at the antique shop and relocated.

June bent until her lower back ached, cleaning moss off the next row of gravestones and shoving aside undergrowth. She had no real experience. The closest she had ever gotten to a garden was the apartment across the courtyard from the one she and Mom shared, where an elderly couple grew orchids, stately and ever so cool, like skinny women in tailored pantsuits. But sometimes she would sit, looking at a patch of tiny white flowers and think, *Those could do with some more sunlight.* Or when she saw the coil of vine around the feet of an angel statue: *That could use a bit of fertilizer to really grow.*

There was a spindly tree growing in the sun near the water's edge. Its leaves flourished fat and green, bigger than her hand, and June knew that if she waited long enough, soon the little late-season green bulbs would ripen, and she could bring Aunt Eliza the fresh figs.

Growth could be violence, ignited by the heating earth. It could be the selfishness of the race to the sun and the agony of new birth. It was aggressive colonialism, the hungry way gooseneck gobbled up every bit of earth. People forgot because flowers were so pretty. But chaos was a blooming thing too. Chaos also wanted to grow. It wanted to spread. But it didn't have to be violent, selfish, aggressive. Maybe this growth could be kind.

"I'm going to make you so pretty," June told the first of two primroses that would be planted in the shade, where only morning light would touch them once their blue-green leaves sprouted. Hours slipped by like dewdrops. June dug deeper under cracked, warm dirt to the moist earth underneath. She pictured black rosebuds, golden cornelias, and huge lily pads flowering at midnight, and something fragrant and vibrant blossomed inside her chest. She didn't fight it.

If it hadn't been so quiet, she would have missed it; in the corner of her eye, she glimpsed something that was no leaf or petal but the figure of a person. There was someone in her garden. June paused, hands on one of the primroses, a wrinkled little shallot half buried in dirt.

There had been no sound, no twigs cracking under someone's feet, no sigh of moving branches, no polite greeting. Nothing at all. It wasn't movement that had caught June's attention because the person hadn't walked up to her. They had not been there. Until in an instant, they were. The two bare, muddy feet shifted. And then walked closer. June kept her eyes trained on her primroses.

Not again. After the fishermen, the sour, vicious way they had smiled while trying to scare her, June didn't want to face whatever was with her now. It was too similar to that bloodred night. She'd been alone today; she'd been sure of it.

And now she was not.

"What are you doing here?" the voice snapped.

June kept her head down, breathing through the anxious

alarm, like an egg was stuck in her throat. "Planting primroses," she said after a moment.

Bare knees stopped close to her, and June steadied her fingers. Cold wrath rushed over her from the figure. "Why?"

"I don't mean any harm. I'm sorry." June was at a loss for what to do, only certain she didn't want to look up—not when she didn't know what she would see. Perhaps June was intruding. She was Goldilocks, stepping into someone's home without permission, pulling weeds and planting flowers with good intentions but not permission.

The air at her neck was cold. Her skin had turned clammy. The feeling didn't relent, but it didn't intensify. "When will they grow?"

What? June swallowed. "You're supposed to bury primroses early in the fall. Let them sleep all winter. Then they come up in the spring." Her eyes watered, and she blinked it back. "I'll go. I can go. I shouldn't be here. I'm sorry."

"If you go, you won't get to see it grow," the girl reminded her. And something in the air had shifted, the pressure of cold winds eased. The storm averted, June's lungs filled with warm, sweet breath. Now the girl seemed pensive. Almost curious. "Don't you want to see it grow?"

"I don't think I can stay." June dared to dig a hole for the next primrose, trowel making soft, dry sounds. It seemed allowed now. "But I hope they grow."

With bloodless fingers, heart still thrumming, June interred the next primrose under that heavy attention. Until the girl spoke again. "I've buried something too. Near here." There was only a misty silence, mournful and encompassing, like the scent of carnations. "Not everything that gets buried grows."

"Maybe it's not in the right place. It could be getting too much sun. Or it could be wrong for this type of soil. What was it?" June pressed the next bulb into the ground, patted soil around it, left it there to sleep.

A soft sigh, strange and quick, a mature kind of sound. "It was a box."

June's hands, almost of their own accord, froze, picturing that heavy frame, the light china-bone tinkle as it plummeted off the church roof. But her voice stayed light. "Oh yeah? What was in the box?"

There was no answer. Only mournful silence. When she dared to glance at where the feet had been standing, there was nothing, not a single bent blade of grass, much less a person. June raised her head. The garden was empty. It seemed to breathe in and then out with her, and the lake rippled, offering no reply.

✧

The hotter the weather got, and the closer the Fourth of July loomed, the more boats Bolt saw pulling up to the marina. The red water was forgotten. People loaded up with gas, gossiped about where they wanted to park their boats for the big show, and stocked their cubbyholes with sparklers, water bottles, and bags of chips. The water was choppy with activity.

Bolt begged out of the breakfast shift at the Destiny to show up early and help tow the ancient fireworks barge out of its place in one of the enormous marina sheds. The old rust bucket sagged low in the water. It was a sturdy platform, as large as a jumbo houseboat but without the cabin, and weighed so much that it took the entire staff to drag it free of the reedy shed interior. The iron felt as rough as burned tree bark under his hands, and when he looked down into the hull, its pocked bottom was littered with spent fuses, abandoned wrappers, and one or two smashed beer cans.

It had been years since a show of this magnitude had gone off on this side of the lake. Usually, the Charlene marina hosted the annual fireworks spectacle. The county turned out in droves, and boats from all over gathered dangerously close in the curves of the lake for a full night of grilling and fire in the sky. This year, Prosper would be competing for all that traffic, hosting their big show over the dam. Daley had been advertising up a storm, though he was nowhere to be found this morning. Today, they were all working from orders left by the old fireworks man.

Dark spirals of Sammy's hair were plastered to her forehead and the back of her neck. The marina workers were all lugging that barge out, except, of course, Rig, who was pretending to load the ice cooler while really playing around on his phone out of sight.

"Hope you got your tetanus shot this year," he teased after the barge was anchored and Bolt was free to return to the shop for water. "That wreck is rank, man. Lucky Dad isn't here to see it."

Usually it was nice to be inside, sheltered from the heat. And yet, talking to Rig, Bolt wished he could be outside again. "Maybe you should put a firecracker in the pit and blow it up," Bolt suggested.

"Ha. I—" Rig seemed to catch Bolt's tone a moment after. He rolled his eyes. "Didn't know scholarship kids could afford to be so squeamish."

The photos and video Rig had caught on his phone from the

night with the body had frequently appeared in the days since. Bolt couldn't avoid it. Every time his eyes wandered, he caught sight of it beaming out of Rig's phone—the sparks, chunks, horror of it all rushing right back. He couldn't let it go, wrestling again with the urge to tell someone, to call the police, to file a report—except he couldn't. He was in those videos, those graphic pictures. The fight was exhausting. Whenever he thought he'd found resolve and the upper hand, fear latched on and dragged him back, an alligator clamped on his ankle.

"Have you ever seen anything in your life you haven't found hilarious?" Bolt snapped at Rig.

Rig was quiet for a moment, and then Bolt felt a hand on his shoulder, giving it a gentle squeeze. "What's this all about, huh?" Rig asked, voice dropping. Sometimes his rough edges smoothed over when they were alone. "Why are you on my case all of the sudden?" His kindling smile flashed. "Thought we were cool."

Cool. Bolt felt the phantom tingle of the blade moving over his skin and met Rig's strange noncommittal eyes. His attention these days was short-lived, eyes moving like he was constantly seeking, always ravenous for something new to consume. For a while, Bolt had been looking for the boy he used to know and hadn't been able to see him. "I don't know you anymore," Bolt realized.

"Whatever." The smile faded, and Rig's expression shuttered. "I don't know what you're even talking about." He turned and fixated on Sammy, who was watching them from over by the sunglasses. On her face was an unbridled hatred so raw, it was almost embarrassing to look at. "Hey," he snapped. "Stop spying on me all the time. Little slut."

"Don't call her that," Bolt snapped back. "I'm getting real sick of your whole thing."

Rig laughed, but there was no real humor in it. The fissure between them had widened decisively. "Chill, dude. God." He threw up a hand in idle farewell and went out, back to the empty cooler and the bags of ice melting on the dock beyond it.

Bolt glanced at Sammy again and shook his head. Yet, bizarrely, part of him was tempted to run after, catch up to Rig. It was probably what Rig expected him to do; Rig liked to be chased after.

He had been the one to give Bolt his first ride on a Jet Ski, his first taste of wakeboarding, even his first taste of whiskey, stolen from Mr. Daley, hard stuff—uncut and uncensored—that went down like lighter fluid.

Bolt had always loved him a little because of those times. But Rig had cut out a piece of Bolt for himself, for kicks, and wouldn't give it back. It was that lost little piece that kept his feet rooted to the floor; he refused to be the one to budge.

For the rest of his shift, he ignored Rig and Woody altogether, though he felt eyes burning on his back now and again. Sammy stuck close in solidarity, and they washed oil stains until noonlight became afternoon light, the dock gleamed, and they had nothing to do but lean on the rail and rest their tired hands, comparing new freckles on their forearms. The fireworks man had arrived about an hour before and was loading all his packages, glittering like huge pieces of hard candy, onto the barge.

"When do you head back home to your parents?" Bolt asked. "Where are they again?"

"Vicksburg," Sammy supplied, shaking strawberry Pop Rocks

into his hand. She wasn't succeeding quite as much at ignoring the other two, who were goofing off just a few yards away. Any sudden sound made her flinch. "I think my mom is coming in like two or three weeks?" She sighed around the candy sizzling on her tongue. "Nonnie will be really sad when I leave, though. I guess I feel—sort of guilty?"

"They don't want to be out here too?" Bolt asked and tipped his palm into his mouth. Pop Rocks snapped against the insides of his cheeks. The fireworks man picked his way back toward his truck, parked catty-corner in the lot. Rig sat on the side of the dock, dangling his legs in the water, his phone balanced on the wood beside him.

"Parents divorced, and my mom has a boyfriend right now." Sammy's voice was dry. "And my dad has a new family, so...I don't see him much." She raised a pale eyebrow at him.

A fast jab of laughter drew their attention. Woody had caught one of the younger kids, Jamie, by the waistband of his swimsuit and was pulling it down. Jamie wore the awful, shaken smile of the bullied, hoping if he played at being friends, Woody would stop. Rig, grinning, had his phone out and trained on the scene. He liked to play filmmaker, liked to be in the role of spectator, there only to be entertained, performed for. Bolt had seen this kind of arrangement from them before, been at Rig's side when he'd say to Woody, *Hey, wouldn't it be funny?* or, *Dude, what if someone...* And then Woody, the good friend that he was, gave Rig a show.

Sammy didn't seem to consider her next move, even for a moment. What had happened out in the houseboat graveyard had changed something. There was no more spectating in either of them. That naked rage was there in her face again, her empty candy wrapper landing in the lake as she darted toward the tableau. Bolt saw it in slow motion, the stretch of her gangly arm, chipped blue polish flashing on her nails as they fastened around the phone in Rig's hand. He wasn't expecting it, and it slid easily from his grip. He stared at her in shock before something in his expression hardened. He hated her then, maybe always had, and the seething rage now carved itself into every muscle in his face. And that was before she gave her wrist a fearless flick and the phone went soaring in an avian arc into the water.

Sammy didn't wait for a reaction. She turned on her heel and marched back to Bolt. "Come on," she said in a soft huff.

"Hey, you dumb bitch!" Woody howled, as Jamie, forgotten, escaped into the marina. "Did that actually just—"

"You'll die for that," Rig said, very quietly.

Bolt threw a glare back at him, then the finger and followed Sammy away from the marina. "He had it coming," he said as calmly as he could despite the prickle of hostile eyes on their backs.

☙

In the yellowed light of a reproduction Tiffany lamp, Cassie flipped the chest onto its side, reading the grain with her fingers for any groove, any dip, any tear, any hint.

Learn a few tricks, get yourself a nice, well-lit table, and there's nothing broken you can't fix, Grandad would have said if he could have seen her there, fishing for clues.

In addition to the word "Pearl," carved so carefully and deeply that erosion couldn't touch it, she'd found a small chicken-scratch symbol of a fish on the chest June had given her, a craftsman signing their work. A swirling pisces, circling itself in the grain.

Cassie looked at the box, where it sat beside her counter.

I wonder, Grandad would have said, running his hand over the top. Wouldn't that be something?

In the Great Depression, Prosper's name must have tasted like cruel irony, fool's gold to sharecropping families who came for the promise of land no one ever meant to give them, to its inhabitants, who scrambled for work building the dam that would flood their homes. They chopped down oaks and whole pecan orchards; they abandoned fields, houses, the general store, the post office, and the school. Strangers came in droves from across the South, hungry for pearls, for construction work, filling the basin with new blood. The Fischer pearls had passed into legend.

Cassie was tracing the curve of the letter "P" when there was a knock at the door. Through the glass, Lark waited, weighed down by a box of telescopes almost as big as she was.

"We're getting close," she panted when Cassie opened the door for her and held it as she hefted the box to her counter. "Three or four more of the big boxes, maybe." Lark turned, pulling off her hat, the floppy kind that protected her from the sun despite the settling dusk. "Hi, by the way." She gave Cassie a winded smile, fanning her face with the brim. "How are you?"

"Fine—here," Cassie said, beckoning her behind the counter, where Grandad had always kept an ancient metal fan that creaked when it started up, but once it got going, it could, as he put it, blow the lipstick off a lady.

Lark sighed in relief as the fan roared into her face, then fumbled for the notepad sticking out of her back pocket. "Here's some more of my chicken scratch—" She stopped abruptly, hand loose on the pad. Cassie followed her gaze to where the box waited.

Emotions flickered quickly over Lark's face. "So it is here," she said. "June...told me she brought that to you." She seemed to stick on the name, stopped mid-sentence to worry it for a moment too long. Her voice was low, as if she didn't want the chest to overhear. "So no luck with it?"

"A little." Cassie picked up a few loose odds and ends from the collection—binoculars and a sleek industrial silver scope.

Lark gauged her expression, then didn't press, dragging her attention away from the box with difficulty. Somehow she sensed the strange privacy of this thing, the precious quiet of it. She wouldn't prompt Cassie for more information than she felt she could share.

But Lark, who had some of Mitch's gentle containment, was a safe place for this secret. The sunset burned beyond the trees. A rush of boldness caught Cassie, and she said, "I have one idea what's inside."

Lark glanced up again. "Really?"

"It's probably silly, but I feel like I could be on to something. She—June—hasn't come by again. She doesn't want it back, does she?"

Lark shrugged, deflating. "I haven't seen her either." She fingered a small magnifying loop—the kind jewelers held to their eye to appraise diamonds—that hung from her neck by a shimmering chain, and for a tick or two, she seemed lost in thought. But soon she roused herself, and her wry smile returned. "What do you—" Again, Lark was stopped short, head whipping toward the window. The sound had been a sudden sharp crack. A dirty metal collision, just a few feet from them. "That car just ran through your sign," she said.

When Cassie turned to see, Lark's beat-up old Explorer was not the only one in the parking lot. Another car was now catty-corner to it, a brand-new, gleaming white Jeep, its hood spewing angry black smoke from where it had struck the sign. The car was familiar, as was the haggard figure stumbling out of it in the bright backlight of the sunset. Jeff Daley, paying another social call. Except things were different this time. She could tell from the bowed, tense curve of his body, his back bent like a barbed fishhook. No friendly greeting crossed the lot ahead of him. Cassie stood up fast, nodding at Lark to go out rather than let him in. Lark seemed to know too, some instinct passing between them. Cassie locked up quickly, the heavy box and Lark's telescopes safely within.

Lark hovered beside her at the locks, squinting over her shoulder as he approached. His car keys swung loosely from his hand. Something in his expression made her take a step back. "I'm picking up a seriously bad vibe," she muttered.

"Mr. Daley," Cassie called across the gravel, taking a few steps toward him. "I'm sorry, I've just closed."

"Change your mind, Cassie," he said, in a voice slightly too quiet for the distance that still separated him. He might've been talking on the phone or to himself. His eyes didn't meet hers but skittered. "Change. Your. Mind. Change your mind."

Lark seized Cassie's hand, her fingertips cold. "This is not good," she murmured.

"Mr. Daley," Cassie repeated, pressing backward with Lark. Cassie's car was behind the shop. Lark's was ahead. But Daley's car blocked the only narrow exit, pinning them in. "You need to go home. I'm closed."

"You don't listen. Change," Daley growled. Shadows purpled his eyes. "You don't care. The lake. Can't you hear what it wants? Change." His hands fisted. Then he moved fast, no longer walking, charging at them with the force of a battering ram.

Lark yanked Cassie into motion.

They hurried away from him, skidding the bricks of the shop as they rounded it and hurled themselves into the deep shade of the woods. Behind them, the pound of Daley's feet was uneven, a half stumble. An odd gurgling roar ricocheted off the tree trunks.

Cassie kept a grip on Lark's hand, horror piercing her throat at the sound of him at their heels. She could hear his fingertips scrabbling over loose tree bark. There was no time to get to the car. It was like a bad dream. Cassie's ankle wobbled over an uneven divot in the land.

Cassie had lived on the edge of the lake all her life. But she'd never known what it wanted, except for one thing. It was hungry. It wanted and it ate, and when it was done eating, only a husk was left. How long had it been eating at Mr. Daley?

"Where?" she gritted out to Lark, not daring to let go of her.

Lark dodged a monumental fallen trunk, scrabbling downhill through feet of brush. The smell of damp soil, leaf mold, and dry pine needles filled Cassie's nose. Daley was larger than they were and probably stronger, but he wasn't nearly as lithe. "We can lose him." Lark's voice shivered like they ran through arctic winds, not tepid July heat. "I think we can hide if I can—just find—" They were too panicked to stop, but as soon as a particularly fetid crack of lake water appeared through the trees, Lark veered them away and toward the sunset. "See that gravel road?" she hissed. "We'll follow that and—"

"CASSIE, CHANGE YOUR MIND," howled the eaten-up thing that chased them from somewhere beyond the last dip in the land.

Suddenly, Cassie knew where Lark was taking her. "Right. Okay." She charged ahead with one last glance back. Soon the two of them burst from the forest into the clearing that was the houseboat graveyard. Cassie had never explored it herself. She had been too terrified of the lake by the time her classmates wanted to go kiss under the moonlight and old motors. But she knew where those husks were, the huge beached boats rusted and spilling parts into the water, across the concrete of an unused boat launch.

Lark allowed herself half a second's pause, clutching her side as she scanned the skeletal silhouettes. "There," she managed, snatching Cassie's hand again and sprinting for the moldering half-drowned dock. It would be the closest Cassie had been to the water in more than twenty years. But for once, she feared something behind her more.

They tripped over soggy planks. Beneath them, the dock creaked out a series of complaints. Here, above the lake, something smelled of rot, a sickly stench of decay so thick, they nearly gagged as Lark towed Cassie farther in. Something dead was near.

"This one." It was the second boat abandoned here, its hull half encased in dried mud and shallow water. The visible half of its rusting sides were spray-painted with diamond shapes, again and again—eyes.

"Cassie." A voice rang over the graveyard, maybe from the clearing's edge. "CASSIE."

They threw themselves over the rails, then slid through one of the narrow broken windows on their bellies. The close, airless cabin pressed in around them. They stared at each other through the darkness, sucking in panicked gulps of oxygen through their noses.

Outside, heavy footsteps. The crunch of rubber sole on gravel. Cassie shrank in her own skin. Please, the most fragile piece of herself whispered. Please don't see us.

The footsteps lurched. They staggered on metal, on ground again. Then: splashing water, the sound of knees meeting pebbles. Cassie met Lark's eyes, wide and silver in the dark. What was he doing?

Lark glanced at one of the windows that faced out toward the lake. She didn't move right away, charting the steps between her and the glass. It was across what remained of a couch, the seats grayed, speckled with droppings, and gaping open, but soft. She checked Cassie's face again. Then, so quietly, breath held, Lark crept over to peer out, feet silenced on the cushions. Her hand clenched the magnifier around her neck.

Cassie followed on her hands and knees, using Lark as her lighthouse, careful not to kick the beer bottles and spray paint cans. Cassie pulled herself up to crouch beside Lark, her grip too tight on the edge of the window. Together, they looked.

Jeff Daley was prostrate in the brown shallows of the lake, half-submerged, his golf shoes ruined, and slacks soaked through in the slime that built up on the water in these stagnant corners. Beside Cassie, Lark's throat worked silently. Daley dipped his head below the surface, remained there for long seconds, and then lifted enough to breathe. Again. Again. His face was rapturous and slack. He gathered another mouthful of the lake and swallowed it, his eyelids fluttering.

Lark raised her hand, the jeweler's loupe still clasped in it. With a meaningful look at Cassie, she raised the magnifier to her eye and focused on Daley again. For a moment, she was still, as airless as this boat's rib cage where they hid. Then she shifted her view a millimeter and started, throwing a hand over her mouth to silence the gasp.

Daley was unchanged, his communion with the water timeless. His chase was apparently forgotten. Wordless, Lark gestured to Cassie and held out the loupe to her. Cassie took it, confused, because this was meant for delicate, close work. But she lifted the curved lens to her eye and looked through the glass.

All the breath left her body.

Through the lens, the world was bent on the edges, and Daley was bent too in his rapture, his legs and hips swept up and out of the frame in a strange optical illusion, like he was being eaten feetfirst by a python. But Cassie only cared about one thing, and it wasn't Jeff Daley. It was past him, it was in the water, it was out there.

She was there. Maybe twenty feet away, she stood in the waist-deep shallows lit by a broken knife of moonlight. She wore a clean summer dress that floated and billowed, ballooned around her middle. Wet hair fell across her forehead in loose curls, and even without light, Cassie would have known her, because only she could rip her breath away like that. Only she could make Cassie want to turn and see Mom standing on the porch behind her, hands on her hips, ready to face the world with her curlers in.

She was exactly the same as she had been when Cassie was five, except Cassie had never seen her so removed, so full of rage that it radiated off her. But it was her—Cassie's heart knew it, torn between wanting to call to her and wanting to shut her eyes and never open them again. It was her. There was the tiny dimple on her cheek, the shoulders that had seemed strong enough to carry the world. There, the face, the hair, the hands, the frame Cassie had seen thrash facedown under the dock as she drowned.

Watching with baleful eyes as Daley gulped lake water was Catfish.

CHAPTER SIXTEEN

HE FEAR HAD LARK BY THE THROAT. SHE COULDN'T get enough air. Her heart, the rush of blood in her veins, was too loud. Her hands were miles away, but somehow, he was *right here*. She could almost taste the silt of the lake water on her own tongue. And that woman—or girl, really, just on the threshold of adulthood—who stood in the magnified swirl of the jeweler's loupe. Even after Lark lowered the loupe and it fell cold and heavy against her sternum, she felt her there. The girl, so full of quiet wrath, her grim, devouring disappointment leaking out over this entire lake.

They huddled there, bodies cramping.

Eventually, Daley pulled himself up and sniffed the air, head nodding this way and that. Lark clamped a hand over her own mouth, glancing at Cassie's frozen face. A muscle in her thigh seized. If he found them now, the girl in the loupe would watch him smother them in the shallow algae. But Daley did no more than nod, nod, nod. Then he was turning, stumbling a step or two on the shore. Without another word or a single glance, he shambled away. The footprints he left behind swelled across the pavement until they were as wide as craters.

Cassie was taut as if she'd never move or speak again. The smell of death was heavier than ever, and now it was too dark to find its source.

Finally, when the pain from crouching was too intense to endure a second longer, they crept off the boat. Lark's legs wobbled as she stepped back onto land. Her adrenaline had leaked away, and now she felt emptied, too exhausted for tears. It took everything in her to open her mouth and force a few words out. They didn't sound right—tilting, hoarse. "What should we do?"

"I don't know. Not the shop. Not home. I don't know where he could have gone." Cassie stood facing the water, hands clasped on her elbows. Then—"Mitch," Cassie said in a broken tone.

"Right." It took Lark a long time to find her phone. Her fingers shook so badly, it was hard to find his number. It rang a few times, Lark urging him silently to answer.

"Hey, Cuz," Mitch said. She heard the boisterous sounds of a packed Grand Destiny through the speaker. "Busy night over here. What's up?"

"Can you come get Cassie and I?" she managed, her voice still odd in her own ears. "We're—at the houseboat graveyard."

"What?" His anxiety couldn't touch her through the blanket of shock. "What happened?"

"I'll explain when you get here," she said. Cassie nodded. "Hurry up. It has been a really fucked-up night."

The sounds of jubilant early Fourth of July celebrations were already gone, which meant Mitch was rushing out to his truck. "I'm coming. Just stay put, okay?"

"See you soon." Lark felt cold all over. More than anything, she wanted to get away from the overpowering aroma of death. They walked to the edge of the clearing to wait.

"You saw her. Didn't you?" Cassie asked after a few minutes. There were a few scratches on her arms from branches. "You saw her."

Lark nodded, swallowing. When she saw Cassie's expression, she nodded more forcefully. "Cassie, who—"

But the headlights of Mitch's truck whipped around the last bend in the road and roared to a stop in front of them. He jumped out of the driver's side and hurried over. "What are you doing out here? Are you okay?" Though he addressed Lark, his eyes kept fixing on Cassie, examining her for any sign of damage, and she tore her eyes off the water to turn into his space.

Lark just headed for the truck. "We have to call the sheriff."

The next few hours were a miserable blur. Cyril, the sheriff's deputy, came to the Grand Destiny to do the interview, while Lark and Cassie sipped too-hot coffee and Aunt Valerie buzzed like an entire wasp's nest around them, running between the late-dinner guests and where they sat on the slouchy couches in the lobby. Valerie scolded Cyril when he didn't seem to grasp what they were saying.

Mitch had spent an hour or two calling every neighbor he could think of, but the few who were answering their phones hadn't seen hide nor hair of Jeff Daley. "I'll put the notice out and try to get a few more guys down here tonight," Cyril said at last, tugging his belt higher on his belly. There was a strange almost reluctance in his manner, in the slow notes he took as they spoke. "You ladies just stay in, all right?"

"They'll stay here tonight," Aunt Valerie clipped out.

Tucked up in one of the Grand Destiny's double beds, the scratchy comforter under her chin, Lark clutched her phone against her chest, finger hovering over her contacts. More than anything, she wanted to call June. She wanted June here. But this wasn't the place nor the time. She was overloaded. Sighing, she laid the phone on the nightstand and turned to watch Cassie settling into the other bed. She'd looked for her brother, Bolt, but he wasn't in his room. So now here they were, just the two of them again, the horrible huge experiences of the night hovering somewhere near the ceiling.

"Who was that?" Lark murmured at last. "I don't mean Daley. His boat's right down from ours. The—the one in the water."

Cassie was swallowed in a shirt that wasn't hers, with the University of Central Arkansas seal emblazoned on it, sitting on the bedspread and picking at a loose string. "Catfish." She had let her hair down into absentminded muddy waves. "I was always told she was my imaginary friend. But you saw her."

Lark nodded against the pillow. "It was the loupe. The spy-glasses…let me see what's just under the surface of this place." She laughed brokenly. "I didn't believe it at first, but they reveal *real* things. The truth." She paused a moment, choosing her words carefully. "Do you know why Catfish was there?"

"I never know." Cassie closed her eyes, bracing her forehead on one pale hand. "But I don't want it. I spent so long trying to tell people, and no one believed me. I didn't want to wonder why anymore. But she's been here all my life. Probably longer. Even if I haven't been looking, she's still been there."

"I don't understand," Lark said gently. "Who is she?"

"She helped teach me to swim," Cassie replied. "But when I

was young, I realized there was something very wrong. I haven't wanted to admit it, but I've known she's dead for a long time. Still here, but dead."

Lark wasn't sure what to say to that. She thought of Daddy again, of how far he'd been willing to go to see the very wrong things here.

"Why me?" Cassie's gaze strayed to the window, even if the lake beyond was hidden behind curtains. "I didn't ask for this. I don't want it." In one sharp movement, she slipped off the bed and crossed to the window before snatching the curtain—but she couldn't seem to pull it back. Her fingers twitched and that was all. "No. Tonight has been more than enough." She let go, smoothing the fabric against the sill and sides until not even moonlight could creep through.

∽

The night before the Fourth of July, June dreamed of her garden, of the one-winged lion raising his head and blinking up at the sunlight, a crown of larkspur growing between his ears. It followed her into the morning, the soft, oily scent of pollen and summertime. When she woke, the first thing she saw was crimson blooming in her hair, and on instinct, she dug for the scissors in her bedside drawer.

But she felt a strange frustrated resistance to cutting them out. She wanted to touch them or take them somewhere safe, where she could replant them in a dirt bed. Poppies would be lovely in the garden.

No. She was being silly. June cut them and swept them under her pillow.

Aunt Eliza was waiting for her downstairs, lemon poppyseed muffins cooling on the counter. The Fourth of July, it turned out, meant loading into her Accord for a trip into Charlene. Charlene was a charmer, perfect for magazine covers of quaint Americana. Healthy old trees lined the streets, where the peaceful similitude of single-family homes with blue doors and flags on the porches was occasionally broken with big historical houses, the kind with wraparound balconies and gingerbread trimming.

The town was also full of people, residents and weekenders there for Ranalli's famous linguine, and they were lucky to find a spot in the square when an SUV pulled out in front of Kimmy's Kornbread Sandwiches. Eliza whipped into the free space.

At the apex of the square stood a big wedding-cake church. GOD BLESS AMERICA! read the marquee. The church's high steeple and stained glass in every window made Eliza's chapel seem small and a little country in comparison.

"They have a cute church," June said, unbuckling her seat belt. "Ever wish you were there instead?"

"This isn't where our roots are," Aunt Eliza replied. "Whole different ball game on this side of the lake. Now come on."

They dropped by the famous general store (since 1921!), which sold Arkansas quartz, jujube divinity candy, and five-cent drip coffee. In honor of the Fourth, there was a special America-themed section where they picked up glow sticks and tiny American flags by the counter.

June squeezed past a couple of women in matching stars-and-stripes visors who were leaning on the counter to talk to the man counting change at the register.

"Heard about poor Jeff Daley?" one asked.

"Yes. Damn shame. The sheriff was calling around about him," the store manager replied.

"I hope Jeff keeps his head down until it all blows over," the other replied. "So sad; the whole fireworks show was his idea. My Stan says—"

June grabbed two huge Uncle Sam top hats—and a bright red feather boa with sparkles woven into the feathers—and wriggled back through the crowd. She found Aunt Eliza again, greeting her by plopping one on her head.

Eliza turned to give her an amused arched eyebrow.

"Hey," June asked, draping the boa around her neck. "I heard some people talking about Jeff Daley. He's that rich guy, the marina guy. Right?"

"He is. I got a call about that this morning." Tension infected Eliza's easy demeanor. "Asked me to check the church for him. Didn't sound good at all."

"Is he *in* trouble? Or is *he* the trouble?" June had seen him around a little, and it was difficult to imagine a man with such a huge boat and manicured life hiding in the pews of Eliza's church. "Probably both."

Eliza nodded. "Listen, I don't want you running off and ending up in the woods late at night again. All right? There are strange people around. That firecracker man, now Jeff Daley. Real strange people."

Maybe because she knew him now—or maybe because June couldn't count the times when she'd been the "strange" one—but irritation flared. What did Eliza know? But June let it go. Eliza wasn't her mother.

They picked up three flavors of frozen custard in big gallon containers and drove home at breakneck speeds to get them into Aunt Eliza's deep freeze.

No matter what was going on with the marina owner, the fireworks show was all paid for and would still go off. As the sun set, Eliza and June drove the half mile down to the shoreline nearest to the dam, a little camping spot with a green stretch of land and a little dock. They lined up on the edge of the water for the big show.

People were already milling along the bank. Families were having picnics at the tables dotting the lawn. A kid popped the bottom out of his miniature bag of potato chips, his brother giggling and swiping for the first chip. Speedboats idled in the shallows. In the distance, the skiers risked the wild churn of the late-afternoon water. Eliza waved to a parishioner bobbing nearby in a fat banana boat. Every so often, someone screamed with delight.

Eliza cracked open a pair of Shiner Bock, and they lounged in their deck chairs, the last of the sun tingling on June's bare legs. She pointed her toes at the lake, and the water glittered.

"See if Lark wants to watch with us," Eliza suggested, clinking their bottles. She'd been wanting June to bring Lark over for dinner ever since Eliza picked June up from Lark's houseboat that night that felt so long ago now, the night they met. Eliza had brought a cooler of beer and several extra chairs in case company happened to appear.

The *Big Dipper* wasn't out with the other boats gliding on the water, blue canvases billowing. Lark never took it out of the dock; its engines might not even run. She was probably in its depths with only telescopes for companions. "Yeah," June said, tipping her beer back. "She won't want to."

"Honey." Eliza huffed, and the mouth of her beer bottle hummed. "I don't know where you got it in your head that you aren't good for people."

"It's more like what I've been told. Over. And over." June shut her eyes, the sun leaving a burning imprint of the lake and sky on her eyelids. "We barely know each other."

Eliza didn't push it—this was one of her gifts. Conversations with her could feel significant without turning tense. She knew when to engage and when to let the quiet speak. Endless commercials played on a nearby stereo. "Your mama called me the other day. I think she was checking on you, mainly."

June hadn't spoken to her in all the time she'd been here, hadn't wanted to bear the brunt of telling her, *Hey, guess what, Mom? I screwed up again!* "What did you tell her?"

Eliza smiled. "I told her about all the work you've been doing for that old cemetery." She crossed her ankles in the grass. "I invited her up for the day, but she had to work. I think she'd like to hear from you, though."

June hummed noncommittally. "I didn't know you knew what I was doing in the cemetery."

"How could I miss that smell of wisteria sneaking in my room? All those flowers are keeping me up at night." Eliza tipped her beer idly. "You have the greenest thumb I've ever—"

"Hey, preach!" A man called from down the shore, a wide grin on his face. "Come see the baby."

"Y'all brought her down?" Eliza bounded up in spry delight, patting June on the shoulder. "I'll be right back."

June stood and waded into the water with her beer. It chattered around her ankles, and a pair of Jet Skis whizzed through adjacent coves, leaving high watery tails in their wake. The water nearest to the dam was empty, except for one platform barge only tethered to land by a long portable aluminum walkway, the kind that could be easily folded and carried off. It was empty. Except for one solitary body.

Jack stood on its back. Around him was a whole arsenal of rockets stocked on temporary shelves and piled around his ankles. Between his fingers was the stub of a cigarette, which glowed in a low, irregular breeze. He seemed to feel her gaze and turned his eyes on her, as neutral as a gravedigger. Then his lips quirked in recognition, and he waved her over.

Curiosity prickling at her neck, June climbed onto the walkway and walked down, steps hollow, until she was far out over water and close to the dam. The sounds of all that summer fun felt deafening, an echo chamber of sound and fury. She paused at the edge of his barge, Eliza just out of sight. The fireworks collection was crouched on the barge and ready to leap. Sweat trickled down the back of June's neck.

"Good night for fireworks," she said. "Even if your benefactor is MIA."

Jack nodded, surveying her as he had the last drag of his cigarette. He flicked the butt into the water. "I came here before, did I tell you that? Tore the whole place to shreds last time. Seems like the aftershocks still get to people. It's a little in everybody tonight."

June curled her toes against the edge of the dock. "When was that?"

Jack laughed shortly. "Ages ago now." He gestured to the tricks arrayed around him in the pocked old hull. "See anything you like?"

"I don't know what I'm looking at," June admitted. "But that red rocket is pretty cool."

He nodded approvingly. "I know a kindred spirit when I see one. That one's a whole nest of snakes," he said. "For the grand finale." He stood aside, offering her a place beside him. "Help me with the show. I'll show you what to do with that spark in you."

She never could resist an opportunity so strange and once in a lifetime. She stepped forward.

Jack smiled. He unhooked them from the dock, and they began their long cruise into the open water.

ᏆᎧ

"Not long now," Valerie called from the back of the rusty old party barge, adjusting her visor over her eyes to combat the fierce sunset over the dam. Diego sat close beside her. She rummaged in their cooler. They'd expected to have Mitch and Valerie's niece Lark along as well, but with everything that had happened—just the thought of it, stories about Mr. Daley that turned Bolt's stomach, too awful to be true and too bizarre to be lies—it had ended up being a much smaller crowd. Cassie hadn't come, of course. It was only the memory of her expression after last night that convinced Bolt Mr. Daley had done what they said he had.

"Y'all want a Coke?" Valerie called.

"Yes, please," Sammy called back from where she perched beside Bolt on the front cushions, opening her hands for the catch.

Bolt took a deep breath. Out there, no one seemed to notice the founder of the feast was at large somewhere, whereabouts unknown. Jeff Daley was missing, but the air smelled like patriotism: some combination of sweat, sunscreen, and the meat that sizzled on a hundred charcoal grills. It was dusky, and the lake was all chop as countless boats laced over one another's wakes, idling into position for the big display. Valerie and Diego's swan paddleboats were all under sail with guests, gliding through the Grand Destiny's little harbor to face the marina. Fishing boats—mostly the rented ones, out on the water for a day only—had already returned from the shallow coves with their catches. They anchored down together, so little space between them that they brushed sides. After the rented boats and cigarette boats came the weekenders, true cruisers, and speedboats polished to a shine. The men who had driven them propped hairy feet on their steering wheels and toasted their Coronas against the setting sun. Prosper was a cacophony of competing radios, iPhones plugged into speaker systems, children shouting. Sparkles erupted at random across the city of vessels, giving the breeze a tang like gunpowder. Some competing fireworks displays were already crackling away beyond Prosper's borders.

Anchors drifted into the depths. Party barges, Jet Skis, and speedboats were rafted together into floating potlucks. Some had come in their houseboats, sharing deviled eggs on their upper decks. People dove in or floated in big fancy inflatables. A girl astride a unicorn. Two kids astride an oversize watermelon slice. People hollered for sunscreen, tossing it from boat to boat. Friends visiting other boats swam between them and in the watery canals that formed naturally between prows; others simply clasped their Tupperware of sandwiches tight and leaped short distances from deck to deck.

Even in the years of Charlene fireworks shows, Bolt had never seen anything like the congregation of boats and people in front of the Great Damnation, this impromptu floating city—Venice built in a day. In the distance, banked against the marina itself, was the platform barge. Valerie and Diego had pulled out their ancient pontoon boat, loaded it with snacks, and chugged out to the chaos themselves, joining the crowd of people waiting eagerly to see the fireworks Jeff Daley had paid for but would not see. Soon boats had tied up on either side, so the party barge was wedged into a long row, just one tile in an eclectic mosaic.

Sammy cracked her Coke and took a drink. They'd been passing a flask, and some of its contents joined the soft drink in the can.

"I don't want to stay here," Bolt said to her, and she nodded shortly. She probably still pictured the horror of the corpse, blown to unrecognizable bits in the shallows. Bolt certainly did.

"Let's hook our nose up to your back," Patty, a Grand Destiny neighbor and owner of a tiny fishing boat, suggested to Valerie as she offered her a piece of lemon meringue pie over the side. "We've got a nearly unbroken connection between banks!" Insanity. That was the entire width of this finger of the lake. Bolt gazed down the thread of connected prows but couldn't discern the end in the deepening evening.

"Don't tell all those folks about this pie, Pat," Valerie warned, producing a plastic fork from somewhere. "I didn't bring enough for five hundred."

"Seems like everybody's been sharing something around," Patty said around a lemony bite. "Folks are acting a little funny. And not like ha-ha funny, either."

"We're going to see how far this thing runs," Bolt told her.

"Okay, but be polite and say hello to people whose boats you're walking all over," Valerie bossed. They'd know just about everyone they encountered anyway. "Ask permission. And don't fall in. And be back before we head in, or I'll worry."

Bolt took off, and though he pushed Jeff Daley, pushed the body, pushed Rig, into deep pockets in his mind, some part of him already worried.

⁊

Lark sat on one of the Grand Destiny's benches, knees pulled up to her chest. She'd told Aunt Valerie she wasn't up to the celebration, not after what had happened. Every so often she saw Daley again in her mind, his crooked footsteps and bloodshot eyes; she could still hear the howl through the trees as he'd chased them. But now the quiet of this place pressed in on every side. Cassie and Mitch had gone back up to her property earlier in the day. Lark felt the excitement of the holiday flowing away from her as everyone else departed for the marina. She could almost see it: webs of lightness that tangled around the happy huddles of revelers, processing out to the show in boats of every size. The air hummed with engines.

Other years, Lark's family would've packed Skip-Bo cards, cheese, crackers, and crispy pecan cookies. She would have worn bangles jingling with stars and stripes and painted her toenails. Doris Ann would sit at the front of the speedboat, ears blowing back in the breeze off the lake. That was her spot. Lark's spot was right in front of the driver, so she could grin back at him, squeeze her eyes shut in the spray off the lake. As the boat sped up, its nose rose high enough that Daddy would have to stand from the driver's seat to see where they were going while they cruised across the lake toward the Charlene side, where the fireworks were usually set off.

Once they were close, they couldn't go very fast, not with the water so crowded. Still, the chop would make them hop like bullfrogs out into the fray, hard landings rattling Lark's teeth as she flipped through their CDs for an alternative fireworks soundtrack to the patriotism blaring over the radio channel. Maybe she'd choose ELO or they'd have an ABBA Fourth of July. Beach Boys?

Tipsy E Dockers would wave to them, and they'd keep their eyes peeled for Aunt Valerie and Diego, maybe hook up with them or a few neighbors if they got there early enough. Dad always brought extra telescopes, extra binoculars to pass around between boats. They'd take a preshow dip, floating with drinks in cozies, waiting for night to fall. It was the only time of year when Lake Prosper had anything in common with New York City. Laughing, catching sight of Daddy's face lit up like Times Square, huge coronas of fire reflected in the pools of his glasses, then fading, sparks doused in water...

Down on the Grand Destiny's dock, Mitch's fishing boat bobbed, almost expectant. Its prow slapped the surface of the lake. *C'mon!* It urged. *You'll miss it! It's never been so close before!*

It was hard to imagine feeling any lonelier than she did right there, sitting with her forehead pressed into her kneecaps, outside a dark motel room, facing the wrong way. Here, Jeff Daley could be roving around just beyond her view, out there in the woods. She was on her own. She should have gone with her family just to avoid this solitude. Anxiety crawled up her arms and legs, and she rubbed at them frenetically.

The Destiny had plenty of boats Diego rented out for little pleasure cruises. They were small but far nicer than her little dinghy, with a real motor and cushioned seats. She wouldn't have to talk to anyone. No one would see her there. And most of all, no one could touch her out on the water. No one could get at her out in the boat. She needed that breeze. She needed to move.

Sighing, feeling the full force of the Earth's gravity, Lark walked down to the dock.

CHAPTER SEVENTEEN

OSSING THE FLASK BACK AND FORTH, BOLT AND Sammy wandered their way along another boat and another, where some adults that Sammy vaguely knew were giving out glow sticks.

"You're getting so big!" one of them exclaimed about Bolt. "Isn't he getting so big?" Once they paid the toll of polite conversation, they hopped along to the next boat over. Now they found themselves amid the marina kids. The adults were inside a fancy glassed living room, sipping a greenish wine, but the deck they had stumbled upon was laden with teenager smell and sound. There was a waterslide off the back, and two girls sat halfway down, complaining at one of the boys who had barricaded the way with his body; there was a discrete cooler of beers on the boat's tail, and their coworkers were making clean work of it. The girls managed to dislodge the slide blocker, and he backflipped into the lake.

"Hey," Bolt said. "Isn't this the boat where those twins from E Dock live?"

"Yeah, it's usually parked three slips down from Nonnie." Sammy scratched her nose, giving the deck a bored appraisal before searching through the darkness for the fireworks barge.

"It's probably about to start. Looks like somebody's helping him." Sure enough, even from way out here, Bolt could see two shadows standing together under the work lamp.

Before they could investigate it further, Jamie from the marina found them, excitedly towing them to the beer cooler.

"Dude, we're putting bets on what Daley did to get the sheriff after him," Jamie said. "Want to put five dollars on skinny-dipping outside Lou's slip?"

What would they bet on if they knew the truth? For a vicious moment, Bolt wanted to throw down what he knew and spoil the game.

"No." Bolt grabbed a beer and shoved his way back out of the circle. By the time he was a beer and a couple of shots down, he'd forgotten the way back across all the boats, and Sammy's laughter was high and off-key.

It was truly dark now, sparklers blazing all through the rows of boats in front of the dam. Several fire boats, their huge hoses at the ready, puttered slowly through the crowds, vigilant for hazards. It was by far the most dangerous night of the year. They'd hand out tickets for boats without their lights on, without enough life jackets for every person present, with parties too wild for safe sailing. At least they'd do their best. It was mostly anarchy out on the black water. This floating city, a little civilization that rose and fell in a few hours' time, could only really exist here, now, under a sky of red stars.

Bolt felt cold, suddenly, exposed to the air—and something else. The weight of someone's eyes, of intention, settled like a hand on his throat. He looked away from the sky to scan the deck.

Across the boat, Rig was watching them. Beside him, Woody

picked at the label of a beer bottle. Rig looked unsurprised to be caught staring, as if it were all prearranged. Bolt raised an eyebrow at him, and almost dutifully, Rig and Woody shuffled through the crowd to them.

"Any news about your dad?" Sammy asked, her voice hoarse and cautious. The threat was still very much in the air between them.

"No sign of him." Rig snorted, glancing at her and away, as if she were merely beneath his notice again. "He's been a real freak lately. Just stares at the lake all day and talks to himself. Seems like he's gotten into some psychedelic mushrooms or some shit." He glanced at Bolt. "But I tried to tell you that."

"Don't blame this on me," Bolt replied. "He's the one who attacked Cassie."

"Your sister—first she just sits on that land and refuses to hear him out," Rig huffed out. "Now she's spreading lies about him. And you just let her, like my dad hasn't been a goddamn father to you and helped you so damn much. It's honestly pretty fucking unbelievable." Rig was drunk, though it wouldn't be obvious to anyone who didn't know him. It wasn't much more than a tiny flush in his cheeks and slight brightening in his eyes. He had a hand shoved almost awkwardly into his pocket.

"You think I wanted this to happen?" Bolt snapped. "He attacked her. Not the other way around."

"That makes no sense," Rig spat. "She's making it up. God. I should've known you'd take her side."

"Cassie doesn't lie." Bolt felt Sammy's hand slip into his and squeeze. This whole conversation felt useless. "I think Valerie wanted us back before the…"

"Oh no," Rig said, eyes sharp as a cat's. Rage boiled off his skin. "You'd be missing out."

"Shut up, shut up. Y'all." One of the twins frantically tuned the boat radio. "It's starting." He got it to the shared channel, and the national anthem blared through a thousand boat speakers around them. Older folks had their hands over their hearts. Lights switched off on every side, the night growing increasingly profound.

And the ramparts we watched were so gallantly...

"You'd be missing out." Rig was not one to be deterred. Woody, usually sickly, practically glowed. He rubbed his hands together with a sort of grim resolve.

And the rockets' red glare...

Sammy was speaking. Still. Barely audible under the tinny sound of airwaves. "What are you talking about?"

...Bombs bursting in air...

Rig drew his hand out of his pocket, and Sammy's nails cut hard into Bolt's skin. Her face was illuminated a ghastly green in the light of the first firework, which had just erupted in the air above the dam, hovering over it. It flared ten times bigger than the sun and just as bright. Horrible radiance pooled in an emerald glow on the knife in Rig's hand.

ɕ

Standing on the barge with the fireworks man, June had never burned so brightly. She was right under the fireworks, safety abandoned for exhilaration, only she didn't feel the danger. Not when she was a part of it.

"Celestial bodies." Jack laughed, fixing the second firework into one of his launch cannons. The air was thick and stinging after only one shot. The anthem boomed around them. "Astronomers watch the constellations. We make them." The fireworks lit up gold on his skin.

What did people once call him? For a moment, June didn't remember, but it came back to her. Yellow Jack. His face was very wry, eyes like two little coffee beans in a weathered ageless face. Almost like the fishermen she'd met on the docks. Were they out here tonight somewhere? The thought would have sobered her if she hadn't discovered that smoke gave more life than oxygen and fire filled her better than water could.

The air was so hot, it was hard to even consider flicking the lighter on. June had sweat running between her shoulder blades. Sparks fell close; one left a dark singe on her shorts. The flashes were so bright, she couldn't see the boats or the shore anymore. But they didn't look like fireworks, in their concentric circles and sparkles. Instead, they screamed like voices and flew on lightning wings, and sometimes, in the flash, she saw things like mouths grinning, faces in screaming rictus. Instinct should have urged her to duck, but they couldn't touch her. "They look—" Everything tasted like smoke. "Why do they look like that? What are these?"

"Lost souls?" His eyes were smoldering cinders, all the light from the spent fireworks catching in them. "Burnt offerings?" He touched the next fuse, catching it between thumb and finger, and snapped once, sharply. A flash—when he withdrew, flame was crawling quickly up the fuse to the gunpowder. June was too shocked to look away as it rocketed into the sky.

All her life, she thought she'd known chaos, thought she'd felt it. But it had been woodsmoke, and this was the bonfire, flavored with kerosine.

"Look at them. Bright enough to illuminate every dark corner. Wake the dead." The fireworks man just winked at her, and with nothing but the tips of his fingers, he lit another. "The fire pulls back the curtain. The world is full of things most people never see."

Fireworks shouldn't move like that, in all directions, swooping down toward the boats and up into the sky, snapping at the people below. But each lighting lit something in her as well.

The fireworks man lit another fuse by licking the end; his skull glowed under his skin. He turned to June, offering a challenge. How hungry she was for a challenge.

June inched closer and then fell to her knees beside the fuse of the next firework, a bright red rocket with a Tasmanian devil grinning at her on the side.

"Go on. You can do it," Jack said.

So, matches abandoned, June touched the end of the fuse herself, taking dry twine between her thumb and finger. With nothing more than a twist of her fingers, it sparked, a hot flash, and she yanked back with ash left behind on her nails. Flame, born of her own hand, greedily devoured the fuse, and the rocket blasted into the sky, then burst overhead.

June swiped soot off her forehead. She reached out, bare-handed, and lit another.

꼭

One moment, Bolt was pushing Rig, who laughed a cold, miserable laugh, close and beery in his ear, and maybe because of the booze, it was sort of funny, the way he looked lit up in red and gold. It was sort of funny, their usual boyish wrestling, until the blade stung Bolt's wrist.

Bolt snapped his wrist back. "Put that away."

The fireworks had brought a change over everyone around them, a strange electricity flowing. Above them, artificial thunder crashed, and cheers soared from the water. One of the Pickle sisters stooped, cupping her hands to gather the light-filled lake water and draw it to her face. Something in Woody's expression and the way, as one, he and Rig both suddenly lunged turned the game sour. Bolt and Sammy—with the instinct of a startled flock—retreated down the deck in a drunken skitter, Bolt stumbling against a foam noodle.

"Come on." Woody snorted, ducking in and back, watching Sammy's every twitch. A green firework crackled over his face. "Lighten up, bitches."

"Go to hell. You're such stupid assholes," Sammy panted, her eyes darting. She feinted, then leaped onto the deck of the cruiser, hooking her legs into its rails to hoist herself up. Woody made a grab for her ankle, a move that could've ended in a split skull for Sammy if he'd caught her.

Bolt vaulted over the rail after her—Rig snagged his shorts, and Bolt twisted back to glare. There were adults everywhere, people he knew everywhere. Why did no one do anything? But all eyes were fixed overhead, on the dazzle above them. With the fireworks erupting in the sky, they were as good as alone.

"Careful." Rig's eyes flashed gold in the light, and he bared his teeth. Metal flashed—hot pain as the knife nicked across his knee. He kicked Rig's shoulder, launching over the rail and dashing after Sammy's dark hair. He caught up at the edge of the boat, glancing back to see Rig scrambling up after them. Eyes flashing, Rig mimed dragging the knife across his throat. No one noticed them, not a single head turned as the fireworks captivated every eye beyond their chase.

"Come on," Bolt said, heart thrumming in his ears. Sammy and Bolt pushed through a crowd of retirees until they could spring across the gap to the next boat amid adults, one of whom chuckled indulgently. A champagne cork soared past Bolt's ear, the party cheering as foam hit the deck. Rig was right there, just a few bodies away—there was a sharp scream from a bystander as his blade grazed flesh. A plastic champagne flute hit the deck and bounced.

In the chaos, Bolt pushed the houseboat's sliding back door open, and Sammy darted past him inside.

"Lost his damn mind," she panted as they crept through the dim interior. It was a thawing icebox, a boat usually kept freezing cold by an air conditioner and now, away from the dock, reached summer temperatures. The fireworks were more a feeling in here, a hard rumble in the pit of their stomachs as they slid over hardwood, past a faded leather couch, the unwashed dishes from lasagna, a strawberry shortcake melting in its dish on the table. Picture frames hung askew on the walls. "Him and everybody else on this lake. Should we just hide in—"

"Get down," Bolt whispered as the door opened a second time, the noise of the night pouring in. They hit the deck, covered by the kitchen island. Some patriotic country music anthem pounded along with the show.

"Nice place." Rig snorted, flipping his knife. He picked up an ashtray resting beside the captain's wheel and turned it idly in his hands.

Sammy glanced at Bolt, her face ashen. Her eyes skittered

down the houseboat. They had to keep moving, or he'd find them there.

Rig whistled a note or two, hefting the ashtray. It was a heavy geode, irregularly shaped, purple crystals sprouting from dark rock. "Let's see. Maybe…" He hurled it, and the ashtray skidded across the island and gashed Sammy's shoulder on the way to the floor, inches from her skull. She gasped, crumpling in pain.

Rig threw himself through the space between them, the knife glinting, and some animal instinct inside Bolt snapped awake. He kicked a barstool out, and it clattered on the kitchen tiles. Rig tripped and stumbled, his face in a horrible twist, his curses lost in the words of the radio and the explosions above, and Sammy was already up, grimacing, as they sprinted through the dock.

"My dad loves you. Should hear how he talks you up to me all the damn time." A vase of blue glass shattered against the wall, tiny splinters spitting at Bolt as they ripped the door out of the way and ran back into the night.

Outside, the fireworks boomed without pause, a row of white flares shooting across the sky. Their light, erratic, flashing on the offbeats from every side, cast the whole scene into bizarre monochromatic animation. The boat, its crowd, their pursuit, might as well have been a theme park fun house ride, the people only automatons and the action only pretend. Bolt saw, briefly, something like a dragon outlined in smoke, a deadly, twisting shape that he didn't believe.

Sammy and Bolt wriggled through a pair of women, slipping on something spilled as they ran down the pitch-black path illuminated in short bursts, strobe light revelations. Bolt gripped

Sammy's hand, and they sprang to a speedboat that nearly cap-sized under them, bucking under their weight.

"Watch it," the captain griped under his Razorback cap, but they were already gone, hurtling onto the back deck of a house-boat. No sign of Rig, not anywhere.

Far behind, Bolt could just hear Woody's half-hysterical guffaw. "Y'all are sunk!"

A line of blood from Sammy's shoulder ran down to her wrist.

"You okay?" Bolt panted.

Sammy huffed, not quite an affirmative.

He threw a glance back just as Woody, three boats back, shoved someone into the water in his rush. Bolt and Sammy bounded over a low back gate and through moldy deck furniture clustered around a tube, abandoned because the inhabitants were in the water. Nothing but empty beer cans watched the two of them scurry across the narrow deck, Woody disappearing from sight as they rounded another corner, past burgundy canvas toward the stairs—

Rig waited around the corner, knife flashing violent orange. A firework screamed overhead, drowning out his words, but Bolt read them anyway. "Got you."

ↂ

It was exhilarating, June laughing in the face of fire, standing on that platform, daring sparks to rain down and burn her. The whole barge was covered in soot, a fine layer of Pompeii dust, and Jack had unending tricks to show her.

All these were his little packages of chaos. How had he done it? How had he harnessed that thing, the mad whirling dervish inside, and found ways to channel it? He had wrapped living flames in paper, and it had held, until now, until he set them free. June thirsted for the answer. She could touch his works, even light them with nothing but her own skin, but she couldn't understand how he had done it or how to do it herself.

As if he could sense her longing, Jack smiled at her with ashy teeth and stroked two fingers along the back of a Black Cat firework. It charged into the sky in gleeful self-destruction.

More. Then more. And more.

June grabbed the fuse of a Roman candle, dug her thumbnail in, and jerked—the fuse caught, and the candle vaulted to the stars, lightning trailing behind.

"Somebody's gonna die tonight," he mused. "Wonder who?"

The words broke through the adrenaline so violently, at first, June must have misheard. But he still smiled at the sky, expectant and unbothered.

"What?" she asked through numb lips.

It was then, in the flash and bang of the Roman candle, that June first saw the little boat and its little passenger. At first, the animal part of her, mesmerized by firelight, didn't even recognize her. But then, June swiped soot off her forehead and looked again. Lark was almost invisible in the choppy waves made by bigger hulls and fancier boats, just a cork on the tide.

June hadn't been looking for her, not in any conscious way. But at the sight of her, June felt cooled, sedated, brought down from the sky, aware of how sore and scorched her throat was, how her eyes burned from the smoke. What had she been doing? Where was Aunt Eliza—surely she would be looking for her?

Yellow Jack had abandoned her, moved down the barge to

attend to spiky black fireworks. They were horrible, unnerving vultures with shrouded wings and hooked beaks turned toward the gathered boats. They looked hungry, ripe for a grand finale. He crouched next to them, and for a flash, he could have been one of them, just as eager for destruction. He touched the first of the flock. June's stomach heaved, bile and beer and cornbread clogging her chest. The firework was off with a burning glow, arcing so close to the boats, it could only have been intentional.

June dropped to her knees, clutching the edge of the barge, and tried not to vomit.

Boom. Crack. The explosion drowned out the cheers. The flash was as bright as daylight, laying them all bare, the boats, the faces. The water.

And under the water. In that night-banishing light, June saw clear into the lake, past scattered schools of fish all the way to the bottom. Only it wasn't just a muddy lake bed waiting for her.

Without a spyglass, June saw the places the record player needle skipped on the scuffed old vinyl of Lake Prosper.

There it was. It had been there all along. Its little streets, its community center, the rows of little houses: the drowned town of Prosper. The anchors from the boats on the surface had settled everywhere, hooked into chimneys and around the cavity in a church steeple, where once bells must have rung. More were buried in the silt, one broken entirely through the First Prosper Bank sign. The water was catfish slick and weedy, but through the churn, she saw the people, down under the water, their hair and clothes drifting in the currents.

It was only an instant. But she saw them as clearly as the people in the boats. June swayed, clenching the edge of the barge.

Like everyone else, their milky pearl-crusted eyes were fixed upon the show with gaunt terror on their jaundiced faces. But they had anchors too. Their ankles, under disintegrating clothing, were tied down, barnacled with strange milky growths. Pearls. The people floated in place but couldn't rise more than a few feet toward the surface.

Trapped on the barge, in the nightmare's cruel engine, June screamed, but the next boom drowned it out. Behind her, the fireworks man was laughing. In front of her—Lark was still there, her face lit in the fireworks glow.

Before she could fear it, she crawled into the water, craning to keep her head over the surface, and swam for her life toward the only refuge she could see, the only possible escape left to her, the little boat with its little passenger, bobbing alone on feverish, hungry water.

☙

Rig should've been grinning, flushed with victory, the winner of a great jest. But his face was still and empty. He lounged in their path, half sprawled up on the stairs they were about to climb. Sammy screamed as she nearly collided with him. His knife was inches from her gut. The next volley of fireworks, a bouquet of blues and violets, exploded above them.

"Is this the chaos you wanted?" Bolt challenged him, daring himself up the first couple of damp metal steps toward Rig. The taste of gunpowder spread down his throat.

Rig closed his fist around the knife hilt and, quick as a cobra, punched Bolt. The world tilted dangerously, steps loose under his feet—but Sammy steadied him. Hot blood dribbled onto his lip.

"Dickhead," Rig muttered, tickling his knife over his own face like a shaving razor. "Y'all are such wastes. Wastes of skin. My dad was wrong to come here and try to save y'all." He flipped the knife once between his fingers. "Oh, hey, Woody."

Woody had caught up, leering at them from behind. They were cornered.

"You've got to stop," Bolt snapped.

"Oh." Rig laughed shortly, and there was no lightness in his eyes anymore. They were flat as the smoke-choked sky. "Because you say so? We're way past that."

Bolt shoved an arm in front of Sammy just as Rig snatched at them. Catching Bolt, he reeled him in until their knees banged together, Rig's eyes bright and rabid. Bolt grabbed his wrist, pushing the moonlight flash of blade away from him. Rig felt stronger than he ever had before, sinewy and strange, nails digging into his skin, staring at Bolt with such focus. Then he snapped his head forward and sank his teeth into the muscle where Bolt's shoulder met his neck. Bolt yanked him away by the hair, and Rig grinned, empty and miles wide, as the blade—the *knife*, he had forgotten the knife—sank into Bolt's side.

But just as quickly, metal hit his rib and grimaced to a shallow halt. They were locked there, holding each other eye to eye. It wasn't heartbreak or pain that froze Bolt but dull disbelief: Rig had done it. He'd actually done it. For a splintered second, Rig looked just as shocked before he let out a soft huff and gifted Bolt a loose, fond smile. The first of warm blood trickled down his side.

Woody yelped—Sammy had nailed him in the groin, and he hit the deck, moaning. Coming alive, Bolt shoved Rig so hard that

his head banged against the door. Sammy grabbed Bolt's hand in a
sweaty vice. As one, they jumped over Woody and veered the only
way left to them, off the front, where the gap was treacherous. They
hurled themselves out over the darkness. The minuscule ski boat
wobbled when they landed, nearly capsizing under their weight, and
Bolt hit hard, landing shin first against the rail and then the floor.

"Watch it!" someone spat at them.

"The water," Bolt gasped. "We're close enough to shore. We
have to swim." It would be darker in the water, away from the boat
lights, the mad fire spinning in the air above them. "My Country
'Tis of Thee" rang out with a jukebox crackle from every radio.

Sammy ran ahead of him, a blur of curly hair and long limbs
diving into the water. Nose still gushing, side stinging, Bolt
leaped after her. He soared, plummeted, dark water slapping
against his cheek like an open hand, and he was submerged.

Distantly, a firework boomed.

"Everything's okay," Cassie had whispered the first time he
remembered watching Grandad stutter into the lake through a
rainstorm. Mom chased after him until both were locked together
in the shallows. Lightning snapped in the sky, and the water was so
rough, Bolt was convinced it was an ocean that would swallow them
whole. But Cassie wrapped around him, her hair full of a scent as
fragile as April rain. "He's having a bad dream. Just hold on."

"Wait for me!" Grandad had screamed and sobbed as he was
pulled away. "Wait, please!"

Only it hadn't been dementia, as Bolt had long assumed. It
was the same trap closing around Bolt. He kicked up, toward the
surface, but something cold and firm latched on to him. Hands.
Hands tugged him down, toward the lake bed mud. He gasped.

It was a rookie mistake; he knew to save his breath if he was ever caught underwater. *Don't panic, or you'll drown faster—*

Bolt felt the glide of cold water moving as something slid over him on the surface, through refracted sunlight. *Sunlight?* Bolt thought desperately, turned around and confused. How could that be? It was a small rickety fishing boat propelled by old wooden oars. Desperate, Bolt reached for the oar passing over him, caught the edge, but it was already stopping, twisting in the water to pull the boat out of motion, into a sideways drift. Bolt clung on, digging his fingers into the rough wood grain.

Everything's okay, he heard Cassie's voice as if she were there too, under the water. *It's just a bad dream.*

A young boy looked down over the side of the boat, water rippling between them. He was as knobbly as a crawdad, with a flop of muddy-brown hair. His skin was freckled. Just like Cassie's. And Bolt knew him. He *knew* the young face of his own grandfather, peering into the water. Grandad's face was tense with pain and old tear tracks. Lungs burning, Bolt pushed himself toward the surface just as Grandad tossed his arm down, and for a flash, Bolt thought he was reaching for him, and he stretched up to meet him. But Grandad grabbed a strand of thin white driftwood. He yanked it out of the mud, and with it, a box of woven wood—a funnel fish trap. There was something in it, three big dark bundles wrapped in cheesecloth. As Bolt kicked for the surface, feeling the water give way, Grandad began to heft them into his boat. One shifted. Out spilled a slim rainfall of small winking objects. They floated past Bolt's nose, a series of white spheres, each a perfect, pea-sized star. Pearls.

Bolt kicked until he broke the surface, but when he scrabbled for the boat, for the pearls, he met nothing but empty water.

CHAPTER EIGHTEEN

HE VIEW FROM THE TOP OF CASSIE'S RV WASN'T PER-
fect, which made it, well, pretty damn perfect. The
show was going on behind them—Cassie's land and the
Destiny were only a ridge away from the dam. Up on Cassie's
hill, then farther up on her RV, they were able to see most of the
flashes lighting up blue, gold, or red. But mostly, they heard the
great earthquake booms of rockets, the yellowish light they cast
onto the growing smoke. Sparks flew over the treetops, seeming
close enough to alight on the double-wide and burn the roof.

Cassie's nerves were still frayed after her run-in with Daley.
She'd been wild and unspooled all day.

And yet she was a woman who loved her own home, who
wouldn't be chased away from what was hers. Cassie had been
resolutely against attending the fireworks show on the water, even
with Daley unaccounted for. She knew where her refuge was, and
she wouldn't be talked away from it. So Mitch had, of course,
gone back to her home with her.

Cassie's shotgun rested beside her on the RV roof, and every so
often, they took turns shining an ancient spotlight at the spaces
between the trees. Mitch had had to be careful as he climbed to

sit on the rounded top of the RV; it wasn't that much larger than he was and creaked crankily under his weight. Now he watched the light from the fireworks animate the freckles on her face. Their cans of Fresca sweated thick rings onto the RV top, but neither of them had remembered to take a drink.

"I think another storm is coming," Mitch murmured, listening to the wind kicking up around them. It had an unseasonable chill in it.

Cassie squinted at the clouds but offered no other commentary on the likelihood of storms. Her mind was elsewhere. She sat with her legs crossed, her can balanced between her slim ankles, and her eyes stayed pinned on the crackling sky above them. "Grandad hated fireworks," she told him offhand. "They always made his eyes well behind his cataracts. He became detached in time, was back in the war. It scared me. How real it still was. As real as I was." It must have been frightening for a child to realize the horrors of his past were not gone but sleeping, able to wake up at a moment's notice.

"This show is like a war," Mitch murmured, his voice nearly lost in the distant booms. And the past felt very close. His mind stuck on her grandfather, on his humorous eyes as he repaired something stubborn. Mitch would stare at those clever, knobby-knuckled fingers, as patient as End Times while he fiddled with gears smaller than a pinky nail. "Cassie, I've always wondered…" He hesitated. He was venturing into delicate territory, brushing against old secrets. "How did he do it?"

Mr. Fairchild had owned a lot of the property around the new boundaries of the lake since the Grand Destiny's earliest construction, all the lakefront the corps didn't preserve. But as far as Mitch knew, he hadn't been rich or power hungry. He hadn't even kept all the land he bought. In a few cases, Mom had told him Mr. Fairchild gave acres away to Prosper residents from the old days. But, when so many had lost everything, how did the son of shop owners get all that land in the first place?

Cassie had been scanning the woods, but she returned her attention to him with a thoughtful frown. "I never asked," Cassie admitted. "I didn't know when he was alive. His accountant called me after he was gone. On my eighteenth birthday, actually." She picked at the hem of her shorts. "I knew about the land that we lived on and that the shop stood on, but I had no idea what he really owned. I still don't. I never wanted to know, really. I told the accountant to stay on, only tell me what I needed to know, and that I didn't want to sell."

Above them, yellow stars split apart in the sky. "I was afraid, I suppose," Cassie said. The reflection of fireworks bloomed reddish on her pale throat. "Overwhelmed. And betrayed. It felt cruel that he didn't tell me or put Mom in charge, that he didn't even explain it to me. There are a lot of things I wish he had told me."

Quiet fell between them as the Fourth of July rocketed on in the distance. Not a single cricket sang, no rustling came from the bank. All the creatures of the lake were hidden away from the two storms: the fireworks and the earliest hint of lightning.

"With everything going on, it may be stupid, but I love being out here with you, Cass," Mitch said at last, looking over at her as the grand finale crackled in the deep of her eyes, its cacophony bouncing between the hills and the trees around them. "I'm really glad—well, you really thought on your feet last night. I don't know what I would've done if Daley had…" The wind tossed the sound around, dark clouds pushing competitively against the leftover firework smoke. A storm really was brewing.

Cassie looked at him then, a kite reeled back to earth. She seemed to read his mind. "It's going to be a bad storm. Worst of the season." Lightning flared overhead as the weather turned, startling them both. Cassie found Mitch again, her face set. "Come inside."

"You're right." Mitch roused himself, oblivious. "Better get to shelter."

"Mitch." In the break between rolls of thunder, her voice was solitary and loud. Her eyes were very soft. "Come inside."

"That's what I—Oh. Right." It was still new, this thing. New and precious and fragile. Numbness gave over to an intense build of heat, of melting. Mitch touched her face, the skin right beside that undeniable stare. He'd never been accused of being a particularly smart man, but she wouldn't have to repeat her command again. He was hers.

Rain began to plop down in large, heavy drops as first Cassie then Mitch descended from the roof of the RV to the ground, where she took his hand. It felt unreal, the smell of the rain, the frankness in her eyes, and the way she pressed against his chest as if the years of distance between them were nothing but a moment and a step.

She pulled him out of the rain.

℘

"Damnation and...hellfire." Hellfire indeed. Lark's eyes burned. Afterimages of the grand finale, which had struck the sky over the dam like a dozen snare drums, still hung above the boat, long weeping willow trails of smoke bleeding onto the water. Now it was a stale battlefield. June was soaked from her dive, the swim she'd taken across the lake, which glowed orange and gold in the glow of the arson above. Lark hadn't thought, had just hauled her into the boat, her hair heavy with water and the scent of gunpowder.

The show was ending. A few engines roared to life behind them as some boats broke formation and chugged toward home, but most hung under the night's spell. The air, which felt wet and humid, buzzed and chuffed and hooted with churning water, horns, and motors. And something else: a growing growl of wind.

June had sooty smears on her cheeks from her labor on the fireworks barge. She was still full of frenetic movement, her muscles trembling with exhaustion she didn't seem to feel. Her face was electrified, eyes darting with energy yet to be spent.

Lark tried to catch her breath, blinking the supernovas in her vision away. The little boat she'd borrowed from the Destiny bobbed as others went by them. People were starting to go in; the smoke of the performance was moving fast on a changed breeze, and everyone was waking up. Lark felt several steps behind, nowhere near ready to operate a watercraft, especially with June, mistress of the night's tricks herself, suddenly there and radiating this energy that got in Lark's blood. "You did that? That was— something else."

June looked sharply at her and nodded with a jerk of her chin. Her fingertips, tapping a rhythm on her knees, were red, pinched. Burned.

"I never wanted to be like this," June burst out. The boat bucked dully under them, and she pressed her hands to her mouth, gaze flicking to the smoke that blocked out the stars, hovering right over the water. "If you think I don't show restraint, I'll tell you I try. I know I said I was going to go, but I didn't. I stayed—I try to stay, I try not to be too much, I try to build a solid life. No one ever believes me, but I do. I try so hard to be—"

Lark could almost sense the words she bit off. *Good. Still. Tame.*

The wind stirred up around them, and June curled her fingers together.

"Jack told me he could help me." Water dripped from her hair down her cheek. "With how I am. He understood, you know? The way I start fires and can never stay out of trouble, and when I try, trouble just bursts out of me anyway. But tonight..." June shook her head. "I saw under the water."

The jeweler's loupe felt heavy around Lark's neck at those words. She nodded, keeping her voice low and even. Suddenly it felt like there might be listeners somewhere close. "What did you see?"

The water seemed even choppier now, and June dropped her gaze. "You know what I saw," she murmured. "I think he knew too. I think he liked waking them up, liked scaring them. He liked setting fire over their heads, over their town down there, when there's nothing they can do. That wasn't ever what I wanted."

Lark stared down at the dark ripples of the water, and her throat ached. Some part of her suddenly wanted to stroke the surface, let the crests of the wakes brush her palm. She turned to the ignition. "We should get out of here." It had started to rain gently, but a distant growl of thunder promised the storm.

"Stop." June caught her wrist gently. "Don't start the motor. I don't—I don't want to stir it up anymore. The wind's towing us back anyway." It was true; the currents set by the swiftly thinning crowds around them meant the docks already loomed nearer, and beyond, the great monolith of the dam.

"Okay." Lark turned back to June and slipped her hand into hers. They bobbed along, nearer and nearer to the bank between E and F Docks as the wakes of bigger boats shunted them into the shallows, the bottom of the boat running aground in soft mud under the fall of a willow tree. The rain was growing fiercer, so Lark gathered up the loose tarps and tossed it over their heads. Inside was warm and still, the rain thumping like fingers on a drum. "You're okay now. You were so brave to jump in that water." Her thumb brushed the angry burns. "I saw you up there, lighting all those fuses..." Up on that barge, dancing between rockets in the fireworks exhaust, June had gleamed like an idol, fire rolling off her like she was a sparkler. It hurt Lark's eyes. "It was—I felt afraid for you, but...you were amazing," she admitted softly. Thunder growled in the distance, and the air felt like rain. Lark's stomach was full of lightning.

June's lips twitched, a cinder of a smile in the darkness. "That's what makes it difficult. It would be easier if it were only terrible. But it's dangerous. And fun. And all-consuming and exhilarating. If I swallow it down, if I pretend it's not there, it comes out anyway, and it comes out explosive. I've always thought I could smother it, but it doesn't die. It only builds." June's eyes, raw and singed as the night sky, found Lark's. "I don't want to be like him."

"You're not," Lark promised, brushing wet locks of hair from June's face. Touching her skin sent a shock through Lark, as if her fingertips had skimmed a hot plate. "You're not." Lark caught her mouth. Even in the rain, June smelled faintly of flowers. Flowers and gun smoke. Lark crowded her down into the bottom of the boat, the tarp pooling around them, dark and hot. June was only surprised for a moment before her fingers seared up Lark's back, shifting her knees so Lark fit herself over her, close enough for the buttons on their denim shorts to clink.

June's voice was a soft rumble, drowned by a roll of thunder, breath on her ear, a hint of teeth. "Sweetheart—"

Lark bit at the soft skin of June's neck, breath ragged, pushed cold hands up under her sooty tank top. Lightning pounded into the water off the back, someone's car alarm starting to howl from shore. Rain was soaking the tarp, the downpour on the lake's surface deafening. There was no way home now; they'd have to wait it out here, tucked into this little cove.

June sweetened, giving with gentle hands, one cupped at the small of Lark's back. They'd been on different rhythms all summer. When Lark had expected her to understand the importance of things, the delicacy of her life, she had swarmed in, wildly offering sweet escape. When she had wanted to be alone, June swam to her boat and clung to the side with damp fingers. Now she matched Lark breath for breath, touch for touch.

Outside, the world heaved on uncertain water. Shadows puddled between them, and they didn't speak anymore.

ↄ

After Mitch fell asleep, cramped on her Murphy bed, Cassie remembered she had left the double-wide open and unguarded. The rain was still coming down, but the wayward sparks from the fireworks that had collected on top of the double-wide still flickered. She ran between raindrops to take shelter in her own doorway, where windows were open and rain fell on the floors.

Mitch was caught, carried through the weather with her in the folds of her shirt, the places high on her neck that he had kissed. She touched one of them and, for a moment, closed her eyes.

Cassie walked through the double-wide, turning lights off as she went. Here was the sink where she had washed the same plates thousands upon thousands of times and where Mom had stood the last time she'd seen her. Here was the kitchen window Cassie had painted over to block the view of Lake Prosper.

Here was the hall she had run through in bare feet, trying to rush out the door when Mom opened it to get the mail. Here was the corner where linoleum had begun to curl up from the floor in the heat of the summer, which Cassie used to grip and pull and pull and pull until Mom put her in her room for a time out. Here was the bedroom where she had waited up at night with her eyes on the woods, hoping to see a fox or a doe silvery and slippery with moonlight, until she fell asleep with her head on the windowsill.

Here was Bolt's room, clean as if the boy himself had just left it, with the radiator that hummed in the window and a mobile Grandad had made hanging over the twin bed, special red cardinals spreading their wings just for Bolt, each one built around a heavy antique key.

Here was Mom's old room, which always smelled like her, where Cassie would go in the evenings to curl against her side and hear stories about the places she wanted to go one day and the one summer she'd followed a boy in a band around Tennessee, when Mom would ask that wonderful question: *Did I ever tell you…?*

When the lights were all off and she reached the very farthest corner of the house, Cassie turned back. The light in Cassie's old bedroom flickered back on.

Her breath left her body. Nothing in the house made a sound. There was nothing in here. No one in the house. Nothing in her old bedroom, no one to be turning on lights. There was nowhere to hide in a double-wide. Nothing but hall and rooms. No one could have gotten past her to the kitchen, not without her seeing. A double-wide's layout flowed one way, along one channel. There were no other routes. She charged down the hall and braced herself in her bedroom doorway.

The box sat on the floor in the center of her room. In the chaos, the fear of Daley, she had never retrieved it from the shop. She had left it there, its secrets unmoored. She had forgotten it. Cassie rushed forward toward it—

But her bedroom didn't wait for her in the space beyond. Cassie swayed on her feet. She was surrounded by the smell of horse manure and dark mineral mud. The rumble of dusty cart wheels filled the air. She took an uneven step, packed dirt soft under her feet. Buttercup-colored light filtered between trees, collided with the sides of modest buildings crowded together beside a shallow, swamp-like lakeside. It was a much, much smaller version of Lake Prosper, its current wide, clean edges replaced with shallow marshes, rain feeding a modest river winding west.

People, a sparse parade of meager faces, walked through the space where Cassie's bed was supposed to be, and on, toward a humble steeple, a huddled town square. And toward her, racing with a colt's agility against the current, came a familiar figure. Once Cassie had noticed her strength, her long muscular limbs. Now all she saw was how young her face still was. She wore a dress made for summertime, white linen that hung loose and free. Under her arm was a basket of Arkansas tomatoes, and there was something else clutched tight in her hand. As she sailed by Cassie, she glanced back once, cocking her chin at her.

There was nothing else to do. Cassie couldn't hear the rain now. The only way out was through. She staggered after Catfish, away from the crowd, down little paths between houses, through narrow spaces like slots between Old Prosper's ribs. Old bones. Catfish rounded a tight corner, and suddenly she was leaping at someone in the gap, someone who was laughing, whose pale face, beneath his fading cap, looked familiar too.

"What do you have there?" he asked, his hand gathering a little of the white linen at the small of her back. Even then, when he couldn't be any older than Catfish, he'd had a slightly bulbous nose. His eyebrows, designed to worry over things, to quirk and press against each other and furrow, drew Cassie up short. How many times had she watched the grayed and bushier version of these brows waggle over their work at the shop's repair bench?

"What, *pomodori*?" Catfish hid the small surprise in her other hand, coy. "Whatever Nonna says, they grow well here. Pastor Hiram gave me these from his patch."

He took one from the basket and pressed its spicy skin to his nose, but his eyes were on her. Full of sunlight, the tomato glowed between them like a carnelian. "Not those," he said finally, in that low voice of his. He nodded at her fist, replacing the tomato in the basket. "What's that?"

Catfish opened her hand to reveal a small brightly colored box. "A man came into town selling these. He's in the square now."

"A firecracker?" Tobias Fairchild examined the gilded paper.

Catfish hung from his neck, smiling. "Best in the world, he says. He just came in from Memphis."

"He gave you this one?" Tobias turned it over in his hand. His other hand still held her against him, here in this tight in-between space, away from prying eyes.

"Free samples? I don't think so, *bello*." In a sleight of hand, Catfish stole it back, and in its place in his palm sat something small, white, and shimmering. "The lake bought it for me."

Tobias held the little orb up before his eyes in wonder.

"I went to dive this morning before the shopping." She stashed her firecracker in the pocket of her fraying smock. "I swear, those little things just follow me around down there."

Tobias kissed her. "I gotta be up on the dam tonight," he murmured against her mouth. "But when I come back, let's you and me set that firecracker off. Make a few more plans."

They would have met young, her running from the slurs, *dago, dago girl,* him from his father's shabby roadside shop. Catfish would have told him stories of her parents as young children carried on one of the last of the rancid steamboats up the Mississippi River from New Orleans, the end of a journey begun in southern Italian hills. So many families had been drawn to Arkansas by the promise of land bought on credit. By the time they made it to the steamboat, they would have known the land was an overpriced trap. Catfish's mother, even decades later, wouldn't step foot on a boat, but her daughter would grow up loving the water. Tobias barely remembered his own mother, who never learned English, only recalling the beautiful Arabic prayers she'd sung in private to soothe him.

Catfish played over the collar of his work shirt. "I got something to talk to you about anyway—"

The sunlight slapped off, and there was a brush of air, like someone sprinting by her in the darkness. Gasping, Cassie found her hand on the switch, standing just as she had been, in her dark bedroom. She gulped in the breath she'd been holding.

It was happening. Again. She was practically a child again, trapped under the dock by her hair, feeling someone else's memory closing in around her, and she couldn't understand why it was happening now.

Outside, Mitch's truck was faithfully crouched in the driveway. He was still in the RV. She could return to him, curl into his warm side, and fall back asleep with him. She could leave the nightmare. If she could just withstand it long enough to get out of the house.

The kitchen light burst on. Between her and escape. Heart lodged like a fish bone in her throat, Cassie followed the hallway to the kitchen, dreading every step. But it was as if the walls of the double-wide had collapsed, folding apart like a cardboard box, and around her now stood the dinky town square of Old Prosper. It was too much, her senses overloading, the past crashing in, crushing the present into rubble to make room for itself, expanding. The town was stripped, a blank face, and nearly empty. The air felt too still and full of water. Somewhere concealed, a baby was hacking.

She didn't see the couple again until they met below a half-collapsed awning. The market was abandoned, the sky gray. "I'm sorry," Catfish said. She was wrapped in a heavy coat that pooled at her knees, and she looked exhausted.

Tobias had his cap pulled lower than ever to hide the tears on his cheeks. He nodded once, sharply. "Not your fault." He reached for her, squeezed her fingers. "Please don't go to the schoolhouse. Not now. Not with—let's go on, now."

The schoolhouse. A blackboard. A row of beds. Desks pushed against the walls. A sight Cassie's young mind hadn't been able to fully fathom, her hair caught in the underside of the dock.

"Don't go, Catfish," she whispered, but there was no sound to her own voice; here she was the ghost. "Don't go to the schoolhouse."

But Catfish shook her head. One hand gripped a wall, dug into the grooves of the brick to steady herself. Her face was pinched. "It'll be for just a few days. Yellow Jack kills you fast if it's gonna kill you, and I've got things to live for."

"Then come with me and live, damn it," Tobias managed, his voice almost too gruff to understand. "Let's hit the road, Kat. We'll never tell anyone we came from here. And no one'll remember this place in a year or two anyway. Not the town, not the sharecroppers. Not the fever. We won't either. I'll take care of you." Two children with two new family names and two new identities each hoping to tie their loose strings together. They would be happy under the name Tobias's father had chosen. Fairchild. More than just a name with an American ring; it was a prayer, his wish. A fairer world for his children. Bolt's world, full of bright hope, far from the lake and the Great Damnation.

"I can't make the trip sick. It's going to be hard enough, don't you see? I need my strength." She trailed off, but he was already nodding. Her voice was far firmer than his. "Get that last pay-check. And—I want you to do one more thing, all right?"

He looked at her, those clever eyebrows trembling.

"You...you know where they are." She held his eyes, blinking not even once despite the fever shine of her skin. "You go and get them and have them ready, right? For our future."

"Right." He took a breath, and for one moment, just one moment, he brushed his fingers along the buttons on her coat. "Our future."

The ground shook. Cassie stood in an immense crowd. Men, women, tripping toddlers, in patched and worn clothes, the best they had for travel, clutching bags and hats, their best things, their only things. They shoved past her, down the road, out of the town. Umbrellas and forearms sheltered them from the rain, but there was no time now to waste. It had been a rainy summer, Cassie did know that.

They parted around her like a river around a stone. Tobias and Catfish were lost in it, and Cassie fought her way through them to the switch on the kitchen wall and slapped the light off.

"Stop," Cassie ground out, clutching her head. It pounded, her blood rushing. "Stop it. Stop—"

And the porch light turned on. It pooled yellow on the grass, stretching buttery fingers toward the lake. The source of Cassie's fears. She backed into the refrigerator, already shaking her head.

The light didn't flicker. It waited.

She could just stay here in the kitchen. She could avoid those final steps and stay where Mom had made hair tonics and sweet tea with mint, where Grandad had sat staring out the window over his lunch. *Just waiting for the light to change,* he'd tell her when she asked him what he was thinking about.

But hadn't Cassie tried to hide? Hadn't she spent years closing her eyes and ears, painting her windows, waiting for it to be safe? And Catfish had waited too. She could wait forever to draw Cassie out, to show her what she had been attempting to communicate all Cassie's life. She steadied herself, breathed in the familiar scent of her home, her space, her time. There was the aroma of honeycomb wreathing up from a pot on the stove. Rain tapped on the roof that liked to leak. She anchored herself in her own body, in all its panic, in all its weakness, as she crept to the open front door.

"Catfish," she whispered. "You were—you were my friend. I loved you. I trusted you. So I have to believe you're not just doing this to scare me." There was no response. The light glowed on. "I'm coming out."

Cassie stepped outside into deafening rain. Water streamed around her ankles. She ran to the edge of her property, where trees and weeds encroached on the narrow path down the hill to the Destiny. At the top, the resort, the shoreline, and their private winding finger of the lake was laid out before her, perfectly positioned for a crack of lightning that almost brought her to her knees.

Someone was in the water.

The path down to the lake from her property was a newborn stream now, mud sluicing as if from an open vein, spilling into the shallows, where a small figure huddled on all fours near the shore.

Cassie inched closer down the bank.

"Hello?" Cassie tried, her voice buffeted by the wind.

There was so much she had never noticed until the day she watched Catfish drown. That Mom never once saw her, that Catfish carried her past the dock and no one ever seemed to notice them gone. That Catfish waved from the water and waited for the five-year-old girl to come to her. That Catfish could float and do the backstroke and dive but never, not once, stepped foot on shore.

Warm tears shuddered down Cassie's cheeks as she knelt beside the water and kept her eyes ruthlessly on the sight in front of her.

Catfish was crying, her shoulders shaking with cold, and though she didn't look at Cassie, she could feel Catfish tugging at her, pulling at her with some wordless, untamable need.

"Catfish." Cassie cleared her throat. "*Catfish.*"

Her head lifted. Her neck turned, and she looked at Cassie with dark, angry eyes, lost in time.

"Do you know me?" Cassie asked her, choked. "We used to play together. A long time ago."

Catfish didn't try to speak, but Cassie could read it in her eyes—horror, desperation and need. A question. *Where?*

Cassie pitched forward—

And fell.

And felt water tug and pull underneath her, dripping in from the ceiling. She was back in the last place she ever wanted to be.

It had been dripping in from the ceiling for three days of rain. Prosper's schoolhouse had been carefully made, but it was poor. Desks, pushed to the sides of the building to make room for pallets on the floor, and people crammed together. After just one day of rain, it began to pool from under the door too. Grady had tried to stop the leak with spare blankets and used to mop, trying to push the water out, but he was too tired now to bother. He floated on his yellow sheets like everyone else, unrecognizable but for his shock of copper hair.

Catfish had been woken by a fever dream of monsters with hammers knocking on the door in the darkest hours. Under the veil of nighttime, they appeared in the windows, looking in at them. Men or devils.

"Not sure about this," one of them had said to another.

"Stop whining. We talked about this," another monster whispered. His skin looked like leather. Through the shadows, he looked like he only had one eye. Cyclops, she thought hazily. "We do what needs to be done to save our kin. This sickness can't spread."

Then she had fallen asleep again, but not before getting a strange sense that the ground was being washed out from under her.

Just a dream. And yet. Later that night, when the night hung like a heavy, warm blanket, Susan, little Susan, had tried to open the door, wanting to use the bathroom outside—but it didn't budge, didn't even rattle. It was stuck fast. Water leaked underneath it.

So cold. It was so cold. And her skin was so hot. She turned her head to the north wall, where water buffeted through, spraying and sloshing with algae and white bubbles. She couldn't stand up anymore. She was too tired. Just days ago, she had been dreaming of far-off city roads. Why was the water so high?

The yellow sickness came from the mosquitos in the lake bed, the doctor said, and the school was where sick people were sent—for the town's peace of mind, see. People were scared it would spread as far as Charlene, that it would become another Memphis. They all knew what had happened when yellow fever came to Memphis.

Sickness came from the lake bed. Panic came from the town.

The basin won't flood, the doctor had said, full of confidence.

"As long as the locks are open, the old town of Prosper will be perfectly safe. There's no better place for the sick to seclude and heal." But the doctor had not come in three days, since the rain started. The rest of the houses here in the basin were empty. Why was the water so high?

One of the school's blackboards had a tired scribble: *Gen. 9:11*.

She faded out for a time and woke suddenly and sharply in silence because something was wrong. Her hair was wet. Everything was wet. Water was a hand high, lapping at her face, her blankets beginning to drag and float. She turned, struggled onto her side, and saw Mrs. Grier was on her stomach, very still, a rosary still coiled around her wrist. She was never still. Her fingers were deft, flour-dusted when she fried pancakes for breakfast, her voice sharp as a bell, but she was facedown and water lapped at her ears. Rising.

Water tickled Catfish's nose, so she turned back and felt the nauseous pull of her stomach, and blood was on her nightgown again, warmth leaching out into the cold, cold water that soaked her blankets. Around her limbs. There had been a break between the wall and the door, and water swirled in; the building shuddered. Could it hold, if the water didn't stop? She couldn't stand, not even when it rose around her where she lay on her back and fell on her from the ceiling. Something in the building's very structure cracked, and now the water rushed, so cold, already a hand high, and she was so tired, in such pain, and if she couldn't sit up—

Cassie fell to her knees in the mud at the lake's edge. Catfish shuddered. Maybe she was still locked in the memory, still feeling herself slowly drown, crawling for the door that was nailed shut, knowing she was too weak to open it.

Cassie was seized by the same impulse to save her that she'd felt as a child, watching Catfish sink—the same impulse that drove her to stand vigil on those nights when Mom fished Grandad out of the lake. But the paralyzing helplessness felt the same too. "Come here," Cassie called to her. "Catfish, get out of the water. I'm here, I'll help you. Please."

Catfish didn't respond but looked at her with such strength, such power, that Cassie felt her refusal settle like sediment in her bones. *No.* The storm shuddered, and rain slashed across Cassie's face, blinding her for a moment. When she rubbed her eyes open, Catfish was leaning in inches from her nose.

CHAPTER NINETEEN

HE THUNDER GREW LOUD AND ANIMALISTIC AFTER midnight. Under the sodden tarp, June lay next to Lark, and they didn't speak. Her skin had been electrified so long, now it was turning numb, bruised from the two of them washing up against each other over and over and over. Every so often, they peeked out. At some point, the lights of the nearby docks had sputtered out, and the perfect darkness was now only broken by the flashing storm.

They would meet there, eyes seeking eyes in the lightning strikes, and sweat-slicked knees tangling and lips catching and Lark's pink hair brushing her shoulders, and then they would recede in silence, not sleep, until they would turn again to each other, hands curled, and pull helplessly on.

"Never seen a storm like this," Lark murmured at some point. "Thank God this boat drains, or we'd be underwater."

"I don't want to go back out there," June sighed against her jaw.

June had always loved the first time with someone. Sex was new again every first time; there was always more, more, and more, as clumsy fumbles turned into rhythm and two figured out how to move as one. The lessons learned while charting a path from navel to hip could only be discovered once. It was fresh falling in love, with the narrowness of Lark's chin and the dip of her spine, with the feel of soft weight settling over her stomach, and the silent way she huffed out her breath in the aftershocks as they rolled away from each other. Brimming, June couldn't help but watch Lark from under her eyelids and wait for the tide to draw her back.

A crack like a falling redwood roused them. It was so loud, the shudder of their little boat so profound, that for a moment June was sure they'd sink. Lark lifted the tarp as she sat up, suddenly alert. "Something's going on," she managed, moving to peer over the side toward the closest houseboat dock. Suddenly she gasped, a painful drag of air. It sounded like panic. "That's him."

"What?" June drew up with her, instinct telling her to stay low. On either side of them, the long docks bucked in the water. People raced around their boats, resecuring the riggings with larger, more elaborate knots, flashlights in hand. The houseboats could have been bath toys, they looked so fragile.

And there, crouched on the shore, where F Dock was anchored, someone was working with bolt cutters. "What's he doing out there in a storm?" June asked.

"It's him. No one else moves that way, no one." Lark was struggling to get a deep breath in, her eyes darting, her hair plastered to her head. She dragged her clothes on in quick jerks. "Jeff Daley. He almost killed Cassie and I yesterday."

"What?" June hooked her arm around Lark's waist. The clothes she'd put on were completely drenched. "Okay, keep your head down. What's—"

Lark lunged back to the wheel and tried to get the boat started up again, twisting the key, trying to intervene somehow. "He's ripping F Dock loose." There was a second horrible boom and a metallic tearing that echoed across the whole basin of the lake. "People could die."

June scrambled for her soaked clothes, tossing her shirt back over her head.

"Look." Lark lifted the little lens she wore around her neck to June so she could see the magnified horror. F Dock was detached, buffeted on the water, ship to iceberg, toward E Dock.

"Are they going to crash?" June asked. "What's happening?"

Lark's silence and her wrestling with the boat's engine were a grim answer.

In the distance, the dam was lit by wild streamers of lightning. The storm seemed to want to pull it up by the roots, and in the flash, June saw them again. Five figures, scurrying fugitives, their destruction sowed long ago, on the distant dam, there—and then gone. She knew them. Just like the night when she'd stood on the edge of the red lake, and those five fishermen told her stories of blood in the Nile—she heard their gravelly whisper from across the water. *The dead have a tight grip on this place.* Did they even know their world was gone and that they were nothing more than the brutal afterimage left behind after a lightning flash?

And those people, trapped under the water, awake—were they reliving horrors all over again? They would not rise tonight, she knew that. There was no divine intervention coming to save the docks. The living were on their own.

Daley stood, leaving the bolt cutters in the grass, and dashed into the water, into a low dive, where he vanished under the frothing waves.

Finally, Lark got the boat started, the engine's roar totally eclipsed in the sound of the rising water, the deep booms of wires snapping in the deep. She grabbed the arm of the accelerator, and the boat hauled across the high surf, struck back and forth by waves. It was all June could do to not be thrown off into the water as they careened forward, trying to get out from between the massive wooden jaws of the two docks threatening to snap around them.

"Can you see Daley?" Lark screamed into the wind. "We've got to—" Then her eyes fixed on something, and she screamed again, this time without words. The dock, as large as a highway overpass, heaved over the water. Great white foam was borne ahead of it, boats torn free and skidding in every direction in the dense rain. The houseboats tossed in their slips like stabled horses, desperate faces trapped behind dark windows. The other inhabitants of Echo Dock had noticed; screams rose, one after another, and a small crowd of a dozen or so of Lark's neighbors rushed to the edge of their dock, huddled together. Through the loupe, June saw two teenage boys with their arms around a woman in a bathrobe. A dog barked hysterically in an older woman's arms, while another furry creature—a ferret?—wrapped protectively around the neck of a bald man. A little girl with leftover blue and red stars painted on her face watched the adults in horror.

Lark steered for the ever-narrowing gap between the two dock ends, trying to get them out of the collision zone. "We won't make it!" June shouted, but her voice was lost in the wind. Two boats crashing on the water would be deadly. But this—twenty, thirty, all at once, hulls splintering, poles cracking, cabins flooding—

Lark, desperate, gave up on their escape and gave the wheel a savage twist into E Dock. "Jump!"

Together, they leaped for one of the arms of the dock, scrabbling against the rough wood for purchase. The Styrofoam under the wood squeaked, crumbling to bits under their feet. In a panicked surge of strength, June got a foothold on the dock and wrenched herself up. Her nails felt like they'd be torn from her fingers by the effort of hanging on to the wooden pillar. She reached for Lark, who was hanging, quickly losing purchase above the water. She screamed again, but it might as well have been a silent film in that noise. Their boat spun in a slow-motion swizzle away, toward the oncoming danger, then, picked up in its approach, it came hurtling back toward them like a missile.

June caught Lark's wrist. All that energy that never knew where to go, all that bundled fire, June unleashed it and yanked Lark up beside her, anchoring them together with an arm around Lark's waist. *Stay.* The word—the need—thrummed through her body. *Stay with me.*

"Brace for impact," a man yelled from the end of the dock. People ran again, abandoning their boats, scattering for safety.

As one bore down on the other, the movement of the dock seemed almost sluggish, a smooth, slow-motion arc. June held Lark closer, bracing them together. The remaining boats of F Dock seemed to strain away, pushing and pulling on ropes that held dreadfully steady.

"Close your eyes," June pleaded. And with a screech that shook the air, the docks crashed together.

Wood splinters the size of tire irons exploded around them, the unholy screech of metal rending against metal, glass shattering, a sudden flare of boat horns. Beneath their feet, planks cracked, and they were suspended in air—then falling—when the dock beneath them folded. And June wrapped Lark tighter until they could have fused, bone to bone, rib to rib, heart to heart.

Still, her body screamed: *Stay. Stay.*

Stay.

Stay.

ℰℐ

Face-to-face with a thunderstorm, Cassie froze. Catfish's eyes, this close, were pieces of flint. Catfish took a breath, and with it, lightning crashed dangerously close, enough that Cassie felt it sting across the surface of her skin.

Catfish didn't want to leave the water. She was not its. *It* was *hers.* She had loved it, and now, she was everywhere in it, and not a thing happened on the lake that Catfish didn't feel.

"Then what do you want from me? If you don't need help, why do you need me? Please," Cassie asked, settled on her heels. "Is it because I'm—I'm his granddaughter? Just tell me. I don't know what to do, Catfish." She was begging now, five years old again and afraid to be left alone by the older girl. "Help me understand."

Catfish's eyes were so intent, boring into her like fishhooks, and Cassie reached farther over the water.

Catfish's lips parted, and though they didn't move, Cassie heard it, a thread of a sound on the storm's back. "*Give.*"

A warm hand touched her shoulder and pulled her back. "Cassie."

She turned, blind with rainwater. Bolt stood on the shore so close behind her that she couldn't understand how she hadn't heard him. Compared to everything else, and the water soaking through her, he was startling, a blanket after a snowstorm, a mug of hot chocolate in the dead of a winter night.

"Come out of the water." His grip on her twitched tighter. "Please. You don't like it."

"But she—but she's there," Cassie pleaded with him. "I swear she is. She's right there, Bolt."

"I know." Bolt's mouth was grim and flat—pained, Cassie realized after a moment. Why was he in pain? His gaze slid past Cassie to the girl in the water and immediately away again, his face blanched and ill, just on the verge of panic. "I see her. Cassie. *Please.*"

But Cassie felt that cold whisper again. "*Give me.*" She let the water draw her back, away from Bolt, to Catfish's angry stare.

And she fell again out of time and into Catfish's grip.

Into a warm, sunny day and dry land, high above a riverbank, where at the base of a flowering sapling, Catfish sat curled around something she held in her lap—a box of smooth, polished wood with bright brass fixtures. There was a knife in her hand. She was carving into the box, and Cassie already knew the word.

Pearl.

And she knew what had stirred Catfish so deeply that the lake had bled, that her fragile peace had shattered, that ghosts long laid to rest had risen again.

Somewhere, either beside her or decades away, Bolt screamed her name, pulling on her shoulder. Cassie fumbled back, found his hand, and squeezed. "There's a box in my bedroom. Please get it."

Pearl.

That pearl rush was like a miracle. Not just an accident, Grandad had said. *Gave us all some hope for the future.*

To mark what the box held? What was it for? Catfish, the girl of the pearls, the girl who could dive fifty feet, the girl who could crack open a freshwater mussel and find riches inside, who had found so many that people said they spilled out of her pockets in a frozen rain.

But when Catfish raised her head from the chest, it was to wipe tears off her cheeks. She bent over it again, working on the curve of the fourth letter.

She was already sick with yellow fever. The end couldn't be far from her now.

Catfish had already dug a hole. Upturned, new dirt piled around the tree roots, a muddy trowel laying at her side. It was a deep hole. Dirt clung to her skin almost to her shoulders.

To bury riches, she must have worried they would be stolen from her. She carved her secret into wood, for everyone to see, but then buried it in as deep a hole as a girl could dig. Was this what she'd urged Grandad to find? A box buried under the tree where the two of them liked to meet? Grandad had said the final lake was bigger than intended after a terrible storm. A problem, he said, with the locks. A freak accident, flooding the land too soon after three days of stormy weather.

It was Catfish's salvation, her hope for the future, never meant to be buried so deep that it might have never been found but for a single girl disturbing the waters for a single night in a faraway summer.

"I don't understand," Cassie said desperately, though Catfish wouldn't hear.

Catfish finished the last letter and kissed the top of the box. Her tears caught in the wood grain. She reached into her collar and pulled out a key that hung around her neck. She held the key to her lips so tightly, Cassie wondered if Catfish was keeping herself from opening the box again to see its treasure one more time. She bent over it again, and silently, her shoulders shook.

White petals drifted to catch in her hair.

Lightning crashed so close, Cassie felt it rattle her spine, and Catfish was there again, her anger shrieking on the wind. She had retreated further into the water, hands clutching at her face, bent like reeds in the wind.

Cassie was half drowned in Catfish's memories and still so lost. "Is it the pearls?" Cassie asked. "You want the treasure back? The one you meant for you and my grandfather?"

For a long, furious moment, Catfish didn't say a word.

"The pearls aren't in the box," Bolt said from behind her. Despite his obvious fear, he'd done as she'd asked. In his hands was the box. He stared down at it, eyes black with pain and fear. "Grandad found them in one of his fish traps. I saw—" He looked from Cassie to Catfish. "This is what she wants?"

Catfish's lips trembled. *"Give me—give back—back to me— give her—give her back to me."*

Cassie looked at Catfish again. Her eyes were fixed on the box in Bolt's arms with fierce need. The water was eternally cold out here, even in the sun, because the lake was so deep, more than two hundred feet in places now, Grandad had once told her. She could still imagine a summer day in her earliest, most sun-soaked memories, her in a puffy life vest, and Grandad, his knobby knees sticking out from damp shorts, fishing worms out of the old

Crisco tin he used as a bait box and tossing lines. *Do you know how deep one hundred feet is, Cassie? I used to fish this lake with my girl, and she could dive almost half that, straight down, no fear.* Cassie had wanted to know if he meant Grandma, and his face had turned worn. *No. Not Grandma. A childhood sweetheart.*

Catfish had come, again and again, to the shore visible from the porch of the double-wide. The porch where Grandad had liked to watch the light change. Where he had been found after the last, biggest heart attack. He was sitting in a lawn chair and gazing at the water. Cassie's mother brought him another beer and went back inside. It had taken finding the bottle sun warm and untouched an hour later for her to realize he was gone.

He had told Cassie so much, without saying what mattered. A childhood sweetheart. His purchase of land along the lake. A secret stash of treasures—*Catfish's* treasures—kept safe in one of Grandad's traps, their plans for a future as bright as hope, as pure as milk.

"Oh." Cassie realized, and in the span of a heartbeat, the rain, the thunder, the lightning, even the waves, all stopped. Cassie had held the chest in her arms. She'd soothed it with every trick she knew, every beeswax lullaby she had in her repertoire, built over years trying to rescue treasures from the deepest places. But she could not mend this hurt.

Catfish didn't take her eyes off that little sacred chest. Why would she? What would her life have been, if yellow fever hadn't come, if she hadn't succumbed to illness and drowned in a schoolhouse, locked in with the sick and dying? She would have made a new start with her lover, with their secret intact and growing inside her. They would have found themselves a new corner of the world, somewhere else with water, and had their honeymoon surrounded by so many pearls, they couldn't all be kept in a cabinet. They would roll underfoot, forming new freshwater constellations on the floor all the time. So many that a little girl with Mediterranean skin, Fairchild eyes, and a swimmer's heart could've used them as marbles, could have looped a few of her favorites on a string and given them back to her mother.

Cassie scrambled up the bank to him. "Give it to me, Bolt," she said.

The rain fell again, clapping against the water, and Bolt shook his head, eyes catching on Cassie. "Don't go out there."

"Bolt." She caught his wrists, noticing blood down the side of his soaked shirt. "It's okay now. She won't hurt me."

He didn't want to let it go, and Cassie fought for a grip on the chest, water catching in the letters Catfish had carved so long ago, the only memorial she could offer. The only gift she could give in her sickness and isolation: a name.

Bolt gave in, his grip loosening, and Cassie cradled the chest as tenderly as she could. She waded out to the water to meet her oldest friend.

CHAPTER TWENTY

ARK DIDN'T OPEN HER EYES.

F Dock's collision sounded like a fifteen-car pileup in the Lincoln Tunnel. There was the roar of the storm, the low, bony boom of dock hitting dock, the twist and shriek of contorting metal. Clinging to each other, Lark's face hidden in June's neck, they huddled in the rain, waiting.

Lark held her breath. She was afraid the next inhale would be water. June was limp in her arms.

She realized, dimly, that it was quiet now. Dragging in a breath of new green air, she finally forced her eyes open. At first, it made no difference; the static chaos of what she saw was more confusing than the noise had been. "June," she rasped. "June. What—"

She didn't answer, but Lark felt her warm breath against her neck, ragged, exhausted huffs. Lark looked about again. Somehow, they weren't dead. A dog was even barking somewhere near. They'd been passed over.

The docks were no longer at the water's whim but firmly caught and held at that point of impact by a series of strong, impossibly thick roots wrapped around poles, clutching dock arms, and braced between E and F Dock like heavy clamps.

In the crash zone, boats still leaked and crumpled; some were even up out of the water completely, with their prows in the air, crunched on top of one another. And yet it all hung there, suspended, the disaster halted halfway through.

And in the center of the new growth, cradled above the surface of the water, June and Lark were sheltered so safely, so securely that there was no doubt in Lark's mind about what had happened. After years of running, place to place, June had found her roots.

Their salvation was half fainted in Lark's arms, June's breath coming out in shallow pants. Several people had screamed, and a child's cry lingered long after the last roll of thunder overhead. Even after the hard shakes of impact and the interminable trembling of aftershock subsided, Lark hid in the ozone scent of June's skin. The damage was bad. But it should have been catastrophic.

With a flinch, June began to come to, a flush already high on her cheeks. Beyond a few scrapes and splinters, no damage done. Her eyes found Lark's like moths kissing the flame. "Are you okay?"

Lark had to laugh. "Oh, sweetheart. Am *I* okay? Look what you did."

June sat up. Tiny pink buds bloomed just behind her ear, blue ones across her forehead. As she inhaled the details of their shelter, gulped in the sight of the docks' new architecture, Lark watched wonder sprout across her face. Around them, people stared, befuddled at the strangeness of the roots that locked the docks down and yet fused them together at that point of impact. One girl—Sammy, Mabel's granddaughter—was bravely stepping over them toward Joe's place, his petrified, trembling ferret held carefully in her hands.

"I...?" June trailed off, overwhelmed.

They might've hung like that forever, in their shelter of roots—except neighbors needed help. Numbed, with one stolen glance at each other, Lark and June hurtled into action, ducking between the tendrils of their protective cage to rush toward the center of the destruction. The ramp down to Echo was loose and rickety, and they slowly descended into the darkness.

Immediately there were things to do. Several pets had escaped, panicked in the darkness. Some people hadn't woken in their boats until the collision. At least one person was trapped beneath a fallen beam. Lark fumbled her phone light on and spotted the twins still reeling in the blackness. "Call 911," she said to them. "Let's see what we can do."

Eventually, dawn pulled itself free of the murk and bloomed on a pale steaming horizon the morning after the storm. She got Aunt Valerie on the phone, and within fifteen minutes, she and Diego were there with giant thermoses of coffee and paper cups. Mitch came a few minutes after, wearing the same clothes as the day before. They all gaped at the sculptural tangle of protective roots for a few moments, found no question worth asking, and then jumped into action.

The rest of the hours of the night were taken up with the first response, and all of them were busy enough to avoid looking at the *Big Dipper* at all. The people of F Dock were in the worst state, and Valerie lent a hand as those who could climbed awkwardly onto E Dock to make it to shore. Diego managed to salvage Lou, a retired veterinarian and eager fisherman, out of his boat, which was leaking gasoline and sucking in water. Mable, who'd slept through the whole thing, found her boat loose from the dock and drifting into the lake, so Mitch went out in his fishing boat to rescue her. Some slips were just empty. The boats closest to impact were already half-sunken, back ends crumpled like tin cans. Through the blur of destruction, one that only became clearer as the sky lightened, Lark helped where she could. Firefighters and the sheriff's department arrived through the deluge about the time that June (against Lark's advice) was clambering up a half-toppled pillar to catch someone's lost parakeet.

There were many injuries. Apparently, as they learned in the minutes and hours that followed, there had been only one casualty. Jeff Daley had dived out into the storm and been crushed between a cruiser and the back of his own boat.

By the time firefighters streamed around Lark, June had returned, splinters in her palms, one hand cupped around the parakeet clinging to her shirt. There was a mark on her neck that Lark had left there. She was so desperate to finally talk with June, to unpack the strangeness of what they had seen, to check her over for scratches, to rediscover themselves on solid ground.

But June's face was tight, and Lark could see before she spoke that she couldn't stay. "I'm so sorry," she said, squeezing both her hands. "I have to go. I promised Eliza I wouldn't run off, and after this storm, she's got to be worried."

"Thank you for staying so long. And for, you know. My life." Lark tugged the jeweler's loupe from around her neck and pressed it into June's hand. "I'll see you later."

"I'll be back as soon as I can," June promised and darted forward, pressing two featherlight kisses against Lark's brows, one over each eye. "First thing tomorrow."

Then the current of people carried them different ways. Lark nearly collided with Deputy Cyril, who was setting up a barrier between the *Godfather* and the rest of E Dock. "I'm sorry, but this end is off-limits," he managed, blocking her. "This is an active investigation."

Aunt Valerie wrapped a bracing arm around Lark. "C'mon, honey," she said, pressing a cup of scorching coffee into her hands. "Time to go check on your parents' boat."

Lark shivered as they walked back to the boat she'd avoided for as long as dusky early morning allowed. She skimmed her hand over the front rails, keeping her eyes down. But at first glance, the *Big Dipper* seemed unharmed. Only one of the fraying old ropes had failed, leaving her skewed in the slip, back end slightly catty-corner. There were several long painful gashes in the faded paint. But the boat was sound—no leaks, no fatal injuries. Miraculously, Lark's dinghy was clinging on by a thread. It was strings away from being long gone, either to the bottom of Prosper or skimming around on its own way in some hidden cove—but it had held on stubbornly and bumped its nose against the dock with every wave when she arrived.

But the telescopes.

Lark's stomach buckled as they picked their way onto the front, where the first of the casualties lay in plain view. Broken glass twinkled in a Milky Way across the deck carpet. Not a single telescope turned on its tripod to watch them. "It's not all of them," Lark said to Aunt Valerie automatically, her throat dry. "I've packed so many. Twenty boxes, maybe—all safe. These are just..."

But there were so many. All silent. They walked through the

glass sliding door, which hung ajar from the jolt of the collision. The inside was a battlefield. The boxy early millennium TV had fallen from its place and lay busted on the ground beside couch cushions, as was the barometer that usually stood beside the neglected captain's chair and the coffee maker. Coffee grounds dribbled under the unreliable dishwasher. Lark's mother's blown-glass vase, once buttressed on the kitchen table by telescope cases, had been thrown against one of the windows and lay shattered on the ground. And amid these things, every telescope Lark had neglected was on its side, unmoving. Stands were toppled, lens caps displaced. Several of the delicate tripods had snapped. Glass crunched beneath their feet. She swallowed, bracing herself on one of the chairs.

"You took great care of this place." Aunt Valerie was stoic, as strong as her coffee. A little broken glass couldn't get under her skin. "Sit and rest. I'll get a broom and get this glass out of here. Mitch will be right back. We can get it all fixed up in no time." She checked the time on Mama's dangling kitchen clock. "Then we're gonna call that realtor and get her in here to take a look."

"But—" Lark's lip trembled. "It's not time yet."

Valerie hunted for a broom in the cramped utility closet. "It's time. Past time."

Lark gazed around at the destruction, this new world throwing the futility of her summer's work into stark relief. "I'm not done. I'm not—ready."

Valerie had fought a broom out from the tangle of appliances. She leaned on it, casting a thoughtful glance around at the *Big Dipper*. Very lightly, she touched Lark's hair. "You've got another home here, baby. It's time to let this one go."

❧

Though the rain had stopped, as if the clouds were simply wrung out, the gray sky was still swollen like a punched cheek. Bolt felt just as finished. Cassie pressed fresh gauze to his side and the honest-to-God stab wound there. He was propped against the dusty headboard, where he'd slept that night for the first time all summer. Faded daffodil sheets. The mobile of red mechanical cardinals Grandad had made him when he was a child. A family picture on the wall.

"The box was—"

Cassie nodded. "Yes."

"And she was…"

"She loved him. And she died too young." Cassie tightened the fresh bandages. On the floor below them lay unused gauze, Cassie's first shaky attempts from the night before, like bits of wrinkled snake skin on the carpet. "You saw her," she reassured him. "You saw everything I did. It was real."

He'd seen Cassie, who could barely look at the lake, take up an eerie burden and wade into the water she'd feared for Bolt's whole life. He'd seen her walk straight toward the girl in the water, a girl so angry and hurt and as dangerous as raw nature. Cassie had held out the chest, and the girl had taken it, cradled it against her body. She'd bent like a willow tree over it, tracing the rough letters carved into the grain. Cassie had stood there, watching as the girl turned away and walked into the water. It had come up to her chest, and her hair had billowed like moss. The water had lapped at her shoulders. But it was tamer, no longer the storm swells it had been, the kind that could drag you under with an alligator's brutality. Cassie had stayed in the wakes, a faithful witness as the girl vanished under the surface and out of sight.

"She was there all the time. She was real, and we didn't believe you," Bolt started, some kind of apology still swirling, amorphous emotion in his head.

"You were a child," Cassie replied. "It was unbelievable. Arms up."

He lifted his arms gingerly so she could wind the new gauze around his ribs. Her hands were gentle and reassuring. "I think I was hearing her call to me," Bolt admitted. "Sleepwalking. Like he did."

"He probably heard her again near the end, when he was forgetting things. I don't believe she meant to hurt us, really," she said. "And she won't now. I think you'll sleep just fine."

If Cassie said so, if she was sure, Bolt could be too. He suspected he'd only witnessed the very end of a long train of horrors. But Cassie was calm to the bone, in a way she had never been before.

She tucked one end of the bandage into the others, pulling it to a neat close. "I'll sell some of the land if you want," she added out of nowhere. "If it'll help you. After all this."

They hadn't talked about it, that last, greatest fight or what they both believed had become of the pearls, what the man they both knew was most likely to have done with a bounty like that, grieving all he'd lost to other men's greed and fear. It had gone unspoken, with everything else.

Before Bolt could think of an answer, his phone buzzed with an incoming message. It was Sammy.

Jeff Daley, king of the lake, she texted him, was dead.

Rig had wandered home after a night on the dam, lost in the

woods, people were saying. No one had noticed him coming onto the wreckage of Echo before he saw his father's arm, wrist-watch still ticking, jutting from between the hulking bodies of his houseboat and the next. Rig's mother was driving up from Little Rock, where she owned a little interior design company, to collect him.

Cassie read the stream of messages over Bolt's shoulder and then tucked him gently against her, like when she'd read him stories as a kid. "What do you want to do?" she asked.

Bolt should have been thinking about the man he'd known and admired once upon a time. But all he could think of was Rig. It was hard to connect the Rig who'd sunk a knife into his side with the one he had met all those years ago in school, the offbeat little artist with too much intelligence and not enough outlets. For all he seemed like a vagabond, a shiftless drifter, like the fireworks man, Rig had never lived away from the security blanket of his wealthy father.

"I want to see him," Bolt decided.

So he let himself into the empty Grand Destiny kitchen early, turned on the ovens, and borrowed one of Valerie's aprons. She'd taught him all her little tricks, how to fold blueberries into sugar and vanilla and then into a piecrust, always made from scratch. Magic, she called it. The magic of her great-grandmother's crust was the cure for all ills.

Cassie didn't understand why he had baked a pie. She certainly didn't understand why he'd want to go see Rig. But she agreed to drive. Bolt held the pie on his lap, and they cruised around the basin to the docks, hopping puddles and dodging waterlogged bumps in the road, jolting his wound. The windows were down, and the day was still and muggy. They hurtled around a craterous bend.

Cassie parked in the lot beside a Ford Explorer, left her engine still rumbling. There was a bee balanced on her ring finger.

"I'll wait here," she said, which wasn't surprising. For all her bravery the night before, there were still quite a few people around, and she didn't thrive in a crowd. "Unless you need me."

"No. I won't be long." Bolt hopped out, pie in hand, and started the walk down to the half-drowned, still-reeling Echo Dock.

The sight was dramatic enough that he paused, sucking in a breath. The neighboring dock hung at the wrong angle, like a broken arm, dislocated entirely from its hinge on land and yet fused with E Dock where it had swung with such force. The water was so high, it had devoured the nearest trees, and the gangplank was low and soggy. Out on the water, workers on boats attempted to disentangle the two docks, doing battle with a new formation of roots that clung on like stubborn old growth. Occasionally a crash or the scrape of industrial ruins echoed over the lake.

Bolt held the pie, the glass dish still warm on the bottom, picking over the patchwork of broken dock and ropey roots. It was dark and silent. No electricity. The houseboaters spoke in low, careful tones. He saw Valerie on her brother's boat, sweeping up glass, and she paused to hug him and peck his cheek.

"I don't know what to say to him," Bolt admitted, gripping the pie tightly.

Valerie laid a hand on his back. Any anger at his disappearance the night before was washed away in relief that he was all right. "There's no right thing to say. That's why you brought the pie."

Jeff Daley's slip was the last on the dock, twice as long as any of the others. Rig had liked showing that off in his typical blasé manner. He'd never explained why he preferred Rig to Ritchard, but maybe the nautical name had been tied to the houseboat. Or perhaps he liked it because it was like naming himself a cheater, a person who could always rig the game. Bolt had never asked about that either.

There were a lot of people on the *Godfather*, or at least, what was left of it. It looked to be a whole room shorter than it had once been, the back deck and back bedroom totally crushed. Daley's family and friends were crammed into the rest, a solemn gathering with his ex-wife, Rig's mom, reigning in the middle. She looked small, her thin face drawn and framed by a gleaming curtain of dark hair. But there was no sign of Rig there among his family.

Bolt found him on the roof, staring out at the crumpled wreck of the houseboat's back end. The frenetic, horrifying energy of the night before had drained away, and Rig was just a kid again, bony shoulders hunched in on themselves, his hands still for once.

"Hey." The pie was making Bolt's hands clammy.

Rig glanced up at him, his eyes dull and red. He took in Bolt, the pie in his grip, and then looked back at the water. "Hey," he said.

"I brought a pie," Bolt offered. "Oh hell. Rig..."

"I told you he'd been acting like a psycho," Rig snapped, wrapping his arms around his legs. "I was at Woody's after we saw y'all." An explanation—an alibi. "That was pretty out of control out there."

"I wouldn't know. Someone stabbed me," Bolt said before he could stop himself. He winced and took a long painful breath. "I didn't mean that."

"Yeah. Well…" It wasn't in Rig to apologize. He gave a forced, slightly soggy laugh. "Weird summer, huh?"

It was all he'd get from Rig, who had never been much of a giver. *We spent our days on the water or shooting firecrackers—* weird summer! *I stabbed you last night, and my dad died*—weird summer! *I don't know what got into me*—weird summer!

And yet what did Bolt have to offer him? Forgiveness for wounds Rig didn't care about? There had to be something. In these situations, wasn't there always something to be done, some comfort to offer?

At a loss, Bolt rested a palm on Rig's back, tucking the pie against his stomach.

It felt wrong.

Pressing his lips together, Rig looked up at him, eyes glassy, and nodded. "Um. Thanks." He swallowed. "For coming."

That felt wrong too. They were just kids playing adult.

"Take care," Bolt said. "You don't have to eat the pie if you don't want to."

Rig snorted and didn't answer until Bolt was halfway down the stairs. "Probably will."

When Bolt returned to the parking lot, Cassie was parked where he'd left her in that dusty old El Camino, her window open. Hadn't there just been one bee? Now two crawled around the collar of her cotton shirt. But she looked happy, twirling her fingers in the wind.

"Okay?" Cassie asked, gaze huge and concerned on his face.

He nodded, pulling the seat belt across his ribs with a twinge. He pictured the return of spring, Cassie's bees building a new hive, exploring a world of wildflowers around grassy fields. He remembered Grandad, who used to take him fishing on his birthdays, and the serene coves where they'd laid down lines under the green umbrellas of those April trees. And those velvet-soft nights when Mom, Valerie, and Grandad would sit with their feet in the Grand Destiny's pool, and tucked safe in bed, he and Cassie would hear them belting out Dolly Parton, all the way up the hill.

"I don't want to sell the land," he admitted in the safety of the cab. "I don't want to wake up one day and not recognize this place." He glanced up at her. "Do you think that'll cost me?"

Cassie smiled as she checked her rearview mirror, and he could tell she was quietly, painfully relieved. "Not even for a second."

☙

Aunt Eliza and June drove cautiously down drowned roads toward the church, Eliza's knuckles on the steering wheel telling the whole story of her long night, her panicked search. There had been power outages and flooding all around the lake, so some people were sheltering at the church. She'd heard where June was from one of the F Dock refugees. She'd heard about the miracle, roots that sprang from the water to hold the docks down. People were already scoffing, saying clearly it was old growth that had been caught up by the swinging F Dock, a trick of luck and nature. June didn't say a word, still feeling the thrum of their creation in her body.

"Phones out, power out, lightning and thunder—" Eliza took a shivering breath, wiping at her eyes again. "What were you *thinking?*" She reached over to give June's hand another tendon-cracking squeeze, anger—but mostly a bone-deep relief—contained in the grip. "You're lucky I didn't call your mama. Another hour and I would've." They whooshed through another puddle so deep, it was nearly a pond in the middle of the road. "Did you hear somebody died? What if—what if that had been you?"

Eliza's mixed concern and anger washed over June, and she closed her eyes. The storm had dried cold on her skin, in her clothes, and the stench of fear was everywhere around her. She was more wrung out than she could remember being in a long time. Listening to the pitch of Eliza's voice, it occurred to June how very rarely in her life she was truly exhausted.

"I'm sorry," she said again. "Really. I should have called."

Eliza glanced at her, reading the fatigue that must've shown in every line of her. "You could've tried," she relented. "Service was out. Let's go home so you can get some…" They were at the corner, ready to turn into the church lot. But across the street, just a little farther down the road, the Bag of Tricks Traveling Pyrotechnics Co. truck curved across the gravel lot of Fairchild's. "There's that truck again," she murmured. "I saw you on his barge last night during the show."

"Yes," June admitted. She pinched the bridge of her nose. "I… paid for it. I was stupid. The things I saw last night made me wish I'd never—" She could still see those under the water, their silent grief. "I didn't believe in ghosts before. Not really. But now…"

Eliza didn't scoff or shrug it off. She watched the truck through the windshield, unblinking. After a moment, Jack came around the back, unrolling the tarps, adjusting a strap. "You never met Great-Granddaddy," she said thoughtfully. Her voice was very calm. "He told some strange stories about this town. Drifters, dealing in magic tricks and trouble." Her fingernails, painted a dusky blue, tapped the steering wheel. "I think it's time for that man to go."

She passed the church lot and turned into Fairchild's, parking alongside the truck. Jack looked up, nonplussed. There was no tent set up now. Had he passed the storm in his truck?

"What are we doing?" June asked.

Aunt Eliza didn't answer, just jerking her seat belt loose before ducking out of the car and striding over to where Jack stood chewing his lip. She was tall, nearly as tall as he was, standing there in the mist.

The car was running. June cracked her window, wet air whipping her face.

"I think you've been here long enough," Eliza said.

Jack reclined on one foot, appraising her, still wearing his quiet smirk. "You're the reverend these days, huh? Trying to fill old Hiram's big shoes?" June's mind flitted to that proud face, those brown hands around the sunflower stem. Somehow he knew. Or remembered.

"That's right." Eliza faced him head-on, so June couldn't read her face, but she could imagine it, the unflappable stare, the stillness. "My great-grandfather watched over this place. We had people here. So I came back." A pause spread out between them. "Why did you?"

His lips only twisted. "That was some show last night. What did you think?"

"I think you better stay away from my niece." Her voice had an edge now, a knife blade beneath a calm surface. It was full of power, maybe a special kind of force she'd learned standing at a pulpit. "You've done enough here. Move on."

He stared at her, and for an instant, his eyes flickered to settle on June, waiting in the car. He nodded to her, and it was to her that he spoke. "I'm all packed up anyways. There are always other places to go." He was a thing that kept on and on. He just carried his tricks from one town to the next, and he never stopped.

June caught the door handle and shoved it open. After the solidity of the earth, she would never chase fire again. "Not for you," she snapped. "No one needs you here, and wherever you go next, they don't need you there. I don't need you."

He didn't have an answer to that, only stood there, very still, holding her gaze as long as she would give it to him. He was very old and shabby.

Eliza turned and walked back to the car at a steady pace. She got in. They used the half-mud gravel to turn around.

When June looked back, she couldn't help but see how lonely he looked there.

"I'm proud of you, honey," Eliza said. They drove. That was the end of it.

She turned to Aunt Eliza. "I want to show you what I've been doing in the cemetery."

June dreaded seeing what havoc the storm had wreaked in her garden. It had ripped F Dock across the water, so what could it do to her new flowers? The sapling fig tree, the dogwood, the stones she'd piled into a makeshift bench: It would be trashed now. All the new flowers would be overturned, their pale roots floating in the water, and all that fertilizer and velvet soil she'd bought and laid would be swept out.

June was always the leaver in her life, the one who roamed. In every breakup, she'd never kept the apartment. No wonder she was more comfortable in chaos, on the road, between places—she never got to be the one who stayed. She never learned how. The garden was the first thing she'd built herself. She hadn't shared it with anyone yet, but maybe that was part of the problem. Maybe good things needed to be shared. Maybe it made a difference.

When she led Aunt Eliza down the path, the air smelled of petrichor: earth and rain.

"I'm amazed we didn't get more flooding over here." Eliza stepped carefully, avoiding the path's muddy edges. This way had started to know June, to clear for her. There were no more logs, no more low-hanging branches threatening to scrape her face and catch in her hair. The path spilled them out into the garden.

Eliza came to a hard squelching stop at the boundary of the cemetery. She gaped, like what she was seeing was the end of a sentence she'd been only half listening to. Now she was drawn up short, eyes shimmering with sheer amazement.

The garden hadn't died but had flourished, and it was nothing like what June had planned, full of strange meandering paths the flowers had forged, spirals that trailed off into nothing, and several arteries that pointed to the fig tree. A jacket of white blossoms covered jasmine vines, still clinging to stone and bark. Small white flowers grew like lamb wool along the ground, and a vine that crawled up the side of a nearby cedar suddenly blinked awake with purple blossoms. Lush azaleas, a sweep of leafy rhododendrons, the dark green foliage of hardy shrubs that would take care of themselves without her help. Hydrangeas flowered their best and brightest in the sunny spots, huge creamy clusters that looked strong enough to bloom into winter.

The storm hadn't totally spared her little plot; water had pooled halfway up the clearing, settling around the angel's feet. Hyssop stalks were up to their chins in the water but refused to bow to it. The fig tree and its ripe little fruits stood, shivering, and most of the snowdrops had been completely uprooted, drifting forlornly among the lily pads.

And that was the largest change. The lily pads were huge and thick. June could have sat on one. She could have lain down on some of the verdant rafts. Eliza knelt to examine a bed of soft clovers—several seemed to have four leaves—and brushed her way through a patch of larkspurs and candytufts that whispered against her fingers as she passed.

Look, they said, *look how we've grown.*

The petunias had gathered in, turning their faces to the water as if to gossip with each other. She toed her shoes off amid a cluster of black-eyed Susans, walking down curlicue paths lined with traveler's-joy, white heather, bright orange blossoms, and resilient, pocked prickly pears.

"June, baby," Aunt Eliza breathed. "What on earth did you think you needed that man's help for when you made all this?"

June felt tears warming in her eyes. "Maybe we should build a little gazebo," she said. "People from the church can come sit out here, give the residents some company." It could be unfinished wood so honeysuckle could climb into it and moss could hide in the eaves.

When she reached the edge of the water, she stepped onto a lily pad, spongy under her bare feet. It trembled, but it didn't sink. It held.

"Lord, help." Eliza took a step after her, careful but fearless in her faith. She beamed at June. "This is a miracle. An honest-to-God miracle."

They stepped to the next, again to the next, and the next. They stretched from the size of tires to the size of coffee tables, and then—

Then one that must have been six feet across. She hadn't known lily pads could grow that big. June and Eliza sank to their knees and then to their backs. Cool water soaked June's shirt, her shorts, from where it had pooled on the lily pad. It didn't sink but held her, and she felt breathless with delight and gratitude.

Aunt Eliza laughed suddenly. "You know, your great-granddaddy was quite the gardener himself, along with tending that old church." She sighed, shutting her eyes in contentment. "He couldn't keep still a day in his life, pouring himself into the people and things that mattered." She reached for June's hand, pressing their palms together. "That energy you've got, I think maybe he had a little of it too."

And suddenly June felt she could tell her anything. She could talk about the girls she had left and the ones who had left her or how often she had to forgive Dad for raising cats better than his own daughter. She could have talked to her about the very first morning she woke up with poppies growing from her hair, her head thick with their elusive scent of dreams. She had followed the bud to that gentle place where it became a part of her, where they felt especially fragile, incongruous and easily dislodged, and she had been so, so proud—until Mom had come with scissors, cut the poppies out, and ordered her not to talk about it to anyone because Mom loved her and was afraid. June could talk about how flowers were changing into powerful trees and the truth of the docks. She could talk about Lark, and the tentative way her heart had started to bloom pink and rose again, and the box that drew them together, one last wrong June still hoped could be fixed.

But there was no rush. In a minute. June smiled at the sky and kept her aunt's hand.

CHAPTER TWENTY-ONE

FTER THE STORM, THE SHORELINE WAS LITTERED
with treasures from below: Old bottles, pairs of glasses,
china dolls, and cutlery, all rusted and muddy. A few
chalkboards that looked like they came from a school; the waterlogged leather-bound covers of hymnals, their pages long since
disintegrated; shoes with empty eyelets, their laces a long-ago
banquet for the fish. But that wasn't all that washed up. Several
old bodies in yellowed clothes had been found on the shores near
the dam. Laid out in almost a perfect line in the reeds, they were
mistaken for mannequins at first. A baffled coroner from Little
Rock could only guess some natural phenomenon, perhaps the
cold at the bottom of the lake had preserved them, all dating
back to the building of the dam, all likely drowning victims. But
everyone knew what she didn't say: they shouldn't have been there
at all, in land doomed for flooding, and they certainly shouldn't
have been preserved all this time, waiting to be found.

Once the lukewarm investigations of law enforcement con-
cluded, with no family to claim them, Mitch had the idea to
bury them in the cemetery, and June's aunt, Eliza, held a tiny
ceremony as they were interred safely in June's garden.

It had been a small service, just Lark's family, June and Eliza, and Cassie and her brother, Bolt. In the name of laying the people to rest, June's garden was nearly demolished, flowers sacrificed to fresh dirt plots.

"It's all torn up," Lark said, dismayed.

June smiled. She had satisfaction in her eyes and soil under her fingernails, reeling Lark in to kiss her knuckles. "It'll grow back. You'll see."

It was days later now, days that had passed as gently as a light breeze around Lark as she spun here and there, trying to finish everything she needed to do. Plans had been made, hasty, heady plans. For Lark, it was time to get going.

"Mitch—do you have any more of those licorice life jackets?" Lark shouted, stuffing Rice Krispies into her army jacket. The worn-out old garment hung to her knees. It was the jacket she always wore to the movies, oversize, full of pockets to tuck snacks in. Perfect for road trip preparation.

Mitch poked his head out of the inventory room. "What I've got is on the table. Try the box turtles. Paula makes good caramel."

Lark tucked a family of chocolate turtles into an interior pocket, along with several slabs of the raspberry fudge. Valerie was in the restaurant, cooking up a storm to cope with her feelings about Lark's departure. At this rate, the Explorer would have a trunk full of fried chicken.

"Got your driving playlist ready?" Mitch asked, tucking her under his arm for an almost-painful squeeze.

Lark grinned at him. "All Memphis groups."

Valerie appeared in the door with Diego, three plastic bags full of food weighing her down. She'd already delivered a breakfast large enough to feed the multitude to Lark's cabin that morning, where she'd been staying during the last week of the houseboat cleanup. She sat out at the rickety little table to eat eggs Benedict. The lake had sparkled, the early morning sunlight casting the opposite bank in a prism of rose tones as she sipped her coffee. It was so easy to forget the truth below. People who benefited from it would always be sure to forget.

Earlier, she'd walked up to Cassie's property from the Grand Destiny. Cassie seemed a bit flummoxed, as always, by the surprise, but then she was happy, pouring Lark a glass of peach tea from a pitcher hand painted long ago. They sat and looked down at the lake together. "Mitch told me you were leaving," Cassie said.

"It's time for me to go," Lark replied. They'd sat together like this most evenings of Lark's last week, finishing up with the telescopes while Cassie told her the whole story in low tones. Of the woman they'd seen together at the houseboat graveyard, of her pearls and her treasure.

"That reminds me." Lark dug in her purse, pulling out the mother-of-pearl binoculars she'd marked for Cassie, too precious to sell, too marvelous to give up to a stranger. "I can never thank you enough for all you've done for me. But—I want you to have these."

Cassie's eyes were very wide and bashful, as if she didn't receive presents all too often. "Write to me," she insisted. "I always thought it would be nice to have a pen pal, and I don't like texting."

Lark chuckled. "You got it. We need some way for you to tell me where all the spyglasses end up."

Cassie had given her a long wordless embrace, the binoculars still tucked between them against her chest.

Now Lark's family walked her out to the Explorer, Diego giving Lark's shoulder a quick pat. Mitch had taken the bags of lunch from Valerie, who didn't seem to know what to do with her hands, hovering restlessly. "Don't forget," she sniffed. "The realtor said she put the signs behind the deck chairs."

"I know." Lark turned and wrapped her arms around her aunt. "Love you. Thank you for everything."

For once, Aunt Valerie melted like butter. "I love you too. You're an awfully brave girl."

Lark waved goodbye to them in her rearview mirror. Diego took Valerie's hand. Lark turned a corner, and the Grand Destiny disappeared in the trees.

The lights were finally back on at E Dock, and a few neighbors waved to her as she passed them. She didn't make a fuss, just said hello and didn't mention leaving. She walked around to the back deck of the *Big Dipper* first and climbed over the railing to gaze out at the cove.

She scanned the familiar vista, the memories inlaid in it. She needed no spyglass to see them play out in shadow theater before her eyes. There where she'd pushed Gil Preston out of a paddle-boat for giving her a wet willy. There where her Girl Scout troop had made s'mores and told ghost stories of the lost souls in the town under the lake. There where she and Mommy had set their pet (for a day) minnow, Buddy Holly, free. He lived in a baby pool for three hours until Lark thought his tiny eyes seemed sad. There where her father had washed her hair in the lake, smushing suds into her cheeks, dunking her until she spluttered. Her uproarious laughter. His.

There where she'd seen a mermaid diving.

Lark dipped her foot in the warm water a final time, heart aching. She would remember it just like this. All of it. Her childhood and happiness and loss, and alongside it the older histories of buried loves and lost places and deep pain. This land was both; it was all. The lake and the town below were both real, pressed together. Lark had needed the spyglasses to see the way the histories were layered like a spiraling shell. Now she would just have to learn to hold both past and present together on her own and try to go on. Not every old hurt could be healed. People, like water, had a way of flowing imperfectly on.

Inside, the boat was quiet, scrubbed, preparing itself for something entirely new. She and Aunt Valerie had completed the job as a team, with Diego helping fix the damage to the hull. With the collection finally gone and the cobwebs dispelled, the place felt a little bare and just a little eager, like a first day of school, long anticipated. The *Big Dipper* might be somewhat nostalgic in its decor, but the realtors had assured Lark that, somehow, this was still a seller's market. This hook, quietly dipped, had already received several bites from weekender-hopefuls. Apparently, the roots, the lore, all of it, was turning into fodder for oblivious tourists and conspiracy theorists. It was just about enough to make anyone a cynic.

Lark had to scrub at her eyes a bit as she rooted behind the deck chairs. She took the FOR SALE signs left by the realtor for her and propped them in the front windows of the *Big Dipper*. "Goodbye," she murmured to the boat, gathering the last of the boxes. In them were photos from the walls, one VCR tape of home movies, her mother's chimes from the front porch. A whole history easily carried away. She locked up and patted the railing.

The hum of things remembered surrounded her. She stood in the shadow of all those roots, June's love, for just a moment longer. But she didn't stay long, and once she was in the Explorer, she didn't look back. There was one more stop to make.

Back behind the church, the path was easy to spot. It had been worn down with repeated footsteps, and it was inviting, opening to her easily, like it remembered her. It curved like a snake, back and forth once, and suddenly, Lark was hit by the colors.

It had been mere days since she was last here, but the garden was already restored. Pale blue cabbage roses the size of her head bent from where they had climbed an awning likely dragged from Cassie's yard of garden sculptures. The lake curled on the far edge, trickling into a small stream, and lily pads spilled into the cove like the train of a long green dress. Lark had never known they could be so huge. The headstones and grave markers were resplendent among clouds of white blossoms and something wild and purple that dripped from a pair of trees. Wisteria? There were vines winding everywhere and flowers so deep and thick, the graveyard would put any arboretum to shame. Spiders spun glassy webs, and there would be lightning bugs every night. Golden honeysuckle strayed nearby.

June had remade all this.

At first Lark didn't even see her. She blended so well with the flowers because there were more in her hair, bright yellow petals. But there she was, in a patch of bright purple berry bushes.

"Yes, you know how I feel about you taking over this corner. Only if you don't choke out my little irises. I like them. They came from Great-Grandad Hiram's seeds I found in a hymnal. Don't you pout over it."

"This is amazing," Lark called, gazing up at a stone angel who wore billowing tangles of white jasmine. The smell was loud, heady, outrageous. "You're amazing."

June jumped, whipping around. She dropped the pair of clippers she'd been holding and grinned. "I told you they'd grow back."

Lark rolled her eyes, smiling. "I don't know how I'm still surprised after all I've seen you do."

"You'll have plenty of time to get used to me." June smiled. Stray clippings stuck out of random pockets, and a sprig of jasmine was tucked behind her ear. The day after the Fourth, Lark had told June the ending of the box's tale. June had listened, tears slipping down her cheeks at the end, and been silent for a long moment.

Then, she stood and clipped a handful of flowers free from a nearby planting, white blossoms with scarlet droplets on the insides of their petals, before gathering them in a bouquet with some twine she'd been using to build a trellis for blush-pink climbing roses. "Alstroemeria," she said, handing one to Lark. The rest, she took to the edge of the shallow water and set to float off between the lily pads. It could have been an apology or an offering. June didn't say, and Lark didn't ask, just brushed the tender petals against her cheek.

"I was thinking about the girl and her box this morning while I was sprucing up the graves again. Catfish." June brushed dirt off her gloves, removed them, and tucked them into the waistband of her shorts. "Was that her nickname or something? Did Cassie give it to her?"

"Catfish?" Why hadn't she asked this? "I'm not—"

June grabbed her hand, twined their fingers, and tugged her through the garden, down one of the meandering paths, and through a patch of clover before bringing her to a stop near a clean white stone surrounded by poppies. "Funny thing, graveyards. You come across all kinds of people here." She turned, giving Lark a nervous, flitting look, and pointed down at a gravestone under the paws of the lion statue, a little cloud of purple flowers growing around its feet.

In letters impeccably carved, the headstone's face bore a name already half weathered away by age. "What do you think?" June murmured. "Could that be her?"

Lark ran her fingertips over the pocked surface of the stone. "Catfish."

Katarina Fischer, 1919–1937.

EPILOGUE

THE MIDDLE OF JULY BEGAN TO ROAST, AND CASSIE'S poor RV was broiling hot even with all her portable fans on. Mitch sweated miserably no matter where they went, and so when even the mornings became steamy, Cassie rolled over to face him and his unhappy pout.

She trailed a finger down his cheek to wake him up. He chuffed drowsily and nuzzled into her. He was such a bear in the morning.

"Let's go swimming today," she said.

That woke him up. He propped up on an elbow in surprise. "You—Cassie. *My* Cassie. You want to go swimming?"

"Yes." She kissed his nose. "I don't have a suit, so I'll wear your shirt." Then his forehead. "You can wear your boxers." The corner of his eye. "I have sunscreen in the double-wide, and I will get it for us on the condition that there is coffee in the pot when I return." Valerie had always said "man hands coffee" was best, and though she stood by her own, Cassie would give it a try. She sat up, stretching, feeling the greasy, unavoidable mats that formed in her hair after a night curled up with another person. "Yes," she agreed with herself. "Let's go swimming today."

Mitch nodded, pondering all this in that way he had, very seriously. He leaned in to catch her mouth for a moment. "Coffee. Coming right up."

There wasn't much in the way of breakfast, only granola with the freshest honey, a peculiar rich blend that was nearly as dark as molasses. The bees whispered of a new source, buzzing about spooling black-eyed Susans, beautyberries blooming purple, Solomon's seal drooping blossoms in the shade, and showy azaleas. She took Mitch's hand, and they rushed down the banks toward water she hadn't wanted to look at. It was still difficult to think about the ragged dock, which she hadn't cared for in years, which might have drifted off entirely if not for Diego's seasonal care. Even with Mitch waiting for her, even though it was her idea, even though she'd braved it on the Fourth of July, Cassie still stopped herself instinctually on the edge of the water, as if a hand might reach out and snatch her, a shard of cruel glass might be waiting for her foot, as if again she would find only torture waiting for her.

Cassie pulled in a deep breath and stepped in.

Nothing but those soft, muddy waves and mossy algae greeted her. She walked deeper, water cool against her skin, welcoming on a hot day. She sank, dropping to her shoulders, and pushed into the water past Mitch. Out in the heart, it was crystal blue, and boats roared now and then, though none came close. The Grand Destiny was closed today. Bolt had returned home. Valerie and Diego were on an exotic vacation to northwest Arkansas, and the place was shut up and peaceful.

Mitch waded out, keeping pace with her, dipping under to get wet. He held her hand, eyes attentive. "I never thought I'd see the day," he admitted, mouth curving.

She cupped her hands, filled them, and poured water over his head, letting it tip down his back. "I didn't either." They swam together, tangled up.

Cassie had told Mitch her secrets, whatever was left. He helped her repopulate the beehives, and she taught him to see the patterns in the bees' dance. She told him about the little Frankenstein miracles Grandad had taught her to make out of scraps of metal and gave him the roaring grizzly bear Grandad had made of some clock gears and springs. Finally, she told him about Grandad's first love and the twisted merging of their lives. She'd talked until her throat was sore, and he'd kissed it better.

Mitch swam now in a perfect breaststroke toward the nearest small island, and Cassie splashed around, imagining the new freckles that would form on her shoulders and how he might try—again—to count them.

She had spent so many years cleaning whatever drowned trinkets she could find, drying them and polishing them, trying to erase water damage and give them absolution. Wholeness. Restoring Prosper, piece by piece. Her life had been spent waiting on shore for the lake to vomit antiques up in a storm or for some intrepid diver to yank old heirlooms from the muddy lake bed, just so she could avoid seeing or touching that water.

Maybe it was time to see what treasures she could pull from the deep—time to dive herself, to trust the place that had raised her. With a final smile at Mitch, she turned on her back and did a backstroke the way Catfish had taught her long ago, propelling herself out past the dock, into where it was blue and glistening.

Once her momentum had slowed to a ramble, she filled her

stomach with air. Just like that, she could imagine Catfish's smile again, her strong arms underneath her back.

I've got you, she would assure her, while they drifted in their little cove, two girls safe in the shallows. *Okay, toes up, arms out.*

Cassie fanned her arms out, fingertips skating on the glassy top the way dragonflies did, those water-skiers in miniature who first taught people to glide.

Good, Catfish would say and step back, gently drawing away. First her support. Then her warmth. And finally her voice would trail off the way an inlet faded into dry land. *Now breathe and rest.*

"Okay, Catfish." Cassie closed her eyes, sunlight warm as a kiss on her face, warm as Mitch's laughter. Whenever she breathed in, the water lifted her.

And she dove.

READING GROUP GUIDE

1. What did you know about the real histories of towns being drowned in "development-induced displacements" prior to reading the book? What ideas or feelings were awakened in you thinking about these true stories while reading?

2. Cassie is terrified to go near the lake, yet she spends her days lovingly restoring objects salvaged from its depths. Why do you think she has devoted her life to this practice? What does it say to you about the ways we are shaped by childhood experiences?

3. What was the significance of the telescopes, and what did they really show to Lark? If you were Lark, would you choose to look through the spyglasses? Why or why not?

4. Lark, Cassie, and June each have a complicated relationship with a parent, whom they both love and yet feel some essential disconnection from. How do they each choose to cope with these relationships? Have you ever had to navigate similar dynamics?

5. June is introduced as a character who has felt pressure to hide parts of herself—like the flowers that grow in her hair. Is the need to hide or reduce some part of yourself a struggle you relate to? How does June's inner conflict unfold through the story?

6. Each of the three main characters is an inheritor of the history of the lake, with familial roots linking them to the past. How do they each contend with this legacy? Where do you come from, and are there any complexities to the way you feel about your own home?

7. The ghostly fisherman retells part of the biblical story of Moses to June. How does that story function in this novel? What did the fisherman mean when he said, "Sickness came, and Pharaoh didn't do a single thing. Didn't lift one finger. Times like that, we do what needs done to save our kin. We let them other people go."?

8. Bolt spends much of his summer with his old friend Rig. But over the course of the book, the dynamics in their friendship radically shift, culminating in violence on the Fourth of July. How are the larger conflicts of the lake reflected in the teenagers' shared tumble into violence?

9. How do June and Lark find each other, and what connects them in the novel? Is it possible to carve out spaces of queer joy in fraught landscapes?

10. The Fourth of July provides a pivotal backdrop to some of the book's most climactic scenes. How does patriotism or the State inflect the events/themes of the novel?

11. Was Jeff Daley a bad person? He came to Lake Prosper with ambitions of building up tourism and "saving the town." How did/didn't he bring about his fate?

12. Who was the fireworks man? What role did he play in the lives of the characters of the book? The fireworks man clearly felt a deep affinity to June. In what ways (if any) was June like him, and how was she different?

13. Near the close of the novel, Lark thinks, "The lake and the town below were both real, pressed together...the histories were layered like a spiraling shell... Not every old hurt could be healed. People, like water, had a way of flowing imperfectly on." How does living near or alongside histories affect the way you live your life? Everyone has been hurt before; how do we honor that pain and still find new joys?

ACKNOWLEDGMENTS

The authors would first like to thank their precious cats, Theo and Prosper, who napped through most of the work we put into this book. To our agent and third Beatle (So, George?), Amy Stapp, a thousand thanks for being our steadfast champion. And to our brilliant editor, Mary Altman, thank you for being Quinn's perfect match in voice, enthusiasm, and favorite drag queens.

Thank you to Sourcebooks Landmark: our production editor, Jessica Thelander; our copy editor, Manu Velasco; our marketing team, Cristina Arreola and Anna Venckus; our amazing cover designers, Brittany Vibbert and Erin Fitzsimmons. And to our thoughtful sensitivity readers, Lashaunda, Margeaux, and Dee, thank you so much for sharing your perspectives and engaging with our work. For input in the course of our research, we humbly thank Cheryl Batts, the CEO and founder of the Uzuri Project in Hot Springs, Arkansas, an organization devoted to preserving local African American history; the Garland County Historical Society; and Dr. Wendy Richter.

Thank you to photographer extraordinaire Frank for capturing our author photo, and to Shelly for flawlessly editing it. Ayana, thank you for loving, for reading, and for always offering your strength and your insights on the publishing process. We may never have even gotten an agent without you.

Thank you to our alma mater, Rhodes College. And finally, gratitude for the other half of Quinn Connor: one always believes when the other can't; one picks up the pieces of our stories the other can't hold alone.

Robyn: thank you to my best friend, my mama. Thank you to Daddy; all the Barrows (what's the next minor holiday I can see y'all for?); Uncle D; my ride-or-die, Kyleigh; until-death, Jessica; my Yorkshire sunshine, Emily; my ever-interlocutor, Erin; my poet, Aylin; my peregrina, Lauren; "hello my dear!" Amanda; Jessi, from the lake; puddin'; Ramey; my strawberry, Ayana (once wasn't enough); Jenny and those Tokheim-Hubbards. Sally Dormer, thank you. To the art history department at Penn, especially my venerable adviser, Sarah, as well as Darlene, Julie, Libby, Shira, Ivan, and Bob. And thank you to my special ones who are gone.

Alex: thank you to my family. Mom, because when I got tired, you picked up the pencil and let me dictate my first story to you. Adrian: because what's a sister, if not God giving you a ride-or-die? And Aunt Loli, for fostering my early love of reading, even when you lived a whole ocean away. (Also Dad, but you already got the dedication.) Thank you to my two very best friends. Nancy, for being the first audience for my amateur, early drafts, and giving me a thousand tiny pushes to keep writing. And Courtney, for being my biggest cheerleader; your friendship carries me through. Thank you to my mentors. Lynn, for your steady counsel; Christian, for your mentorship that transformed my journalistic work; and finally the late Mark Behr, whose fiction writing lessons (monologues) guide me to this day.

ABOUT THE AUTHORS

Quinn Connor is one pen in two hands, Robyn Barrow and Alex Cronin.

Both writers from a young age, Robyn and Alex met at Rhodes College in Memphis and together developed their unique cowriting voice. An Arkansan and a Texan, they can often be found arguing about the differences between queso and cheese dip. Whether Robyn is wandering the Far North for her PhD or Alex is chasing down homemade pasta in Prospect Heights, they write all the time. It's their preferred form of conversation.